Praise for the novels of *New York Times* bestselling author HEATHER GRAHAM

"An incredible storyteller."
—*Los Angeles Daily News*

"Graham wields a deftly sexy and convincing pen."
—*Publishers Weekly*

"There are good reasons for Graham's steady standing as a best-selling author. Here her perfect pacing keeps readers riveted as they learn fascinating tidbits of New Orleans history. The paranormal elements are integral to the unrelentingly suspenseful plot, the characters are likable, the romance convincing...."
—*Booklist* on *Ghost Walk*

"Graham's tight plotting, her keen sense of when to reveal and when to tease...will keep fans turning the pages."
—*Publishers Weekly* on *Picture Me Dead*

"Graham builds jagged suspense that will keep readers guessing up to the final pages."
—*Publishers Weekly* on *Hurricane Bay*

"A roller coaster ride...fast paced, thrilling... Heather Graham will keep you in suspense until the very end. Captivating."
—*Literary Times* on *Hurricane Bay*

"Refreshing, unique... Graham does it better than anyone."
—*Publishers Weekly* on *Hurricane Bay*

"Spectacular and dazzling work."
—*Booklist* on *Eyes of Fire*

HEATHER GRAHAM

THE VISION

MIRA®

ISBN-13: 978-0-7783-2915-2

Recycling programs
for this product may
not exist in your area.

THE VISION

Copyright © 2006 by Heather Graham Pozzessere.

For questions and comments about the quality of this book please contact us
at Customer_eCare@Harlequin.ca.

www.MIRABooks.com

Printed in U.S.A.

In memory of
Victoria Jane Graham Davant, my sister.
She has gone on before me
but there isn't a day that goes by
when she doesn't speak
to me in my heart

Prologue

The form drifted eerily.

From a distance, it almost appeared to be a woman.

At first Genevieve Wallace didn't know what she was seeing. There it was at the bottom, drifting ever so lightly with the current, looking almost like…a woman.

She looked to her left and saw that Vic Damon was just feet away, concentrating on a jutting coral ridge that created a cavelike effect in the pristine waters. With what they had recently learned about the *La Doña*, they were trying to see what might be hiding more or less in plain sight.

The easy, rhythmic sound of her own breathing filled her ears, and she looked at her air gauge. She still had twenty thousand psi, and her depth monitor showed she was hovering between forty-five and fifty-five feet beneath the surface. She could check out the strange form without compromising her own safety.

The water was like crystal, a shimmering color between blue and green. The temperature, too, was absolutely perfect. It was a wonderful afternoon in which to take the time to explore the smallest detail that drew her curiosity.

Last week, when they had started working the area, it had been different. Their first day out, three members of their five-person crew had been violently ill, including Marshall Miro, the owner of Deep Down Salvage. Gen didn't get seasick, but with everyone around her heaving…it hadn't been pleasant. But now the winds had died down completely. The surface was nearly as smooth as glass. The sand had settled.

Visibility was good.

It was almost as if the shape in the water was beckoning to her. Still hearing the rhythmic sound of her own breath, she gave a kick of her fins and started toward whatever it might be.

As she drew closer, she thought that someone had dropped a mannequin in the ocean. From a distance, it had looked like a woman. The closer she got, the more that impression became set in her mind. Yes, it was some kind of mannequin. She wasn't easily frightened, but she could feel a frown of curiosity creasing her brow as she moved closer.

Blond hair floated freely in the water, creating a halo effect around the mannequin's head. There was something soft and beautiful—eerily lifelike— about it. Kicking to propel herself directly in front of it, she saw that it was dressed in a white gown, which billowed with the movement of the water.

The serenely molded face stirred a feeling of deepest sadness in her.

She almost reached out in sympathy.

Almost…

With a shock, she realized that it was down here on the ocean floor because it was weighted. There was rope around the ankles, connected to a canvas bag full of what seemed to be bricks.

The sound of her breathing stopped abruptly.

She had to force herself to breathe again.

It wasn't a mannequin. The body was real.

The blood in her veins turned to ice. Sickened, she did reach out, knowing she had to touch the face. There was no hope the woman was alive. There were no escaping air bubbles; there had been no other boat for her to have come from…and yet she knew she had to touch her, find out if there were some way she might be saved.

Just as her fingers were about to make contact with the woman's lifeless skin, her head rose. Her huge blue eyes opened and rested on Genevieve's. They were filled with sadness.

Her flesh was grayish-tinged white. Her lips were blue.

She stared at Genevieve, her mouth forming a silent O, and she lifted her hand, reaching out to Genevieve, as if seeking a touch of consolation.

She started to smile, as if heartbroken.

It was a terrible smile, a knowing smile. A lifeless smile.

Then she formed a single word with those blue, dead lips.

Beware.

1

"Hey, no one ever said the sun made people sane," Jack Payne, an old-time and expert diver, said, staring at Thor Thompson with an amused cant to his head.

Thor, in turn, was staring at the woman.

He'd first seen her earlier that day, when his boat, *The Seeker,* had met up with the group the state had hired. They were both involved in the same exploratory mission, and there had never been any reason, as far as Thor was concerned, not to co-exist with other companies and other divers. Especially on this project. The state of Florida, along with the environmentalists and the historians, was solidly against some of the methods treasure seekers had used in the past. Coral reefs were fragile. It was one thing to disturb a little nature when there was a verified find; it was quite another to rip the sea floor to shreds in the pursuit of a find. Though the historians were the ones who had set this project into motion, they were going on a theory, and there had to be proof of that theory before the state allowed in any of the big machinery that might tear up the beauty of the reefs—the state's real treasure, as far as tourism went.

Thor was working for the federal government, not himself, and since the Deep Down Salvage group was working for the state, it wasn't as if one of them was going to seize the treasure from the other. If it turned out to be true that the *Marie Josephine* was hidden beneath sand and coral and the continuous reef life, and they did discover a pirate cache, they would both make out well, but it wasn't as if the proceeds wouldn't be divided, or as if the state and U.S. governments— and maybe others—weren't going to be taking the majority of the haul. As a diver who'd spent his career working on old wrecks and salvage, he had done well, and it wasn't that he didn't appreciate his creature comforts. But he had never been in it for the riches that some salvage divers continually sought. He liked the work, the history and the thrill of discovery.

With the recent discovery of the wrecked *La Niña* just off Calliope Key, all sorts of people had once again become excited about the fact there were thousands of undiscovered wrecks off the Florida coast. It was more than plausible that at least some of those wrecks had been hiding pretty much in plain sight. Too often, people simply didn't know or wouldn't recognize what they were looking for. The sea could totally camouflage the remains of a ship after centuries, something researchers had learned much more about in the recent past when vessels of various kinds, having outlived their usefulness, had been purposely sunk to help create artificial reefs. Along with the passion, however, had come the cautionary voices of the historians and environmentalists. A number of the search areas where archives suggested the *Marie Josephine* might be found were marine sanctuaries. Solid proof of a find—more than a few pieces of eight, some ship's silver, or even cannons—would have to turn up to allow for any dredging, hauling or sifting equipment to come out.

Thor's group, known as the Seekers, along with their lead research boat, wasn't on call for just fantastic finds. There were times when the work was far more painful than exciting, when they went looking for survivors or the remains of a crash, times when they didn't dive into the extreme beauty of the Caribbean, the Florida Straits or the Gulf of Mexico. There were dives into swamps, as well, and those were excruciating. The work here, though, was something he enjoyed—at which he hoped he excelled. They were on the trail of pirates. The initial work, done by the state historians, had sent them straight into some of the most beautiful water he had dived anywhere in the world. He liked what he was doing right now. It was the intimate kind of work that was the most exciting. Because they were going on speculation, this was real underwater exploration. Sure, they had sonar and radar, but because storms and time could play such havoc with the remnants of the past, they were also going back to basics, using their own eyes, their own instincts.

Big money—despite the possibility of a big pay-off—was hard to get in the speculation stage. Still, people were more important than equipment right now. That was why he was there, and that was also why *she* was there.

The woman he was watching was an expert diver, so he'd been told. But he and his crew had been about half a mile from the Deep Down Salvage boat when he'd seen her bob frantically to the surface. He would have rushed in for a rescue, but her own people had been quick to recover her. When they had come broadside just to make sure everything was okay, she'd sounded like a lunatic, going on and on about a body in the water. He'd gone down.

And found a lot of parrot fish and tangs.

Since they were all staying at the resort, she was there now, with her buddies, and from the look on her face, they were still ribbing her. The whole thing felt strange to him, because she looked like the last woman in the world who would ever lose her cool. Frankly, she had a look that instantly aroused whatever was sexual and carnal in the male psyche. She was very tall—five eleven, at least—and everything about her was elegant. Even now, she appeared both calm and confident. She had long auburn hair, striking green eyes, dark, well-formed brows, a heart-shaped face and features that exemplified the phrase "perfect symmetry." He'd seldom seen anyone look better in a bathing suit. She would have made a hell of a model, then again, she also would have made a hell of a stripper.

Her mere presence in any room was enough to draw the eyes of any red-blooded male within range.

It was a pity she seemed to be certifiably crazy.

"Conchs are the worst of the lot," Jack said, breaking into Thor's thoughts.

"What?" Thor looked back at the older man.

"I said," Jack told him, lighting his cigar, "that Conchs are known for being crazy. You know, Conchs. Like me. Native Key West folks."

"Well, I'm glad you added a subcategory there," Thor told him.

Jack shrugged. "That's right. You're a Jacksonville boy. North of the state—might as well be a different breed."

"The sane breed?" Thor said, offering a dry smile.

Jack puffed on his cigar and watched the flame. He was somewhere between fifty and sixty years old, hair still long and iron-gray. He wore a huge skull-and-crossbones earring in one lobe and a chain with a Spanish doubloon around his neck. He was built like a man half his age who spent hours at the gym. In his own words, he'd been diving since the rest of them had been in knee britches. He was a man who knew what he was doing.

"Ever hear of Count Von Cosel?" Jack asked.

Thor stared at him.

Jack smiled. "He was a German immigrant—not a real count—working down here in the hospital. He fell in love with a Cuban girl named Elena. He knew she had tuberculosis. He made up some weird kind of cure, but despite his efforts, the girl died.

Family had her buried. A few years later, he decides she should be buried in a great mausoleum, so he builds it, and supposedly that's where the girl's body is interred. But as time goes by, folks start to notice odd things about his place. Like it looks as if he's dancing with this huge doll. Turns out the poor bastard dug up Elena and tried to put her back together again so that he could try some whacked-out thing to bring her back to life. Bastard slept with the corpse for years, repairing her constantly. Finally the family got wind of it, and the sister goes to see him. There was an uproar, but there's a statute of limitations on whatever crime they figured it to be, so he gets off. This is Key West, after all. He not only gets away without being charged, he winds up with people sending him money to survive."

"You're a lying sack of shit, Jack," Thor told him.

"I swear to you, it's a true story. Ask anyone. Look it up. Newspapers all over the country carried the story." He paused and took a puff of his cigar. "The point is, comparatively speaking, the young lady you're staring at is as sane as they come. And damned better looking than any other I've ever seen with these old eyes."

Thor shook his head and lifted his beer. "I saw her out there today, and when you're diving, the last thing you need is someone going off the deep end, no pun intended. Ask her out on a date, Jack, but don't bring her on my boat. There's too much at stake."

"I've gone diving with that girl many a time,

Thor. She knows what she's doing. As far as hooking up with her, hell, I could be her father. And I've known her forever, since she was a kid."

Thor shook his head again and turned his focus to the water. Late summer. Hot days, gorgeous nights. There was always a breeze coming off the ocean. And the sun, when it set, was glorious. It was eight at night, and the sky was getting ready to change. Now it was light. Soon it would be pink, purple, gold, yellow, blue…streaks of color that would slowly deepen. Then, around eight-thirty, it would suddenly go dark.

He was staring at the water…and then he was staring at her again. It was hard not to stare at her, he thought, realizing what it was about her that drew him so powerfully. She emanated a natural, easy sensuality. It was evident in her every movement. Nothing forced, nothing overt. Something she herself wouldn't even know she possessed.

"Sun's going down now," Jack commented. "You could take off the shades."

Thor smiled again. Hell, no. He liked the ink-dark Ray-Bans. No one could tell when his eyes kept turning toward the other table.

"Can't take your eyes off her, huh?" Jack asked.

"What's not to appreciate about eye candy? I just don't think any rational man—especially a diver—should get too close to a loose cannon."

"Want to hear about the guy who thought his doll was alive and all the folks who think it's cursed?"

Thor groaned. "Jack, give it a rest."

"Hey, it's all real stuff. Know where the name Key West came from? When the Spaniards first arrived, it was one big boneyard. An Indian tribe that died out? Killed in a massacre? No one knows. But there were bones everywhere, so they called it Cayo Hueso, *Island of Bones*. The English didn't bother to translate the Spanish, just turned it into words they knew. I'm telling you, Thor, Key West is a unique place."

Thor smiled slowly. "Jack, if you're trying to convince me that she's totally right in the head, you're not getting anywhere. The woman claims she saw a body in the water. And that it talked to her."

"Hey...for every tale out there, you'll find a grain of truth."

"Have you heard about a missing person in the area? Anybody looking for a murder victim? I had the news on—far as I can tell, everyone's accounted for."

"You're sounding like a callous son of a bitch, and I know better," Jack told him. "What you are is so focused on diving that you don't mind going through women like Kleenex."

Thor arched a brow. "Yeah? Haven't seen you settle down."

"Never knew a woman could keep up—in my generation. They probably existed somewhere. We just didn't cross paths."

"I don't play where I work," he said softly.

Jack let out a guffaw. "That's 'cause the one

woman on our team is married and an Amazon to boot."

"Now, who's being a son of a bitch?"

"Me? I think Lizzie's great, but she's all business. Tough as nails, and I think she could take me if we were arm wrestling. And if she couldn't, well, who the hell would want to mess with Zach?"

Thor shrugged, amused. Lizzie—Elizabeth Green— was not a woman to be taken lightly. She wasn't an inch shorter than his own six-three. Her husband, Zach, had been a professional basketball player, and between them, they were a daunting pair. Lizzie waged a lot of the company's battles when they were seeking permits for projects. She could best almost any man. "Lizzie's tough. And down to earth. She isn't going to fly off the handle, seeing corpses that aren't really there."

"Come on. Everyone's been spooked by something once or twice."

"Maybe."

"And you're a pile of crap yourself, Thor."

"You think?"

"You'd have your tongue on the pavement if she crooked her little finger."

"Yeah? Bull." He spoke coolly, but he knew he was lying. The nutcase was almost explosively hot. But he hadn't been lying when he said he didn't fool around where he worked. Even on a long haul, they put into port somewhere, and that's where he did his playing. Complications on a job were something nobody needed.

"I call 'em like I see 'em," Jack said flatly. "No one's ever accused me of lying."

"Hell, I'm accusing you right now," Thor said.

Jack laughed, noticing that Thor was watching the other table again. "Remember, Thor, the mighty can fall," he said.

"Yeah, yeah. I've been hearing that 'mighty Thor' shit all my life," Thor told him, then waved to the bartender, the owner's son, ordering another round.

"We all looked, Genevieve," Victor said. "There was nothing there."

"I'm telling you, I saw a woman's body," Genevieve repeated stubbornly, her jaw set. "Look, I don't know if it was some kind of a joke, or if there's a real murder victim down there. But I didn't hallucinate. I saw it."

Bethany Clark touched Genevieve's knee. "Hey, honey, all of us see things down there sometimes. It's the mind playing tricks. The water playing tricks, causing visual distortion."

"Have another beer," Victor said dryly. "It will make everything better."

Genevieve groaned, gritting her teeth. She couldn't say they hadn't tried. She had kicked her way to the surface with the speed of lightning. Thankfully, she hadn't been deep. The moment the woman had opened her eyes and smiled, she had felt such a sense of sheer panic that she had rocketed to the surface, which could have been deadly if she had been down deep. When she'd reached the surface, she had nearly choked on salt water, spitting out her regulator and waving her arms madly.

Marshall Miro, head of their unit, had been on board, and she knew she'd been babbling as he'd helped her out. Victor had surfaced right after her, having seen her ascent. Then Bethany and Alex, not too far distant, had come up, and Bethany had stayed aboard while the others had gone down, searching for the woman's body. *The Seeker*, one of their fellow ships, had been in the vicinity, as well. Her crew had gone down, too.

And none of them had seen anything.

Maybe she had imagined the eyes opening, the woman reaching out, but she *had* seen a body. She just didn't know what had happened to it.

Unfortunately, she had babbled something about the eyes and the fact that the dead woman had moved, even tried to speak, and now even Bethany, her best friend, thought she was crazy.

She glanced around the small resort in the old-town area of Key West where they were staying. She actually owned a house not even half a mile away that her great-great-however-many-greats-grandfather had built on the island years before the Civil War.

But this place was a local hangout. Jack kept his beat-up old fishing boat here, and there was one slip where three of the area cops kept their boats berthed. They liked to come here just to have coffee, or drinks in the evening.

She'd stayed here on purpose to be able to work

this project at the blink of an eye with the others. Their dive boat was right there, where they needed it, along with *The Seeker*. There was no spa or twenty-four-hour room service, but what it did have was true old Conch charm. The main house had been built in the 1800s. Bungalows had been added right around World War II and were spread out over a sandy beach, and each offered an outside table and chairs on a little individual patio. There was also the tiki bar and "munch house," as they called it, which opened at seven in the morning and stayed open until midnight or so. The night bartender was the owner's son, so he kept it open as long as he was having fun. The menu wasn't gourmet, but it was fresh and delicious.

Despite the fact the divers following her garbled directions hadn't found a body, Genevieve had insisted on reporting what she had seen to the police—by then calm enough to report the body but not the fact it had seemed to move of its own volition. It had been late when they had actually returned to shower and change and meet here at the bar to dine on fresh fish sandwiches, and the resort's own coleslaw and potato salad.

"Okay, guys, laugh at me all you want. I saw a body," she said firmly.

Bethany lowered her sandy head. Victor, Alex and Marshall all stared at one another, trying not to smile.

"Hey, Gen," Victor teased her. "There's a lady at the bar who wants to buy you a drink…look—

Whoops, no, sorry, you didn't act fast enough. She's disappeared."

Genevieve glared at him through narrowed eyes. She wanted to wring his neck. Of all people to be so taunting… They'd gone through school together. He was a year older, but she'd matured faster, and having a shape in high school had been tantamount to being cool back then. She'd taken him with her to every social event in their adolescent past.

In college he'd finally filled out and grown a few hairs on his chest. He'd grown into his features, as well, and now he was tall, dark and good-looking. They'd never ruined a good friendship by dating, but he could irritate her as thoroughly as if they were a married couple.

"Victor…" she began.

Grinning, he waved a hand. "Yeah, yeah, I know what I can go do with myself."

"Hey, kid, it will be all right," Marshall said, but he, too, was still secretly smiling. At least someone was amused, she thought. Marshall was the owner and founder of Deep Down Salvage as well as a local. As a kid, he'd been fascinated by the history of Key West, which was inextricably entwined with tales of wreckers and salvage divers. It was a mixed history. Sometimes they had saved the lives of the poor souls on a ship that came to ruin on the dangerous reefs.

Sometimes, however, they waited like vultures— hoping ships carrying rich cargos would flounder and sink. Such a system had created many a rich man throughout the centuries.

Marshall was at least ten years older than most of their group. He had made his name by working in the northern waters off Massachusetts, doing heavy-duty, cold-water salvage. But Key West was his home, the place he loved. He had used his earnings to come back and open his own company, buy his own boat and equipment, and set up shop. He made a good income, but he was always pleased to work on any historical effort, and he had a tremendous respect for the reefs, the water and the past. Deeply tanned and buff, and dead even with her own height, he kept his head shaven, a look that went oddly well with his almost ebony eyes and dark brows.

Sitting with his feet up, shades on despite the setting sun, he grimaced. "We'll find out that there was something down there. You know…flotsam and jetsam of some kind."

Alex hummed a version of *The Twilight Zone* theme song. "Yeah, flotsam and jetsam with a face and hair," he teased.

She glared at him, hiking a brow. Alex was from Key Largo, a different world from Key West, since the city of Miami was barely an hour north. He was blond, bronzed and a child of the sea and sun, a graduate in history and a master diver, but she'd shown him secrets of the reefs here that only the natives knew.

"Oh, you—" she said, then broke off in aggravation and rose, taking her beer with her to the little fence that looked out over a deep channel where the resort's pleasure crafts and fishing boats were berthed.

"Don't go away mad!" Alex called.

She spun around, shaking her head and forcing a smile as well. "Just wait, my dear, devoted friends! Somewhere along the line, you *will* get yours. I'm not going away mad, I'm just going away."

"Hey, don't be mad at *me*," Bethany said.

"I'm not mad," Genevieve insisted.

She walked on down to the dock, nursing her beer, looking out at the sunset. It was beautiful and tranquil, but she was roiling inside. Why had she been so panicked? She'd twice worked rescue situations that had become retrieval situations, and they had found bodies both times, once after a plane crash in the southern Glades, and once after a boating accident off Key West.

But the dead hadn't looked at her then.

Digging a flower bed at her house, she'd dug up bones once—but that hadn't been as shocking as it might have been elsewhere, not in Key West, the Island of Bones.

But those bones hadn't disappeared.

She felt a presence next to her, tensed and turned, certain that one of her friends had joined her to continue the torture.

"You all right?"

She turned at the soft masculine query to see Jay Gonzalez. He was still in uniform, hat low over his forehead, sunglasses dark and concealing his eyes.

She smiled. She liked Jay a lot. He was in his late

thirties now, and had been young himself when she had first met him. He'd pulled her and a few friends over when they'd been in high school, and, admittedly, there had been a few beer cans in the car. He hadn't brought them down to the station, though. Instead, he'd taken every one of them home.

He was one of the cops who kept his boat here. He didn't go out on it often anymore. He'd been out on it when his wife had fallen overboard and died. But he still kept it up. Maybe he even visited it now and then because he somehow felt closer to his wife when he was on it.

But he wasn't there now for the boat, she knew. He was there for her.

"I'm fine—if you think having all your friends convinced you're crazy makes you fine." She hesitated. "Thanks for listening to me today."

He nodded, leaning against the little wooden rail next to her. "I know you're not a ditz," he told her, grinning.

"Bless you."

He stared out over the water. "I just wish I could help you. I don't have anything that would correspond with what you told me. Then again, someone might be missing and it hasn't been reported yet. I sent some men out after I talked to you. They couldn't find anything, either." He hesitated. "Bizarre as it may seem, given the amount of drinking that goes on down here, Key West itself doesn't have much of a murder rate. I deal with boozed-out kids and car accidents more than anything else."

"Jay, I saw a woman down there." She hesitated before going on, hoping he wouldn't take what she was about to say as a slap on his professional knowledge. "It's not like no one ever gets killed here. There was the husband who went nuts and shot his wife a few years back. And there was that almost-supermodel who disappeared when I was in high school. No one believed she would ever be found alive. Oh! And just last year, in the middle Keys somewhere…another young woman disappeared."

"I didn't say we never have murders, but in comparison to Miami, our numbers are low—single digits. And, Gen—"

"I know. There's no missing blonde on the radar right now."

"We could find out later there is," he said gently. "But let's hope it was a prank of some kind, huh?"

"I am definitely hoping that's the case."

He nodded. "There could be a bunch of frat boys laughing their asses off somewhere. We may never know. But I believe you saw something. In fact, it's you, so I *know* it."

She smiled her thanks. "Can I buy you a beer?" she asked him.

He shook his head. "I'm still on duty. I just wanted to make sure you were all right." He made a face. "There's some trouble up on Mile Marker 6. You take care, all right? And call me—whatever comes up. I don't think you're crazy."

He brushed her chin affectionately with his

knuckles, then walked away toward the sand-and-gravel parking lot.

She thanked God for him. At least he believed her. He was an interesting guy, she mused. He was a perfect sheriff's deputy. Tall, dark, quiet. He exuded an air of competence and assurance. She always felt a sense of sympathy for him; his wife had died about five years ago, when they'd been on vacation. He'd kept pretty much to himself after that.

But he was a good guy. And it was comforting to know he had taken her seriously.

Upsetting, though, to know that no one had found any sign of anything.

Staring back at the horizon, she took a long swallow of the Miller Lite she'd been holding so long that it was growing warm. When she felt someone beside her again, she thought that Jay had returned.

Wrong.

"Hey, cutie. Long day, huh?"

It was Jack Payne, one of her favorite people in the world, though he was working on *The Seekers* this go-round. Crusty as a crab, Jack was weathered and leathered by the sun. He wore one of the coins he had found around his neck, a Spanish gold piece hung from a chain, and in one ear a gold earring in the form of a skull and crossbones. He worked out of the area a lot, but they'd shared several assignments, and he was a great diver with whom to work.

She flushed, seeing the semi-smile on his face.

"I know, I know, Jack. Give it a good laugh, okay?

But thanks for calling me cutie. At my height, I don't hear that word too often," she said wearily.

"Hey, I believe you saw something. And maybe 'cutie' isn't the right word. How about, hey there, gorgeous? And, as to the other, there's nothing else anyone can do right now, huh?"

She nodded.

He slipped a fatherly arm around her shoulders. "Maybe we'll hear something soon about someone going missing."

"I hope not. I'd much rather it have been my imagination," Genevieve said.

"Right…well, this is a pretty kooky place. We'll probably discover that some prankster did sink a mannequin in the water."

"Yeah, well, I've got to get past it right now," she murmured.

"You will. It will be fine."

"Really?" She swung around, leaning on the wooden railing as she surveyed him. "I'd swear you've been sitting there with your hotshot friend, trying not to agree I should be taken off the project."

"Me? Never. I'd dive with you any day, Genny."

She risked a quick glance at the man remaining at Jack's table. *Thor.* Who the hell had a name like Thor? Yeah, yeah, he had a reputation. And in another place and time, he might have fit the name well, having the height and build and rugged features of some ancient thunder god. But this was Key West, and they were living in the real world, and down here they didn't care how many times someone had managed to make it into the newspapers. She didn't know why—maybe it was because he had been so ready to rescue her that afternoon— she felt an instant dislike for the man. Pretentious. Arrogant. Those adjectives definitely applied. And it wasn't because she had a thing about working with other groups. She just didn't like *him*.

"Come meet him. He's really not such a bad guy."

"Could have fooled me," she murmured.

"Hey," Jack said lightly. "Your buddies are doing a pretty good job of ribbing you right now, too, aren't they?"

Genevieve shrugged. Yes, this one was going to take a very long time to live down. No—they'd *never* let her live it down.

"Come on, come meet Thor."

She rolled her eyes but followed Jack back to the table.

To his credit, the man stood. She could see little of his face because he wore a pair of Ray-Bans, but he had the kind of high-set cheekbones and strong jaw that certainly defined his personality. No-nonsense, rugged, probably fearless. Totally confident and determined. She decided that even without what had happened today, she probably wouldn't have cared much for him. He didn't appear to be the kind of man who worked and played well with others.

"Thor, meet Genevieve Wallace. Gen, Thor Thompson."

He offered her a hand. He didn't smile, however.

He wasn't treating her experience with the same amusement as the others. Apparently he found it dangerously annoying.

"Thor," she murmured, shaking his hand but extracting her own quickly. "Interesting name." She couldn't help the bit of disdain in her tone.

The hint of a smile curved his lips at that. "Sorry—my grandparents were Norwegian. They started out in Minnesota. It's common enough in those circles. Genevieve, huh?"

"Family name, as well. St. Genevieve. My antecedents were old-school Catholics, I suppose," she murmured.

"Gen. It's easier," Jack said cheerfully. "Sit. I'll get you a beer. Ah, you already have one. Well…sit."

"Um…" She hesitated. She should have been quicker with an excuse. *Anything. Actually, I'm already sitting with friends over there. Excuse me, but I think I'm wiped out, I'm going to my room. There's a cat in a tree I have to rescue… Anything!*

But she hadn't thought fast enough. Jack already had a chair pulled out for her.

"Strange you two haven't met yet," Jack said.

Genevieve saw a tawny brow shoot up over the Ray-Bans. "Jack, it's a big world."

"Yeah, but you've worked the Keys before," Jack said.

Thor nodded. "I haven't been down this far south that often, though."

"Well," Jack said cheerfully, "it's a great project to be working."

"Right. Working," Thor murmured.

Genevieve stiffened instantly. Despite the Ray-Bans hiding his eyes, it was more than apparent that he thought of her as a liability. "I *am* working, and I take my work seriously, Mr. Thompson," she informed him coolly.

"Mr. Thompson?" Jack said. "Gen, we're all working together. He's just Thor."

"Interesting work method," Thor said, as if Jack had never spoken.

His voice let her know he was staring at her as if she were a total flake.

"I would be willing to bet, Mr. Thompson, that I know these reefs far better than you ever will."

"Really?" he replied, leaning forward. "Just what is it that you think you know about these reefs, *Miss* Wallace? That you mysteriously see the past? People floating down there? Strange, if that were the case, one would think you'd know exactly where to look for all the sunken ships. Wouldn't that be great?"

"Come on, guys," Jack demanded. "What's with this *Mr.* and *Miss* stuff?"

It was her turn to ignore Jack.

"My reputation as a diver is absolutely spotless, Mr. Thompson."

"Hey, why don't I go over and say hello to your buddies, Gen?" Jack murmured.

His chair scraped back. He was definitely in a hurry to quit their company and the wave of tension that had seemed to materialize around them.

Thor Thompson was still staring at her. Then he

leaned forward suddenly and removed the sunglasses so he could stare into her eyes. "Spotless?" he asked softly. "Maybe until today. We might as well get this right out into the open. I don't give a rat's ass about your reputation. Even though we're not working at great depth, every man has to pull his weight. I've seen too many 'experienced' divers pop up dead. If you see dead bodies that open their eyes and try to communicate with you, Miss Wallace, we've got serious problems ahead. You might want to get some help before you go down again."

For several long moments Genevieve stared at him, so shocked by the hardball vehemence of the attack that she didn't even blink.

The man had blue eyes sharper than jagged ice and a jaw that seemed set in concrete. Her heart pounded. He didn't know her; didn't know anything about her.

He'd simply judged her.

She sat forward, as well, met him eye to eye, and smiled.

"I'm a better diver than you could ever hope to work with again. And I'm known to find what I'm looking for, so if you don't like me, well, then excuse me for being crude, but I really have nothing to say other than 'Fuck you, asshole.'" Still smiling pleasantly, she stood and walked away.

Jay Gonzalez drove down Roosevelt, wondering why the situation had left him so perplexed.

Nothing. There had been nothing down there.

Hell, he'd been in and around the water long enough. Vision was distorted beneath the waves.

The crime rate was low, just as he'd told Gen. Most of it had to do with petty theft. Some grand larceny, and of course there were the drugs. But murder didn't happen often.

There couldn't be anything to it. Genevieve thought she'd seen a body. The body had been gone. A prank, perhaps? According to Marshall, there hadn't been any other boats in the immediate area. But, hell, he knew kids, and they were willing to go to great lengths to play a trick.

Still, it disturbed him. He liked Genevieve, really liked her, and always had. He hated to see her upset like that.

Ghosts were big business in Key West, as they were in many places. Hemingway was said to walk around town, and sometimes it seemed as if every house on Duval Street claimed to have a ghost, thanks to the Indian bones and the wreckers and plain old human frailty. But Genevieve wasn't the type to make up a story for the fun of it.

What the hell had she seen?

Murder wasn't common in Key West.

But it did happen. Had happened.

Hell, yes, it had happened. He knew damned well it had happened.

He gritted his teeth; he was already reaching US1. His siren blaring, he wove through the stopped cars. There was an accident just ahead.

He looked at the cars as he approached and prayed he wouldn't be seeing any bodies himself. Not that night.

2

The following day, Thor was one of the first divers up and about. The plan was to meet early every morning at the tiki bar to grab coffee and a light meal. Just fifty feet from the little hut, the resort offered a small dive shop, where their tanks were filled and any damaged piece of equipment repaired. He stood on the dock for a few moments, enjoying the sunrise. It promised to be a beautiful day, or at least a beautiful morning. They planned to spend the next couple of weeks taking the boats out early and calling it quits by about three, when the late summer rains traditionally rolled in. Those afternoon storms often came on with ferocity, but generally they raged for half an hour or so, then were gone.

He sipped his coffee, aware that others were beginning to emerge from their cottages. Marshall Miro's crew was impressive. They were all in excellent shape, and comfortable in the water no matter what the circumstances. They had the proper respect for the ocean's power. Which was good—he didn't intend to lose any divers. Even Genevieve

Wallace had sounded sane enough when she'd snapped back at him. He liked her air of determination, in fact.

He saw her walking from her cottage, meeting up with Bethany, the second woman on Marshall's crew. She was the opposite of Genevieve, probably a respectable five-five or five-six, but next to her friend, she appeared short. She was attractive, compact but nicely muscled. She also seemed to be far more cheerful and easygoing than her long-legged counterpart and was waving to Lizzie and Zach even as she met up with Genevieve. Lizzie made even Genevieve look short, and when Zach moved up, he dwarfed them all. Jack was already over by the tiki hut, and Clint—long and lanky at twenty-two, bronzed, his hair flopping in his face—was setting out platters of doughnuts and fruit. Rounding out the group, Vic and Alex came running up along the beach, heavy packs of equipment over their shoulders. They were of an age, and, like the others, physically fit and mentally sharp.

"Hey! Thought you were lolling around in bed. Didn't see you down here," Marshall called to Thor, walking down the dock.

"We're in search of the find of the century," Thor said dryly. "I wouldn't want to oversleep and miss all the excitement."

"You don't think we're going to find anything?" Marshall asked, rubbing a hand over his bald head and squinting against the sun.

"I didn't say that. I wouldn't be here if I didn't

believe there was something to find. I'm just curious what the state guys have planned if nothing shows up here. People have been diving this area for years. Admittedly, we've been finding signs of metal down there, but hell, that could mean just about anything."

"All we need is proof that she's there, and then it's up to the ecologists and historians to start arguing about the next steps," Marshall said with a shrug. He stared at Thor. "To be honest, I'd just like to go down in the books as having been in on a real find. If determination means anything, we'll find something for sure."

"Determination is always an asset," Thor murmured. He was looking back at the others. Victor Damon gave Genevieve a teasing bump as they walked along the path. She turned and pointed a finger at him, saying something. They were probably still ribbing her. He said something else, and she stole his baseball cap, then slammed it back on his head. Still, they were all laughing. That cop, Jay Gonzalez, seemed to hold her in regard. If she'd been a fruitcake, it was doubtful the man would have listened to her so attentively or sent divers out in search of a body.

"You've got a tight-knit crew," Thor commented.

"Those two," Marshall said with a nod toward Genevieve and Victor, "and Bethany all went to school together. Best friends. Poor Alex is the new guy. He's only been around for about three years. All the way from Key Largo," he added dryly. "What about your people?"

"The best," Thor assured him. "Lizzie and Jack have worked it all—rescue, recovery, salvage. They're a great team. And you must know Jack. Probably better than I do. The invitation to join this search came kind of suddenly, and several of my people were already committed to other projects. I'm missing some of my regulars, but I've known Jack forever and I'm glad to have him on my team."

"Jack has more experience than all of us put together," Marshall said.

"We should get going," Thor said, checking his watch.

"I'd like to be down before nine to take advantage of the visibility before the storms roil up the sand." He let out a whistle, drawing the attention of his crew, who hurried for their coffee.

Genevieve Wallace walked by, her eyes like sharp crystals as she assessed him without a word.

"Nice morning, wouldn't you say, Miss Wallace."

"Yes, a perfect morning," she replied politely, and hurried on by.

It was a perfect morning, and the day passed uneventfully. Three different dives, hours under water. Just before three, with the regularity of a factory whistle, the storms started rolling in.

Thor had seen the sky change on the horizon, seen the rain when it had begun farther out at sea. When the divers came up for the third time, he motioned to Marshall that it was time to call it quits. With the boats lashed together, he could hear

Marshall's people talking as he waited for his own crew to stow their gear.

"I think we were closer yesterday," Genevieve said.

"Why? Because of that woman you saw?" Alex teased her.

She slapped him on the arm. "Because I have a hunch. I think we need to back it up a bit, Marshall. We didn't give yesterday's location a thorough search. I mean, a relic isn't going to just jump out of the sand into our hands."

"We'll talk about it," Marshall assured her.

By then the motors were purring, they had cast off their ropes and weighed anchor, and were moving away.

"Think Genevieve might be right? Should we move back?" Lizzie asked.

He shrugged, though privately he admitted that they should retrace the area. There had been too much excitement yesterday—too much time spent looking for a woman's body are not enough for signs of a wreck.

"We'll see," he said. "I'll talk to Marshall about it tonight."

He was startled when his cell phone started to ring. "Excuse me, guys," he told them. When he moved forward and answered, he shook his head when he recognized Sheridan's voice. "Yep, that will be fine." He hung up and swore. The preliminaries had been done. But now…well, hell. It wasn't his nickel. If Sheridan wanted to come down and talk again, so be it. "Meeting at the tiki bar tomorrow morning—seven-thirty sharp!" he called to the others.

Thor felt suddenly irritated. He didn't know why exactly, but Sheridan bugged him. The man had even hinted that perhaps Thor should find another diver for his team. He didn't like bringing in someone he didn't know well. Maybe he'd have to hire someone else, he decided. They were looking for needles in a really giant haystack, and he wanted to do more of the actual diving himself. Well, tomorrow, at least, he would have an extra body around, if needed, with Sheridan there. That would work, for now, although he wasn't sure how long he wanted Sheridan on his boat. Maybe it would all work out without bringing in untested strangers.

The day had yielded nothing, but Genevieve still felt on top of the world.

She had slept with every light in the bungalow on, dreading the darkness. But she had drifted off at some point and actually slept reasonably well.

She had tried to appear completely calm, competent and rational throughout the morning, even allowing the others to joke at her expense. She simply wasn't going to live this down for a while. And yet, despite her apparent calm, she had been terrified all morning, praying silently not to have any visions this time, not to see a dead woman telling her to beware.

All day, she had stayed closer to Victor than

usual, all the while trying not to let him know what she was doing. But if she saw something, she was determined he was going to see it, too.

There had been no finds. But there had been no corpses in the water, either. That made the day a great success, as far as she was concerned.

By five she had washed down her own equipment, helped with the boat, showered and changed. She wasn't fond of hanging around by herself, so she hurried out to the tiki bar.

She was the first arrival from either of the crews. Clint saw her, and brought over a Miller Lite. "You do want a beer, right?"

"I do. Thank you."

He grinned. "It's the only appropriate libation for kick-ass women."

"Bethany likes piña coladas," she reminded him.

"Well…some chicks can get away with it," he assured her. "Ah, the big guy himself."

Genevieve thought he had to mean Zach—she hadn't met many people in her life quite as tall as Zach. But then she turned and realized Clint wasn't referring to Zach. He was talking about the man she had personally dubbed *asshole*.

To her displeasure, he headed right for her. Then again, the only other guests enjoying the thatched shade of the tiki bar right now were an elderly couple who had told her earlier they hailed from Ohio. A nice couple, but not exactly people any of them knew.

Not that he exactly knew *her*, Genevieve thought as he approached.

He didn't ask if he could join her, just nodded—eyes shaded behind dark glasses again—and slid into one of the chairs. By the time he was seated, Clint had returned with a beer.

"One of these days, do you think I can head out with you guys?" Clint asked him.

Thor shrugged, accepting the beer with a quick "Thanks." He looked up at Clint. "What kind of a diver are you?"

"A good one. I have a master's certification."

Thor gave Clint a long assessment, not a muscle in his face so much as ticking. "Sure. Take time off next week. But out on the boat, I'm not just captain, I'm God Almighty. If you can live with that…?"

"Shit, yes," Clint said, then caught himself. "Sorry, Genevieve."

"I think she's all right with the word," Thor said, smiling. Evidently he hadn't forgotten a single one of her words to him.

"No problem, Clint," she replied. "And if you want, I'm sure you can go out with us, too, one of these days." She hoped her sunglasses were every bit as opaque as Thor's and her smile every bit as pleasant.

"Cool." Clint was still looking at Thor, as if for approval. After a moment, he moved away awkwardly, giving them a thumbs-up sign.

"So, how was your day?" Thor asked her once Clint had moved on.

"Fine, just fine."

"Nothing down there, huh?"

"If there had been, I would have reported it."

"Nothing strange, I meant."

She forced another smile. "You know, I really don't know who you think you are. I've been out on these reefs all my life. I know every landmark. And I'll bet I make a discovery before you do."

He sat back, a small smile curving his lips. "You think you can outdo me, Miss Wallace?"

"I know I can."

He shook his head, amused. For a brief moment, she wondered what the hell she was doing. He had a sixth sense when it came to finding what was lost beneath the sea.

"Interesting," he said. "You're really throwing down the gauntlet."

Yes, she was. And that, she realized, seemed to take him from believing she was nuts in one way to believing she was nuts in another, *saner*, way.

"Well?" she demanded icily.

He shrugged. "Is this a dare? For real?"

"You bet."

"You're on."

"Good."

"We're talking about a real relic—not imagined," he said.

"Absolutely," she agreed.

"All right. What's the bet?" he asked.

She shrugged. The stakes hadn't entered her mind.

"A round of beers?" she suggested.

He shook his head. "Far too cheap."

She arched a brow. "I planned on a friendly wager."

"A *friendly* wager?"

"Okay. So we're far from being friends."

"Do you have so little faith in yourself?"

"Should I be betting my house?" she inquired lightly, feeling ever-so-slightly ill in the pit of her stomach.

He shook his head, his smile deepening. "I wouldn't dream of taking your house."

"What makes you think you'd take it? And what would I be getting—when I win?"

He laughed out loud then, truly enjoying himself. "I have a nice place in Jacksonville."

"But I have no desire to leave the Keys."

"As I said, I have no intention of taking *your* home, either."

He was intent on winning, she knew—despite the fact she couldn't see his eyes. There was a tightening, barely visible, in his muscles. His male ego was taking over. Testosterone was racing. It was pathetically immature, she thought.

She had started it.

"You won't get a chance to take my home," she assured him coolly.

"Well, a round of beers is too paltry, claiming your house too serious. I guess we could give this thing some thought overnight, hmm?" he suggested.

"Whatever you wish, Mr. Thompson," she said stiffly.

"No, whatever *you* wish, Miss Wallace," he replied mockingly.

"Tomorrow morning, then, we decide the bet," she said.

"I've got an idea," he murmured, looking amused. "But you won't like it."

She was suddenly certain she knew the nature of his wager. It should have infuriated her. Instead, it just made the challenge greater.

"Really?" she murmured, suddenly aware of her own muscles tightening with the same tension, the same sense of challenge and ruthless determination, as his. Worse, his air of sexual innuendo only increased her fighting spirit.

"You really don't want to know. It's a pretty wacko thought."

"I think I *do* know, Mr. Thompson. The question is…what do I get when you lose? Sorry, a night in the sack with you isn't my idea of a prize."

He laughed softly. "You made quite an assumption there, didn't you?"

She fought the wave of crimson that threatened to splash her cheeks and tried to bluff her way out of it. "What kind of prize would be wacko to you?" she asked sweetly.

He smiled, for once a simple, deep and, she had to admit, very nice smile. "Wacko doesn't necessarily mean… *The Seeker*," he said suddenly.

"What?"

"*The Seeker*. You'd get *The Seeker*."

She frowned. "The boat is yours?"

"From bow to stern, yes."

"But…she's your livelihood."

"I won't lose."

Genevieve sat back, totally confused. "You'd wager your dive boat? Against…?"

He smiled again, and this time it was far too sexy and seductive. "Well, it was *your* suggestion."

"Never!"

"My mind wasn't moving in that direction until you said something."

"It sure as hell was."

"I never would have voiced it if you hadn't."

She wasn't sure what she felt at that moment

"You *are* joking, right?" she asked softly.

He leaned forward; she found herself doing the same. The bet was between them; no one else would be in on it. "I'm not joking. If I lose, I'll pay up. Will you?"

"You'd risk your boat for a woman you think is crazy?" she asked. "You have to be crazier than you think I am."

He laughed. "Not really. I won't lose."

"We'll see, won't we?" she murmured.

"So it's a bet?"

She noticed that Jack had made an appearance and was dragging another table over. She realized that in a few minutes the tiki bar would be crowded, as the crews from both boats all began to put in an appearance. In fact, she could see Lizzie and Zach approaching. Bethany, Alex, Victor and Marshall would no doubt be over in another few minutes.

"People are coming," she murmured.

He gripped her wrist where it lay on the table. "Is it a bet?"

"Yes," she hissed quickly.

"One of us will have to lose," he said, stating the obvious.

"It won't be me," she assured him. "But don't worry. I'll take excellent care of *my* boat."

A touch of dry amusement entered his eyes, and he leaned close.

"Don't *you* worry. I'll take excellent care of *you*."

The others were there before she had a chance to reply, and she rose to greet Elizabeth and Zach.

Maybe she was just being paranoid, but it seemed as if Elizabeth and Zach were looking at her oddly. Then again, it might not be paranoia. She hadn't been in great shape when she had surfaced yesterday. But Elizabeth had sympathy in her eyes as well as the same speculative look that Thor Thompson usually wore. "You doing all right? Everything okay today?" Elizabeth asked, taking the chair her husband offered her and drawing it up beside Genevieve's.

"Fine. I'm really sorry I caused such a commotion yesterday."

"Hey," Elizabeth said. "I've had a few weird experiences in the water, too."

"Lizzie ran into a head once," Zach said.

"We were diving a small plane crash in the Everglades. It was pretty grisly."

Genevieve nodded, staring across the table at Thor, who was smiling at Bethany. *Asshole.*

"I've done some recovery in the Everglades, and it is brutal," Genevieve said.

"The muck…you can't see anything until it's in your face—then, suddenly, you've found a body part," Elizabeth agreed. "But…well, you must have seen something. Maybe we'll find whatever it was in the next few days."

"I hope so," Genevieve said. She looked at Thor again, clenching her teeth. "I haven't worked rescue and recovery all that often, but we've gone up to the Glades a few times. I don't know what this was." She waved a hand in the air. "It had to be someone's idea of a joke. A mannequin or something." She didn't believe it for an instant, but she was sick to death of the topic.

"Hey, anybody want to head out for dinner?" Bethany asked as she and the others came walking over.

"I was thinking about eating here," Alex said. "We were planning a pretty early morning, at least three dives. I'm going straight to soda water after this beer."

"You?" Genevieve inquired skeptically.

"We should call it an early night," Thor said. "We're supposed to meet back out here on the patio tomorrow at seven-thirty."

"Seven-thirty?" Genevieve said. "I thought it was eight-thirty? All we have to do is get up and walk out to the boats."

"Our advisers are going to be here in the morning," Marshall said. "Preston from the Coast Guard and Professor Sheridan, from the university."

"Oh?" Genevieve said.

"Thor got the call when we were out today. Sorry, I missed telling you," Marshall said.

Had her own boss decided she was too far gone to receive information like everyone else? she wondered. Didn't he want her in contact with the higher-ups?

"Great," she said. "I guess we should call it an early night." She started to rise, but Marshall smiled, putting a hand on her shoulder to stop her.

"I say we let the crew of *The Seeker* buy us dinner tonight."

"Sure," Elizabeth said cheerfully. "The hamburgers here are cheap enough. We'll let you guys buy us steaks after our first discovery."

"I'll go give Clint our order," Thor said, rising. "Though what Marshall isn't telling you is that all our meals go on an expense account. Hamburgers, cheeseburgers? Any vegetarians in the group?" He looked at Genevieve.

Of course, she thought. He already considered her a bit strange, so no doubt she must be a vegetarian in his red-blooded, rough-and-ready, American-male world. She suddenly wished she were a vegetarian, just so she could see the look on his face when she told him.

She decided not to answer him. Instead, she rose determinedly. "I think I'll skip dinner. I'll see you all at seven-thirty in the morning. Good night."

Elizabeth looked at her in concern. "You really should have some dinner."

"Yeah," Bethany said, frowning.

Easier for you all to talk about me, if I just disappear, she thought, forcing a convivial smile.

"I've got snacks in the bungalow," she said. "Thanks."

She left then. Thor, ordering the food from Clint, didn't even glance her way.

The bungalows were set no more than twenty feet apart, but they managed to feel private. They were nestled against a thin forest of sea grapes, pines and spindly oaks that shielded them from the rush of Duval Street and beyond. A stretch of beach lay in front of some, while the deeper water and the docks flanked others. The property wasn't big; there were only three piers, one with local boats and two for guests. She could see Jack's ramshackle fishing boat and Jay's pleasure craft rocking gently at one pier, their work boats at another, awaiting the morning.

She entered her bungalow and looked around, admiring the casual plan. Each unit offered a refrigerator, microwave and wet bar, with a screen between the parlor/kitchenette/sitting area and the bedroom.

She turned on the television, feeling restless and eager for the sound of a human voice. Luckily, the television wouldn't rib her the way her so-called friends had.

She had a package of breakfast bars by the sink and decided they would have to do for a meal. She would be seen if she tried to leave their small resort, and she didn't want anyone to know she had just been seeking her own company—or company other than theirs, anyway.

Munching an oat-and-honey granola bar, she stared at the television, then started flicking the channel changer. Nothing drew her attention. The sound of laughter filtered to her from the bar area, and she found herself annoyed that they all seemed to be getting along so well. She'd been disturbed enough that her own friends were making fun of her. The Thor Thompson thing was more than she could stomach. The man was arrogant beyond belief.

She threw herself on the bed, staring up at the ceiling. She *had* to make the first discovery now.

The bet was ridiculous. Totally immature. She should just tell him in the morning that it was off. Except that she was the one who had started it.

Eventually the exertion of the day began to take its toll. She left the television on for company but changed into an oversize T, turned off the lights and tried to get some sleep. At first she could still hear the sounds of conversation and laughter, just as annoying as before.

But she needed rest. Last night she had slept at last but not long enough. At least today, she hadn't seen a thing in the water except fish and coral.

The world was well, she told herself.

A little voice crept in. Bull!

At last she drifted to sleep.

In her dreams, she was diving again. The sound of her breath through the regulator was soothing. The water was clear. Tangs and clown fish darted by. A very large grouper, a good six feet, hovered by the reef. The sun struck the water, the rays arrowing down. Anemones wafted with the current.

And then...

She saw the woman. Hair drifting in golden streams. Head bowed, arms lifted in the easy current. White fabric drifting against the length of her body Feet tied to the weight that held her down.

Her head lifted. Her eyes opened. Her mouth worked. No sound came, but her eyes pleaded, filled with an infinite sadness.

Then, from behind her, they rose....

Skeletal forms with decaying flesh cloaking their bones. Skeletal forms brandishing knives and swords, bodies rotting, clothing streaming from them in oddly colorful tatters.

They marched. Marched across the seabed, sightless eye sockets staring at Genevieve, bony jaws locked with determination.

She was frozen at first, unable to move.

She had discovered something, she realized. Something she wasn't meant to know.

And now...

The sound of her breathing stopped.

The army of skeletons was almost upon her. She turned to swim away, only to discover that she was surrounded. There was no escape.

A rotted arm in a tattered jacket reached out for her. Suddenly skeletal arms were rising all around her, bony fingers nearly touching her flesh.

She sensed the girl's soundless warning. Beware…

She could almost smell the overwhelming scent of decay.

Rotting flesh. A breath away…

It was impossible, she told herself. Impossible to be smelling death and decay beneath the surface, breathing through a regulator.

She awoke, jerking bolt upright in the bed, filled with dread and panic. She forced herself to breathe deeply. It was a dream, only a dream. Inhale, exhale.

She gritted her teeth. Ridiculous. She wasn't like this!

She felt thirsty, anxious for a glass of water, for something tangible. Tea. She could make tea. Maybe it was close enough to morning that she could just stay awake.

The television was still on. Paid programming. Some buff guy talking about his new cardio machine. She could see him past the screen dividing the room.

She let him keep talking. She liked the voice, and the light cast by the television. Actually, she needed more light. She turned on the bedside lamp.

It was only when she stood that she realized she was wet. And salty. As if she'd really been in the sea. Swallowing hard, she rushed into the bathroom, turning on the main lights on her way. She started to splash her face with cold water, then looked into the mirror of the medicine cabinet above the sink.

Her heart thudded; her breathing ceased.

There was seaweed in her hair.

3

The strangest clattering noise was going on, as if someone was throwing pots and pans—or as if chains were being furiously shaken.

Marshall Miro was aware of the sound, deep in the fog of sleep. He twisted and turned. He almost awoke. The sound was unsettling. It reminded him of…

What?

Something…unpleasant.

He fought the sensation and the noise. His body clock informed him it was too early to wake up.

So he didn't.

Jack Payne was vaguely aware of a noise. It fit right in with the video game he was playing in his dreams. The game was called Kick-Ass Karena, and kick-ass it was. Gorgeous animated women battled one another and the player for supremacy. And when a guy won, it was all his: the booze, the women and the victory, hot or ruthless.

The sound just seemed to be part of the game.

* * *

Victor heard a noise and woke up with a start. For several seconds, he just sat up in bed wondering what the hell had woken him up.

He heard nothing. Nothing at all.

Groaning, he lay back down and prayed for a little more shut-eye.

Jay Gonzalez never quite made it up. The noise seemed to be coming from a distance. He wanted to get up. Wanted to stop it. But there were times when he fell asleep with the lights or the television on, then wanted them off but couldn't quite rouse himself enough to do it.

He didn't even open his eyes, despite the fact that the sound disturbed him deeply. It brought to mind things that were…uncomfortable. Painful. It touched memories that….

That he wished would remain lost.

Ignore it, he told himself. Sleep.

The sound would be gone by morning.

Thor bolted up. What in God's name was going on?

He slid his legs over the side of the bed. He didn't turn on a light, having learned it was better to cloak oneself in darkness to check whatever might be going on in the light. Barefoot, he walked softly to the door of his bungalow and looked out.

A benign moon fell over the sand, water and nearby cottages. It was a serene picture. A semitropical night in paradise, all as it should be.

So where the hell had the noise come from?

Looking at the next bungalow, he saw that it was alive with light. It was Genevieve's bungalow, he was certain. Okay, so she liked things bright. Couldn't hang her for that.

Not that he wanted to hang her. Just…

Why the hell couldn't the woman be normal?

He started, suddenly certain he had heard a scream.

Or not.

It almost seemed as if the sound had come from inside his own head. He studied the cottage next to his own. If anything was wrong…

Swearing, he strode toward her lighted window.

Genevieve stared at her reflection in the mirror, all but paralyzed.

Okay, this was frightening. A dream was one thing. Hopping out of bed to plunge into the water in the middle of the night was another. What the hell was happening to her?

She nearly jumped out of her skin when she heard a hurried knocking at her door. She glanced at her watch. Five-thirty-five. Not as late as she had wanted to sleep, but early enough to get up for the day. Early enough for someone to be knocking at her door?

Then she heard her name called, softly but urgently. "Genevieve?"

She froze, recognizing the voice.

"Are you all right in there?"

She strode to the door, opening it to see Thor Thompson, as expected.

But for once he wasn't laughing at her; he actually looked concerned.

"Uh, good morning," she murmured, holding tightly to the door. "Of course I'm all right. Why are you asking?"

He stared at her as if she were suffering from something contagious. She realized she still had seaweed in her hair. Self-consciously, she reached for it.

"You didn't hear a…racket?" he asked her.

"What?"

He sighed, pointing to the neighboring cottage. "That's me, next door. It sounded as if something was…clanking over here, and then it sounded like a scream."

"Clanking?" she repeated blankly.

He shrugged, looking ill at ease. With her—or himself? "Yeah, clanking, clanging…like chains. You can't mean to tell me you didn't hear anything?"

"I'm sorry. I must have been sleeping," she murmured.

"Or swimming."

"Pardon?"

"Swimming. You're all wet, and you're wearing… seaweed."

"Oh. Well, I like a morning dip now and then."

"Right," he murmured, staring at her flatly. "You just wake up, feel the urge and plunge right in? In the dark?"

"Now and then," she said lightly. *I am losing my mind*, she thought. But he was the last person in the world with whom she would ever share that information.

"Interesting," he said. "Well, if you're sure you're all right, I'm going back to bed."

She wasn't all right at all. But there was no way in hell she was going to tell him so. "I'm fine." She smiled. "Are you all right? It sounds as if you're hearing things. You know. *I* see them, *you* hear them."

"Something was making a racket," he told her flatly.

She shrugged. "Well, it wasn't me."

"Couldn't have been. You were swimming."

"I was about to make coffee. If you'd like some…?" she added, praying her words were perfectly casual. Indifferent.

Hands on his hips, he looked at her as if she'd just made another entirely insane suggestion, but then he shrugged. "Hell, I guess I'm up for the day."

He followed her in. She went straight for the coffeemaker and then the sink, filling the pot with water, then setting the premeasured bag into place to brew. He'd taken a seat on the futon that served as the sofa— or guest bed. She realized he was studying her, and she was pretty sure she made an absurd picture, dressed in the long, soaked T-shirt, seaweed still in her hair.

Act like it's perfectly normal, she warned herself.

"How do you like your coffee?"

"Black."

"Macho, huh?" she murmured.

"Nope. Best way to learn to drink it when you might be out for a while with milk that goes sour and a crew member who forgot to buy sugar or creamer."

"Right. Perfectly sensible."

She sensed his shrug.

"We crazy people like it light," she murmured.

"Hey, it's a new day," he said politely.

The coffeemaker chimed. She poured two cups, handed him one, fixed hers the way she liked it and sat across from him on one of the two wicker chairs that faced the futon.

"I saw something down there," she said flatly. "Today I'll figure out for myself what it was—while discovering the first relic."

"You're not just going to find it, you're going to find it today?"

She shrugged nonchalantly.

"And you think *I'm* arrogant," he murmured.

She lifted a hand. "When the shoe fits…"

He looked as if he was going to rise. To her deep annoyance, she realized she didn't want to be alone. "What are they going to talk to us about this morning?" she demanded quickly.

"The usual, I imagine. Stuff we've already heard about preserving the reef while we excavate."

"We're working as carefully as we can," she said.

He grinned. "They just want to keep putting in their two cents, that's all. And I have to hand it to Preston—his research was top-notch, and his logic appears to be the same."

"I know. I read the letters written by Antoine D'Mas, the pirate who watched the *Marie Josephine* go down. It all makes sense to me, too."

"There you go. We agree on something," he murmured.

They both heard the sound of footsteps pounding on the sand and the knock at the door. "Hey, you up in there?" Bethany called.

Genevieve stood and opened the door. Bethany was ready for the day, it appeared. She was wearing cutoffs over her one-piece Speedo. Her hair was tied back, out of the way.

"Good, you're up early!" she announced. "I didn't want to sit around alone any longer. There's nothing on the TV—hey!" she said suddenly, seeing Thor on the futon.

"Hey yourself," he greeted her, standing politely.

Bethany suddenly stared at Genevieve, as if really seeing her for the first time. "You're soaked. And there's seaweed in your hair. What the hell…?"

Genevieve looked meaningfully at her friend, her back to Thor Thompson. "You know me. I woke up early and just couldn't resist the lure of the water."

"By the dock?" Bethany said incredulously.

Genevieve made her stare fiercer. "On the beach side," she snapped. "I can't resist the water sometimes, and you know it."

"Oh. Um. Right," Bethany murmured.

"Do you want coffee?" Genevieve asked quickly, changing the subject.

"Sure, thanks."

Bethany plopped down on the futon, where Thor joined her. "You still on for tonight?" she asked.

Genevieve nearly spilled the coffee.

"Yeah, why not?" he asked.

"Barhopping," Bethany told Genevieve. "We're all going."

"Should we be barhopping?" Genevieve asked.

"We don't have to drink at every bar. But Thor, Lizzie and Zach haven't spent much time here. We're going to show them the must-do tourist places and then our own favorites. Hey, we're always in by four o'clock. We can shower, eat somewhere cool, show them a few spots and be back by eleven-thirty. Marshall's coming, and Thor's the boss of his team, so…" She shrugged. "It'll be great."

"I'm not so sure," Genevieve murmured.

"When did you suddenly turn into such a stick?" Bethany demanded.

"Here. Take your coffee. Entertain yourselves. I'm going to shower," Genevieve said.

"You're going to shower—to go diving?" Bethany asked.

"Yeah. I want fresh seaweed in my hair," she said, and left the two of them together on her futon. She walked into the bathroom and closed and locked the door. She stared at her reflection in the mirror again. She realized she was deeply irritated and didn't know why.

She also didn't want them to leave.

Determined not to dwell on the situation, she hopped into the shower, washed her hair, then hopped out. Her suit from the day before was on the rack, and she slipped back into it, then found shorts and a denim shirt, and slipped them on over the suit. When she emerged, the two were still talking.

"It was weird. I thought it was coming from here, too," Bethany was saying.

"What are you talking about?" Genevieve asked sharply.

"Weird noises." Bethany laughed. "If I didn't know you better, I'd have said you were cooking!"

"You heard noises, too?" Genevieve demanded.

"Yeah, a real racket. I don't usually get up way before I need to—especially when I'm hoping to have some energy left at night," Bethany told her. "What were you doing?"

"Nothing. I was swimming, remember?" Genevieve said curtly. It was enough to make her nuts. She saw a body, no one else did. Thor heard noises, so did everyone else.

She felt a disturbing, creeping sensation along her spine. How much did that matter when she had awakened wet with seawater? And she didn't remember a thing about leaving her cottage.

"They've probably got the tiki bar open by now. I'm hungry," she said.

Thor and Bethany rose at her obvious suggestion that they all leave. He headed off to the cottage next door, waving a hand behind him. "See you in a few minutes."

Bethany stared after him. "Cool," she murmured.

"Yeah, he's just great."

Bethany looked at her in surprise. "What's the

matter? He's got a great reputation." She giggled. "And damned good buns, too. And pecs. And biceps. And those eyes…"

"Bethany…"

"What?"

"Go for it."

"Oh, no. I'm not flirting with him or anything. He never fools around on a job."

"Who the hell told you that?"

"I read it. There was a magazine article on him not long ago. He's the kind who's married to his work. He grew up on the wrong side of town. Father walked out on his mother, she wound up dying of a heart attack at forty, trying to raise the kids on her own. He just doesn't want a family, I guess."

"How noble," Genevieve muttered.

"What is the matter with you? I'd think you'd want to work with someone who wasn't hitting on you all the time. Everything with him is all business. Though I guess he's been a little hard on you over the…what you thought you saw in the water."

"A little hard? He thinks I'm certifiable."

Bethany giggled, sobered quickly and apologized. "Genevieve…we've all seen what we haven't really seen in the water at some time."

Yes, but have we all awoken soaked in seawater, with seaweed in our beds? she nearly asked aloud.

"Let's get something to eat. We have to make the first discovery. And we have to make it today," she said, catching her friend's arm and urging her toward the tiki bar.

* * *

Thor knew the history; he never went into anything without studying every shred of information about the project. Still, for some reason—perhaps to enforce the part about avoiding destruction of the reef in any way—they were seated on and around the picnic tables and benches by the docks, listening to what they knew already.

If ever a man had looked like he should be a professor of history, it was Henry Sheridan. He wore the kind of glasses that had Coke-bottle lenses, black frames, and, sure enough, he must have broken them, because they were held together between the eyes by a Band-Aid. His hair—a combination of mousy-brown and gray—stuck up in tufts from his head, without benefit of mousse. His face was very thin, ascetic, and his form was equally meager. Thor had the feeling the man seldom thought about eating, so lost was he on some intellectual plane.

Coast Guard Lieutenant Larry Preston was the antithesis of Sheridan. He was big, tall and hardy. He could swim and dive with the best of them, and though his job was to see that they followed the dictates of the state, Thor was pretty sure that history itself bored him. Preston liked action. He was wearing sunglasses and a uniform hat, along with his white shorts and shirt, and beneath those glasses, Thor had a feeling the man was keeping his eyes closed.

To the credit of the divers from both boats, they

were at least putting on the pretense of rapt attention.

"As you all know, I'm certain, we estimate that there are at least two thousand undiscovered wrecks in the waters around the state. But the sea is harsh. Ships don't usually sink intact. Winds and rains crack masts, and timbers split. On the way down, ships are at the mercy of tides and currents and their own weight and construction. Sometimes small vessels fare better, but huge ships—even broken up—can be an easier find. A ship such as the *Marie Josephine* might have left a field of discovery a mile long. She was brutalized by pirates in the midst of a storm. It's more than likely her remains are in far more than two or three pieces. Despite that, and as you're aware, we're not going in with any vacuuming devices. Especially since we're working on nothing more than speculation right now. It's likely that, should you succeed in finding the ship's resting place, you'll begin to find small relics. Coins, of course. Pottery, porcelain. Last year, as Thor can tell you, we unearthed a Civil War barge in the St. Johns river because an 1860s razor was found. By Thor." Sheridan nodded his way in acknowledgment. Lizzie applauded, and Alex Mathews let out an appreciative whistle.

"Cool," Bethany murmured, offering him her generous smile.

Thor felt restless, anxious to be out on the water. He found himself studying Genevieve Wallace, who was staring straight ahead at Sheridan, her face betraying not so much as a flicker of emotion. The woman was fucking weird. She walked out in a nightshirt and jumped into the water?

While all kinds of noises were coming from her cottage?

"Raccoons," he heard someone whisper.

Victor Damon was leaning casually against the edge of the next table over. He wasn't listening at the moment; he was grinning as he looked at Bethany.

"Excuse me?" Lieutenant Preston snapped.

"Sorry, sir," Victor said. "Bethany heard some kind of commotion last night. She forgets just how many cats and raccoons we have around here."

"Well, they won't be under the water!" Preston reminded him.

"Right, sir, absolutely not," Victor agreed.

Sheridan cleared his throat. "I think it's important that you all understand the full history of this wreck. The Spanish settled Florida in the early 1500s—St. Augustine is the oldest continually inhabited European settlement in the United States. The English got nervous about the Spanish being so close, and the French were trying to get a piece of the action, too. In 1763, Britain gained control of Florida in exchange for Cuba. Then came the Revolutionary War, and Florida remained loyal to the mother country. In 1784, the Spanish gained control again as part of the peace treaty that ended the American Revolution, but in 1821 they ceded Florida to the United States."

Alex yawned. He caught the others staring at him and sat up straight.

"Hey, sorry, but I grew up here. I learned all this stuff in school," he said.

"Yeah, but were you listening then?" Victor asked.

"This is important," Sheridan said impatiently. "It explains why our ship is where it is. During the American Revolution, the French helped the U.S. Unofficially, the Spanish helped the French give us help. Before he was a pirate, José Gasparilla was in the Royal Spanish Navy. He knew these waters from his military experience, and he continued his career as a pirate until he died in 1821. Rumor has it that before his ship could be taken, he cast himself overboard with weights tied to his feet—one of his favorite ways to do away with prisoners. But shortly before his death, he heard of the *Marie Josephine*." He paused dramatically.

"An English ship, despite her name," Genevieve said into his silence.

"Yes, and Gasparilla was loyal to Spain. Unless, of course, there was a good Spanish ship to be attacked." He laughed, then continued. "At any rate, he heard that the *Marie Josephine* was nearby, having taken a late exchange of prisoners to Cuba, and heading back to jolly old England laden with the ransom that had been paid," Sheridan said.

"He probably felt he had a right to steal it," Marshall said with a shrug.

"Exactly!" Sheridan agreed.

Thor was startled when Genevieve disagreed. "I don't think that was it at all. Gasparilla had fallen in love with the captain's daughter, Anne, who had managed to travel with her father and the prisoners to Cuba, because she wanted to be with a young Spanish nobleman they were exchanging. He and Anne had both been Gasparilla's prisoners previously—that's how they'd met—and had been ransomed together by the English, who then made the young Spaniard, Aldo Verdugo, their own prisoner. Rumor has it that Anne tricked her father and managed to become a passenger on the ship once again to remain with Aldo. And Aldo, who should have been safely in Cuba, had stowed away on the ship so he could remain with his beloved Anne. Gasparilla, however, had also fallen in love with Anne when she was his prisoner. He had returned her to the English because of the ransom, and his fellow pirates wanted the money. He, however, wanted her back. *That's* why he went after the *Marie Josephine*."

Alex snorted. "Gen, that's nuts. Let's see…all that ransom money—in gold—or a woman. Come on! Women would have been a dime a dozen to a pirate."

Genevieve waved a hand in the air dismissively. "He wrote letters about his love for her," she claimed.

"Where are these letters?" Sheridan demanded, frowning.

"*Your* university," Genevieve said. Everyone was

staring at her. "Hey, I made a trip up and studied everything in the library about the *Marie Josephine*, Gasparilla, the storm, everything. I was cross-referencing, and that's when I found the letters."

"Come on, you can't put a romantic spin on pirates," Victor teased her. "They were dirty, nasty thieves."

"You should have read the letters," Genevieve said. "Even a nasty, dirty pirate can fall in love."

"He could have had tons of women," Victor insisted.

"Yes, but she was the one he wanted. Who knows why someone falls in love. Or maybe it was only an infatuation. The one he couldn't have. Anyway, he wrote about her in those letters, and he said he was in love."

"Leave it to a girl," Victor countered, rolling his eyes and sighing.

Genevieve laughed. "Leave it to a girl to beat the pants off you," she countered lightly.

Thor sensed camaraderie in their teasing. It was apparent this group knew one another well, that there was a deep underlying friendship between them. He realized that he envied it. He had a damned good crew, but they didn't always work together. Zach and Lizzie were totally reliable, but they were too close as a married couple to bond with anyone the way Marshall's people were bonded, even when they were teasing and testing one another. He'd thought he liked it when business was business, but there was something approachiing an actual family relationship between Marshall's divers, and it not only appeared to be fun, it clearly worked.

"Hey, baby, please don't beat me up," Victor said in mock fear. "Hey, Alex, watch out. Our Gen is tough." He paused, grinning and sliding closer to her on the bench to set an arm around her shoulders. "Except, of course, when she's seeing things in the water."

Genevieve shook off his arm and smiled sweetly in return. "Eat shit and die, Victor."

"Hey, hey! Knock it off, all of you. This is serious business," Marshall said.

"Hey, I meant it," Victor protested innocently. "She's the best. Ouch, Gen! That wasn't nice."

"Yeah, yeah, yeah," she said, staring at him sharply with those mercurial eyes that could so easily light with laughter, then narrow on a dare. "I did my homework."

"Of course. Obviously…I haven't read everything in our archives," Sheridan said. Thor had the feeling the man would be finding the letters immediately on his return to the university.

"If Gen says they're there, they're there," Victor said, suddenly dead serious.

"Come on," Marshall said wearily. "It doesn't matter *why* Gasparilla attacked the ship, only that he did. And right as he was savaging her, a storm came through. Gasparilla got away, but the *Marie Josephine* went down. He purportedly came back to find the treasure, but the storm had shifted the sands and he couldn't find her, so the ship remains at the bottom of the sea with her complete treasure, or so we imagine."

"Yes, well, that's about it," Sheridan said, sounding somewhat huffy. He'd always been a nice-enough guy, if a little geeky, but it was obvious he hadn't liked being shown up by a diver. "The letters I do know about were left by one of his men, and from his descriptions of their position while awaiting the *Marie Josephine*, and calculating the currents, the effects of the storm and the natural shifting due to time, I firmly believe I have you exactly in the right area. But you need to find proof positive of the ship's final resting ground before we allow any disturbance of the reef."

"How many times do you think we'll have to listen to this speech?" someone murmured softly. Thor looked around. Jack Payne was shaking his head.

"As many times as Professor Sheridan wants to give it," Marshall said, staring at them. "We're being paid by the state," he reminded them. "Money raised mainly by the efforts of Professor Sheridan."

Thor leaned forward to speak at last. "We took more than simple pirate history into account while plotting our coordinates. When the ship sank, remember, half of what is land today wasn't then. The area has been dredged, filled in, blown away and literally remade by the army, the navy—and Henry Flagler. When he was building his railroad, they didn't have a place for a depot, so he told them to make one. All that has been taken into account, along with weather charts and the tidal phenomena over the years. One of the main points we need to remember is that our ship's probably broken into many pieces, most of them entirely unrecognizable without careful scrutiny. And she's probably spread out over a wide expanse of ocean floor."

He was pleased to see that he'd captured their full attention. And they remained riveted when Sheridan spoke again.

"And the state will take full possession of the find, with each of you receiving a percentage," he reminded them.

Marshall rose suddenly, arching a brow to Thor. He nodded, knowing what Marshall was about to say. Sheridan had advised them both of the plan. For some reason the man seemed very wary of the divers he had chosen. He wanted the two crews mixed up, so there wouldn't be any chance of one group hiding anything from the other. Sheridan was not a trusting soul. The names had been mixed in an old bait bucket last night, to be drawn at random this morning, before the meeting.

"We're mixing up the crews today. We've done it by lot, so there's no complaining—there shouldn't be complaining, anyway. We're all in this together. So forget your old buddy system, because you're getting new buddies. Here's the roster for today. Bethany, you're with Zach. Vic, you're with Lizzie, and I'll be the man on deck. Alex, you're teaming up with Jack Payne, and, Gen, you're with Thor. Preston will be staying topside."

He was going to be working with Genevieve?

That was something Thor hadn't known. Great. Just great.

Well, at least he could quickly dispel the notion that she was seeing dead people smiling at her in the water.

"We're retracing ground we've been over where the sonar has indicated there is metal somewhere beneath the water. We may find a lost diving watch from last weekend, but hey, we're looking for a needle in a haystack, so...everyone ready?" Marshall asked.

If he was unhappy, it certainly didn't seem Genevieve Wallace was thrilled with the arrangements for the day, either, Thor noticed.

But as they walked, heading out for the boats, Jack Payne slipped an arm around her shoulders. "Should I grab that equipment bag for you?" he offered.

"Jack, I've been hauling my own gear forever, you know that," she said, but she smiled at him as she picked up her own bag and they all made their way down to the docks.

So he was partnered up with her, Thor thought.

He still felt the uneasy sensation of waking to the strange noises, then seeing her, soaked, salty and wearing seaweed in her hair.

She was a wild card, no doubt about it.

So why the hell was he so damned fascinated with her?

On shore, fine.

In the water?

He shook his head.

It was going to be one hell of a day.

4

Neither Genevieve nor Alex had been on *The Seeker* before, and Thor couldn't help a moment's pride when he watched them survey his boat. She was nice, with a great cabin, powerful motors and a large dive platform, allowing for easy exits and access.

He took the helm himself as they headed out. Lieutenant Preston was at his side. "Sheridan's a jerk," he said above the roar of the motor.

Thor shrugged. "He's all right. He's just really passionate about history, I guess."

Preston snorted. "Yeah, but did you see his face when Genevieve knew something he didn't? Thought he was about to have a stroke. I guarantee you he's on the phone right now to some grad student, reaming them out for missing a cross-reference."

Thor shrugged. "Hey, finding the ship is the important thing, right?"

"Man, she's nice," Preston murmured then, studying the console. "There a second helm in the cabin?"

"Yep."

"Radar, sonar, GPS...she all but drives herself, huh?"

Thor turned, aware they were no longer alone. Genevieve was standing behind him, wearing her wet suit. Beyond her, the other divers had already attached their buoyancy control vests to their tanks, and tested their regulators and air, ready for the water when they reached the reef.

Gen had a touch of challenge in her manner. "Great boat," she told him seriously. "I'm really going to enjoy it."

He had to smile, then glanced down at his instruments to hide his pride. Marshall was leading at the moment, and in fifteen minutes, they would be dropping anchor and tossing out their dive flags.

"You're point man," Thor said to Preston, who nodded. Thor headed back to don his own gear. One of his fellow divers had already taken care of his BCV and his tank. Nevertheless, he checked out his regulator and air, along with the security of his tank.

"Don't trust me, eh?" she said softly, next to him, sliding down on the seat to secure her vest.

"Never trust anyone when you're getting into the water," he said.

"Don't worry. I don't. But if you're with any of us, that's all you have to do. Final checks. We take care of each other."

He felt his teeth grate. Was she suggesting that he'd never dived with anyone trustworthy before?

She stood, balancing perfectly with the weight of her tank. Preston hurried up behind her, but she was already moving. "Hey, we're partners!" Thor called after her.

She waved. "I'll be hanging at the surface. Waiting. Take your time," she added sweetly.

Sweet? Like hell.

He was quickly ready, stepping off the dive platform to land beside her in the water before sinking slowly.

Ten feet away, Jack and Alex gestured, indicating their parallel paths.

Thor believed strongly in the methods they'd used to determine the location for this search, but down here now, their depth a little over fifty feet, he wasn't at all certain they would make a discovery. They were a little west and south of the customary beaten dive areas, but they might as well have been pleasure divers off any tour boat. The reefs were majestic here, dangerous for anyone who didn't know the path to navigate through them—or forced onto them in the midst of a roaring storm. There were areas where the coral outcrop—with its rich abundance of life—gave way suddenly to greater depths, and then fan coral would suddenly shoot sharply toward the surface. The colors seemed brilliant today. Purple fans, then a riot of fire coral. Blue-and-yellow tangs. Clown fish. A huge grouper…a lone barracuda. Something seemed to glisten in the sand deep below, and he propelled himself past the coral and downward.

The object was covered in sand. He dug, adrenaline racing through him. His fingers curled around the object, and disappointment washed through him. There was nowhere near enough sea growth on the object for it to have been in the water any length of time.

He had found someone's lost dive knife. A nice one, actually. But definitely new.

He looked back, ready to let his dive buddy know it was nothing. She was right behind him, as ever, perfectly still and buoyant. She nodded her understanding.

He swam on.

No! Good God, no.

She was there. Thor was just ahead, but *she* was there. The woman with the long blond hair.

I don't see you! Genevieve raged inwardly.

The woman's head rose. The woman smiled with poignant, aching sweetness.

She was a ghost, Gen told herself. She wasn't there. But she *was*. She reached out…but didn't touch Genevieve. Then it seemed that a ghost of a ghost, an image of the woman but even paler still, rose from the creature weighted to the bottom. Rose…and pointed.

Thor looked back. Genevieve tried to stare back with perfect calm. She pointed.

Apparently he saw nothing. He frowned and looked in the direction of the woman, then swam toward the area bordering the coral where Gen indicated. He stopped just to the side of the ghost and gently began to sift through the sand.

So she *was* insane.

But the ghost's specter or aura or whatever was pointing, as well. Genevieve forced herself to breathe, listening to the lulling sound of her regulator. Okay, she was crazy. But the ghost wanted her to go in a certain direction.

She went.

Nothing. Nothing at all. Sand, without a hint that something might be lying beneath it. He looked back again. His partner was moving. She looked back at him and indicated that he should follow her.

She had the strangest expression on her face.

Shit! The woman was seeing things again. He was sure of it.

He waved, determined to get her attention, to snap her out of whatever strange hallucination had seized her. He had no idea where she was going, or why.

She nodded to acknowledge him but ignored his signal, indicating that they should circle around the coral outcrop rather than move on.

She didn't appear to be distressed; maybe he was jumping to conclusions. But neither did she seem willing to allow him to take the lead. With a controlled motion of her fins, she went shooting on farther to the southwest.

He followed her. She had stopped again, as if following some unseen guidance.

She dove deeper, past a strip of high fan coral, down to the seabed, another fifteen feet or so. He followed. It was as if she knew exactly where she was going. There was no hesitation in her movements.

At the bottom, she stopped and stared at the sand, then began searching.

She had lost it, he decided. Completely.

It was just sand. No different from the sand she had pointed to moments ago.

All right. He would give it a go. They were searching for a pack of needles in a pile of very large haystacks, so what the hell.

He began to search, as well, carefully, trying not to roil the sand. He unearthed a small ray. Disgruntled, the creature shot away.

She was sifting the sand, as well. She dug calmly, at first, but then she began to search frantically.

He watched her, ready to haul her up and, once they reached the surface, explode. Hell. He wasn't diving with her anymore, and that was that.

He reached out for her. She was strong; he hadn't planned on that. She wrenched her arm away from him. When she did, her hand hit the sand, hard. The granules danced up into the water, darkening it. He was about to go for her with a more powerful grip when he noticed something that didn't quite belong. Something that looked like a black, crusty blob.

He reached for it instead of for her.

When the object was in his hand, he felt the familiar—and pleasurable—adrenalin rush. He wasn't sure, but...

He reached for the dive knife in the sheath at his ankle, snapped it out and scraped carefully at the piece. He looked up as the black coat of time, oxidation and sea growth slowly gave way.

She was staring at him, waiting. Dead calm, perfectly buoyant, as if she were floating in air. Those eyes of hers, behind the mask….

She knew.

He looked at her and nodded slowly.

Gold.

"I don't understand," Bethany said, seriously confused. She untangled a length of her freshly washed hair with her fingers. "You should be on cloud nine. That was a Spanish gold piece you found. Minted in Cuba, Marshall thinks, though he admits he isn't sure yet. But if so…then it has to have come from the *Marie Josephine.*"

Genevieve nodded, brushing her own hair out before the mirror. "I *am* delighted." Delighted? Did she dare tell the truth, even to Bethany?

"Well, Thor picked it up, right?"

"What?"

"He's the one who actually found the piece."

"Like hell!"

"Don't bite my head off. You two were together. The first discovery goes to you as a team. That will teach them to rib you! As if you could possibly be crazy in any way. They'll be sorry." She giggled. "I'll bet you Victor is sorry right now. I mean, you are *his* diving partner, really. I'll bet he's kicking himself right now for what he said."

Genevieve's brush paused halfway through the

length of her hair. She turned and studied Bethany. "What if I told you I saw her again?"

Bethany laughed, flinging herself back on the bed. Then she realized Genevieve wasn't laughing and sat up soberly. "You're kidding. Please tell me you're kidding."

"If you repeat this, I will call you the worst liar in the world," Genevieve said forcefully, taking a seat on the edge of her bed. Bethany was staring at her with worry in her eyes.

"Oh, Genevieve…you *are* teasing me, right?"

"No."

Bethany closed her eyes. "I don't think I want to hear this."

"Then…then I won't say any more."

"No! You have to talk to me…. I just don't think I want to hear it." She hesitated. "Please, Gen, go ahead."

Genevieve sighed. "I was down there with Thor. He was moving a little ahead. I felt as if I were being called, so I looked back, and…there she was. Exactly where I saw her before."

Bethany frowned. "I…wow. I don't even know what to say."

"Here's the thing. Have you ever seen one of those movies with…astral projection, except that it wouldn't be exactly that…or heard about people who died on the operating table and were floating above themselves, looking down at their own bodies?"

"Now you're seriously scaring me. What are you talking about?"

"It seemed as if her…her ghost left her where she was weighted down. And led me—pointing exactly to the place where I should look."

Bethany just stared at her.

"Did Thor see her?"

"No."

"Gen…"

"It's the honest to God truth."

"You saw the woman again? A dead woman. Then her…ghost pointed out the exact spot where you found the coin."

"Exactly."

Bethany just stared at her again.

"Say something."

"Oh, God, what do you want me to say?"

"That you believe me!"

"Uh…"

"Oh, never mind. Just don't repeat anything I've said. He'd have me locked up."

"Who?"

"You know who. Thor Thompson."

"Oh, Gen, I don't think—"

"He'd manage to get me thrown off the dive, I guarantee you."

Bethany walked over to her, setting a hand on her arm. "I think you're right. I think…I think you'd better not talk about any of this."

"I swear to you, everything I'm saying is true."

"True in your own mind," Bethany whispered gently.

"I saw her. I promise you, what I saw was real."

"But Thor…?"

"No, you're right. Thor didn't see her."

"And today you weren't…scared?" Bethany asked.

"No. Yes. I was terrified at first. And then I had to pretend I wasn't seeing anything."

"I'm confused. The first day you nearly choked and drowned, it shook you up so much. And then…today…it's become your friend?"

"I don't exactly know. Maybe today I gave her a chance because I was more afraid of Thor than I was of seeing a ghost. Bethany, I know this will sound strange, but I think she wants us to find the ship."

"Great," Bethany murmured. "*I* want us to find the ship, too." She stared at Genevieve anxiously. "So this is…"

"I guess."

Genevieve hesitated. She was still afraid. And not just of what had happened in the water.

She was afraid of what had happened this morning.

Waking up soaking wet, wearing seaweed.

"I'm going to slip out during dinner and see Jay Gonzalez."

Bethany sighed. "Oh, good move. Like Jay doesn't think you're crazy, too. You talked to him, remember? He wanted to help. He couldn't find anything."

"He can try again. Some poor woman is snatched somewhere every week, maybe every day. And there are always runaways who end up dead and unidentified," Genevieve reminded Bethany.

"Genevieve…if you're seeing a body, a…ghost who seems to want to help you find a lost ship, don't you think the ghost should be someone from that era? I don't believe this. We're talking about a ghost. As if it's…real."

"She *is* real," Genevieve said, wincing. "I swear, Bethany. I don't think Thor Thompson would admit to seeing a ghost—even to himself—if one smacked him in the head. I don't understand what's going on, and why *I* should be seeing this…*her*, but I am. And it…it has to mean something."

"Actually, I know who you should see," Bethany murmured.

"Who?"

"Audrey Lynley," Bethany said.

"Audrey? The We-went-to-school-with-her Audrey Lynley?" Genevieve said. It was her opportunity to stare at Bethany as if *she* were completely mad.

"Yes," Bethany said firmly.

Genevieve shook her head. "Oh, come on, Bethany. She doesn't even pretend that anything she does is real."

"Excuse me, but aren't you the one telling me you're seeing a ghost?" Bethany demanded belligerently.

"She reads palms, Bethany. Or she pretends to read palms. And she does tarot cards. I think she even has a crystal ball and pretends to see the future in it sometimes."

"You're acting as if you don't like her," Bethany said.

"I like her fine—mainly because she uses her act

for tourists and she entertains them—she doesn't pretend she really has any answers."

"What could it hurt to talk to her?"

Genevieve sighed. "If it got back to the guys that I was talking to her…"

"Hey, she's an old friend. There's no law against talking to old friends."

Genevieve shrugged and started to speak but broke off when she heard a voice calling them from outside her front door. "Hey, in there!" It was Victor. "Are you guys ready yet? I'm starving. Let's go."

"We're ready," Bethany called back. Then she turned back to Genevieve and spoke more quietly. "I've got Audrey's number, if you want it. Then again, she's got it posted all over Key West. If—"

"I have her number. We live in a really small place, remember?" Genevieve said softly, shoving Bethany toward the door. "And don't you dare whisper a word of what I've said."

"Of course not," Bethany said.

"Do you believe in ghosts at all, Thor?" Bethany asked, sitting across from him at one of the group's favorite seafood places on Whitehead Street.

She was cute, he thought, and apparently an excellent diver, as well, with a round, charming face that made her appear even younger than her twenty-something years. There was a simple eagerness and honesty about her that was very appealing. Different, of course, from the way Genevieve Wallace was appealing. Genevieve seemed to throw off a musk of sensuality and sophistication without the least awareness. Bethany was like a puppy, ready to be cuddled.

"Ouch!" Bethany cried suddenly, reaching down for her leg.

He'd felt the kick. Genevieve was seated next to him, so there was no way he could miss knowing that she had kicked Bethany beneath the table.

"It's an innocent question," Bethany said.

He glanced at Genevieve. She stared at him, her expression unfathomable. She was close to him. Very close, in the small booth. Once again they'd ended up together. Not that he would normally have had anything to complain about. Her perfume was subtle, an underlying tease. She'd worn yellow, a halter dress that contrasted perfectly with her dark hair and bronze skin, and set off the elusive green of her eyes. Her every movement aroused his baser instincts, a fact to which she seemed indifferent, maybe even unaware. She was accustomed to being with friends. She obviously took pride in her appearance but did little to enhance what nature had given her. He was in a polo shirt and shorts. The sleek feel of her leg—stretching out as she kicked Bethany— had rubbed along his like a brush of living silk.

She smiled. "Sorry. After the other day…you know." She stared firmly at Bethany. "We're not going to talk about ghosts."

"I just asked if Thor believed in them," Bethany said.

"No," he said flatly, and stared at Genevieve again.

"Pass the bread, will you, please?" she asked.

"Have you been to our cemetery?" Bethany persisted.

"Bethany, drop it," Genevieve warned. "He doesn't believe in ghosts."

"I didn't say he did. If he hasn't been there, it's kind of a cool place, that's all," Bethany said.

"We used to try to walk the girls by there late at night and scare them," Victor put in from across the table, next to Bethany. "It *is* a cool place. It was established in the 1840s, after a hurricane washed up a bunch of old coffins. You should check it out. The graves aren't set up like in New Orleans, though there are a bunch of mausoleums. They're stacked on top of one another. There's a nice little memorial to the *Maine*. And if you go by at night…it's creepy. I tried to make out with Genevieve there the first time."

Genevieve let out a sound of exasperation. "The first time?"

He laughed. "Okay, the only time. It was sad. She was three feet taller than me at the time. I needed a ladder."

"Very funny," Genevieve told him.

He blew her a kiss.

"We could take the ghost tour," Bethany suggested.

Genevieve groaned aloud. "I do *not* want to take the ghost tour. I thought we were going barhopping?"

"We *are* barhopping," Alex said from the end of the table.

"Actually, that's when most people see ghosts," Jack chimed in ruefully.

"Yeah, the Hard Rock Cafe is supposed to be haunted," Bethany said.

"We're not going to the Hard Rock," Genevieve said. She had sounded a little impatient and looked at him with just a hint of apology. "The Hard Rock is fine, and the building is supposed to be haunted. One of the Currys committed suicide upstairs and a prominent citizen shot himself in front of the fireplace. The staff tends to be super nice and the food is fine. But you don't believe in ghosts anyway. It's still a fine place. It's just that…we're going to our local friendly favorite places. Hey, Clint is playing tonight, you know. We've got to take our guests to hear Clint." She looked at Thor again. "He can do anything. His own stuff, country-western, Buffett, the Eagles—and U2."

"Hey, the girl down at Duffy's is good, too!" Marshall called.

"Yeah, she's great," Genevieve agreed.

Their entrees came, some fish, some chicken, some steak. Just like the appetizers, their main courses were delicious.

Just then the check came, and Thor picked it up.

Genevieve turned to him. "Are you going to put it on a card? I'll just give you cash."

"Don't give me anything."

"It's not as if we're all on a date."

"And it's not as if I'm paying. We get reimbursed for meals," he said.

"We'll divvy it up later?" Marshall called to him.

"Doesn't make any difference. I'll just put it on the expense report."

Marshall gave him a thumbs-up sign. Genevieve flushed uncomfortably and hoped no one noticed.

By the time he had paid the check and returned to the table, the group had risen and was milling outside the front door. This town wasn't as insane now as it was during Fantasy Fest or the dead of winter, when the snowbirds flocked down, but the streets in Key West were busy year round. People did what they called "the Duval crawl"—just shopping and barhopping up and down Duval Street—into the wee hours. In Old Town, shops, restaurants and bars often kept their doors open, air-conditioning wafting out onto the street. With the amount of people around them as they headed to the first bar, Thor didn't realize at first that both Bethany and Genevieve had disappeared.

In the bar, they found tables near the street-side door, far enough from the singer to be able to talk, enough inside that they weren't deafened by the crowds outside. "Champagne all around," Marshall said. "We can toast our first find."

"Great. Where is the rest of our party?" Alex asked. "Genevieve and Bethany are gone. Why would Genevieve disappear? She and Thor were the ones who made the discovery."

"They'll be right back," Victor said.

"Where'd they go?" Alex demanded.

Victor shrugged. "Some errand...I don't know. They know the path we're following. They'll find us."

"Well, hell, I say we toast without them," Alex said, rolling his eyes.

"We should wait," Lizzie said politely.

"Toast," Marshall said, shaking his head. "They'll get here when they get here."

"Champagne will give me a splitting headache tomorrow—mind if I toast with a beer?" Zach asked.

The sentiment went around. Marshall shrugged. "Beer will be a lot cheaper. All right, beer all around."

"Order two extra—if our delinquents don't show up soon, we'll drink them anyway, I'm sure," Victor said.

Thor glanced out the open door, letting the conversation flow around him.

Thanks to Genevieve's height, he was certain he saw her.

She was just passing into an alleyway at the far end of the block.

"Be right back," he said, and left to follow her.

"This is nuts," Genevieve told Bethany.

Bethany stopped walking to stare at her. Genevieve had explained pretty much everything that had happened to her. She'd had to, since Bethany knew she wasn't prone to simply walking out into the surf in her nightshirt. Bethany had been practical at first.

"No pirate bones are going to rise up and come

get you," she had said thoughtfully. "I mean, think about the time and the conditions. The sea, storms, sand…those skeletons are not intact anymore. Unless, of course, the pirates were buried. But then why would they be coming at you from the sea? Can you imagine being here after that storm when all the bodies floated up? Ugh!"

"I'm sure the skeletons were just a dream," Genevieve said.

"But you were all covered in seawater—and seaweed," Bethany said. "And then you saw the ghost again."

"But she was trying to help me. That's what's so weird."

"And that's why you have to talk to Audrey. I called her and told her we'd have about ten minutes. She's waiting for us. She's a great researcher—that's where she gets all her ghost stuff when she tells visitors who's following them down Duval Street—so she may know something after all. Hey, what can it hurt?"

They had come to a small wrought-iron gate that led to a walkway between two buildings. A small cottage from the late nineteenth century was sandwiched in at the end of the walk. On the sign above the gate were written the words: Oracle; Tarot and Palm Readings. Appointments Suggested, Walk-ins Welcome.

Genevieve let out a sigh and opened the gate. Bethany followed her through.

Audrey was, as promised, waiting for them. She

was standing at the wooden door to the house, opening it wide as she saw them arrive. "Hi, guys! Amazing, we live and work in the same town and hardly ever see each other. But your new project must be really exciting, huh? Welcome. Come in, come in."

Audrey wasn't quite as tall as Genevieve, but she was a respectable five-nine, and she bowed a bit to give Bethany a hug, then reached up just a shade to welcome Genevieve. She was a pretty woman, with long dark hair and flashing dark eyes. Genevieve had been afraid she would find her old friend dressed up in a shawl and scarf, calling herself Madam Zena or something. But Audrey was wearing a simple, fashionably casual cotton skirt and halter top, with sandals.

"It's great to see you, Audrey," Genevieve said, feeling guilty. They did live in an incredibly small community. Why didn't they keep up with old friends?

"You look great," Bethany said.

"So do you two. But then again, you're athletes, huh? Living in bathing suits, diving, diving, diving. So what's up? I can't believe you came for a tarot reading," she said, and looked curiously at Genevieve. "Bethany said you only had about ten minutes."

"She's seeing ghosts," Bethany said cheerfully.

Audrey's brows shot up as she looked at Genevieve. "You?" she said incredulously.

"No, not really—"

"Good God, tell her the truth!" Bethany exploded.

"All right, I think I'm seeing a ghost near the site where we think a wreck is lying. But she's turned out to be a helpful ghost," Genevieve said, feeling ridiculous.

"I can do some historical research for you, see what I can find." She shrugged and grinned, looking at Genevieve. "I've never, uh, seen a ghost. I mean, this is a cool way to make a living, but…" She shrugged wordlessly. "Anyway…I'm sure I can find something if I look into your wreck more deeply."

"I've done all kinds of research," Genevieve said. "I'm still not sure who this woman might be."

"Wait," Bethany protested. "You said Gasparilla was in love with the captain's daughter. Maybe that's who you're seeing. Maybe she spurned him and he drowned her."

Genevieve stared at Bethany. She didn't know why she hadn't thought of that possibility.

Yes, she did. She hadn't believed the first time that she'd really seen a ghost. She'd been looking for a prankster—or the victim of a recent murder.

"I don't know," she murmured. "That's an idea, certainly." She winced, looking back at Audrey. "When I didn't freak out at the sight of her the second time I saw her, she led me to the first find."

"Really?" Audrey said, staring at her.

"Don't you dare tell any of this to anyone, please?" Genevieve begged.

Audrey shook her head. "Don't worry, I won't. But if anything comes out of this…I'm working on a book of Key West ghost stories right now. If there's something to this Gasparilla connection, can I use this?"

"Sure. But for the moment, if my co-workers think I'm seeing a medium so I can communicate with the dead, I won't be working on this project much longer," Genevieve said.

Audrey smiled and said softly, "I'd never betray a friend. But, hey, let me see your palm."

Genevieve was tempted to lock her hands behind her back like a frightened child.

"Give her your hand," Bethany said impatiently.

When Genevieve did so, she was instantly disturbed.

Because Audrey seemed disturbed. She frowned deeply, her mouth pursing. "Interesting," she said at last.

"What?" Genevieve asked warily.

"Oh, nothing, really. I just go by the books. It's all a lot of bull."

"Audrey, what the hell do you see?" Genevieve demanded.

Audrey stared up at her for a moment, then shrugged. "See your lifeline? It doesn't stop here... but it suddenly gets very jagged."

"What does that mean?" Bethany asked.

"Um. Well...a tremendous disruption."

"Like what?" Bethany asked.

"Listen, like I said, it's all a load of shit."

"Like what?" Genevieve persisted.

Audrey shrugged unhappily. "A disruption in

life…catastrophic illness—or a deadly peril. According to your palm, you're going to face an incredible danger. And there's a break that means you may survive it and…"

"And?" Genevieve demanded.

"And you may not."

5

"Oh," Audrey continued, "wait, it's…it's not really all that bad. It looks as if the line does continue."

"Great," Genevieve murmured.

"She's not going to die and come back to life, is she?" Bethany asked.

"Bethany!" Genevieve snapped.

"I'm sorry. I'm trying to help."

"Well, you're not helping."

"No, you're not going to become a zombie," Audrey said. "I…well, I've just never seen anything like that line."

"This just gets better and better," Genevieve said.

"It probably means nothing at all," Audrey said with a shrug and a smile. "I've told you—this is just how I make my living." She grinned. "We have ghost tours down here, too. Do you think all the guys leading those tours believe in ghosts? We're all vulnerable to the power of suggestion. It's how I keep 'em coming back. And if you repeat that…" She tried—and failed—to look threatening.

"Let's have lunch soon," Bethany suggested. "We're not diving on Saturday. Can you meet us?"

"Sure. Let's shoot for late afternoon. I don't open until five on Saturday, when the tourists are filling the bars," Audrey said. "I give my very best readings to drunks," she assured them with a trace of wry amusement.

"Saturday, then," Genevieve confirmed. "And, Audrey…thanks."

"Sure. See you two then," Audrey said.

She stood in the doorway, watching as they left.

"That was kind of stupid," Genevieve murmured.

"Seeing Audrey?" Bethany asked.

"Seeing Audrey for five minutes," Genevieve said. "I feel guilty."

"And freaked out," Bethany added.

"I'm not freaked out," Genevieve protested.

"Well, what she said—"

"What she said was that she's a fake," Genevieve said sternly. "And I feel guilty for not being a better friend and keeping up."

"We're going to see her for lunch," Bethany said. "And I'm getting a little worried, even if you're not." She held open the wrought-iron gate to the walkway so Genevieve could follow.

"That I'm cracking up—or that a ghost is after me?" Genevieve asked wearily, closing the gate behind her as they reached the street.

Then she froze.

He was there.

Thor Thompson. Casually leaning against the wall. He smiled as they saw him, nonchalantly glancing up at the sign that announced Audrey's business.

She could have held her temper, she told herself afterward. *Should* have held her temper. He hadn't said a word.

He didn't need to. She saw the way he looked at the sign, then looked at her.

She walked up to him furiously. "You followed me," she accused him.

He seemed a lot taller. She wasn't short, especially in heels, but he was able to look down at her.

"We ordered your drinks for you. We didn't know where you were. Nothing quite as bad as warm beer."

"You followed me," she repeated. "You son of a bitch. You had no right."

He arched a brow. "Maybe I followed Bethany."

"I think Bethany ought to be getting out of here right now," Bethany said nervously. "If you'll both excuse me—"

They turned to her simultaneously. "No."

"Oh," Bethany said, acutely uncomfortable.

"For your information, Mr. Thompson, we were just stopping in to say hello to an old friend from school," Genevieve advised him. "Not that it's any of your concern."

He looked up at the sign again, then cast her a disdainful look. "Everything you do right now concerns me. I need you sharp and on the ball."

"*You* need me sharp and on the ball? Have you forgotten something? I don't work for you. I work for Marshall."

"You didn't know?" he asked.

"Know what?" she demanded.

"Your group got hired because I recommended you," he said quietly. "Marshall and I make decisions together, sure. That's how good work is done. But I get the final say. On everything."

Genevieve narrowed her eyes as she stared at him. "Is that a threat?"

"I never threaten people. I take action."

"Did you have any difficulties with me today?" she demanded.

"Not at all."

"So why did you follow me?" she demanded again. "Never mind. But don't do it again. I'll quit before I'll stand for being treated like a prisoner."

Not a muscle twitched in his face. She was suddenly afraid the man wanted her to quit. "Don't be melodramatic. It's immaterial to me whether you stay on or not, but if you do…then it's important that you live in the real world."

"You son of a—"

"Genevieve, whoa. Come on, you two. The others will be missing us by now," Bethany said lightly. "This was a great day. Can't we just be happy with that?"

"For the moment," Thor said. His eyes hadn't left Genevieve's.

"Let's go," Bethany urged, slipping her arm through Genevieve's.

"Right. Fine," Genevieve said tightly.

She managed to walk a full five feet before spinning around to point a finger at him. "Stop it. Just stop it."

"Stop what?" he demanded.

"Judging me, worrying about me, following me. Thinking that I'm crazy and dangerous and shouldn't be on this project."

His hands went to his hips, he tilted his head, and his jaw seemed to lock. "At the moment I'm walking behind you and that's it. If that disturbs you so much, maybe you shouldn't be on this project."

"I'm better than you are. I proved it today."

He arched a brow. "I actually found the gold," he said quietly.

She gasped. "Of all the insufferable assholes! I led you to it. I knew where we should be digging. I'm the one who made the find."

"Once again, I repeat, I picked it up."

"You're pathetic. A man of your reputation stooping to such a desperate attempt at glory."

"I picked it up. That's a simple fact."

"Excuse me, but you two are both missing something. We're working as a team here. Does it matter who actually picked up the gold?" Bethany demanded

It mattered. Oh, yes, it mattered, Genevieve thought.

"We really need to join the others," Bethany continued. "We might have taken the first step today toward a historic discovery. Let's go celebrate with a drink. You two can fight later, if you have to."

"You're right. I can fight with this asshole later," Genevieve snapped.

To Thor's credit, he kept his mouth shut, making

Genevieve wish she'd had the control to do so, as well.

This time Bethany stepped between them, joining arms with both of them and determinedly making her way down the street.

Genevieve strode into the bar quickly. The singer was on break; the sound system was piping out something with a beat, and couples were filling the floor. Without hesitating, she headed straight for Victor, dragging him out on the floor.

"Where were you guys?" he asked.

"Just down the street," she said, swirling beneath his arm. One good thing about Victor: they'd known each other forever and danced well together. She didn't feel badly about using him tonight; he dragged her out on the floor whenever he wanted to make sure some hot female knew he was capable of moving to the music. Right now, spinning about in a high-speed hustle was definitely a good way to release some of the energy she was feeling. And the anger.

"What the hell is the matter with you tonight?" Victor asked quizzically. "I'm the one who should be in a huff. You're my partner, but you wait until you go off with the stud to come up with the goods."

She turned under his arm and faced him again. "I'd rather dive with you, believe me," she assured him.

"Why didn't we come up with something before? Oh, right. Because you were busy seeing bodies in the water."

"Can it, Victor."

He grinned. "Boo!"

"Victor…"

"Come on, Gen. Ease up."

Ease up? Yes, she needed to. She didn't want to quit. He might be in charge, but this was her home. She wanted—deserved—to be a part of this.

And *she* was the one who had found the relic.

"Gen?" Victor said, breaking into her thoughts.

"Yeah?"

"Everybody looks ready to move on."

"Let's go then."

Unfortunately, they had to pass under Audrey's sign to reach their next destination. Genevieve made a point of ignoring it and walking ahead. She linked arms with Marshall, keeping up with him, ahead of Thor Thompson. She tried to talk with Marshall as casually as she always did, but she could tell she was talking too much. She tried to slow herself down.

She'd never touched a drop of her beer in the first bar. When they entered the second, she hailed the bartender and made a point of buying the first round and delivering the drafts to each member of their party—even Thor.

She didn't want to remain at the table, but Victor shook his head when she tried to get him out on the floor. When she tried again, he pleaded exhaustion.

"I'll hit the dance floor with you," Thor said, standing.

"Oh, that's all right."

"No, it's cool."

"I'm not trying to *make* anyone dance," she said.

"The hell you're not," Victor piped in.

Flushing, she found herself spinning out on the floor. The band was playing a rumba. She had no idea what to do, but apparently Thor Thompson had—somewhere, sometime—learned how to dance. He knew what he was doing, leading her, not pushing her around. Under other circumstances he would have been an exceptional partner, even the perfect height for her.

"You don't have to do this," she murmured.

"It's good music. A nice place."

"This is a great place to live."

"I believe you."

"Strange. You don't believe much."

"You don't tell the truth all that often."

"Maybe we all see different things as truth."

"Then you're not even telling me what you see as the truth," he informed her.

"You don't want the truth," she said quickly, looking downward. Then she stared up at him again, "And you're not great at telling the truth yourself."

He drew back slightly, looking at her, lips twitching. "Oh?"

"I made the find. You lost, but you don't want to give up your boat, so you're believing what *you* want to believe."

He laughed. "I made the find, and you don't want to have sex, so you're believing what you want to believe."

She was startled to find herself blushing to her roots. "That's not the point."

"Maybe it is to me." He laughed. "All right. On this matter, let's call it a draw."

She arched a brow. "Because I won?"

"Because *I* won."

She shook her head. "Look—"

"We'll call it a draw," he said firmly.

She didn't know why she felt so comfortable about that. She certainly didn't want to take the man's boat.

And she didn't want sex—did she? Not with him!

Why not? a voice at the back of her head teased.

Because he was an idiot. Because of the patronizing way he treated her.

Still…sex, just sex…he was great to look at, would be exciting to touch….

"A draw," she managed to say. "Great. With you trying to get me to quit."

"Genevieve, I'm worried. I think you're exceptional, but…you're just not on your game."

"Don't worry about me. I'm a big girl. I've been on my own in the world for a long time."

"Oh?"

She turned beneath his arm. "My folks were killed in a car crash when I was nineteen. I'm an only child," she explained.

"I'm sorry."

"It was a long time ago."

"Bad things, hurtful things, are never long enough ago."

"But we learn to live with them."

She realized suddenly that the music had ended and they had stopped moving, but she was still leaning against him.

She stepped back. "Truce. But please, don't follow me, and don't worry about me. Not unless I do something terrible, and I won't. I swear, I'll be courteous, hardworking and entirely professional."

"When we're working?" he said.

She didn't quite understand. "Of course while we're working," she said, nodding.

They headed back to the table. She took a seat between Alex and Victor. Bethany was across from her, beaming.

"You two looked great out there."

"Hey!" Victor protested. "She looks great with me, too."

"But they were getting along so nicely," Bethany said.

"They don't get along?" Alex asked.

Genevieve took a long swig of her beer. "We get along just fine," she said, staring hard at Bethany.

"Of course," Bethany said.

"Of course," Jack echoed, lifting his beer. "To all of us. One big happy family," he said, and grinned.

A toast went around the table, and Genevieve finally let go and felt comfortable. Eventually she danced with Jack, then Marshall. Lizzie and Zach got out on the floor, too.

Finally Marshall broke it up. "Okay, time to go home. Tomorrow is a workday."

The streets were a little quieter as they walked back to the resort. By then Genevieve had ditched her shoes. When they reached the cool sand leading to the cottages, it felt good beneath her feet.

The night was beautiful. The dead heat of the sun was gone, and there was no hint of rain. A soft breeze blew in from the water.

"Good night. Tomorrow at eight sharp, guys," Marshall called.

"Eight?" Victor protested. "Oh, God, not another history lesson."

"No, but we're seeing a few computer printouts of how the ship might have broken apart," Thor informed them.

Alex groaned. "Don't they know we've all been on a zillion wreck dives?" he asked.

"Hey," Marshall said. "It will be useful. You'll see."

"Yeah, yeah," Victor said, giving a wave and heading off. They all began to do the same. Genevieve hurried toward her own cottage.

She was suddenly anxious to get inside.

Before she was left out on the sand all alone.

Once inside, however, she found she wasn't any happier. She was afraid to go to sleep.

Since it was her cottage and she was alone, she could do whatever she wanted to, so she turned on all the lights and the television, and forced herself to brush her teeth, wash her face and get ready for bed.

It occurred to her that anyone noticing her place would realize she kept it brilliantly lit all night, but she was going to operate on the premise that it simply wasn't anyone else's business. She thought about calling Bethany and suggesting they share a place for the night, but she was loathe to do that if she wasn't in an actual panic. And she wasn't—not yet, anyway.

She found a good movie on the SciFi channel. She didn't believe in aliens, so the creatures taking over the earth didn't scare her. She kept the remote in hand though, just in case she dozed off and awoke to something about ghosts.

She prayed she would be able to get a decent night's sleep. She desperately needed it if she was going to be the ultimate professional on this dive.

"That would be cruel," Alex said, his hands cradling a bottle of beer. He, Jack and Victor had decided on one last drink, just hanging by the tiki bar. It wasn't late, not even eleven, and none of them had consumed more than two beers during their supposedly wild night of barhopping.

The night was really nice. A cool breeze, no mosquitoes. It felt good to chill out at the tiki bar. No one else was around, just the three of them.

Jack was staring at Victor as if he'd entirely lost his senses. "You want to what?" he demanded.

"Look," Victor said, leaning forward, a mischievous glint in his eyes. "Gen thinks she saw something, so we set something up to scare her, she sees that it's not real, we all get a laugh, and she feels better about the whole thing. It's not cruel at all."

Alex shook his head. "Victor, you are one sorry liar. You want to scare her. Face it. You've had a hard-on for Gen since you've been kids. Now she's getting into Thor, and you're pissed."

Victor frowned, sitting back. "That's bull. She's my best friend. We'd never mess up our friendship. And she hates Thompson. Can't stand him. Can't you tell? Wait. Don't repeat that, Jack. I keep forgetting you're with his crew."

Jack arched a brow. "Haven't you heard? We aren't two crews anymore. We're one crew. One big flippin' happy family. But I've got news for you, Victor. I don't think that's really hate we're seeing."

"Then what is it?"

"Heat," Jack said, grinning. "You mark my words— something is going on there."

"He thinks she's a lunatic," Victor said flatly.

"And you've never wanted to sleep with a woman you thought was off the wall?" Jack asked. "What man out there hasn't found himself dying to bang someone gorgeous, no matter what he thought of her sanity, brains or anything else?"

"She resents him. Big time," Victor said flatly. "And she doesn't sleep around."

"Listen to you," Alex said, laughing. "You're getting all big-brother over there. And you're the one who wants to trick her?"

"You in or out?" Victor asked him.

"Just what the hell do you intend to do?" Jack demanded.

"Nothing major. Just put a blond mannequin on

her porch for when she wakes up," Victor said. "Honestly, don't you think she'll get a laugh out of it, too, and then she'll be past all that panic the other day?"

"Where do you think you're going to get a mannequin at this time of night?" Jack demanded.

"I'm from here. I know half the shopkeepers on Duval Street," Victor said, grinning.

Sometime, right around when the aliens had managed to evolve from being pod people, Genevieve at last managed to drift off.

She never knew just when restful sleep departed and the dreams began. She saw nothing but darkness.

And then, from the darkness, the woman emerged.

She strode forward with purpose. In her dream state, Genevieve groaned.

Go away, she begged.

The woman moved in a cloud of white. It was some kind of beautiful, floating negligee. Her hair was long and blond, drifting as she walked, as if she were perpetually touched by the sea's current, or by a breeze off the shore. Her eyes were large, tragically sad.

"*Beware…*" she mouthed.

"*Go away, please! Oh, God, please, go away. I can't help you, I don't understand. Why are you torturing me?*" Genevieve pleaded silently.

"*Beware…*"

"*Beware of what?*"

There was no answer. She was roused from sleep by a small noise that was real enough to jar her from the nightmare.

Dragged from sleep, she lay on the bed, blinking. The lights remained on, as they had been. On the television, a space ship was whizzing by planets and stars. She blinked and looked around. Everything looked the way it should. She couldn't tell what had awakened her.

She rolled over to look at the clock on the table. Five-thirty. Late enough to get up.

She crawled off the far side of the bed and headed for the bathroom. She was loathe to look in the mirror—afraid she would find seaweed in her hair again. But there was nothing disturbed about her appearance, other than the state of her hair, which was in wild tangles. With a breath of relief, she leaned down to brush her teeth and wash her face. She grabbed for her towel, dried her face, then hesitated, once again afraid to look in the mirror, wondering if a face would appear beside her own.

But there was nothing. She headed into the living area and started her coffeepot brewing, still wondering what had woken her up. While she waited for the coffee, she walked back into the bathroom, found one of her bathing suits, slipped into it, then tossed on one of her terry cover-ups. The coffee was done.

Outside, the pink-and-yellow streaks that heralded morning were beginning to shoot nicely across the sky.

She opened her front door to step out and check the weather.

Sheer panic seized her.

She was staring at a face. At a woman her own height. She nearly screamed at the top of her lungs.

But she managed not to. Then she gritted her teeth, fury replacing abject fear.

The blond wig was slightly askew, the part somewhere over the ear. The dummy was arranged at an odd angle, one arm raised as if it were double jointed.

"Assholes," she muttered. Then she said it more loudly, just in case the culprits were hanging around to catch her reaction. They were probably somewhere like a pack of adolescents, waiting for her to scream.

She swore, dragging the mannequin to the far side of the porch. "I hope it's ruined, and I really hope whoever lent it to you charges you big bucks," she said more loudly. "Are you guys out there?" she called. "Funny, very funny, ha-ha."

She stood, tense and seething, for several seconds, then decided that Victor—it had to be Victor—and whoever had joined him in this prank had to pay. She dragged the dummy off the porch and across the sand, then dumped it into the water. She dusted her hands and returned to her cottage, irritated that no one seemed to have been waiting to watch her reaction. She had hoped Victor would come running from some hiding spot, alarm on his face when he saw she was about to destroy the mannequin.

In the cottage, a sense of satisfaction guiding her, she poured a cup of coffee and wandered back into the bedroom, planning to catch a bit of the morning news.

As she reached the near side of the bed, she came to a halt, a feeling of deep apprehension seeping into her.

She looked down at the rag rug that lay beside the bed and beneath her bare feet.

It was soaked. A glacial chill began to sweep through her. She closed her eyes. *Don't panic*, she told herself. *One of those idiots got in here, too. That's all it is*.

No. They couldn't have known about her dream. They couldn't have known she had seen the walking dead woman, heard her warning.

Beware.

She groaned, sinking down on the bed.

It was then that she began to hear the shouts and the bloodcurdling scream. She raced outside, her fingers locked around her coffee cup.

From the cottage next to hers, Thor Thompson had emerged, as well.

He was looking down at the beach, a fierce frown knitting his brow.

"What the hell?" he breathed.

She looked over at him, then at the cluster of people down by the water, hovering around something she couldn't quite make out.

Her heart sank. Bethany was down by the water. So were Marshall and Bert, the owner of the resort.

Lizzie and Zach were there, too, staring down at the mysterious form.

"Call 911!" she heard Marshall bellow.

"What…?" Genevieve said.

"It's a body," Thor said, watching the shore, not even glancing her way. "They've found a body."

"Oh, God! No, it's not a real body. One of those idiots was playing a joke on me with a mannequin. I dumped it in the water."

He glanced at her, his frown deepening.

"No. It's a corpse."

"It's not, I'm telling you!"

He shook his head, as if he should have been aware before speaking that she wasn't sane. Then he started to sprint toward the group by the water.

She set her cup on the porch railing and started toward the water herself, ready to point out to them that they were all victims of a cruel joke— just as she had been.

"Don't you see—" she began, brushing impatiently by Bethany.

But then she saw for herself.

It was no mannequin lying on the shore, tiny crabs crawling over it, seaweed draping it.

It was a woman's body.

Mottled, gray…eaten away in places. She lay faceup, her sightless eyes turned toward the cottages.

6

For hours there was no discussion about anything other than the body found on the beach. They were horrified, saddened—and glad. The woman had been a stranger. She had been brought into their lives by her death, but they hadn't known her in life.

By ten o'clock the body had been removed. Despite the excitement previously generated by finding the coin, they were breaking off operations for the day. The discovery of the body was a police matter. None of them had known the woman, and as yet, no one even knew who she was. Still, with detectives and forensic units combing the beach and the docks, yellow crime-scene tape everywhere, and the police struggling to keep curious tourists and locals at bay, there was too much confusion going on and no point trying to work.

Hours passed. None of them left the tiki bar unless they were asked to talk to Jay or one of his officers.

Jack—who had actually been the first one to see the body—had spoken with Jay Gonzalez the longest, while the others had provided what they could, which was pretty much nothing.

The woman had been in the water several days, at least, before she had washed up on the beach. Where she had gone in, no one knew. In the next few days, forensic techs and medical examiners would analyze clues on and in the body, as well as currents and tidal patterns, trying to discern just where she might have gone in to arrive on the beach where she had.

A computer image was already being created from a photograph of her face. It would be shown on the evening's news, not just locally but all over Florida, and ultimately, around the country if necessary, and with luck they would soon know her identity.

Though the police hadn't made any announcements as yet, Thor was pretty sure he knew part of her story. Ragged marks at her ankles indicated that she'd been tied to some kind of weight—alive or dead, he didn't know. A medical examiner would be able to answer that question, however.

"Boy, and we all thought you were seeing things," Jack said suddenly, looking at Genevieve.

She had been deep in thought and started when he spoke to her.

"Pardon?"

"Well, you saw a woman in the water. And there *was* a woman in the water," Jack said.

Thor thought at first she would nod—not pleased, because who could be pleased by such a circumstance?—but at least glad she hadn't been crazy.

But she just stared back at Jack.

"Though God knows, we all searched exactly where you had been, and we couldn't find her," Jack said.

"Maybe she lodged in the coral somewhere," Victor said. "But I don't see how." He looked glum and quiet.

Genevieve hadn't offered an opinion. She had turned toward the beach where police and bystanders were still milling. Only the little patch of sand where the body had actually lain was still cordoned off.

"Amazing," Lizzie murmured.

Genevieve turned her attention back toward the group. "I wonder what happened to the mannequin," she said, staring at Victor.

He flushed, then frowned. "Who told you what we were planning?" he asked, staring accusingly at Jack.

"Hey! I didn't say a word," Jack protested, adjusting his big skull-and-crossbones earring. "I thought we all decided not to do it."

"We did," Alex said.

"So how did you know what we were up to?" Victor asked. Thor was surprised to feel a sense of growing unease. So that was what she'd been talking about, spouting about a dummy when there was a pathetically dead woman lying on the beach.

Genevieve stared at him, shaking her head. "You

asshole, Victor! When I woke up, there was a mannequin on my porch, right in front of the door, waiting to greet me. I threw it in the water." She looked decidedly uncomfortable.

"She became real," Bethany whispered.

"Oh, good God," Marshall groaned. "What the hell is the matter with all of you? Victor, did you put a mannequin on Genevieve's porch?"

"I swear to God, I didn't," Victor protested.

"Oh, yeah? Well she was there," Genevieve said flatly.

"I didn't do it," Victor protested, staring at her. "Alex said it would be cruel. I just thought it would give you a jolt, make you laugh, get you over the whole thing."

"Yeah, right. Get her over it," Zach said, fingers curling around his wife's as he gave her a grim smile. "It's bizarre, though, isn't it? Somehow, Genevieve saw a woman in the water, and now…"

"Damn," Victor said, shaking his head. "I was diving with her and didn't see her."

"We all went into the water and didn't find the…the woman," Alex said.

"I sure as hell didn't see anything," Bethany agreed.

"The sea is amazing," Lizzie reminded them. "What she can do—the secrets she can hide. But we should have been able to find that woman."

"Hey, the police divers went in, too," Zach pointed out. "The fact is, no matter how well we think we know it, the sea is huge, the coral is treacherous…things disappear. Hell, we're looking for a *ship* that no one has seen in nearly two hundred years."

"There you go," Jack said to Genevieve. "And we all gave you such a hard time."

She offered him a wisp of a smile. "Excuse me, you all. It looks like that reporter we've been dodging all morning is heading back in this direction. I'm going to get out of here. If we're off for the day, I've got errands to run."

She headed back for her cottage. Thor quickly rose, as well. "Yeah. It's become a good day for errands."

Marshall groaned, rubbing his bald head, a sure sign that he was irritated. "Maybe this was a mistake. Maybe we should be out on the water."

"Aren't we supposed to be listening to another one of Sheridan's speeches?" Alex asked, grinning. "About ships. And how they break apart in the water. As if we're all two-year-olds."

"If you were going to steal a mannequin and put it on Genevieve's porch, you all *are* like two-year-olds!" Marshall chastised.

"Hey, we didn't do it!" Victor protested.

"Thor, think we should still head out? Sheridan canceled when he saw all the cop cars out there, but we could still dive," Marshall said.

"No!" Alex protested. "You can't give people a day off, then haul them back to work," he argued.

"Yeah, I guess you're right," Marshall agreed glumly.

"We'll be fine starting up again Monday," he said. "I guess."

"Monday," Thor said, and left them. He strode to his own cottage, certain Genevieve had yet to leave hers. He couldn't shower and change and keep his eye on her cottage at the same time, but at least he could clean up quickly.

Hell. He was following her. Becoming obsessed. Why?

At the moment, he told himself, it was because she had behaved so strangely when Jack had connected the woman she had seen in the water with the corpse on the shore, which certainly seemed to have vindicated her.

Dressed, he stood in his living room, looking out the window.

Hell, he wasn't just following her. He was becoming a damned stalker.

She came out of her cottage wearing a pale yellow halter dress that complemented the golden color of her skin and the rich, radiant darkness of her hair. She set off on foot, heading out of the resort.

He paused, gritting his teeth, then went after her.

One by one, the others had drifted away. Frowning, Victor noticed that only Bethany stayed. But then, it wasn't usual for Genevieve to walk off without waiting to see if anyone had a plan or wanted to join in on whatever her plan might have been.

This was one weird day, he thought.

At last he got up and headed for his own cottage.

He strode in and paused, startled that the floor just inside the entry seemed to be wet. The watery trail led around the half wall to the bedroom area. He followed it.

Staring at the bed, he nearly let out a scream. He stopped himself in time.

There was a soaking-wet mannequin lying across his bed.

Sightless blue painted eyes stared up at him. A scraggly blond wig was soaked and askew. Plastic arms were lifted up toward him, as if pleading for his help.

What the hell…?

Victor felt a strange sense of panic. If he were caught with this thing in his cottage…when there had been a real dead woman on the shore…shit!

He had to get rid of the damned thing, and fast.

How? How the hell was he going to do that with no one seeing him?

He wondered how the hell someone had gotten it into his cottage in the first place.

Who had brought it?

And why?

She was heading south on Duval Street.

Since Genevieve seemed to be distracted, it wasn't difficult to follow her. She greeted some of the shop-keepers she passed but didn't pause to look at anything. At the La Concha Hotel, she ducked into the Star-bucks. He held back, leaning against the building.

"It's haunted," a woman said, huge sun hat atop her head, dark glasses in place, tour book in her hands. "Herb, it's haunted. It's the tallest building in town. People have jumped from the roof."

"Yeah, yeah, it's haunted. Can we check in?" Herb asked. He was leading two large suitcases by their straps and wore a heavy backpack. He grimaced at Thor. Looked like a nice guy.

"Oh, Herb, I'm sorry," his wife said, and Herb shrugged, still looking amused. The two looked as if they'd been together forever. Happily. Nice thought.

He gave Herb a thumbs-up sign, and Herb grinned and moved on.

Genevieve reappeared with a paper cup of coffee. She started south again. He followed.

Just a few blocks farther along the road, she made a sharp turn. He followed. The street was lined with old houses, all handsomely kept. A few advertised rooms for rent, or had signs announcing that they were bed-and-breakfasts. One dared to proclaim, "Best breakfast in Key West." Genevieve went past, then turned up a walk. Three steps led to a handsome porch and a door that boasted a beautiful cut-glass window in the upper half.

She pulled a key chain from her pocket, opened the door, then let it swing closed behind her.

He stood on the street and surveyed the house, slowly walking closer. It was a striking Classical Revival mansion. It was two stories, with an arched attic, and had wraparound porches on both the first and second floors. There was Victorian gingerbread on the rails, and it looked as if Genevieve lovingly tended the place—the paint was fresh, the lawn mowed, and there wasn't a flaw in sight. As he stood there, he was surprised to see the door fly open again.

She walked out on the porch, hands on her hips as she glared at him. Great. He wasn't just a stalker. He was a stalker who had been caught.

"Were you just going to stare at the place, or did you want to come in?" she demanded.

"Well…"

"I know. You were just on a walking tour of Key West, right?" she said dryly.

He shook his head. "No. I followed you."

"Why?"

"I was worried."

She lifted her hands. "Why? I'm not crazy. There *was* a body in the water."

"I was just worried," he said, and added honestly, "because of your reaction."

"We're all human, and that kind of thing is…horrible. It doesn't matter if you've been on a hundred search-and-recovery missions, or that we've all seen a human body turned into such a grisly mess before. It's still horrible."

"Yes, of course. It just seemed…as if you were disturbed beyond…never mind. You're right. It was a tragic discovery."

She stared at him for a long moment, then shrugged. "Do you want to see the house? Though

I didn't take you for the kind who'd know much about architecture or old buildings."

He smiled, following the path to the house. "Sorry, you're wrong. I like history. And this house has got to be one of the oldest in Key West."

"Definitely not the oldest—the oldest house is a museum now. The Wreckers Museum. This house was built in 1858. My great-great-whatever-grandfather built it. He was a wrecker." She grinned. "He almost lost the house and everything else when the Civil War rolled around. Fort Taylor stayed in Union hands, but most of the people were Confederate sympathizers. Grandpa Wallace decided he could best serve his country as a blockade runner. At the end, he was caught by a friend—a Yankee, stationed at Fort Zachary Taylor. Luckily his friend was a bit of an entrepreneur, as well. The two split the proceeds, my grandfather didn't hang, and I still have the house today."

He looked around the parlor area. The house had the typical southern breezeway—a hall that went straight from the front door to the back, allowing for the air to circulate and cool the rooms. The entry and parlor took up the front portion of the place; there was a Duncan Phyfe sofa beneath the window, a spinet piano, and upholstered chairs on a knit rug before the fire. A staircase to the left of the hall led up to the second story.

"Down here," she said, starting down the hall, "is the library—once upon a time an office, when Gramps was in the wrecking business. And the kitchen. Originally it was a downstairs bedroom, and the kitchen was outside. The kitchen burned down in the late 1800s. But there's still an outhouse back there. My grandmother had that made into a birdhouse," she told him.

She was chatting nervously, he thought. Smoothly, charmingly—but nervously.

"A rude comment here," he said, going along, "but this place must be worth a fortune in today's market."

"It is," she agreed.

"Aren't you glad I didn't agree to let you use it as collateral in a bet?" he queried.

Her lashes fell; a grin twitched on her lips. "You know I really won that bet," she told him lightly. "And I've been on *The Seeker* now. That boat must be worth a fortune, too." She turned, heading back for the stairway. "There are four rooms upstairs, and an attic. There are definitely bigger places on the island. Have you been to Artist House? It's an absolutely gorgeous bed-and-breakfast now. Once Robert, our very weird Key West doll, lived there. He took the blame for all the bad things that happened to his owner and now he takes the blame for all the bad things that happen in Key West. He's in the East Martobello museum now, ruining the tourists' film."

They had come to the top of the stairs. "My office," she said, pushing open a door that had been ajar. White eyelet drapes shaded the windows, and even her computer desk was antique. There were pictures on the walls, many of them. He didn't need to be told which pictures were of a young Genevieve with her parents. The older Wallaces had been tall, as well; her mother had been the one with the full head of rich auburn hair.

"Hey, that's Jack," he said, eyeing a group of children with snorkel equipment standing around an older man.

"Yes, that's Jack. About fifteen years ago. He was great. The PTA liked to hire him for special field trips. We believed he was really a pirate. He loved to tell stories."

Thor walked closer to another of the pictures on the wall. It was Genevieve and the group from Deep Down Salvage. Marshall, bald head shielded by a straw hat, was in the center. Bethany and Alex were on one side of him, Genevieve and Victor were on the other. Genevieve had an arm around Marshall, while Victor had an arm across her shoulders. They looked like a happy, close-knit group, which it certainly seemed they were. Except....

Did it look like Victor was just a very good friend? Or was he a bit too possessive?

And what about Alex? Being from Key Largo made him an outsider. Was he really just the good old boy he pretended to be?

And why the hell was he suddenly wondering about all this? Because a body had been discovered on the beach, he answered himself.

"That's actually my favorite piece in the house," Genevieve said, pointing to a very old brocade daybed. "My grandmother called it a 'fainting couch.' She taught me all these things about the way young ladies behaved. She was actually the toughest thing I've come across in all my life." She started out of the room.

"I've turned this room into a media center. Being technically challenged, I'm very proud of it," she told him.

He poked his head in. She had huge speakers and a great stereo system, a wide-screen television, a DVD player and comfortable furniture. Shelves held hundreds of books, magazines, DVDs and CDs.

"Great place," he told her.

"What's your place like in Jacksonville?" she asked him. "Don't tell me. Ultramodern. Every convenience."

"No. I think my house actually has a few years on yours. But, sadly, I've never taken the time to fix it up the way you have yours."

"*You* bought an old house?"

"I meant to fix it up. I'm just never there enough. I probably shouldn't have bought the place. The historic board would probably like to do me in."

She smiled vaguely and started back down the stairs. He followed. She turned at the foot of the stairs and started along the hall, then on out to the backyard. Though not heavily planted, there were flowers here and there. It was simple and attractive.

She pointed to a raised bed that sported a riot of bougainvillea. "When I was digging to create that little stand, I dug up bones," she told him.

"Oh?"

She turned and looked at him. "Very old bones. I called all the right government agencies. Forensic anthropologists came out. They decided that the bones were Calusa Indian, a tribe that disappeared hundreds of years ago. No one was terribly surprised. When the Spaniards first came, there were bones everywhere."

"Right. *Cayo Hueso*. Island of Bones," he said. Her eyes seemed troubled still, and her tone, when she spoke, was strange. She didn't seem to mind he was there. In fact, she seemed almost grateful for his presence.

Not because it was him specifically. It was as if, although she had chosen to leave the group, she didn't really want to be alone.

"You're getting at something," he told her. "I'm just not sure what. Feel free to spit it out anytime," he said, wondering if he had spoken with the right tone.

Apparently he hadn't. Either that, or she simply didn't intend to divulge what was really bothering her.

"Don't be silly. Do you want some coffee?" she asked.

He laughed. "I had enough coffee standing around at the tiki bar to last until I'm old and gray."

"Soda, beer, anything else?"

He hesitated slightly. "How about I take you to lunch?"

She cocked her head, as if thinking, then determining lunch just might fit into her plan. "I'll take you."

"You're kind of touchy about that meal thing. It doesn't have to be a date. Don't forget, I can put in for expenses."

She shook her head. "I just want to choose the place."

"Choose away."

"All right. Thanks."

She locked the back and started toward the front again, pausing only to sift through the mail on the Victorian occasional table by the door. "Nothing dire," she murmured. "Let's go."

She locked the door as they left, and started back down Duval Street.

"Where are we going?" he asked her.

She glanced at him with a trace of amusement. "The Hard Rock Cafe."

"I thought you preferred your Conch insider places."

"It's a cool Hard Rock," she told him.

He wasn't surprised when they arrived and she knew the young people acting as hosts at the door. He wasn't surprised, either, when she opted to sit inside—Deep South natives of any kind usually preferred air-conditioning to the charming notion of dining in the sunshine and garden atmosphere of an outdoor café.

The restaurant was located in a handsome historic home, late 1800s, with some of the old incorporated with the customary decor of the chain.

After they walked up the stairs, she pointed out a guitar signed by Jimmy Buffett, and a number of pieces of Elvis Presley and Beatles memorabilia.

After they had ordered drinks—she opted for alcohol that afternoon, choosing an island concoction with an umbrella—she told him the place was supposedly haunted.

"Is anywhere *not* haunted here?" he asked her.

She shrugged. "Ask our waitress," she told him.

He did. Their waitress was a pretty young college girl whose eyes widened when Genevieve encouraged her to tell Thor about the ghosts.

"The place really is haunted," she assured him.

"Oh?"

"One man committed suicide here, and suicides always return to haunt the place where they died."

"I see."

"Honestly. Another man died downstairs…but I personally think it's only Mr. Curry doing the haunting. His father was a millionaire, but he managed to go broke in a year. And then his wife left him."

"That's adding insult to injury," Thor agreed pleasantly.

"I've been up here alone when a black shadow kind of sweeps around…cleaning towels move. And Brett set up a table one time only to have all the forks and napkins moved to another table," she said, eyes wide. "Trust me—I do not stay up here alone at night."

Thor thanked her for taking the time to tell her

story. After she left, he looked at Genevieve, lifting his glass, arching a brow. "So you think that the place is haunted? You've seen shadows, things moving around?"

She shook her head. "No, I've never seen a thing."

"So?"

"They tell good stories here," she said. "But lots of people believe in ghosts."

He reached across the table, frowning, barely aware he had set his hand over hers. "There are shadows at night. Shadows when the light changes. People might forget which table they've set up—or someone else might move the table settings."

She pulled her hand away, picking up her glass. "Absolutely true," she told him.

Once lunch was served, Genevieve determinedly changed the subject from ghosts, asking him when he first got into diving.

"I had this great book when I was a kid," he said. "Story about a sunken ferry discovered right in the St. Johns, near where I lived. I was hooked. How about you?"

"Family vocation. My grandfather was a frogman in World War II. I think I was thrown in the ocean before I could walk."

"So that's how it goes, growing up as a Conch, huh?"

She shrugged. "For lots of people. I have friends who hate the water. Some of them still love Key West. They just love the streets and the atmosphere, the sunsets. A lot of people just kind of find Key West. And then stay here." She tilted her head at an angle, smiling ruefully. "You know, we really are the Conch Republic. In 1982 there was a big stink about the number of illegal aliens and drugs that seemed to be flowing into Miami from the Keys. The Border Patrol set up a blockade on US1 in Florida City, trying to get a grip on the problem. Traffic was so backed up, people couldn't get in or out. The mayor of Key West went to the Miami courthouse to seek an injunction, but nothing was done, so Key West seceded from the United States. After a few minutes of rebellion, the 'prime minister' surrendered to the admiral at the navy base and demanded a billion dollars in foreign aid and war relief." She shrugged. "He made his point, and now it's great for the local businesses. You can buy Conch Republic passports, T-shirts…you name it." She smiled.

Thor grinned, glad to see that her mood had lightened.

The check came just then, and she reached for it. "Expense account," he reminded her, taking it from her.

She stood as he laid money on the bill. "Come on, then. I'm taking you for an after-lunch drink. And I *am* paying for it."

A few minutes later, he found himself in Captain Tony's Saloon.

"Are you taking me on a tour?" he asked her.

"This is where Sloppy Joe's was originally, although

it wasn't called that then. If I remember the story right, Joe Russell refused to pay the extra dollar a week when the rent went up in the thirties. All his patrons just picked up their drinks and the furniture and moved down the street to where Sloppy Joe's is now."

"I see."

"What would you like?" she asked, indicating a table by a tree trunk. The tree grew next to the bar and disappeared at the ceiling.

"I'm sticking with beer," he said.

He took a seat at the table by the tree while she waited at the bar for their drinks. Looking up, he saw that the rafters were covered with hundreds of bras, some signed.

A table away, two women were sitting with two children, a boy of about six and a girl who was maybe five years old. The kids had drinks that looked like Shirley Temples, while the women were nursing more exotic concoctions. One of the women noted him and flushed—he guessed she was embarrassed to be in the bar with children. "We're trying to cover the hot tourist spots," she said.

He smiled back and pointed to a table closer to the street. A man there had two boys with him who were about eleven or twelve. "It's my guess it's fine," he said.

She looked relieved. Her companion turned to him and smiled, as well. "I told her it would be okay." The second woman stared at him for a minute. Her eyes widened in recognition, and she leaned forward and whispered to her friend. They both stared at him and flushed, then looked at each other again and started whispering.

They both stared again and smiled. He heard the mom whisper, "…really handsome…." He had enough of an ego that he couldn't help a moment's bemusement—and deep appreciation.

But where the hell did they know him from? They didn't look the type who were into diving magazines.

Then again….

He wasn't sure why, but he felt uneasiness settling in. There had been a number of news crews down by the beach that morning. Most of their group had politely refused to be interviewed—neither he nor Marshall particularly wanted their project associated with the tragedy of the young woman's death. But he was pretty sure he had seen Alex and Lizzie answering a few questions before managing to escape the reporters.

Genevieve joined him then. He waved a hand toward the bras.

"Have you got one up there?" he asked.

"No."

"Interesting," he said.

She grinned. "We're here for the tree," she explained.

"We are?"

"There's a legend that a woman was hanged from that tree."

"Legend?"

"She supposedly haunts this place."

"More hauntings?"

"Ghosts are all over in Key West," she said with a shrug. "They say."

"But you've never believed in them?" he asked.

"No," she told him.

As she spoke, the little girl at the nearby table began shrieking. "No! No, Mommy, no! There's a lady in there."

"Ashley, shh. Honey, that's just a story," the mother said, distressed. "Ashley, please, let me take you in there. We'll have an accident."

"Excuse me," Genevieve told Thor, then walked over to the other table and hunkered down. She flashed a smile to the woman. "You need to go to the bathroom, huh?" she said to the little girl. "And you heard the story about the ghost lady who haunts the bathroom, right?"

"She tried to hurt a little boy once," the little girl told her, wide-eyed. "A man told us the story, and how the lady is still in the bathroom."

"Now, think about it," Genevieve said. "If you were a ghost, would you really want to come back and hang around in the bathroom? Ugh! There are much better places to haunt. I've lived here my whole life, and my mom and dad came here with me lots when I was little. I've used the bathroom. Your mom will go with you. It will be fine, I promise."

The mother looked at Genevieve gratefully. "We really shouldn't have let them hear quite so many stories," she said apologetically.

Genevieve laughed. "You'll be fine, won't you?" she asked the girl.

Ashley laughed suddenly. "Ugh! Who would haunt a bathroom?"

Genevieve rose. The woman stood, too, taking her daughter's hand. "Thank you so much." She paused. "You people are divers, aren't you? And you're *the* diver."

Genevieve frowned. "I'm *a* diver," she murmured.

"You were on television." The woman lowered her voice. "We saw you."

"Oh?"

"You saw that body they discovered this morning. In the water. You saw it days ago, but the police divers couldn't find it—and then it washed up this morning," the woman said softly.

"Mommy!" Ashley tugged at her hand, apparently really ready to go to the bathroom now, ghost or not.

"Um…have a lovely time in Key West," Genevieve said. She spun around, her face pale. She hadn't touched her drink, and she didn't reach for it then. "Let's go," she said to Thor. "Please."

She was halfway down the block when he caught up with her, even though his strides were long and he moved fast.

"Genevieve!"

She stopped, turned around and looked at him.

"Hey," he said, taking her by the shoulders. "You knew there were news crews crawling all over the beach this morning!"

"I didn't give anyone an interview saying I'd seen that woman in the water," she protested.

"Then someone else did. Why are you so upset? I mean, you *did* see her down there. So what's wrong?"

She didn't answer right away. She just stared with fixed interest at a middle-aged man walking his dog down the street.

"I…it shouldn't be so sensationalized," she said.

"A woman has been murdered," he said quietly. "That's serious news. Especially in a place where that isn't—thankfully—a daily occurrence. People are going to talk."

"We shouldn't be involved," she murmured.

Gen shook her head. He kept his hands firmly on her shoulders, forcing her to look at him.

"Genevieve, it's tragic, but it all makes sense, and you were right all along. There *was* a woman in the water."

She stared back at him, and her eyes suddenly held a veiled shield of bitterness. A dry sound, almost a rueful laugh, escaped her. "You don't understand."

"Understand what?"

"I saw a woman in the water."

"Right."

"No, *wrong*. I saw a woman in the water. *But not the same woman!*"

He stared at her blankly. She wrenched away from him and, nearly running, disappeared into the crowd on Duval Street.

7

Jay had been a cop a long time.

He'd seen pretty bad stuff. Not much could compare to some of the auto accidents he'd seen on US1.

But that afternoon...

He'd been the city officer on the scene, while Charlie Grissom had been the lucky one from the county. They'd stood in the cool, antiseptic morgue alongside the medical examiner, Dr. Freeland, while the M.E., brusque and businesslike on all occasions, had pointed out the most important features of the body.

The ankles—what remained of them—were given a lot of attention. Despite the many things he had witnessed through the years, Jay felt ill. Maybe it was the smell in the morgue. It was clean, but it had a chemical odor that reeked of death. Maybe it was the fact that the bloated body had filled with gas that was now escaping, and there was no disinfectant on earth that could disguise that fact. Maybe it was the girl's face, which was now almost a caricature of life. Nothing seemed real, and yet it was painfully real at the same time.

"When she went into the water, she was alive," Dr. Freeland told them. "She drowned. That was her cause of death. She fought the ropes that were holding her down. If you'll look, you'll see where the skin on her ankles is ripped. And then there are her fingers. She tried desperately to free herself. I set the rope aside. I'm sure the crime lab will be able to discover something useful about it. This here—" he indicated the torn flesh and white bone at the ankle "—is where she broke free at last." He gave them a weary grimace. "We all know the sea is a pretty brutal place. The fish ate away at the flesh and the fiber and…that's how she surfaced." He stared up at the two men. "Gentlemen, I'd guess, based on the tides, she went into the water off the southwest side of Key West. She was probably in deep water when she went in. It was five to seven days ago."

Freeland had a few more comments for them. They'd scraped her nails, but would have to wait for the lab results. She'd had a sexual encounter shortly before death, whether consensual or not, he couldn't say from the evidence, but he tended to believe *not*. However, their perp had protected himself, and they weren't coming up with any DNA.

Freeland looked up at them. "I'll have more for you in the next few days. I'm sorry to say this, officers, but it looks like you've got a murderer on your doorstep."

* * *

Jack enjoyed watching the news report over and over again. He thought he looked pretty damned good.

He stared up at the screen in the bar. Every imaginable channel had showed footage of the morning's discovery of the corpse—well, not the corpse itself. They showed the beach, the sheriff's men, the crime-scene units and the people milling around. They had recorded several tourists' reactions, the very brief seconds that Marshall had grudgingly given them, and then they showed him. It was great. As he spoke about the fact that one of their divers had actually found the corpse, they had caught a good picture of Genevieve, auburn hair billowing out behind her in the breeze, eyes sad, *haunted*, as she stared out at the water. The editor who had cut the segment had made good use of the footage. As Jack explained that the sea was an unforgiving resting place, so the killer's intent to keep her hidden might well have worked, Genevieve, leaning against one of the support beams at the tiki bar, looked as if she might have been a sea goddess herself—or the figurehead from an ancient ship, fearing such a fate herself. He looked good, too, and they'd done a hell of a job making it into something more than a simple murder. Not that a murder was ever really simple. The dive hadn't actually had a thing to do with the murder. And, cold as it sounded, people died on a daily basis. Even so, murder generated excitement. And he couldn't help it—he was a publicity hog. He loved it.

He didn't notice at first when Bethany slid into the seat beside him. He hadn't realized any of the group were still around.

"Hey, Jack," she said lightly.

He turned to look at her. She was staring at the television screen. "How sad. Her whole life ahead of her, and she ran into the wrong person. It was hard to tell, but she looked young."

He looked up and felt a little pang. The woman who stared back at him was lovely, with a wistful look in her eyes.

"Twenty-five to thirty…I would imagine," he said. She gave a little shiver, looking back at him. "Jack, do you think she was killed here? In Key West?"

"Anything is possible," he said. "But most likely she was killed up the coast. Probably one of the beautiful people hitting the clubs on Miami Beach. You don't need to be afraid. You've got a pack of he-men around you all the time, right?"

Bethany laughed. "Yeah, I guess." She stared back at the television and shivered again. "I might be hanging pretty close to you guys in the near future."

He set an arm around her shoulders and hugged her. "You can hang with me any time you want, cutie." She *was* cute. She and Genevieve had always made a nice complement to each other. One tall and sexy, one small and sweet. In appearance, anyway. He gazed at Bethany with affectionate amusement. She'd had her wild times in high school, just like a lot of kids. But she'd grown into one damned fine woman, and he enjoyed her.

"So," she murmured, nodding a thank-you to Bruce, the evening bartender, as he handed her a light beer, "what have you done all day?"

Jack thought for a moment. "Hmm. Ate lunch, had a beer. Sat here, had a beer. Ate dinner, had a beer. How about you?"

"Oh, I ran home. My place is on the northeast corner of the island, off Roosevelt. I'm not as close as Genevieve." She shrugged, grinning. "Actually, most of us could go home at night, but it's a lot easier and kind of cool staying at the resort. You still live on Stock Island, right? That's not much farther than me."

"Yeah, I'm still on Stock Island," Jack said. "I'd sure love one of those old Victorians like Genevieve's, but who the hell can afford one now?"

"Maybe we'll all be able to afford one—if we find the ship," Bethany said.

"Yeah, maybe."

Jack was startled when a hand fell on his back. "Jack, old buddy. You going to buy me a brewsky?"

He turned. Victor had arrived. One thing about their group and Key West, at some time during the evening, they were all going to show up at the bar.

Victor had spoken lightly, but he looked strained. Like he needed a beer.

"Sure. Draw up a chair."

Without being asked, Bruce brought over another

beer. "First round is on the house tonight. From the look of the news, you guys need it."

"Thanks." Victor took a long swig from the bottle.

"So what have *you* been doing?" Bethany asked him.

Victor shrugged moodily. "Oh, this and that. Stuff to take care of—you know."

They all stared silently at the television again. Alex arrived just as an artist's rendition of the dead woman's face appeared. He took the beer Bruce offered him. "At least with that picture out," he said, "they might find out who she is. Someone must be looking for the poor woman."

"There's Jack," Victor said as the interview was shown yet again.

Jack didn't feel quite the same pleasure he had earlier. He didn't like the way Victor had spoken. His words had carried a strangely bitter edge.

"Jack, you're famous," another voice commented. He looked up to find that Marshall had arrived. His arms were crossed over his chest, and he sounded weary.

"I thought it was better to talk to the woman than piss her off," Jack said defensively.

"I'm not sure we needed to tell her that Genevieve had spotted the corpse earlier, but then none of us could find it," Marshall commented.

"Come on. Not even the police divers saw it that day," Jack told him. "Bruce, get Marshall his beer, huh?"

They were all still staring at the television, even

though the anchor had gone on to report an accident in Florida City, holding up traffic in and out of the Keys, when Jay made his way into the bar. He was there, standing beside Jack, for several seconds before anyone noticed he'd arrived.

"Sad day, huh?" Jay said after a moment.

"Do you know anything more?" Bethany asked.

"Preliminary reports. The M.E. said she'd been in the water five to seven days," Jay told them.

Bethany swallowed. "Was she…drowned? Or… killed first, then weighted down?"

Jay looked at her, wincing. "Weighted down… and drowned."

Bethany trembled. "She must have been terrified. I mean, she must have known…must have been desperate for breath…."

"Do they have any idea where she was killed?" Victor asked.

"In the water," Jay said dryly.

Genevieve came in then, and they all turned toward her as she neared the bar. "Gen!" Victor said, raising his beer bottle.

Jack watched her walk in. Jeez, she was something. Casual and elegant all in one. She perched atop a bar stool next to Jay.

"Anything new?" she asked him.

Jack couldn't hear his reply, because he lowered his head to speak with her. She said something back to him, her expression anxious, but Jack couldn't hear that, either.

"We'll talk. We can have dinner some night this

week," Jay said, his tone normal. "You don't have to hang with this sorry bunch every night, do you?" he teased.

She shook her head. "No. And I really need to talk to you."

Though she had spoken very softly, Jack was able to make out the words.

Just then Thor Thompson arrived. Jack studied his employer. Thor wasn't the tallest guy he'd ever met, or the buffest. But he had something. A presence. A way of walking, maybe, or just *being*. When Thor entered a room, no matter how softly he moved or how quietly he spoke, everyone knew it.

"Hey," he said simply, taking a seat on a bar stool.

"Bruce, a beer for our northern comrade!" Alex called.

"Northern?" Thor said.

"Jacksonville. You're practically a Yankee."

Thor shrugged and laughed, but Jack thought he looked distracted. He noticed as Thor glanced toward Genevieve and seemed relieved to see her sitting next to Jay. He had clearly been anxious about her. Jack couldn't help but wonder why. Genevieve certainly didn't look like a lunatic now, in light of the day's grisly discovery.

The newscaster returned to showing a picture of the murder victim, asking the viewers for help in discovering the woman's identity.

"Go figure," Alex said. "I didn't want another lecture from Sheridan, but I sure didn't want to get out of it this way."

"You're still getting the lecture from Sheridan," Marshall said dryly. "Monday morning."

"It won't be that bad," Thor informed them all, his eyes on the television. "He's made a model of the ship. Sounds kind of cool."

"Hey, has anybody seen Zach and Lizzie?" Marshall asked.

"They decided to play tourist," Victor informed them. "They were going to do the Conch Tour Train, Audubon house, Hemingway's place—all that stuff. And then they were going to take a sunset dinner cruise."

"How romantic," Bethany said.

"Bethany, if anyone invited you on a sunset cruise, you'd look at him as if he'd lost his mind," Victor informed her.

"Not true. I don't care if I've been here my whole life. A sunset cruise is still romantic."

"I'm glad you think so, because we'll probably stay out a lot later Monday to make up for this," Marshall said. "It will be a great sunset cruise as we all head back in."

Jack watched as Genevieve slipped from her bar stool and said something to Bethany, who nodded. Then Genevieve gave them all a wave, saying she was heading out.

Jack noticed that everyone in their group watched her leave. Odd. Everyone still seemed concerned about her or…

Suspicious.

He shook his head and swigged his beer. Genevieve. What the hell was going on with her?

Thor made no pretense of doing anything else. As soon as she left, he followed her.

Okay, he was a stalker. Definitely a stalker. But he was more worried about her than ever.

She stopped a block from the bar, turned and waited for him.

"I'm all right," she told him.

"I'm really worried about you," he said flatly.

"Don't be." Strange, after the day they'd spent, the last thing she wanted was for this man to be *worried* about her. She didn't want to like him, but she did. She wanted admiration and respect from him. She even, she admitted to herself, wanted him to think she was cool, savvy and sexy. What she didn't want was for him to be worried about her.

"You walked off on me all of a sudden," he reminded her. "You ran away. Great way to end a date."

"We weren't on a date."

"Great way to end lunch and a drink with a friend, then."

She flushed. "I'm sorry. It was just…well, this hasn't been a great day."

She started walking again, not that she really knew where she was going, but just because she felt awkward standing around on the sidewalk. He fell into step beside her, silent for several minutes.

"Genevieve, what did you mean that…the

woman you saw in the water wasn't the woman we discovered today?"

She shook her head. "I must have been mistaken."

"You really might have been," he said gently.

"Please don't tiptoe around my feelings as if I'm really ready to be committed," she told him.

She saw him half smile, shaking his head. "At the moment, I'm not. Any time you're in the water, you can be taken by surprise. The water can play tricks and she was, well, she wasn't in good shape. You might have seen seaweed or fish moving around her, and that might have made her seem alive, hard to recognize when you saw her again later."

"Right," she murmured.

"But you don't believe that."

"I said you could be right."

"Then again, maybe you did see a different woman, and that's a much more frightening and serious thought."

She stared at him sharply. "What do you mean?"

He sighed. "I mean the killer might have had more than one victim," he said.

A chill snaked along her spine, and she shook it off.

"Sorry," he murmured.

"No, no…you're right."

"Actually, at the moment, it doesn't seem as if anyone in the area is panicking. It's sad, but it feels distant to people. I certainly hope there won't be any panic, but I think women need to be careful," Thor murmured. "Um, where are we going?" he asked.

She paused, half laughing. "Frankly, I don't know. I guess I just needed to get out of there."

"Strange day," he said. "You keep going into bars, then running out of them. It's as if you don't want your own company, but you're not sure you want any other company, either."

"You're right. I'm not sure what I want," she told him, then hesitated. "I'm also certain that either Victor or Alex played a prank on me this morning, and that's still driving me crazy. There was a mannequin on my porch when I got up, and I dumped it in the water. Then it was gone—and the real corpse was there."

"Don't let it bother you," he told her. "They were talking about it this morning. Victor denied it, but after what had happened, who would want to admit it? The point is, Genevieve, don't drive yourself crazy. There are explanations for the things that have been happening. You just have to wait and find out what they are."

"Hey!" someone called from behind them.

They turned. Bethany was hurrying toward them, the others following. Jay had come with them, and he was talking to Jack as they walked.

"We're going to get some dinner," Bethany said, catching up. "Do you two want to come with us?"

"We just ate lunch," Genevieve said.

Thor looked at his watch. "Actually, we ate lunch six hours ago."

"You two had lunch…together?" Bethany said.

Genevieve felt color threatening to flood her cheeks. "I found him wandering the streets of Key West," she said lightly. "He's a northerner," she added. "He might have been lost."

"Anybody into Italian?" Marshall asked, breaking into the awkward conversation. "There's a new place and the owner-slash-chef is the son of one of my first diving instructors. I feel the urge to be supportive. I've also heard it's really good."

"Is the owner really Italian?" Alex asked.

"No, but he really likes Italian food," Marshall assured them.

"Sounds like an important factor," Victor said. "Gen? Sound good to you?"

Bethany fell into step with them as they headed for the restaurant. When Thor paused to say something to Marshall, she caught Genevieve's arm and whispered, "Are we still on for tomorrow?"

"Meeting Audrey, you mean?"

"Yes."

"Of course. Why wouldn't I be?"

"I thought maybe you had plans. Which would be fine."

Genevieve frowned, looking at her friend. "Why would I make plans when I already had plans?"

"Well, you just took off today. I was worried about you. I'm still worried about you. I would have thought you'd be happy—no, not happy, relieved— to find out you weren't crazy. Or seeing things."

Genevieve hesitated. The others were too close

for her to want to continue this conversation. "We'll talk tomorrow, okay?"

"Sure. But…well, I wasn't even sure you still felt you needed to see Audrey anymore."

"We're seeing Audrey because she's an old friend."

By then, Marshall and Thor had caught up to them. "The restaurant is around the corner."

As they entered the restaurant, Victor finagled his way into the seat next to Genevieve. Jack wound up on her other side. As everyone else got settled, Thor's cell phone rang. Genevieve could hear him speaking with Lizzie, telling her where they were, and saying she and Zach should come over. They must not have been far, because they arrived almost immediately, having apparently decided to forgo their cruise. While they took seats at the head of the table, Jay caught them up on the murder, until Marshall said they were having dinner and it was time to talk about something more cheerful.

The owner was a young man named Bill Breton, who thanked them for coming, and suggested he do appetizers and a family-style meal for them, and they all agreed. Alex, who claimed to be a wine connoisseur, chose a Bordeaux for their table. After that the conversation turned to Zach and Lizzie's day.

"We saw Robert, that doll," Lizzie announced. "That's one creepy toy. What parent would give that to a child? They had all kinds of letters on the wall about him—one from the mayor, thanking him."

"Thanking him for what? Being a creepy doll?" Alex asked.

"For taking the blame for everything that's gone wrong in the area since the turn of the last century."

"We had something like that at home," Bethany said. "I was one of five kids," she explained. "And we all denied doing anything wrong all the time. When my mom couldn't figure out who had done what, she'd stare us all down and demand to know if we were really living with an invisible jerk."

"It seems there's always an invisible jerk around," Genevieve said, staring at Victor.

He stared back at her. He looked hurt, angry and, she thought, strangely afraid.

"Hey, when I'm a jerk," he said quietly, "I own up to it."

"There *was* a mannequin on my porch this morning," she told him.

"I believe you. But *I* didn't put it there."

"Hey, will you look at that?" Jack said, breaking the tension by indicating the huge plates of food that were being set before them. "Wow, Marshall, you done good. Look at all this."

"Calamari," Bethany said. "That's for me."

"These peppers look great," Lizzie announced.

The platters were passed around; more wine arrived. Gen knew that anyone watching would see what appeared to be a comfortable gathering of friends. And why not? She'd worked with her own group forever. Jack was as much a part of their lives in Key West as anyone, and it was good to have Jay with them. Lizzie and Zach were great. And she had even found herself not just drawn to Thor Thompson but almost painfully attracted to him. Except…

Except she felt Victor's presence next to her the entire meal. And not as she always had. He really was just about her best friend, other than Bethany. He didn't say anything about the mannequin again, and neither did she, but the whole time, it was there between them. *Someone* had put it on her porch, and if not Victor…

"Alex," he said softly at her side.

"What?" she murmured.

"It must have been Alex. We were talking about it together. And Jack was there, too."

"Victor, you know what? It doesn't matter anymore. It didn't scare me then, and it doesn't scare now me. Okay, so someone played a trick. Then there was a real corpse and the trick wasn't so funny. But it's over, and the stupid mannequin has disappeared, so it can't really matter anymore, right?"

Victor let out a breath and stared at her. "It *doesn't* matter…if you really believe me."

"I believe you."

"You want me to believe you believe me," he murmured.

"Victor, please, I just don't care."

"I don't want you not to care. Don't you understand?"

She slipped an arm around his shoulders for a quick hug. "You're like my brother. I care very deeply. Okay?"

He remained tense. There seemed nothing she could do. Across from her, Marshall and Thor were deep in discussion on where they should anchor and how they should extend the search. Jay and Bethany were talking together, and Genevieve was somewhat surprised to see what a close little tête-à-tête they seemed to have going on. At the far end of the table, Lizzie was speaking excitedly about Key West architecture."

"You should see Genevieve's place," Jack advised her.

"You have a historic home?" Lizzie asked her excitedly.

"I do," Genevieve told her. She leaned on an elbow, glancing across the table at Marshall and catching Marshall's eye. "Maybe I should have a barbecue on Sunday at the house."

Marshall grinned. "You're asking for my blessing?"

"Your opinion would be fine."

"I say great."

"Cool," Lizzie announced. Then the pasta arrived, lasagna, angel hair with shrimp and pesto, and ziti with marinara sauce.

Genevieve passed a plate across to Alex. He seemed to be studying her strangely.

So *had* he played the trick with the mannequin? Was he worried she wasn't going to let it go?

But she already had.

Sometime during the meal, she realized that everyone seemed to be staring at her strangely.

Tonight, the night of her vindication. When everyone had supposedly decided she wasn't crazy, because there *had* been a dead woman in the water.

Just not the dead woman she had seen.

She decided she was going home. Not to her cottage, but *home*. She wasn't going to sleep where mannequins appeared on the porch, corpses were cast up on the beach—and ghosts came to her, dripping, giving dire warnings in the middle of the night.

It was late when the meal ended. After the pasta, there had been fish, chicken and meat platters, then dessert, coffee and liqueurs. Finally, they ambled out to the street. When everyone else turned toward the water, Genevieve stood still. "Hey, guys, I'll see you tomorrow. And don't forget, barbecue at my place on Sunday."

Thor was staring at her, frowning.

"Gen, you're going home?" Victor asked; he sounded worried.

"Yeah, home," she said lightly.

"You all right?" Marshall asked, sounding a bit concerned, and yet not sure himself why he should be.

"I'm fine. My house is just down the street."

"We should walk you there," Alex said suddenly.

"Actually, not a bad idea," Jay agreed.

"There are tourists still out everywhere," Genevieve said, laughing. "I'm fine. Good night. Go away, all of you."

But Thor strode past Bethany, Marshall and Jay to reach her side. "I'll walk you to your place," he told her. "It's all right, go on," he told the others. "It would be ridiculous for all of us to walk her."

"Right. As if we're incapable of being ridiculous," Victor said dryly.

"Oh, my God, I didn't mean to create this big a deal. I'm sorry," Genevieve said. "I've lived here my whole life. I'm only a few blocks away. I'll be just fine."

"It's not a bad idea to let Thor walk you home," Jay said. "Or I can walk with you, if Thor wants to get back."

Genevieve shook her head. "I'm going, guys. Later!"

She started down the street. But she could hear them talking as she left.

"It's all right. I'll walk her," Thor said, and in a split second he had caught up with her.

She glanced at him, shaking her head. "I'm okay. Really."

"Don't worry. I'm not following you. I'll just see you to your door. There *is* a killer out there."

Genevieve shook her head. She knew she should be more concerned about the very real dangers out there. But she wasn't. She just didn't want to see any more ghosts. "The streets are full of people. You don't need to do this." She hesitated. "Sadly, and most likely, we'll find out she was a prostitute, or running with a drug crowd. Or she was a trophy wife seeking excitement on the side. I doubt that, since we're not in any of the same circles, we're in any of the same danger."

"Just walk. We'll be there before we finish discussing the situation."

He led her straight to her door. She unlocked it and looked up at him. He was standing very close. Large, powerful. She felt almost as if they were touching. She breathed the scent of him, a pleasant cologne, something of the sea, something of bronzed flesh. Her heart was pounding far too quickly. There seemed to be something magnetic, electric, in the space between them. She was sure he was going to touch her, and if he did…

"Lock your door once you're inside," he said sternly, stepping back. "Go on. Get in."

She nodded and opened the door. "Thanks."

That was it; he was gone, and she was surprised by the measure of loss and disappointment she felt. She didn't want to question her feelings too closely. It had been so much more comfortable to hate the man. He didn't become involved; he didn't date where he worked. So Bethany had said. She had read it. Then again, he had bet his boat against a night with her. A whim? Or sheer ego? Surely that meant the man at least found her appealing….

There was a difference between sex and love. She

didn't want to become a number in a list. She gritted her teeth. She wasn't going to torture herself over a man any more than she was going to torture herself over...

Ghosts.

She checked her doors, but first she got out one of her dive knives, and then she searched the house, down to the closets. She felt a little like a fool, but at least she knew she was alone. She felt resentful; she'd never been afraid in her own house before. She had wished once upon a time that there *were* ghosts, so her parents could have appeared, could have come to her and whispered that they were okay, that they were together and watching over her.

No such ghosts had ever come to her, though.

After a while she felt more comfortable with being home, though most of the lights in the place were on. This was home. Everything was real and familiar. No ghosts, she was certain, would darken her door.

She went through her mail and paid bills, then studied some of the copies she had made of documents regarding the *Marie Josephine*. Her interest was drawn not so much to the ships involved, as to Gasparilla the pirate. He'd had a real streak for cruelty, it seemed.

Had he fallen in love, been rejected...and murdered the beautiful young woman who was the object of his affection? Thrown her into the water, her body weighted...

As the current killer had apparently done?

Even if he had, what could be the possible connection to what was happening now?

Coincidence, she told herself. Or sheer insanity.

She didn't want to think about it, and she pushed the papers away. Then, after she'd walked away once, she returned and slammed them into the drawer of the desk. She fixed herself a cup of tea and headed into the living room. She intentionally kept the television off. She knew about the murder. She doubted she was going to hear any good news.

At last, she went to bed. She was surprised to find herself critically studying her choice of night attire. A large T-shirt. Cotton, worn, extremely comfortable. Dopey on the front, holding a cup of coffee. Hardly the apparel of a femme fatale.

The same thing she always wore, she reminded herself. And, anyway, she was sleeping alone.

But in bed, just as she had for the past several nights, she couldn't bring herself to turn the lights out. And she wanted the noise of the television. She turned it on, careful to choose a station that didn't carry the news.

She was desperate to sleep and simultaneously terrified to do so, but at last she drifted off.

The pirates came again. Tattered and filthy as they walked through the water. Ragged clothing fell from skeletal arms. Shimmering weapons were raised. Rotted teeth showed through decaying lips.

They encircled her. Staring at her, moving closer...

And then the woman came. With her drifting hair, long white gown. Her sad smile. Her whispered word.

Beware…

Sheer panic set in, rousing some instinctive place where the human psyche fought to survive.

She awoke, gasping, sitting up.

The room was empty. The lights were still on.

The TV was showing an ancient sitcom.

Shaking violently, she forced herself to breathe. And then to rise.

And as she did, she saw the water.

Gallons of it, surrounding her bed.

8

Thor didn't go straight to bed. On the walk back to the resort, he discovered that Jay Gonzalez had stayed with the group, which was making a final stop at the tiki bar before splitting up for the night. And Jay interested him.

He was able to get a seat next to Jay at the bar and ask, "So, what do you think?"

Jay, sipping a beer, stared at him, well aware what he was talking about. "What do I think?" he murmured. "I think there's a maniac out there. Of course, there's always a maniac out there, but this one is close to home."

"Do you think the killer is local?"

"No, I don't. But then, I don't *want* the killer to be local. There's no reason to expect the perp to be from here, of course. These waters are a playground for a lot of South Florida." He hesitated, lifting his beer. "But was she killed around here? Yes. For the body to have surfaced where it did…she was killed somewhere off the islands, close to Key West. But she was definitely dumped off a boat, and that boat could have come from almost anywhere."

"She was weighted down. Surely that gives you some clues."

"Pieces of rope, but I have a feeling we're going to discover it's the kind that can be found at any hardware store or any boating-supply place in the country. We have no idea what kind of weight was used to keep her down." Jay stared at Thor with serious eyes. "I'll send police divers down again at the coordinates where Genevieve first saw the body. If we can find the weight that was used, it will be another piece in the puzzle. Of course, finding out who she is should help a lot, too."

Thor kept Genevieve's conviction that this body was not the woman she had seen in the water to himself. "We'll be keeping an eye out, as well," he assured Jay grimly. He hesitated. "Any chance I can see the body again, speak with the medical examiner?"

Jay seemed surprised, and he studied Thor for several seconds. Then he grimaced. "I imagine I can arrange it. Since you're in charge of the hunt for the *Marie Josephine*, what you discover underwater could be as important to our current crime as to your own search. I'll get back to you tomorrow." He handed Thor his card, and Thor returned the gesture.

At that point Bethany crawled off her bar stool and said good-night. Alex and Victor had followed suit, along with Lizzie and Zach. Marshall, too, yawned and left, and only Jack, Jay and Thor were left. Jack groused over the fact his beloved home had been besmirched by a vicious murder, and then,

shaking his head, departed. The bar was empty—
even Clint had gone to bed—when Jay and Thor
said their goodbyes.

Thor was back in his cottage barely long enough
to shower when there was a knock on his door.

It was two in the morning. Not so late for island
barhoppers, but still…

A towel wrapped around his waist, he went to see
who it was.

"Thor?"

He was stunned to hear Genevieve's voice.

He opened the door. She shot in, apparently not
noticing the fact that he wasn't exactly dressed.

But then, she looked a little strange herself. Her
hair was wild, as if she had been asleep, the rich
auburn length sexy with just-out-of-bed appeal. She
was wearing a long, cotton nightshirt similar to one
he'd seen her in before. She had on sandals with
heels, and she was carrying a casual evening bag.

"Uh…yes?" he asked.

She sailed past and right on to the futon in the
living area, taking a seat and staring at him.

"I…couldn't sleep. I was hoping you were up."

"Did something frighten you?" he asked.

"No," she lied with a flat smile.

"I see. You left your house, where you were safely
locked in, and walked back through the city—
where the victim of a nasty murder was recently
found—because you felt chatty in the middle of the
night?"

She stared straight at him. "Yes."

"Okay." He stared straight back at her. "Well," he said after a moment, "I guess I'm flattered."

She looked a little startled, as if suddenly realizing how strange it was that she had come to him, of all people.

She was frightened, he could tell, no matter what she said.

"Did something happen?" he asked.

She shook her head slowly, as if considering. "No."

"I see." He sat down on the futon, a foot away from her, folding his hands idly. "You just couldn't stand being away from me?"

Her eyes narrowed. "You're actually fine," she murmured, "when you're not being insufferable."

"Wow. Thanks."

"You're welcome."

"You're actually okay, too," he said.

Her eyes shot to his. "When I'm not being insane, right?"

He smiled at that. "You're a lot more than okay, but I'm sure you know that. You not only look like you walked out of some teenage boy's wet dream, you have a smile that lights up a room, you're bright, curious and—" he smiled "—an excellent diver."

Her eyes widened as he spoke, as if she were genuinely surprised at the compliment.

"What? You know I'm attracted to you. Very attracted. I wouldn't bet my boat for a night with just any woman," he told her with a wry smile. Maybe he shouldn't have spoken quite so honestly while wearing a towel, he thought.

She flushed and looked away. "As if you have difficulty with women," she murmured. "The magazines call you…what was it? Oh, yes. A bronze god. A Viking adventurer. Indiana Jones of the sea."

"I'm careful never to believe the press," he assured her.

She smiled.

"But you didn't come here to sleep with me, did you?" he asked softly. "Or maybe you did. Except I really don't want you to decide to sleep with me only because you're afraid and it's a better alternative to sleeping alone."

That brought a deep flush to her cheeks, and she didn't look at him. "There's the fact that I really did lose the bet," she murmured.

"I admit that's debatable. And that's not an easy admission, because I'm not good at admitting defeat," he assured her.

"What if I admitted that I find you attractive?" She turned to him at last.

He was a fool, he thought. A sad excuse for the male of the species. Here she was…smelling divinely, alone with him, inches away. Her body warmth and that scent seemed to reach out to him, attack his senses. But for some stupid reason he just didn't want her this way. Though he did want her. He felt the blood throbbing in the erection beneath his towel.

He damned himself. Her skin was golden. As soft as the cotton of the thin T-shirt that covered her body but did nothing to disguise the shape and curve of it. What the hell was the matter with him? He'd never made such ridiculous rules for himself before. If a woman he wanted wanted him, that had always been enough.

"You can stay here, sleep here," he said softly, "without having to sleep with me."

He could almost feel her heart beating. A few inches, and he could touch her. A few minutes, and he could have her, take her with the kind of excitement that swept away time and circumstance, that pounded and pulsed with carnal pleasure. Had he lost his own sanity?

She looked up at him, something that might have been a wistful, even poignant, smile curving her lips. "I thought you found me attractive?" she said. Her voice was a whisper, as if he wasn't already in enough agony. The sound seemed to touch him. Reach out, seep into his bloodstream, brush against the *inside* of his flesh.

"I don't believe in sex for any reason other than pure desire," he told her.

"You don't desire me?" she asked.

Again that sound in her voice. Something husky, almost like purring.

"I like the concept of being wanted for myself," he said.

"Who wouldn't want a bronze god?" she inquired.

"I'm trying to be a decent human being, which isn't all that easy right now," he told her.

To his astonishment, she stood up and pulled the T-shirt over her head. She wore a delicate lace thong beneath—and the strappy, low-heeled sandals. Her auburn hair, like a cascade of night fire, fell over her naked shoulders and curved around the fullness of her breasts. She was long and sleek, with curving hips, a concave abdomen, and a tan line that seemed as provocative as all get-out.

It was the shoes that did it, he decided, emphasizing her long legs and…upward.

"A woman doesn't usually bet a night of sex with a man unless she finds him appealing," she informed him, and smiled, a come-on smile that rocked his libido and bit into his soul. And with that, she strode into the bedroom area of the cottage, where her silhouette, dimly outlined, beckoned insanity into his mind.

He was so stunned that for a second he just sat there. Then he shot to his feet and followed.

The bedside light glowed softly. They stood across the bed from each other. She stepped out of the sandals and walked around to his side of the mattress, straight up against him, her arms snaking around his neck, fingers threading into his hair. The towel fell. He made no move to retrieve it.

She barely had to stand on her toes to find his lips. He dipped his head, allowing her to ease back to her feet. She could have no doubt of his desire for her as they seemed to meld together, the toned flesh of her body hot and vibrant. He caught her chin, formed his lips over hers, pressed deep into her mouth with his tongue, and felt the spiraling tightness within himself. Purely sexual sensations ripped

through him like a storm surge at sea. He felt as if
he were consuming her mouth, his blood electric
with the response to her taste, scent, touch.... She
was sweet, so sweet, everything his dreams had whispered and he had been so determined to deny. Vital
and passionate, the shape of her body was simple sin.

He kissed her, felt that he died a little with the
pleasure, his hands sweeping over her. He felt her
quivering and he drew his lips away from hers.

"You're not afraid?" he asked softly.

"Of you?" she whispered. "Oh, definitely." It was
a teasing statement, but it was the truth, though in
what way, he wasn't certain.

"Of...the night?" he persisted.

"That, too," she admitted.

He wanted to know why. What demon plagued
her. But stark desire overrode sanity. He didn't care.
At that moment...screw decency. His mouth found
hers again. He felt her fingertips riding down his
back, over his buttocks. He held her fiercely.
Dragged her down to the bed, rose above her. Her
breath was coming in heady bursts. Her eyes were
glittering as they touched his. And that smile curled
her lips again, an expression of pure sex. She
reached for him. Her fingers swept down his chest,
curled around his erection. He gave a low groan,
then lay against her again, catching her mouth as
his hands swept over her skin, his lips following
suit. He caressed her with fascination, finding the
line of her collarbone, touching it with the delicate
brush of his fingers and tongue. His hand curved

over her breast just before his mouth fastened over her nipple, his lips circling the peak. His palm slid over her midriff, felt the tautness of her abdomen, lowered to feel the curve of her pelvic bone and the delicate lace of the thong. His body rubbed erotically against hers as he lowered himself, fingers sliding beneath the lace, tongue moving sensually atop the thin wisp of fabric between her flesh and himself.

She rocked beneath him. He caught the slender strand of lace, removed it, found her again beneath it. Caressed, ravished…felt the shiver of excitement that ran down the length of her, moved to spur her to an ever more desperate fever. She cried out and was up, meeting him, crashing into his arms, seeking his mouth with her own. They held each other while the world thundered out the beat of their passion. He caught her thighs, wrapped them around him, and thrust into her with a staggering hunger. Locked with her, he felt her inner pulse reach a frantic edge, fought his own desire to explode, felt the fantastic, delicious agony soar, felt her stiffen, shudder, shake in his arms, and allowed himself to catapult into final climax. He couldn't let her go, nor did she seem to mind. Tremors rippled through her as he embraced her, adjusting himself to lie beside her, to allow himself to grow soft within her, still hungry to touch, to maintain their connection. His body cooling at last, he felt the slickness of heat that covered them both and cradled her even closer. He listened as the pounding of their hearts lowered to a normal speed, felt every little quiver and movement within her, buried his face in the wealth of her hair.

Then he forced himself up, looking at her. Her eyes remained steady and wide on his.

"That was…" he whispered, then ran out of words.

She smiled. "Not bad," she said, a slight smile teasing her lips.

"Not bad?"

"Kind of like being with a Nordic god for real."

"That's better," he assured her.

"Thunder and lightning and all that," she murmured. She reached out, touching his face. "Too much like a god, maybe…"

"Never too much," he assured her. Her lashes swept to her cheeks, hiding her thoughts. "Then again, never put a man on a pedestal," he warned.

"You don't want to be on a pedestal?" she asked lightly, meeting his gaze again.

He shook his head. "I wouldn't want to fall off." Then he asked her seriously, "Why would you be afraid of me?"

"I'm not afraid of you, exactly," she murmured.

"What *are* you afraid of, then?"

"Myself," she murmured, looking away once more. Then she stared up at him again. There was a very strange—given the circumstances—prim and almost shy tone in her voice as she asked, "May I stay?"

"Are you joking?"

"I—"

"I would somehow dredge up the violence of my ancestors, conk you over the head and bodily hold on to you if you tried to leave," he assured her solemnly.

The gratitude in her eyes touched him to the core, tore at his heart as deeply as her sensuality affected his desires. Deeper, if at all possible.

"Thanks."

"It's a pleasure."

She laughed and eased into his arms. He rested on an elbow, fascinated just to let his fingers stroke down the length of her back. "I don't suppose you're going to explain what you meant before."

"What I meant about what?" she murmured.

"Being afraid of yourself."

He felt the subtle tension in her as she tightened in his arms. "Nothing," she murmured.

He wanted to press the matter, but he didn't. Right now, he wanted her at ease and comfortable beside him more than he wanted the truth. He laid his head down by hers, still stroking the long and elegant line of her back. In a while, he realized she had fallen asleep. He wasn't sure what kind of a comment that was on his sexual prowess, but he was gratified she had found the serenity to sleep at his side.

Later in the night, he awoke when she shifted against him. That time their lovemaking began with the brush of her fingers against his stomach, then a slow fusion of their bodies. Soon he was fully awake, just as impassioned, as desperate, as volatile as before. The climax was just as shattering, the aftermath just as sweet, as lazy, with no words spoken— just her body curled against his trustingly as she drifted to sleep once again.

He lay awake while she slept. She was incredible. Hot, bright, electric. He was crazy, letting himself become involved with her. Because she was…

Seeing ghosts. And he was being swept into her world as if into a vortex. He was crazy to let this happen, because…

Because it was crazy to fall for someone who might be totally insane.

There was no way Genevieve regretted what she had done. She had never become involved with anyone lightly, never without feeling something real—except, of course, when she entered into the ridiculous bet with Thor. But even then…as incredibly arrogant and obnoxious as she had found him, she had also found him compelling, even if only sexually at the time. Sadly, she mused, awaking in the morning, still comfortable and ridiculously secure in his arms, she had discovered she found him fascinating, not as arrogant as she had assumed, and not at all obnoxious. She cared about him. Worse, she really *liked* him and admired him.

He had been kind to her last night.

Kind? She didn't want kindness. Although, she mused, they also had incredible chemistry. Which didn't mean he wasn't still questioning her sanity.

After all, she had literally stripped for him and asked him to bed. Not too many men would have turned her down.

So they hadn't sworn eternal vows. She wouldn't have wanted such a relationship, anyway. Real involvement meant so much more than sex, a true learning about each other. But…she did care about him. She didn't want this to be an "I'm afraid and you're great in bed" situation.

But no ghosts had darkened her dreams when she had been with him. She had been completely involved, felt completely protected, even in sleep.

He rose. She heard him enter the bathroom, heard the shower start. A few minutes later, he walked out in a towel—damn, he wore a towel well—and strode out to the kitchenette to put coffee on. She rolled out of bed, headed into the shower herself, and emerged in a towel, as well, just in time to be offered a cup of coffee.

"Good morning. Are you sorry you're here?" he asked her.

She shook her head. "I came here of my own free will, remember?"

"I'm still not sure why," he told her.

She was tempted to ask him if it really mattered so much. She refrained. "Good coffee," she said instead.

"It's hard to mess up when it comes premeasured," he said, studying her. He set his cup down and put his hand on her shoulders. "I actually thought you'd try to disappear by first light or something," he told her.

"No," she said softly.

"Should I slip you out somehow, pretend you were never here?" he asked, his voice pleasantly soft, a bit amused.

"No. Not unless you don't want people to know I was here," she said.

That brought a deep smile. She wasn't sure what it meant.

"I do have a lunch date, though. With Bethany. We're going to see an old friend."

"Ah, yes. The mystic." He made his voice spooky for the final word.

She hoped she kept her tone level and her voice indifferent. "Don't go telling anyone else, but Audrey is the first to admit she doesn't see a thing. She does what she does to make money, and apparently she does well. Not a bad business to run in Key West."

He nodded, waiting.

"Actually, though," she admitted ruefully, "I didn't exactly dress to be seen, and I imagine others are up and about now. Then again, I did walk through town in high-heeled sandals and a nightshirt."

"Ditch the sandals. The nightshirt could just be a bathing suit cover-up," he told her gravely. "It will be just fine. Or, if you'd rather, you can give me the key and I'll walk over to your cottage and get whatever you'd like. But first, you might want to tell me why you decided to walk through the streets of Key West in high-heeled sandals and a nightshirt."

She ignored the last. By morning's light, he seemed taller and far more solid and entirely businesslike—sane, no-nonsense, living in the real world—more so than ever before. And, as she stood there, feeling his eyes on her, his hands on her shoulders, even more arresting. She was startled by the little pang that teased not just her senses but her heart. He was perfect. He loved what she loved. He seemed to have ethics she had never suspected. She wanted to…

Sleep with him, yes. But also have breakfast, walk on the beach…curl up to watch a movie, go horseback riding…spend endless time with him.

"If you'd go to my cottage for some clothes, that would be really great," she told him.

"All right."

But he was still staring at her. Then he began to smile. And she knew from that smile just what he was feeling. Like a current, the heat of arousal raced through her, quickening her muscles.

He took the coffee cup from her, and then she was in his arms again. The towels were lost somewhere before they reached the bed. His every whisper, every move, was erotic. She wondered vaguely if that was simply because he was such an incredible lover, or because it was *him*. His breath against her flesh was a rapid-fire arousal. The brush of his fingers…the liquid of his kiss. And touching him… each ripple of muscle, pulse and tightness she created in him seemed to deepen her own sense of urgency and desire. In the end there was wildfire, sweet excitement, agony, longing, a climax that was violent and shattering…and the feel of his arms around her, as if she were the most wonderful woman in the world, the most cherished.

And then, a soft sigh of regret. "I guess we should try the coffee thing again," he murmured. He rose; she heard the shower again. She was tempted to rise, to slip in with him.

But she had plans for the day, and they were important.

Desperate, actually.

He emerged, and she was somewhat surprised to see him dress as if for a casual business meeting, wearing black trousers and a short-sleeved tailored shirt. But he had refrained from pressing her, so she decided it wasn't her business to ask him what he was doing.

"Give me the key and tell me what you want, and I'll try to find it," he told her.

Thirty minutes later, he returned, bringing her a choice of clothing. She thanked him, showered and dressed. He was sipping coffee on the porch when she emerged.

"I imagine everyone is going to know we're having an affair," he told her, looking out across the sand. "I ran into Jack and Alex when I went to your cottage earlier." He grinned at her. "They'll all be talking about us today."

She shrugged. "I don't mind if you don't mind."

She was surprised when he studied her gravely. "I seldom, if ever, do anything I'd have to hide," he told her. "Unless I was asked." Then his smile returned. "Are we having an affair?"

For some reason, the simple question seemed to give her a little thrill, a renewed sense of warmth.

"I'd certainly hate to think I wasn't going to be with you again," she said softly.

"I'll see you later, then."

She smiled and started across the sand. Then she paused and turned back. "I'll be at the tiki bar later, I guess."

"I have some things to do today. But I'll make sure to end up there."

It was frightening to feel such a burst of happiness at his words. But she merely waved casually and started over to Bethany's cottage.

Bethany must have been watching, because the door opened before Genevieve even reached the porch.

"Hey," Bethany said. She was grinning from ear to ear.

"Hey."

"That's all?" Bethany grabbed her by the arm, practically dragging her inside. "'Hey?'" She took a moment to stare into Genevieve's eyes. "Oh, my God—you slept with him!"

"Bethany—"

"Details!"

"No way."

"I knew it. I knew it from the first second I saw you two together. It was in the air. I got hot just watching the two of you stare at each other."

"Okay, okay."

"Was he incredible?" Bethany asked eagerly.

"Bethany!"

"Was he?"

"Yes. Now can we go to lunch?"

"Lunch? You wound up in his cottage for a night of total abandon, and you're worried about *lunch*? I can't believe you're actually here."

Genevieve groaned. "Bethany…" She hesitated. "Bethany, I still need help," she said softly.

Bethany sobered instantly, putting her arm around Genevieve and pulling her tight for a minute. "It's going to be fine. Really. But…wait," she said, studying Genevieve's eyes. "Something else happened. Oh, my God! That's why you wound up at his cottage. You'd gone home, so what happened that made you come back here?"

"Nothing happened. I just decided I wanted company."

"You're a liar."

"I just didn't like being alone."

Bethany looked at her shrewdly. "Let's see. You've known me all your life. And Victor. And Alex is on our team. Marshall is like, well…he's practically Uncle Marshall. Hell, you've even known Jack since you were a kid. But who did you run to? Thor Thompson."

"Bethany, we have to get going."

"So let's go. You can give me the details as we walk."

"So you finally got Gen over to your place, huh?" Jack said, grinning. "You should feel privileged. That girl doesn't play around. She's seriously discriminating. She is one woman who can pick and choose. But she's great, huh? Sorry, that's not from experience. I just remember watching her grow up. She always promised to be extraordinary."

"She is a beautiful woman," Thor said, regretting the fact that he'd stopped at the tiki bar before taking off. A phone call from Jay had come less than ten minutes after Genevieve had left. He was to meet him at the station at Stock Island in an hour. He was only here because he'd known he could get breakfast fast. But Jack had been here already, savoring an omelet. Victor appeared just as Jack finished speaking.

And it was hard to escape when he'd just ordered food.

"Hey, hey, hey…so those who discover together sleep together, huh?" Victor teased, taking a seat at the bar alongside Thor and Jack.

Apparently, it didn't matter that Jack had been talking about Genevieve; the fact that she had walked into his cottage late last night and walked out that morning might as well have been on wide-screen TV.

"As long as our Gen is happy," Jack said. He was still grinning, but there seemed to be a paternal warning in the words despite the fact that he was working for Thor.

"If she's happy, I'm happy," Thor said smoothly.

"Yeah?" Victor accepted a cup of coffee from the morning bartender and turned to Thor. "But you think she's crazy, right? What the hell. If I met a stranger who looked like Gen and she was willing, I'd give it a go—even if I questioned her sanity. I mean, you don't have to be sane in bed. In fact, I think it's better when there's a little insanity going on."

Screw breakfast. Thor stood, trying to remember that these people were her friends, that they cared about her. And he had to admit, he *was* feeling a little guilty.

Part of him did want to keep his distance. He didn't want to find himself inextricably involved with someone who hallucinated on a regular basis.

"I have an appointment. I think I'll skip breakfast," he said.

Alex came walking toward the tiki bar just as he was leaving. "Hey, hey, hey. I hear you've got a new thing going."

"Have a great fucking day, Alex," Thor muttered, and headed for the parking lot.

9

Audrey looked pretty and completely normal—just as she had always looked—when they met. They chose Pierre's, an off-the-beaten-path local place up by the Bahamian village. Anthony, Audrey informed them as they waited for the owner to prepare them a special table, believed in her powers.

"What powers?" Bethany asked. "Exactly."

"The powers I don't have," Audrey explained ruefully. "Oh, there we go—the table by the fountain." As they were seated, she introduced them to the tall, thin Bahamian who owned the place.

He smiled and shook Bethany's hand, first, but when he took Genevieve's hand, his smile faded and he looked worried.

"You've come for help," he said gravely.

She shook her head, suddenly uneasy. "I'm just here for lunch with my friend," she said lightly. "And what a lovely place. I can't believe I haven't been here yet."

He didn't take her comment lightly. He didn't even thank her for the words. He shook his head, muttering something in a language she didn't understand, then told her, "I will pray for you, our special prayers. We know the dead walk among us. Others are blind. They are afraid. They think pretending not to see things will make them go away. They are mistaken. The dead come back for a reason."

He nodded somberly at her, then gave himself a shake and offered them a broad white smile. "Enjoy your lunch."

After he left, they all sat in stunned silence for a minute.

Bethany reached across the table, covering Genevieve's hand with her own." That was the luck of the draw. He had to say something like that to one of us. He happened to pick you."

"Bull!" Audrey exploded. "Anthony knows things."

Bethany stared at her wide-eyed. "You're a fake. You told us so yourself."

Audrey sighed. "*I'm* a fake, yes. But that doesn't mean I don't know people who are real, that I don't hear the buzz on people who really do…know things."

"What the hell does that mean?" Bethany asked.

Audrey looked at Genevieve. "I've taken the liberty of calling in…a man."

"Oh, no," Genevieve groaned softly.

Audrey shook her head. "No, no, you don't understand. I got his number from a friend who got it from a friend…he handles investigations for the government, for God's sake. He's the real thing."

Genevieve sighed. "How do you know that?"

"Because I read all the articles, and I go to meetings and… Trust me, the only way I pull off any of this is because I know what's going on. It's like any job. I do my research. I know when I'm reading about a bunch of fakes—like me—versus the real thing. Go ahead and look him up yourself. His name is Adam Harrison, Harrison Investigations. He and his company don't troll for business. He isn't in it for the money."

"Then why…?" Bethany asked skeptically.

"He lost someone years ago. Anyway, he has a knack for knowing when people are seeing someone, getting a message from someone beyond the grave. He doesn't have the gift himself, but he can recognize it in others. Even though he doesn't see them himself, he isn't blind, like Anthony said. He *knows*." She reached into her handbag and handed Genevieve a folded sheet of paper she had apparently ripped from one of her psychic journals. "You'll see, once you read it. Look, weird things are happening to you, right?"

Their waitress arrived, so Genevieve didn't answer until they ordered.

"Yes, weird things are happening to me," Genevieve murmured once the waitress had gone.

"So weird she wound up in a hot new relationship with Thor," Bethany said, grinning.

Audrey stared at Genevieve. "Thor Thompson, huh? Cool. Except that…well, it will probably be different with you."

"What will be different?" Genevieve asked.

"Well, he's not known for sticking around anywhere," Audrey murmured. "But then, you're different."

She was different, all right. She was worse. Far worse. She was crazy.

"Thanks," Genevieve murmured.

Audrey shook her head. "I'm sorry, that came out wrong. You know what's freaky, though?" Audrey asked her.

"What?"

"Well, you know how I keep telling you I'm a fake? But I don't even know everything that's happening to you, but…I get a creepy feeling. As if there's an aura around you. In fact, when you two left the other night, I was afraid. As if some kind of dark shadow remained when you were gone."

"It's her, not me," Bethany said quickly.

"Bethany!" Genevieve snapped.

"Sorry."

"Anyway, don't worry. Like I said, Adam Harrison is coming himself. He'll talk to you, probably bring in a few investigators."

"Audrey, no! I can't let that happen. I'll be thrown off the project so fast you won't believe it," Genevieve told her.

"These aren't the kind of people who come in and make a big splash. Trust me. Adam will be discreet."

"You're acting like you know the man, but you don't. You got his number from a friend, who got it from their friend," Genevieve said.

"Genevieve, please, have some faith in me," Audrey implored.

"I do. I just wish you hadn't asked anyone in without talking to me first," Genevieve murmured.

"Do you want to go on just being scared and miserable?" Audrey asked.

"It will be okay," Bethany said quietly. "Look, as long as people are discreet, who's to know what they're doing?"

"I don't have a great feeling about this," Genevieve said doubtfully.

Audrey waved a hand in the air. "Most people think ghosts are fun. They enjoy being a little bit scared."

"That's because they're not really seeing ghosts," Genevieve said.

"Open up a little. That ghost is probably trying to help you." Audrey sighed. "I wish a ghost would help me find a treasure."

"I found one coin," Genevieve said. "Not exactly a treasure."

"But she's leading you to the treasure. Let her," Audrey said. She reached down into her bag again and brought out a stack of papers. "I looked into the ship you guys are trying to find. Which I know you already did, but I had my own reasons." She stared shrewdly at Genevieve. "You don't believe the woman you're seeing is the poor dead girl they found on the beach, do you?"

Gen stared at her in shock. "How did you…? No, never mind. I don't want to know."

"I knew it," Audrey said. "So listen, Gasparilla had quite a crush on this one woman. Interesting, because he could kind of plunder, pillage and rape at will. Maybe all guys just want the girl they can't have. Anyway, apparently he had a real thing for the captain's daughter, Anne. But even when he got hold of her, she spurned him for her young Spaniard, Aldo. Gasparilla was known for his violent temper and you're talking about a time when people were hanged for the least offense. Life was cheap. To Gasparilla, execution might have seemed like the right punishment for a woman who spurned him. So maybe your ghost is Anne, the captain's daughter."

"Maybe," Genevieve heard herself say.

"You know it makes sense. She likes you. Maybe she knows you care about more than just the treasure. Whatever. I truly believe once Adam gets here, he'll find a way to explain things and make you comfortable with what you're seeing. Your days are going to be a lot better."

"And what do I do about my nights?" Genevieve asked.

"Easy," Audrey grinned. "Keep sleeping with the stud."

Despite the savage damage done to the body by the sea, salt, exposure and hungry ocean creatures, it was still possible to see that the young woman had been pretty. Once. Even the fact that she had been sewn back together after the autopsy couldn't hide the fact that she had been blessed with great bone structure. Her hair had been a soft, natural blond. As the M.E. discussed the way the marks at her ankles gave evidence of her desperate effort to free herself, Jay's phone rang. The M.E. continued speaking unemotionally to Thor, detailing the water in her lungs, and the blood marks in her eyes. Because of the man's dispassionate tone, Thor was surprised when he met the doctor's eyes across the width of the gurney and saw sadness there. "Poor thing," the M.E. said. "All that potential, lost. She was young. She wanted to live," he added softly. Looking up at Thor, he told him, "I have a daughter just about this age. And as long as I've done this, there's a part of me that is still staggered by man's inhumanity to man."

Jay came back into the room. "She has a name," he said. "Amanda Worth."

"Family?" the M.E. asked.

Jay shook his head. "None known. We got her name because some guy called in anonymously to tell us who she was. What she was."

"And what *was* she?" Thor asked.

Jay looked at him, troubled. "A working girl from Miami. Drifted south from somewhere up north. I guess she started out as a cocktail waitress on the beach, then found out that in certain clubs she could make a lot more money by being a little bit friendlier. The years went by. Younger girls came in. Then guys with the bigger bucks weren't so interested. Business had begun to slide for her." He shook his head. "Old and used up—at thirty. She'd picked up a cocaine habit, too, and started hitting the streets."

"None of that seems surprising, even if it's sad," Thor said. "She got mixed up with the wrong guy in Miami, I guess. He took her out on a boat and…hell, boats in Miami. There's a needle in a haystack for you."

Jay shook his head. "The caller seemed to know her pretty well. He said she had been all excited about a week or so ago, thought she was going to hook up with someone who might turn out to be more than a john."

"And…?" Thor prodded.

Jay stared him, then sighed.

"According to the caller, she said she'd be heading south. The guy wanted her to see his home. In Key West." Jay shook his head sorrowfully. "It sucks. I'm looking for a local murderer."

"Then people need to be really careful," Thor said softly. He was disturbed to feel a deep sense of unease. He tried to talk himself out of his fears. After all, the people he knew, the people he worked with, weren't hookers and coke addicts. Even so, he found himself thinking with relief that the dead girl was a blonde, not a redhead, like Genevieve, not that that was necessarily even a factor. Besides, Bethany was a blonde, so maybe she needed to be especially careful.

He was bothered by the bizarre turn his thoughts were taking. He found himself realizing he was becoming involved, something he wasn't sure he'd intended to do, and it made him feel…disturbed. It was the only word he could think of. He was falling for a woman who saw ghosts. And there was a murderer on the streets.

None of it connected, he told himself.

He and Jay thanked the M.E. When they left, he asked, "Think your higher-ups would let me use a police computer?"

Jay shrugged. "Sure. With your connections… don't see why not. Just what are you looking for?"

Thor hesitated. "Disappearances…murders."

"We don't have much of a crime rate down here," Jay said, his tone slightly defensive.

"Should make it easy, then," Thor told him.

Marshall didn't know quite what possessed him that day. He knew that any significant discovery could take not just days, but weeks or months. Sure, they had a coin, but the debris field could stretch well over a mile, taking into consideration the battle was fought just before the storm delivered the coup de grâce.

He didn't believe in diving alone. Even top-ranked divers died that way. And he had a crew, a great crew.

A crew that included Genevieve Wallace, who despite having suddenly gone off the deep end on him—no pun intended, he assured himself—had made the first discovery. So…

So everyone had Saturday off. And God knew what they were all doing. Trying to take their minds off things, probably. It wasn't every day a body washed up on the beach.

His own mood wasn't great, but the urge to dive was on him. It was like a senseless itch, as if someone were pushing him to do something he didn't want to and knew he shouldn't. He fought it for a while. Then, just after lunch, he took off by himself. He found his coordinates, set out a dive flag and plunged in.

The reefs here were familiar to him, as familiar as the back of his hand. For people who spent their time in these waters, there were landmarks, just like tall buildings, statues, even curves in the road. He knew where Genevieve and Thor had found the coin; they had left a bright blue marker to identify the spot.

Staghorn coral covered the seabed beneath him. Beds of brain coral also found a home in the area. The fish life was rich and varied, as well. Fish in a myriad of colors darted all around him. He kept close to the bottom, searching the sand for any little ripple or oddity.

He had painstakingly covered about twenty feet of the ocean bed when he felt the first bump against his right thigh.

He straightened instantly, reaching to his calf for his dive knife.

His first thought was, *shark*.

He wasn't frightened by the thought; he'd been in the company of sharks—lemons, hammerheads, blue, reef tips—on many occasions. This was the ocean; it was where they lived. They preferred to stay away from divers most of the time. Every once in a while though, a shark would become curious and get close. Sometimes one would even butt a diver. But it was true, in his experience, at least, that clanging a knife against a dive tank or simply landing a good punch on the creature's nose would quickly send it away, even if it was a pretty big boy.

Or it could be a grouper, which could grow to huge sizes. They could be friendly. In fact, divers often found a grouper hanging around the same reef on a daily basis; they would name it, and sometimes tourists would come and pet the damned fish.

But when he looked around, he saw nothing. There was no six-hundred-pound grouper nearby that could have given him a friendly nudge. And if it had been a shark, it had disappeared damned fast.

He took his time, surveying his surroundings in all directions. *Nothing.* He turned back to his study of the ocean floor. He covered another twenty feet.

And then it came again.

A feeling that he'd been…

Pushed. Shoved.

And that he wasn't wanted here.

Which was absurd. He was too old, too experienced and too levelheaded to believe anything so foolish.

But the sense of unease had settled in, just like the itch to get into the water had settled over him earlier. He told himself that he was a rational man.

He held still, listening to the sound of his own breath through the regulator.

After a moment, he went on once again.

The next shove came almost immediately. And it was hard. It sent him flying through the water.

Marshall didn't pause to think at all. He didn't even look around. He shot to the surface, then swam for all he was worth until he reached his boat. Even as he threw his flippers up on the dive platform and wrenched off his mask, he felt a tug. On his leg. A forceful pull that threatened to drag him down into the depths…

No, he thought. *Not like this*.

Another jerk, hard against his ankles…

"God, no!"

There was a screaming, keening sound that seemed to tear across the blue sky, scattering the powdery clouds…

The sound was him.

There was no one at the tiki bar when Genevieve and Bethany returned from their lunch. Bethany yawned. "I think I'm going to take a nap," she said, then looked at Genevieve. "No, no, I'm not. I'm not going to leave you alone."

"Bethany, I'm fine. I can't spend my entire life around other people," Genevieve told her.

"Yes, but let's wait until you meet that Adam guy, huh?"

Genevieve, staring down the docks, noticed that Marshall's boat was gone. She turned to

Bethany, ignoring her friend's last comment. "Marshall went out."

"Marshall is impatient," Bethany said.

"He was the one who said we should take things slow, that this job was going to take time, and we shouldn't forget to have lives, so we wouldn't get sick of the work," Genevieve reminded her.

"Maybe he went fishing," Bethany suggested.

"Alone?" Genevieve asked.

"How do you know he's alone?"

"Good point. I don't."

Bethany yawned again. "Damn it. Go take a nap," Genevieve told her.

"No, we can do something lazy, like watch a DVD."

Looking around, Genevieve saw that Victor's door was ajar. "No," she said firmly. "Look." She set her hands on Bethany's shoulders, turning her friend so she could see Victor open the door. "I won't be alone. I'll go visit Victor. Quiz him about his latest conquests. He'll enjoy that. I'll be fine. You go and take a nap."

"How do you know he isn't entertaining a conquest right now?" Bethany demanded.

"Because his door is open," Genevieve told her.

"Okay, now *you* have a good point. But if you need me—"

"If I need you, I swear, I'll be on your doorstep. Promise."

Bethany at last gave her a hug, yawned again and started off for her own cottage. Genevieve turned to head toward Victor's.

She walked across the sand, then paused on his porch. There seemed to be a lot of thumping and banging going on inside. As she stood there, debating whether to knock, the door started to open.

"Victor," she said.

Then she gasped.

He was standing there with a head in his hands. A mannequin's head. The hair was stiff and flattened to the skull. Wide, blue, unseeing eyes stared out at Genevieve.

Her eyes narrowed instantly as she stared at her friend.

Victor appeared stricken. "Genevieve, I'm—"

"You son of a bitch," she said softly, and started to turn.

"No!" he cried.

He tried to catch hold of her shoulders, but she shook him off. He raced around in front of her, the offending head still in his hands.

"You don't understand," he told her anxiously.

She stopped dead, staring at him coldly. "I don't understand?" she said coolly. "Right. Get away from me, you son of a bitch."

"Genevieve, please, I swear to you. I'm not the one who did it," he pleaded.

She gritted her teeth, staring at him. She'd known Victor forever, and she wouldn't have put the joke past him. And the fact that he had fished the mannequin out of the sea, once the real body had surfaced, was only common decency.

But he was staring at her with what seemed to be sincere apology and complete honesty.

"I see," she said smoothly. "The mannequin just appeared in your cottage."

"I swear to you, it's the truth. We can go to church and I'll swear to you right before the altar, I didn't do it."

Was she an idiot to even consider believing him? While he was standing there with a head in his hands?

"Okay, okay. I thought it would be funny to put a mannequin on your porch. But not to hurt you. You're like my best friend forever. I would never hurt you. Ever. I thought it might smack you back into reality, that's all. *But I didn't do it.* Honest."

"Then who did?" she asked softly. "And how did it wind up back in your cottage?"

He shook his head. He'd either gotten pretty damn good at acting, she thought, or he was telling the truth. "I don't know."

"Why are you holding the head?"

He flushed, looking away for a moment before turning back to her once again, eyes steady, cheeks flushed. "I didn't want to be caught with it. I was dismantling it so I could take it to some Dumpster piece by piece."

"I see."

"Genevieve, you can ask at every store on the street. I never went to anyone trying to borrow or buy a mannequin."

"I *will* check on it, you know," she told him.

"I didn't do it," he repeated pleadingly.

Glancing down the beach, Genevieve saw that Alex was out, walking toward the tiki bar. She hadn't noticed them arrive, but Liz and Zach were seated there, as well.

"Maybe you'd better hide the evidence then," she said softly.

He swallowed, following her glance toward the tiki bar, and nodded. "Gen, I swear…"

"All right, I believe you. But if I ever find out you're lying to me…well, friends don't do stuff like this to friends. A joke is one thing—even if it wouldn't have been funny to me in the least. Lying about it…"

"I'm telling the truth."

"Then hide that head. Especially under the circumstances."

"Yeah." He headed back toward his cottage, trying to nonchalantly tuck the head under his arm. He looked back at her. "Are you coming?" he asked hesitantly.

"Yeah," she told him. And followed.

It looked like a strangely bloodless massacre had taken place inside. Arms lay atop his bed, legs were strewn on the floor. The torso had been tossed on the futon. The white gown lay crumpled and ruined beside it.

"My God," Genevieve breathed.

"Hey, it was a mannequin. Not real," he reminded her.

She shook her head. He had a box of heavy-duty

garbage bags by the coffeemaker. Standing by the door, Genevieve watched as he bagged an arm.

"Are you going to help?" he demanded.

"Victor, you shouldn't be getting rid of it. We need to find out who did this," she said.

"Why?" he asked.

"Why? So that we know!"

He shook his head. "If I showed this to anyone, I'd be blamed. You know that."

"I'm the one the trick was played on. If I'm not mad, what does it matter?"

"You believe me, but who else will? Not your new Romeo, that's for certain!"

"But, Victor—"

"Are you going to help or not?"

"No. You're my friend, Victor, and I believe you. So it's important to find out who did this."

Again, he stubbornly shook his head. "It was a prank. It was put in here afterward just so I'd be blamed. We need to make it disappear. Whoever did it will eventually start to get nervous and want to know what happened. He—or she—will start asking questions."

Genevieve folded her arms across her chest. "*She?* What woman could have done this? Not Bethany, I can assure you."

"I put that in for political correctness," he said indignantly. "But what do we really know about Lizzie or her husband?"

"Oh, please!"

"Okay, so forget the *she*. And Zach. I don't think

he'd have done this. They don't seem to have a sense of humor."

"Right, because this was so funny."

"Will you please just help me, before someone else shows up?"

She stared at Victor. Was she a fool to believe him? "All right. But like I said, if I ever find that you did this…"

"You won't," he said flatly.

"Okay, once the body parts are bagged, what next?"

"Then we take a little walk and start to get rid of them. I'll even buy you a drink along the way."

"What a deal," she murmured. She was surprised to feel queasy when she picked up a disconnected leg.

It wasn't real, she thought to herself.

Then again, were ghosts?

Jay got Thor started on the computer, showing him how to run the program. There hadn't been a problem. Jay's superiors seemed to believe that Thor had government connections, and that as head of the current salvage project, Thor should have access to information regarding criminal activity in the area.

Thor wasn't exactly sure why, but he found himself looking back over the last twenty years.

Some of the files contained crimes that had spanned both Miami-Dade and Monroe counties. The frequency of violent crime in the big city was

frightening; but heading south, into Jimmy Buffett-
ville, violence decreased. Live and let live. But there
were still a number of murders on the books, most
of them solved. Husbands who had killed wives.
Wives who had killed husbands. Drug deals gone
bad. Accidental killings. There were also files that
contained crimes that hadn't been solved, or where
the solutions were questionable. A two-year-old,
drowned in a swimming pool. The child had suffered
from severe birth defects. Had the agonized mother
decided death was better than life? The police had
been suspicious, but they had found no proof, and
she had never gone to trial, with the death officially
ruled accidental.

After a while, Jay excused himself, explaining he
had paperwork to do.

After Jay left, Thor began to wonder what he
was doing, just what he was looking for.

He moved on to missing persons reports.

Many of the missing had been found. Children
were not always abducted; sometimes, they were
runaways, and the Keys were a nice place to run
away to. Warm weather, easy work, tourists willing
to give handouts. Dina Massey, a blue-eyed blond
sixteen-year-old from Ohio had made it down on a
bus. After two months of panhandling, she had been
questioned by a police officer. She had broken
down, eager to go home but afraid of how her father
would react. A picture showed tearful parents who
had come for her, forgiving all. Donald Leto, of Fort
Lauderdale, hadn't been so lucky. He, too, had run

away. He, too, had been sent home. A notation at the bottom of the file noted that he had died back in Fort Lauderdale, a victim of vehicular homicide.

His father had been driving the car that killed him.

Thor decided he was looking for victims over twenty-one.

Right before he switched screens, however, he found a missing persons case that hadn't been solved. The bulletin had been sent from Miami. The girl in the picture, Maria Rico, was a beautiful blonde. She had disappeared just the year before. Friends suspected that either her abusive stepfather had killed her—though police had found no evidence to support such a scenario—or that she had run south. A "friend" she had met on the Internet had suggested he could give her a haven from her abusive stepfather if she afforded him the opportunity.

No one knew the identity of the friend. And she hadn't been seen in Key West, though her photo had been plastered across the island.

Thor stared at the girl's picture. She had been seventeen at the time of her disappearance. Every inch a woman. He wondered why no one had suspected the woman found on the beach that morning might have been this runaway. He needed to ask Jay. Filing away the mental note, he went on.

The first unsolved disappearance he could find that was directly linked to Key West had occurred almost eight years ago. The woman's name had been

Shea Alexandria. She'd been born Mary Brown, but since she had intended to be the world's next supermodel, she had changed her name accordingly. She was blond and beautiful. Her picture seemed to jump off the page with attitude and humor.

Work in New York had led her to bathing suit jobs on the South Florida beaches. A promotion with a liquor company had brought her to Key West. After a party at which the attendees had imbibed heavily, she had vanished. She had left the party alone and never returned to her hotel room. There had been no signs of violence along her route.

She had left the party alone.

Somewhere, in a five-block area, she had simply disappeared. The case remained unsolved.

Thor flipped back through the files. There were two other still-unsolved missing persons cases that had been flagged by the locals, but there was no specific information that the women had been heading for the Keys. Both cases, however, were definitely on the curious side—especially in light of the morning's findings.

He started searching the murder files again, looking for cases that specifically referred to Key West.

Then he stopped.

Hope Gonzalez.

Dead at thirty-two. Survived by her husband, Jay Taft Gonzalez.

Jay's wife?

Because of the suspicious nature of her death,

Hope Gonzalez had been autopsied. The final verdict had been accidental drowning.

Thor sat back, still staring at the particulars. Hope and her husband had been out on their boat. While they'd been snorkeling on one of the reefs, she had suddenly disappeared beneath the waves, according to Jay. He'd dragged her up and performed CPR after calling in desperately for help.

The death had raised flags. But Jay Gonzalez had never faced trial, an internal investigation, or any repercussions from her death. Not according to the case file.

Thor had a creeping feeling that he wasn't alone. He looked up. Jay was standing by the desk. "You knew that I'd find this," Thor said.

"Of course."

"Why didn't you just tell me?"

"Because I knew you'd find it. Anyone could have told you, anyway. Hope…Hope has been gone several years now. No one has ever forgotten her. No one should ever forget her."

"No one suspected that…"

"That I killed my wife?" Jay asked.

Thor lifted his hands.

"I loved her," Jay said. He rolled back his sleeves. Thor saw the scars on his arms. "I loved her."

"You tried to commit suicide—and the department let you stay?" Thor asked skeptically.

"Don't be ridiculous. I had an accident. I was on medical leave for a few months."

Thor nodded.

"I'm a good cop," Jay said quietly, and with conviction.

Thor nodded, rising. "Are you off? Want a drink? There are some questions I'd like to ask you about some of what I found."

"Sure."

They walked out of the building. Thor felt as if the picture of Hope Gonzalez had been emblazoned in his mind.

Because she, too, had been blond. And very beautiful.

10

"Do you have enough ketchup?" Bethany asked.

Genevieve hadn't really needed help shopping, but after having disposed of the mannequin with Victor, she had found herself at the tiki bar where talk had turned to her planned barbecue, and that in turn had reminded her that she had to have something to put on the barbecue. She, Bethany, Victor and Alex had wound up at the grocery store together.

"I've got ketchup," she said.

"Lots of it, I hope," Alex said, grinning. "Victor puts ketchup on everything in sight. Including grilled fish."

"Hey, it's an American vegetable, remember?" Victor said defensively.

"Whatever, I have ketchup," Genevieve assured them. She swept out a hand, indicating the cart. "Beer, wine, soda, water. Ribs, chicken, hamburger, and we'll stop at the fish market for whatever's fresh. Fruit salad, coleslaw…"

"Salad salad," Victor said. "Without any of that weird grassy stuff the restaurants all seem to think is gourmet now."

"French fries, corn on the cob, onion rings," Genevieve continued. "What else?"

"Hey, where's dessert?" Alex demanded. "And appetizers."

"Bethany is baking a Key lime pie. And making conch fritters."

"And we're having conch chowder," Bethany put in.

"You're cooking?" Victor said dubiously. "Want to grab some cookies or ice cream, just in case?"

Bethany slugged him lightly on the upper arm. He grinned.

"We'll stop at that new pastry shop, too, how's that? It's not like we'll have to throw a bunch of stuff away. We can bring it all back to the cottages if we have leftovers. Pack up some ice chests to take out on the water Monday," Genevieve said.

Alex groaned. "Ugh. Monday."

"I'll actually be glad to go back in the water," Genevieve said. She meant it, and she was actually surprised. Was the ghost going to show again? she wondered. The ghost who was not the unearthly remains of the poor woman found on the beach.

She was also anxious to find out why she kept seeing the vision—and just what the vision wanted from her. She wasn't sure how she knew it, but she felt sure the ghost had some kind of message for her. A trade-off? If she helped the ghost, the ghost would help her find the treasure? But she wasn't in this business for the riches, though naturally she wanted to make a living, just like everyone else. Still…

I'm being haunted, she thought. And it was better to face it than to…what?

Be terrified, time and time again.

"I'm going to be happy to get back out in the water, too," Victor said.

"Me, too," Alex agreed. He made a face. "But first we're getting another of the professor's lectures Monday morning. The one we didn't get on Friday. Could he possibly be more boring? His students must be ready to jump out the window. And when we're trying to find an old wooden ship that's decayed and covered with sand and coral, is it really going to matter if we know exactly what she originally looked like? Wait a minute! We already know that. We've seen pictures." He shook his head in disgust.

"It matters," Bethany said.

"Why?" Alex demanded.

Victor clamped a hand on his shoulder. "State financing, buddy. State financing."

Genevieve wound up in line with Alex, while Victor and Bethany headed out to bring Victor's truck around front so they could pile the groceries into the back. She started stacking their purchases on the conveyor belt. She was startled when she turned to see Alex watching her with concern.

"What?" she said.

"Are you okay?" he asked her.

"Yes…why?"

He shook his head. "None of my business."

She sighed. "What?"

"No, no…nothing."

"Okay."

"But…."

"Damn it, Alex, spit it out."

"You're scared, right?" he asked softly.

She frowned. "In what way?"

"In a 'you freaked out in the water' kind of way, and it's not like I'm the one you usually spill your guts to, but I'm here and I care about you and…well, hell. Gen, you're not sleeping with that guy just because you're scared, are you?"

Genevieve felt her jaw clench in anger and shock.

"It's none of my business, except that…hell. It *is* my business. We're like family. You could sleep on my couch without me so much as making a bad joke if you need to. Hell, I'd give you the bed and take the futon."

She couldn't stay angry. His eyes were so filled with concern.

She started to smile, but a niggling suspicion still teased at her. If Victor hadn't played the joke with the mannequin, the next best suspect was Alex.

"If you don't want me to be scared, why did you play the joke with the mannequin?" she asked bluntly.

He didn't flush or betray the slightest guilt. "What?" he demanded. Then he did flush slightly. "Hey, we talked about it, but we nixed the idea."

She stared back at him, wishing she had the skill to know if he was telling her the absolute truth.

The clerk cleared her throat to get their attention. "Credit card, debit or cash?"

"Debit," Alex said, producing his card.

"No, this is my invite," Genevieve said.

"You're supplying the house."

"But it was my idea."

"Doesn't matter to me," the clerk said, popping her gum, "but there *is* a line."

"Let me, please," Alex said.

"All right. Thank you," Genevieve said.

Victor and Bethany hopped out of the truck when Alex and Genevieve reached the street, and the loading went quickly.

As planned, they stopped at the pastry shop to pick up dessert—just in case.

"Even though I've actually been making Key lime pie all my life?" Bethany asked indignantly.

"Doesn't hurt to have extra munchies when we're diving," Victor told her. "Although I have, um, complete faith this is going to be the best Key lime pie I've ever had."

"He doesn't get any," Bethany said huffily.

"You know *I* can actually cook," Victor said.

"Never mind, we're not putting you to the test. The kitchen is too small, and Bethany has already called dibs on the baking," Genevieve said, lifting a hand as if she were interceding in an argument between siblings.

At her house, with the four of them unloading, the kitchen was soon filled with bags.

Victor, who, as one of her oldest friends, felt totally at home in her house, mumbled some excuse and lazed on the sofa, flicking the television on. He was looking for sports, she knew. Alex quickly joined him.

"We'll have to get ice tomorrow," Bethany commented, lining up the bottles of soda and beer on the counter. "This stuff won't all fit in the fridge."

"Hey!" Alex called.

"What?" Genevieve responded.

"Come out here. They've identified the body on the beach."

"Where is everyone?" Thor asked. He'd headed straight for the tiki bar when he got back to the resort.

Jack sat alone, looking depressed as he nursed a beer. He looked up like a puppy when Thor talked to him. "Don't know. Thought I'd find someone to talk to here," he said. He pointed across the tables. "New couple at the resort. They're here on their honeymoon." He lowered his voice. "The guy is some kind of an Indian, I think."

Thor glanced at the attractive couple across the way and sank into a chair opposite Jack. He waved to Clint for a beer.

"Where have you been?" Jack asked.

"Around," Thor replied vaguely. "You haven't seen anyone?"

"You're really asking if I've seen Genevieve, right?"

"I'm really asking if you've seen anyone," Thor said levelly.

Jack grinned. "All right. I think Zach and Lizzie

went up to the Dolphin Research Center on Grassy Key. You know how Lizzie loves dolphins. They were talking about doing that at one point, anyway. And Marshall…his boat is gone, so I'm assuming he's out on the water, somewhere. The Conch kids and Alex? I don't know."

Thor's beer arrived, and he smiled his thanks, wondering why he felt so on edge. *Why?* How about because there was a murderer on the loose in Key West.

He had barely taken a sip of his beer when Jack slammed a fist on the table and laughed. "Hell, I'm an idiot. I know where they are!"

"Where?"

"Genevieve's place. Barbecue tomorrow, remember?"

Thor stood. "I'll give it a try."

Jack rose, as well. "Wait up. I'm not sitting here by myself anymore."

When they arrived at Genevieve's, Victor let them in, eyeing them both warily. "Hey, hey, half the gang's all here," he muttered. He stood in the doorway, as if loathe to let them enter. Thor had the definite feeling it was him; after all, Jack was a Conch.

"What's up?" Jack asked jovially. He swept past Victor as if he had every right to be there.

"We were just watching the news," Victor said glumly. "They're warning single women in the Keys to be careful. The victim on the beach has been identified. Haven't you guys seen a TV anywhere?

Shit, every bar in town must be running the coverage."

"What makes you think I sit around bars all day?" Jack demanded gruffly, then smiled. "So, got a beer?"

"Help yourself, Jack," Genevieve called from the kitchen.

Jack headed that way. Thor took a seat on the sofa, staring at the television. The news had moved on to the weather, though. There was a storm in the Gulf, but it was headed west.

"Creepy, huh?" Victor murmured, taking a seat next to Thor.

"The storm?"

"The cops thinking that the killer might be from around here. Hope it doesn't hurt tourism any, the way they're talking."

"People rarely see themselves as potential victims," Thor told him. "Especially since the dead woman was a prostitute."

"Hope so. We survive on tourism," Victor murmured.

"No worries," Jack said cheerfully, coming from the kitchen and tossing a beer in Thor's direction. Taken by surprise, he was glad to catch it. "Up in Miami, a few years ago, a guy killed a bunch of prostitutes around Eighth Street. It didn't cause a scare, though, since he only killed prostitutes. Now, if I'd been a hooker, I'd have found some long-lost relatives to visit until the guy was snagged."

"Jack, how can you be so cold?" Bethany demanded,

appearing in the doorway with a mixed drink. "You saw that poor dead girl."

"I'm sorry to say it, but in my line of work, I've seen dead people before. We all gamble with our lives. Girl like that, she gambled more than most. Hey, are we having dinner here tonight?" he demanded.

"There you go," Alex laughed. "The last of the great sympathizers."

"I'm hungry and lonely. Every one of you took off today. I saw the professor this morning, and I was almost desperate enough to have lunch with him."

"You guys are mean," Genevieve offered, coming out of the kitchen. Her eyes met Thor's. "He's not that bad a guy. He's an academic, that's all."

"Armchair diver," Alex sniffed. "Can't cut the mustard himself, so he thinks he's going to tell us all what to do."

"Be nice," Genevieve warned him.

"What about food?" Jack asked, fingering the skull and crossbones in his earlobe.

"We bought lots of food," Victor said.

"For tomorrow," Bethany said firmly.

"Let's go somewhere with upbeat music," Alex said thoughtfully. He looked around. "Jack is right, you know. I don't want to say anyone deserved such a fate, but…she was a prostitute."

"You were right the first time," Genevieve said firmly. "No one deserves what happened to that girl."

No. No one deserved it, Thor thought. So what

about the runaway who had disappeared, and the almost-supermodel?

And Jay Gonzalez's wife.

"Thor, what's up?" Bethany asked, catching his thoughtful look.

He shrugged, forced a smile. "I'm with Alex. Let's find some good food and good music."

"All right. Let's do the Hog's Breath tonight," Bethany said. They all stared at her. "Hey, someone has to make decisions around here."

Thor rose. "Hog's Breath it is."

They opted for a table near the lone musician, a guitarist and singer. Thor had seen many talented singers with synthesizers at their sides, but this guy was a cut above. He joked with the crowd between songs. He wasn't a Conch, he told them, just a wannabe. At the end of his first set, he proved himself to be a decent human being, as well, speaking on a somber note. "Ladies, gentlemen, you are in Key West. And Lord knows, we want you here. We want you to buy lots of booze—and my CD of original songs, of course—but we also want you staying responsibly sober and careful. Know the one you're with, ladies Take care out there. Help us out. If you see or hear anything helpful to the police, let them know. I want you coming back to see me. And I want you to buy more CDs and eat more Key lime pie. Thank you all."

Thor rose. He felt Genevieve's hand on his— he'd made sure that this time *he* got the seat next to her when they sat down. She was looking at him with a frown and a question. He smiled at her. "I like this guy so I'm buying lots of CDs."

She gazed at him with a smile. Something in him did a flip. He was falling too deep. Drowning. But he liked it, and couldn't quite stop himself. "Be right back."

He found out when he bought the CDs—he picked up three: one for his secretary in the Jacksonville office; one for himself; one for Lizzie and Zach, who he thought would enjoy it—that the singer knew all about the dive. "You're working with Marshall's crew, right? And Gen?" There was something soft in his voice when he said her name. "Watch out for her, huh? She's a Key West treasure, kind of like the sunset."

When he got back to the table, Bethany was saying, "I really hope they catch this guy. People need to be warned, but our whole economy is tourism."

"There's the navy, too," Victor said without conviction.

Bethany shivered. "Just think. There's a killer here. He could be right here on the patio listening to the music and having supper, just like us. He could be right next to us when we walk down the street."

Just as she said the words, Thor looked up to see Jay Gonzalez, in a casual long-sleeved shirt and jeans, walking in.

Could it be…?

No, the guy had let him into the autopsy. He'd arranged for him to access police files.

Cover-up?

All he knew was that he would keep his eye on the man until…when?

There were killers out there who were never caught.

Thor didn't realize just how long he'd been staring at Jay until Genevieve nudged him. "Ready?"

"What?"

"We're all set," she said, her expression curious. "The bill?"

Victor cleared his throat. "My turn. I already picked it up."

"I can expense meals," Thor reminded him.

"Yeah, but I was starting to feel like a kept woman or something," Victor said, grinning easily. "And tonight was probably the cheapest opportunity I was going to get. Reasonable place, and we're minus Lizzie, Zach and Marshall."

As they left, Jay Gonzalez raised a hand in greeting. Genevieve pulled away from Thor for a moment, walking over to Jay, giving him a hug, exchanging a few words. Thor realized he didn't like it. He wanted to drag her away from the man. He refrained, forcefully holding himself in check.

As Genevieve started walking back, Jay Gonzalez smiled and waved to him. He found he was forcing a smile in return. It was probably not a good thing to let the local cop know he was considering him as a candidate for the possible serial killer they were seeking. The guy had been good to him, getting him in to see the body, letting him search through police files. He owed him.

Still…

This was getting ridiculous. He was becoming suspicious of everyone.

Maybe that wasn't so bad. Because the killer had to be *some*one.

Maybe someone they knew well.

"We'll see you tomorrow, Jay," Genevieve called out to him.

"Yeah, see you tomorrow," Thor repeated.

"You got it," Jay called back.

Thor kept his smile glued in place. Fine. The guy was welcome to see them all anytime. Welcome to see Genevieve. Just as long as *he* was with her.

As they left, Genevieve linked her arm with his. "I was thinking of going home tonight," she said. "You know, to be ready for the barbecue tomorrow and all."

"Is that an invitation?"

"Yes."

"Sure." He turned to her, smiling slightly. "We're walking with the others toward the resort, you know."

She laughed softly. "Yes, I am aware of that fact. I just want to make sure Marshall's boat is back," she told him gravely.

"Sure."

When they reached the resort, however, Marshall's boat wasn't back.

Genevieve was worried and said so.

"You know Marshall. He had the time off, so he went off somewhere. That's all," Victor said. "Hey, we'll call his cell, okay?"

But Marshall didn't answer his cell.

"We should put out a missing persons report," Genevieve said.

Victor groaned. "Honey, he's a grown man. He hasn't even been gone twenty-four hours. He knows what he's doing. He has plenty of fuel capacity. He could've headed up to the mainland for all we know."

"I'm still worried," Genevieve said.

"Gen…" Victor set his hands on her shoulders. "Marshall is a big strong guy. He'll be fine. He's not a pretty blonde like the killer seems to be after. We'll see him tomorrow. Okay?"

"No," Genevieve said. Then she sighed. "But I guess there's no choice."

"Honey, it's really okay. Victor is right. We found a dead *woman*," Jack reminded her gruffly. "Not a man like Marshall. He can take care of himself. The guy who killed that woman…he likes the ladies, not gorillas like Marshall who can fight back."

They were all silent for a moment. Then Bethany said, "Victor, I'm on your couch."

"You can come to the house," Genevieve said. Did she sound a little nervous? Thor wondered, or was he imagining it? And if she *was* nervous, was it because she'd opted to be alone with *him*, or because Bethany was going to be alone with Victor?

"With the two of you? No, thanks!" Bethany laughed, then yawned. "Come on, Victor. Let's go to bed. I'll just get a few things from my cottage for the morning."

Victor groaned. "Your cottage isn't a minute's walk from mine."

"I need my toothbrush," Bethany insisted.

"All right, all right," Victor grumbled.

"Hey, me having a toothbrush is for your benefit, too."

"Really? Are we getting that close?" Victor teased.

Bethany stared back at him. Victor laughed. "Don't worry. It would be gross, like sleeping with my sister."

"Now I'm gross?"

Victor stared at the others. "I can't win here, can I?" he demanded.

They laughed, but Thor wondered why Genevieve still looked uneasy.

They said their good-nights. Genevieve was quiet as they walked back to her house.

"What is it?" he asked her.

She looked at him, startled. "Nothing—well, other than the fact that the police believe the killer comes from the Keys."

He shook his head. "Are you worried about Bethany?"

"Of course not! She'll be with Victor," she answered too quickly.

"You suspect Victor?" he asked very softly.

"Don't be silly! I've known him my whole life." She smiled. Her words were both sincere and, somehow, a little uncertain.

He stopped walking.

"If you're the least bit worried…"

"I'm not," she insisted. She stared at him, shook her head and smiled. "Really, I'm not. We all know exactly where Bethany is."

He nodded, and they started walking again. "I wish I knew where Marshall was," she said softly after a minute.

"Marshall is a big guy. I'm sure he's fine."

Again she was silent for a minute. Then she looked at him, and he was certain her worry was just as much for him as for Marshall. "The biggest, most confident, toughest guy in the world can fall…if taken by surprise."

"Marshall is fine," he assured her. He believed that, right? So where the hell was the guy?

And just *what* was he doing?

Thor gritted his teeth silently, forcing an expression of complete calm over his features. He slipped an arm around her shoulders as they walked. "Marshall will show up tomorrow. I promise."

"He knew about the barbecue, so if he wasn't planning on coming, he would have said so," she agreed. "Right?"

Despite her words, she still seemed uneasy. When they reached her house, Thor tried to reassure her again. "Marshall is fine, and so are we."

She hesitated, then nodded. "Thor, if he doesn't show up tomorrow, I want to look for him, okay? And we'll call Jay, too. I can't help it. I'm worried. Marshall is a social creature. He always hangs around with us."

"Look," Thor said softly. "You're all friends, as close as a pack of siblings—but you don't date one another. Marshall is a good-looking guy. Maybe he went out on a date, huh?"

She smiled at that. "Yes, that is a possibility."

"Would you have been so worried if all—" he weighed his words before opting to say "—*this* wasn't going on?"

"No," she admitted.

"All right. Tomorrow, if he doesn't show for the barbecue, we call the cops, and we look for Marshall. And when we find him, he'll probably be surprised, and maybe a little pissed, thinking he needs a life, too, and we should have respected that. So let's give this place a really good once-over—or twice-over, if it makes you happy—and make sure we're locked in, alone and safe and sound, okay?"

His words seemed to help her. And once they got inside, he did walk through the entire house twice, with her following right behind him.

"Nothing in the closets or under the beds," he swore. "She's locked up tight. You're safe and sound. Except from me," he teased.

"You still think I'm crazy," she told him.

He found himself standing in front of her, his hands on her shoulders. "I think you're beautiful," he told her softly.

His words were the right ones, and they were true.

He didn't notice how they made it up the stairs and into the bedroom. It was as if she was instantly in his arms, their clothing melted away rather than taken off, with something like pure, wet, hot, primal fusion taking place. At one point some sense of sanity returned, and he murmured, "I know you're worried. We don't have to…we don't have to…"

Her eyes touched his. A slight smile teased her lips. "I'd crawl into your skin, if I could," she said, and her lips fell against his again instantly while their flesh burned together and their limbs entwined.

He wasn't sure how other thoughts managed to stay in his mind as his sexual desire rose with volatile speed to madness. But she was beautiful in so many ways, body, mind and essence. Tall, vital, muscled, competent, proud, unique…lips full and sensual, hips capable of such extraordinary movement… His mouth savored and teased her flesh, his body, heart and head pounded…

It seemed he climaxed in a million ways, that he came to life when he should have been limp, her slightest movement awoke every erotic impulse in his system. Time seemed unending. Then she curled against him. And they slept.

He would never understand what happened then, in the middle of the night. He prided himself on his awareness. He'd started that in the navy, on guard in the Middle East. He'd made it a way of life when diving in foreign ports where safety wasn't even a suggestion. He usually awoke at the drop of a pin.

Instead, he woke slowly when he felt her shivering, trembling at his side. His mind seemed fogged.

He became aware by degrees that he was surrounded by a strange dampness.

It seemed that he could smell the sea.

At last, somehow, he roused himself enough to realize he wasn't actually holding her, that she was a breath away from him. He wrapped his arms around her, listening then, fighting the mist in his mind.

"Genevieve?"

She didn't reply. She moved closer. Flesh on flesh so tight she might have crawled into his skin.

"What is it?"

"Nothing," she whispered.

"What…?"

"A nightmare. But you're here. Nothing…I'm all right. I'm all right." The first statement was said with a quiver. The second was stronger.

Her conviction allowed him to draw her tighter. "I'm here," he said.

"I know," she murmured. She was silent a minute, close against him. He was amazed to realize how incredible it felt just to sleep beside her.

Just to hold her.

He kissed her forehead, drew her closer.

He was still tired. And sated. And ready for more sleep.

The fog returned. Darkness. Exhaustion. He fought it, waiting for her trembling to cease. And when it did, he gave way to sleep.

He knew when she awoke in the morning. Just as he should have been, he was alert at her first shift, as she slipped from his arms and arose.

She knew he had awakened. She planted a kiss on his lips.

He reached for her, but she slipped away. "It's late," she said. "Nearly noon. We'll have company soon."

He lay in bed for a few minutes longer, closing his eyes, oddly tired. True, they had spent a lot of the night awake.

But he felt as if he'd been...*fighting* all night. There was a feeling of exhaustion after sex, but that feeling was good, sated....

Damn, this was strange.

At last he rose himself.

As he did, he paused. There was a hint of something in the air. A teasing scent. He paused a moment; then he knew.

Seawater. The distinctive scent of the ocean.

He gazed at the bed. It was still...damp. He tried to tell himself they'd indulged in some strenuous lovemaking, the kind that couldn't help but dampen the sheets.

He walked around the bed.

The floor was soaked next to the side where Genevieve had slept. He hunkered down and touched the Persian rug. The scent rose more strongly around him.

Seawater.

11

"This is my uncle, Adam," Audrey announced, entering Genevieve's house. "And Uncle Adam... this is everyone."

They were virtually the last to arrive. Jay Gonzalez had been first, with Bethany and Victor right behind him. Zach and Liz had been next. Then Jack, proud as a peacock as he arrived with a perfectly sized grouper, freshly caught that morning. Alex had arrived just seconds before Audrey and her uncle.

Only Marshall still remained among the missing.

And as for Uncle Adam, Thor was suspicious of him from the start, mainly, he had to admit, because he had arrived with Audrey.

Why Audrey irritated him so much, he couldn't say. It was just the entire idea of being a medium, a soothsayer, a tarot card reader, whatever.

Uncle Adam was tall, thin, almost gaunt, a man of perhaps sixty-something to seventy years in age. For all that, he was a handsome man with strong features and fascinating gray eyes. He was soft-spoken, polite, interested at every introduction.

Except, Thor thought, the guy stared at him a little too long. Made him feel uncomfortable. He'd never in his life felt he was being *read* before, but that was the impression Adam gave him. He didn't like it. He liked it even less when he saw the older man speaking with Genevieve, who was smiling back and chatting, looking at the man as if he were *her* long lost uncle.

"Hey, want to give me a hand with the grouper?" Jack asked.

"Yeah. Sure."

He didn't really want to, of course. He wanted to eavesdrop on whatever was being shared between Audrey, good old Uncle Adam and Genevieve.

Hell, he had to get a grip.

He went outside with Jack. Genevieve had a nice setup for cleaning and preparing fish. The knife Jack handed him was sharp, and he was able to gut and fillet the fish as if it were butter.

"Where do you think Marshall has gone off to?" Jack asked.

"What?"

"Marshall, remember? Your co-worker. Co-boss of our operation. This isn't like him. He loves a barbecue, and he loves Gen's place," Jack said.

"I don't know. But we've got a cop right inside. Maybe it's time to report him missing," Thor said.

"Yeah, and maybe he'll have us all by the balls if we do," Jack said dryly. "Maybe he's off getting hot and heavy with some woman." He grinned. "Could be why he's not answering his cell. I mean, who wants to be interrupted in the middle of something, if you know what I mean?"

Thor didn't reply. He was anxious to finish with the fish.

Victor, cradling a cold bottle of beer, walked out to join them. "Need any help out here?" he asked.

Jack indicated the pile of fillets they had just cut. "You're too late."

"Sorry."

"It's all right," Jack said. "I think I could cut up a fish in my sleep."

Victor looked distracted as Jack pulled out a box of aluminum foil. "Trust me, these fillets are going to be great. Loosely wrap them in the foil, add a pat of butter, a squirt of lime, dash of salt and pepper, and one clove of garlic...can't get any fresher. They're going to be great."

"Yeah, great," Victor murmured.

"What's wrong?" Thor asked him.

Victor stared at him, startled. "Uh, nothing."

Thor shrugged and started wrapping the fish according to Jack's instructions.

"It's that guy," Victor blurted.

"What guy?" Jack asked. "Audrey's uncle?"

"What's wrong with him?" Thor asked casually.

"He's...creepy," Victor said.

"He need a bath or something?" Jack asked.

"No. He's just...creepy. Those eyes of his...kind of pale. And his skin is almost white."

"He's just not from the land of sun and fun, I guess," Thor murmured, though he felt uncomfortable, too. But the guy himself wasn't creepy. Rather, the guy gave him the creeps. Strange. Who the hell was he?

Then again, a lot of things were making him uneasy these days. And he didn't believe in feeling uneasy. Not like this. The world was full of known dangers. It was okay to be uneasy about going out in heavy seas. It was all right to have a sinking heart when you were going into a swamp after a plane crash.

But this…

"Here you go, Victor. You want to be useful? Give Jack a hand. I'll go check up on Uncle Creepy, how's that?" Thor said.

He didn't wait for an answer but headed on into the kitchen to wash his hands. Genevieve came up beside him. Her eyes were sparkling; she seemed more alive, easier, *happier*, than he had yet seen her. She glowed. His stomach seemed to pitch and toss. She hadn't said anything about last night to him, and he hadn't had a chance to say anything to her. When he'd gotten downstairs, guests had already been arriving.

She smiled at him, wrinkled her nose. "Tastes much better than it smells after cleaning, huh?" she teased.

He slipped an arm around her, and brushed her lips with a kiss, heedless of anyone else who might be nearby. She didn't seem to mind. She hugged him back enthusiastically.

"What's that all about?" he asked.

She shrugged. "I don't know. I just feel as if a weight has been lifted."

She started to walk away.

He pulled her back.

"Who the hell is Uncle Adam?" he asked.

She pulled back and looked him in the eye. "A very nice man, that's all."

He dried his hands and walked into the living room. The stereo was playing. Adam was sitting on the sofa, next to Audrey. Bethany and Alex were trying some kind of a dance step. Lizzie was laughing at the two of them, and Zach was warning her that he would make her learn if she wasn't careful. Jay was just watching, nursing a beer.

Thor sat down next to Adam.

"So, Adam, where are you down from?" he asked politely.

"Virginia. You?"

The man had a smooth, cultured accent that seemed reminiscent of mint juleps, Southern breezes and total refinement.

"Jacksonville," Thor answered. "What brings you down this way? Or have you come just to spend some time with Audrey?" he asked. On his other side, Audrey flushed. He hoped she was a better actress when doing readings for her clients. She couldn't have looked more guilt stricken.

"Key West is a great place to visit," Adam said.

"True," Thor agreed. Like hell. This guy didn't look like a boater or a fisherman. Definitely not a diver. He didn't even look as if he was particularly fond of heat. And he was too old for the more ribald shenanigans Key West was known for.

"I'd love a chance to talk with you alone, under quieter circumstances," Adam said. Again Thor had the feeling he was being read. *Being* read? Hell, no. This guy had taken one look at him and it was as if he had finished the final chapter. *Creepy.*

Thor shrugged. "We're diving again as of tomorrow. No lunch breaks on land, I'm afraid."

"Are you fond of breakfast?" the older man queried, a slight twist to his smile.

"You bet."

"Shall we meet early, then?"

He hadn't realized he had hesitated until Audrey looked at him. Her eyes were wide, sincere. "You should. You two should get to know each other," she said. Her tone had a hint of a tremor.

He decided grimly that he would definitely meet with the man. Alone. They needed to have a discussion before the man tried to convince Genevieve she merely needed to commune with the dead or something equally ridiculous to banish her nightmares.

Seawater. There had been seawater beside the bed.

No. She had showered, then dripped on the rug, and the seawater smell was coincidence. The air of the Keys smelled like seawater in general, a good smell, one that was everywhere.

This was ridiculous. They were sucking him into some bizarre fantasy world. He wasn't going to let it happen. "I'll see you early then. I have to be on the dock by seven-thirty, so let's say 6:00 a.m."

"Works for me. I'm staying at La Concha. Let's eat there."

Thor nodded and rose, wondering if he looked as grim as he was feeling.

He went to find Genevieve, who was in the kitchen, setting raw vegetables on a tray. She arched a brow as he caught her hand. "The carrots can wait a second," he told her. She smiled back, bemused and still curious as he pulled her into his arms for a kiss.

They were interrupted when Victor announced that the fish was ready, and suggested everyone grab a plate and step out back, where the burgers and chicken were already waiting.

"I'll be out in a second. Let me throw out some of this garbage first," Genevieve said, heading for the living room to clean up the empties. Thor followed to help.

Victor had left his empty beer bottle sitting on the coffee table. Thor picked it up, then froze and stared at it in shock.

The label had been viciously shredded, almost as if torn apart by the talons of an enraged bird.

Beyond a doubt, it was an interesting day. Genevieve wasn't sure why. Nothing had changed, but just meeting Adam Harrison had somehow made things better.

She wondered if she would still see the ghosts in her dreams.

The pirates, clothes tattered, bones sticking out of their rags, faces grim, weapons in hand, marching silently through what seemed like the deepest regions of the sea, stalking her...

The beautiful woman, white gown flowing, hair wafting on an invisible current, standing protectively between her and the decaying pirates, whispering her warning...

Beware...

Haunting her mind, her soul.

Fighting the dream each time, waking.

And then, for terrible seconds, the fear gripping her like a vise. Hard and torturous, squeezing her heart. Each time, she fought to breathe. To believe again in the light of day. She dared to say nothing, questioning her own sanity even when the visions faded and she knew she was alone. She thought gratefully of the solidly real man who had been at her side this morning. His being there gave her strength, made her long to describe each second of the strange, terrifyingly real dream, but she didn't dare.

She knew she would lose if he questioned her sanity much longer.

Somehow, she believed, Adam Harrison would change...everything. And so, during the course of the barbecue, she felt as if she were on cloud nine.

Except for one thing. She thought she was the only one worrying about it until Bethany's Key lime pie and coffee were served.

"Hey, Jay," Victor said. "I'm kind of worried. Marshall didn't show up today."

Jay looked at him, forkful of Key lime pie halfway to his mouth. "You're worried about Marshall?"

"None of us has seen him in a couple of days," Jack explained.

Jay didn't look particularly worried. "Marshall is…Marshall. He has a private life. I know you guys share a lot, but I'm sure he doesn't feel he has to tell you if…"

"If he's getting some?" Alex finished dryly.

Jay shrugged.

"I think we need to file a missing persons report," Genevieve said.

"I think," Bethany said, "that we've waited this long. But if Marshall doesn't show for work tomorrow, it's definitely time to worry."

There were murmurs of agreement all around. Gen tried to convince them otherwise, but by then everyone was too busy with dessert to listen.

Shortly afterward they all began to split up. Jay left first, hugging Genevieve warmly, thanking her, warning her gruffly to be careful.

"I'm always careful," she assured him. He looked over her shoulder at Thor.

"Well, I guess it's good that…I think," he murmured.

She smiled. "He's one of the good guys, I believe," she said.

Jay nodded. "Sometimes we have to go on logic *and* belief, huh?"

She agreed, and bade him good-night, promising him that they were still on for a dinner sometime during the week.

Audrey and Uncle Adam were the next to leave.

As Jay had done, Audrey hugged her, but Audrey's hug was fierce. "You take care. And thank you. This was great. It's been too long since we spent time together."

Genevieve hugged her back, just as fiercely. "Thank *you*," she said.

Audrey grinned. "My pleasure. *Uncle* Adam is cool, huh?"

"Absolutely."

Uncle Adam was the next one to say goodbye. Just feeling his handshake and meeting his eyes made Genevieve feel better. "Tomorrow night, then. We'll talk."

Suddenly she glanced uneasily over her shoulder, wondering where Thor was.

"It's okay," Adam said. "I'm having breakfast with him."

Her eyes went wide with alarm.

But Adam Harrison shook his head. "Trust me. And don't worry. I already have people down here to help."

"Oh?"

"My son is with me, and there's a couple at the resort. Nikki and Brent Blackhawk. You'll like them. He's worked with me a very long time. And Nikki…Nikki has what it takes. You'll get to meet them soon. And though I don't have the gift, I have a hunch. Everything will be fine."

She stepped up and kissed his cheek. She was surprised and embarrassed. He just smiled, squeezing her hand. "We need to learn how to listen," he said softly. "That's all." Then, arm in arm with Audrey, he was gone.

There was a sudden silence. Genevieve turned around. All her remaining guests were silent, staring after the two who had just left.

Then Victor blurted out, "That guy is fucking weird."

"I've gotta agree," Alex said.

She could see Thor standing, grim and silent, just behind the two.

He agreed, as well. She could tell.

"Then again," Jack said, "Audrey's a little weird herself."

"You're all nuts," Genevieve informed them. "To you guys, anyone who isn't a diver, who doesn't live to spend half their days underwater, is weird."

"Need any help?" Bethany asked Genevieve. When Gen shook her head, Bethany said, "I guess we should all head back, then. Tomorrow is an early day."

"Lecture day," Alex groaned.

"Lecture day, and let's pray Marshall shows," Genevieve murmured.

"Marshall will be there," Victor said, setting a hand on her shoulder. "He'll show. You know he will."

He gave her a warm, brotherly hug. She smiled at him. "Right."

"Hey, Victor, don't you dare leave without me," Bethany said.

"Of course not," Victor said, rolling his eyes jokingly.

Genevieve realized that, amazingly, they had spent the entire day without mentioning that there was an unknown killer loose right there in the Keys.

There was another moment's silence. "Okay, well, Zach and I are out of here," Lizzie said firmly. "Genevieve, thanks. This was great."

Genevieve grinned. She liked Lizzie and Zach.

"Out, out, everyone out," she said with a laugh.

"Oh, this is so cute," Alex said with a sigh as everyone headed toward the door. "Look at the lineup—Lizzie and Zach, Bethany and Victor, and me and…Jack."

"Hey, no way I'm sleeping with you, bud," Jack announced.

"Out!" Genevieve said again, laughing even harder.

At last, she managed to close the door on them all. Even without turning back to face him, she felt Thor's silent presence, felt him watching her.

She turned to stare at him, crossing her arms over her chest, leaning against the closed door. "What?" she asked defensively.

He cocked his head at an angle, staring back, speaking softly, "I hate to agree with Victor, but…"

She pushed away from the door, heading for the kitchen. "I liked him," she said flatly.

She went to the sink, ready to do the last of the dishes. He followed her, setting his hands on her shoulders. "Don't you see?" he asked softly. "This guy is…some kind of a…well, let's get serious. He's as loony as Audrey. He'll feed into every fear and fantasy you've been breeding."

She dropped the sponge and turned around. "That's what you think, isn't it? That I've got an imagination that never ends, and that I'm just letting it run wild." She hesitated, hating what she saw in his eyes. She thought he cared about her and that what was going on between them was a lot more than sleeping with her. But there was a crystal over his eyes. She could just hear him thinking she was crazy as hell, and he wouldn't be sticking around if she insisted on keeping it up.

She didn't want him to go. It hurt like hell to say the words, but she managed to speak them with tremendous dignity. "Don't let me keep you where you don't want to be."

His answer came slowly. "I'm exactly where I want to be," he said. He let out a long breath. "Look, we're tired and tomorrow is going to be a long day. And…"

"And what?"

"There's a killer out there," he said very softly.

She shook her head. "I don't want you staying because of that," she said.

The warmth she so loved and craved touched his eyes again. "I'm kind of big to throw out," he said.

Then he stepped away, as if any more conversation between them could cause him to leave after all. "I've got a *really* early morning. I'm setting the clock for five-thirty. I'll reset it for six-thirty. Will that work for you?"

"Sure," she told him.

"I need to check my e-mail. Mind if I log on in your office?" he asked her.

"Of course not."

"Unless you want some help down here?"

She shook her head. "I've got it under control. Thanks."

He left her. She washed up the last few dishes, hesitated, then dried them and put them away. She didn't like leaving things out, since she might well wind up spending the rest of the week at the resort. Her last few little chores wound up taking longer than she had anticipated, but when she walked up to her bedroom, he still wasn't there. She was tempted to go into the office and read over his shoulder.

She hesitated, then chose not to. She washed her face, brushed her teeth, then slipped into the shower for a minute; she felt she was wearing the scent of barbecued fish. Once out, she dried and hesitated. Presumptuous to slip into bed naked? Or ridiculous to slip into bed clad?

She closed her eyes, biting her lower lip for a minute. She was falling for him so hard. He was everything she could want in a man, her dream counterpart, sharp, intelligent, fun…a diver, a lover of the sea. And it didn't hurt that he was built like Atlas, with such striking features, and that he had a way of touching her, of making love, that was exciting beyond measure and still, somehow, achingly tender.

She slipped into bed, turning off the lights, then stared into the darkness. There was light coming in from the hall.

And he was there, just down that hall. So close to her, and yet so far.

She was just about to get up and turn the lights back on when Thor came in at last. He moved silently in the darkness, not about to wake her if she slept.

When he, too, had slipped beneath the covers, she rolled against him, fingers light as they moved down his chest. He took her into his arms.

He made love as he always did. Erotically, slowly, teasingly... He elicited and teased, and she lost all fear of the darkness in the madness of desire. She was aware of the feel of his lips against her, so intimately, the tremendous power of his frame, the frantic beat and soar of touching and rising, writhing, thrusting, rocketing into the volatile realms of sex and sensuality. She longed for release, longed to stay forever....

As always, he held her.

And yet...

She sensed something different. He was silent, as if lost in his own thoughts. She was afraid then. Afraid she had lost him, that this was his way of saying goodbye.

She started to inch away, alarmed to realize her heart was so tender, that she was already on the defensive.

He pulled her back, kissed her forehead. She thought words hovered on his lips, but if they did, they went unsaid.

The real thing.

That was how Captain Raul Terry, a good friend

in Naval Intelligence, had described Adam Harrison. The real thing.

There *was* no real damned thing, Thor thought.

But the Internet had yielded the name Adam Harrison in a number of articles concerning unusual occurrences. There had been no Web site for Harrison Investigations. There were no advertisements. In fact, it was impossible to find. Except the articles had referred to the government, so he had hunted until he had found Raul online, and the man's response had shocked him.

The real thing.

Impossible. They were living in the real world.

At his side, Genevieve shifted slightly. He pulled her closer, damning himself in the night. He would not be taken in.

And yet…

He found he was afraid. He had never been under the delusion that his size made him tough, but he believed in his reason and intelligence, and it was frightening to feel with a greater sense on a daily basis that she was slipping away.

That he couldn't protect her.

He gritted his teeth in the darkness. There was a killer on the loose. Hard, solid fact. The guy was probably a coward, victimizing the weak. There was no reason to believe Genevieve was in any danger. The man had killed a prostitute.

But there were the other disappearances.

Seawater…

The scent of salt water suddenly seemed to be upon them again.

"Genevieve," he whispered urgently, pulling her close. Her eyes opened. She stared at him in the shadows, smiling, still half asleep. "Stay with me," he murmured urgently. A slight frown crossed her brow. His words made no sense, he knew. She obviously had no plans to.

But he repeated the words, anyway.

"Stay with me."

He cradled her to him. Made love with a ferocity that bordered on the violent. Held her against him, flesh to flesh.

He realized he didn't want to sleep, even as she drowsed in his arms. But in time, despite his desire to remain awake, he slept. Completely entwined with the woman he realized he loved.

As if his very flesh could keep away the demons in which he did not believe.

It came again.

The smell of the sea.

Salt, waves, wind.

And she knew they were coming. Men, marching slowly, grimly. Tattered frock coats in many colors. White unbleached cotton shirts that were in rags.

Decaying bodies.

Rotting flesh.

The white gleam of bone.

Eyeless sockets that still seemed to stare…

Marching. Coming closer, closer…

Here a blunderbuss, there a saber.

Shreds of hair from bony heads topped by angled hats. And there the remnant of an earlobe, gold hoop dangling precariously.

She fought the fear. Fought the conviction that they meant to surround and entrap her. But still they came closer…closer.

And then, as usual, the woman. The beautiful young woman. Hair floating around her. White gown drifting in the invisible water.

Her eyes, so sad. Her lips, forming the word.

Beware…

Genevieve fought against her innate panic; the survival instinct that begged her to awaken. She knew she needed to wait, to let them enter her unconscious mind.

To let them have their say.

Beware of *what?* she entreated in silence.

The woman's full, rich, beautiful lips, so miraculously preserved against the absolute decay of her companions, began to move.

But her words dissipated at the ear splitting blare of the alarm.

Genevieve bolted upright. She gasped, drawing a deep breath, more panicked by the noise than she had been by the dream. She looked around. The room was in shadows.

Thor was gone.

She couldn't remember hearing the alarm earlier. He must have awoken on his own, then, as he had promised, reset it. She let out a long breath, closed her eyes tightly, steeled herself for the day. She started to rise.

The bed was soaked. When she stepped onto the rug, it, too, was drenched. She stood there, naked and shaking, fighting the urge to burst into tears.

She hunkered down, smelling the sea. "What?" she cried out. "What do you want? What are you trying to tell me? What?"

There was no answer in the shadows of the early morning.

Swearing, she headed for the shower.

There were two men sitting together in the dining room when Thor arrived. Adam was wearing khaki shorts in concession to the heat and a tailored short-sleeved shirt, while the younger man was wearing jeans and a T-shirt that advertised a nineties rock group. Before Thor could greet Adam, the younger man spoke. "Hey. I'm Josh. Adam's son. It's a pleasure."

Thor nodded somewhat curtly and indicated that the men should sit, then took a chair himself.

"Mr. Harrison, I'll start right off by saying I did some investigating myself last night."

The younger man's eyes widened. Adam Harrison smiled. "Of course. I would have expected no less."

"I admit my former colleagues have only good things to say about you."

The waitress stopped by to pour Thor's coffee

and take their order. The younger man waved a hand, indicating he wasn't eating. Adam ordered an English muffin and orange juice. Thor opted for eggs and toast. Though it wasn't good to overeat before a dive, it could be worse not to eat at all.

Thor sipped his coffee, staring at Adam. "You've come here to ask me to leave," Adam said.

Thor arched a brow, setting his mug down with precision. "You're not going to convince me that our project is being hounded by ghosts."

"It doesn't disturb you that a young woman you obviously care about is suffering?" Adam asked.

"I think you insinuating that she really is seeing ghosts is just going to make matters worse," Thor said quietly.

"You do know I've worked for the government?" Adam said.

"Oh, yes." They were engaging in a staring contest, Thor realized. "And I know some presidents have sworn that Lincoln haunts the White House."

"He does," Josh Harrison commented.

Thor ignored that.

"Mr. Harrison, the body of a woman was discovered on the beach. There is a serious danger in the Keys. It's coming from a real killer. Messing everyone up with talk of ghosts and things that go bump in the night isn't going to help anything."

"Ghosts are not necessarily evil," Josh said seriously, his brow furrowed. "If you let them, they can help with the real, the present."

"Thank you," Thor murmured, stopped from saying more when the food arrived. "You've got to see my position," he went on when the waitress had gone.

"I do," Adam Harrison said. "And my people and I will try very hard to stay out of your way."

Thor chewed his food without tasting it. "Don't disturb my divers," he said at last.

Adam Harrison leaned forward. "Look. You've checked me out. You know I'm honest. Give me a chance to be around. And we're not talking about divers, plural. We both know we're only talking about one. And she's more than a diver to you."

"She's scaring you," Josh said.

Thor shot the young man a withering stare.

"Don't let what's happening turn you against a wonderful woman," Adam said softly.

Thor wondered if the guilt the words made him feel was clearly written across his face. Yes, all this made him uneasy. It made him want to hold her, protect her. It also made him—*him*—want to run. To get out before...

"I don't believe in ghosts," he said firmly.

"But you will," Josh said softly, almost sorrowfully.

Thor sighed. "I know I can't convince you to leave today. So be aware I don't believe in what you're doing for a second. And tread lightly."

Adam shook his head. "I'll do my best to stay out of your way, but I have a job to do, too. And I honestly believe you'll wind up grateful for my presence."

Thor was surprised to discover he had eaten his eggs, apparently, much like a normal, unenraged human being. He rose. "I had hoped we could come to some kind of an agreement," he said tersely.

Adam Harrison's slow, easy smile was grating. "No, you had hoped to intimidate me into leaving. But I do understand. I harbor no resentment. Good day, and good diving to you."

Fortified by a long, hot shower, Genevieve dressed for a day of diving, throwing on a suit and a terry cover-up.

Downstairs, she discovered Thor had left her coffee. She smiled, wondered how she could feel so touched and poignantly sad at the same time.

Because he would never stay with her. Because she really was going crazy.

She washed up in the kitchen, angry again. Until they locked her up, she had to work, had to keep going.

She gathered the few things she wanted to take back to the cottage at the resort and locked up the house.

As she turned the key in the lock, she froze, a prickling sensation suddenly sweeping up her spine to her nape.

She looked around. It was still early. Not full light. Shadows everywhere.

And from the shadows, she felt as if there were eyes. Staring at her.

She swore aloud. This was really getting ridiculous.

Determinedly, she started down the path. Bushes and trees seemed to rustle behind her. She found herself hurrying.

She was alone on the streets.

She started to walk, still feeling as if she was being watched. She stopped, angry, spun around. There was no one. And not a sound. Not even a bird cheeped.

She started forward again.

Then she heard the footsteps. Running footsteps, hurrying over grass and pavement.

She turned quickly. Yes, there by the bush…a shadow.

She started to run, afraid to turn back to look.

And hit Duval Street.

And there, coming from one of the bed-and-breakfasts, was a deliveryman.

She nearly crashed into him.

"Good morning," he called cheerfully.

She came to a halt, swallowing, heart pounding. She dared to look back.

The street was empty.

12

Genevieve wound up being just a few minutes late—the last arrival of the morning. The deliveryman had realized she was shaking and worried about her, even getting her a bottle of water. She had quickly regained her composure and bought him a Starbucks latte in thanks.

Still, the morning should have been good. The skies were clear, the breeze soft. Perfect diving conditions.

Professor Henry Sheridan was ready with his model and his lecture.

There was one flaw.

Marshall wasn't there.

His absence had already been discussed when Genevieve arrived. Thor appeared to be so completely irritated—though whether about Marshall or something else, she couldn't tell—that she immediately determined to keep her distance from him.

"This isn't like Marshall," Victor insisted.

"Not at all," Alex chimed in.

"I'm really worried about him," Bethany said.

While Marshall was absent, Jay was present, as were a pair of handsome strangers, the woman a beautiful blonde, the man with striking features that denoted Native American ancestry. Sliding into a seat on the bench at the picnic table next to Bethany, Genevieve demanded in a whisper, "What's going on? Who are those people with Jay? I don't understand anything here. Marshall isn't here—Jay is. With strangers. But I take it someone knows *why* Marshall isn't here?"

"Unavoidably detained on the mainland. That's why Jay is here. Evidently Marshall called the police station last night, too late to call one of us, afraid we might be worried, and asked that someone come out here and explain, and relay his promise to be back as soon as possible."

"So that's why Jay is here?" she asked.

Bethany shrugged and nodded. "And probably why Thor looks like ye olde thunder god. He's disgusted. I guess. He's used to running a tight ship, and so far this dive has been anything but."

"If we could quiet down, please? I miss Marshall like the rest of you, but he's a a responsible man, so if he says he's unavoidably detained, well then, we move on," Thor snapped.

They all fell silent.

"All right, here we go," Professor Sheridan announced. He indicated the ship with his pointer as he spoke. "The *Marie Josephine*. Launched in October 1803, purchased by the British in 1816. Displacement, one thousand eight hundred pounds, length one hundred and sixty feet, depth 14.3 feet, in the hold. She carried thirty long guns and two twenty-four-pound bow chasers. Those guns are down there somewhere. She had her masts blown to bits, and holes in the hull. She was mortally wounded before the storm ever began. Using descriptions of the damage written in one of the pirate's journals, we reconstructed her sinking via the computer. I believe she took on water in such a way that she split in half as she began her descent. It's estimated that the storm that caught them was gusting up to two hundred miles an hour. That would mean huge pieces of her might have been carried more than a mile, so we're looking for a truly vast field. Your clues will be the guns and…" He pulled out a sheaf of paper from his briefcase. "These are computer illustrations, showing what pieces of the ship might look like now."

"Looks like coral," Alex murmured.

"Precisely. You might be staring right at a piece of the hull and not even see it. That's why this morning's lecture is important. You need to learn how to see what's hidden from the eye. Take a really good look at these pictures. She's there, and judging from that coin you found, you're right on top of her. You just have to find her. Well, that's it. I'm done for the day."

He stepped back, looking pleased. The divers were studying his pictures, and no one had yawned.

"Thank you, Professor," Thor said firmly.

The others looked up. As if on cue, they started to clap. Professor Sheridan flushed a deep red.

"Thank you. And good luck."

"Hey, Professor," Jack said. "Do you want to go out on one of the boats today?"

Sheridan lost his color, turning white. "Thank you, but I'll leave the diving to the experts," he said.

Genevieve noticed that Jay was talking to Thor, who still looked grim. He turned to the couple who had come with Jay, barked out a few questions, then shrugged, as if nothing were of the least importance to him anymore. Then he turned suddenly, as if aware Genevieve was standing there. His frown deepened. "You're with me," he said.

"Hey, who's my buddy?" Victor demanded. "Jack?"

"Me. I hope you don't mind," the blond woman said, smiling as she approached him. "How do you do? I'm Nikki."

"Hi, Nikki." Victor suddenly seemed thoroughly pleased with the situation.

"Sorry, guys," Jay said. "I should have made the introductions earlier. Nikki and Brent Blackhawk work for the government. Now, don't let me hear any groans. They're pitching in because we're short a man and a boat. Jack and Brent will be topside on Thor's boat, and I'll be staying up on the police cruiser."

"We can take my boat," Jack offered.

"Gee, thanks," Bethany teased.

"Hey, all she needs is paint."

"Trust me, the cruiser has everything you'll need," Jay said.

"The cruiser is great. We appreciate it," Thor said.

"Right," Alex muttered, shaking his head. "What the hell is Marshall thinking?"

"Let's do the best we can for the day, shall we?" Thor asked. "Now, let's get going."

He grabbed the bag holding his diving equipment.

Genevieve realized that Nikki had fallen into step with her. She flashed her a quick smile. "Hi, I'm Genevieve. Nice to meet you. So you're an experienced diver?"

The woman's smile matched Genevieve's. "I dive." She paused. "Actually, I'd prefer diving with you, but…I'm grateful just to have gotten on the boat."

"I see," Genevieve said, though in reality she didn't see anything. "Victor is my usual partner. Don't let him fool you. He's a top-notch diver."

"I'm sure."

"You are?"

"He wouldn't be on this project if he weren't."

Genevieve found herself smiling in turn. That was true.

They split up when they reached the dock and neared the boats. Genevieve stared at the woman suddenly, frowning. Adam Harrison had mentioned he had people coming, people who were acquainted with the kind of difficulties she'd been having.

She had feared he meant psychiatrists.

Now she knew he had meant ghost hunters.

Ghost hunters with government connections? Maybe that wasn't so strange.

"Wait!" she called.

Nikki paused, looking at her with an expectant smile.

"I know you're with Adam," she said softly. "He told me."

Nikki nodded, but her eyes shot to Thor, who was ahead of them.

Genevieve almost laughed aloud. She felt ridiculously relieved. "Not a word," she swore.

On the way out to their coordinates, Thor was entirely uncommunicative with her, but she heard him speaking softly with Brent Blackhawk. The man had a smooth, easy voice, and she could understand why Thor seemed to take to him so easily. He was a man's man, his authority quiet and unassuming. His smile was quick. He had the appearance of someone who could withstand any storm.

And yet, when he glanced Genevieve's way, he was quick to offer a smile, and a wink.

Looking at Thor, she realized that he knew. Somehow, he knew why Nikki and Brent were there, and, despite that fact, he was behaving decently.

Why? Was he just waiting to throw them to the sharks?

The motor sputtered to a stop. Brent Blackhawk came to help her up once she had buckled on her tank. She caught his eyes again. They seemed to offer reassurance. She thanked him, then met up with Thor at the stern. He stared at her for a long moment, then stepped out to the platform and jumped in. She followed suit.

He was leading. She followed.

As they moved deeper, she glanced at her gauge. Fifty feet…fifty-five…sixty. There was coral to her right; ten feet to her left, there was a drop-off leading down another ten to twenty feet. Glancing through the water, she could see Victor and Nikki about forty feet away.

She moved slowly. The water was clear, the current easy. Thor kept looking back at her. She stayed about ten to fifteen feet behind. The sound of her regulator was as soothing as the clear warmth of the water. Neon-colored fish shot by her. A huge grouper hovered by a staghorn coral, making her feel a bit guilty about last night's meal. He was a friendly fellow. He swam straight toward her. She reached out and she ran her fingers gently over its huge body. The fish outweighed her by about a hundred and fifty pounds, she decided.

Thor had paused and was looking back at her. He seemed pleased that she had been waylaid by nothing more than a friendly fish.

Again he moved forward.

Genevieve stared after her fish as it departed.

And then, in its place, she saw the woman.

Genevieve stopped breathing. Her heart hammered in a slow, dull thud.

She swallowed. Forced herself to breathe. The woman stared at her with her great sad eyes. Blond hair and white cotton trailed in the water. Through her, Genevieve could see the bright bodies of a dozen tropical fish.

The woman beckoned.

Genevieve followed.

Entranced, she had forgotten Thor—until she felt his grip on her ankle, jerking her back. He stared at her furiously through the lens of his mask.

She stared back and pointed. He shook his head. She pressed her gloved hands together, prayer fashion.

Then, without waiting for a reply, she shot away from him.

Ahead of her, the woman waited.

There was a sand shelf beneath her, and Genevieve began to dig gently. She felt Thor behind her. *Felt* that he didn't want to believe.

Even so, he came beside her and began to help her with her task.

She didn't know how long they worked there, only that they displaced a tremendous amount of sand. The water around them had become silt. But he didn't leave her. And he didn't stop working.

She didn't think he was even as amazed as she was when she hit something hard.

A box!

It was a metal box. Small, no more than a little chest, something that must have held only the dearest mementos, or perhaps the most important papers. It was finely etched; not the sea, the sand nor time itself had managed to entirely erase the delicate tracery of flowers and birds, visible through the sea growth that clung to the box.

Thor stared at her. He should have been jubilant,

but she winced, because the look in his eyes told her that he thought of her as something beautiful, but best kept at a distance.

He picked up the chest and gave the sign to head back. She nodded and followed. Turning wearily to thank the ghost, Genevieve saw that the apparition had already disappeared.

A few minutes later, they were topside. Thor handed up the treasure to Jack as he slipped off his fins, and tossed them and his mask onto the deck. On the platform, he reached back to assist Genevieve, but he didn't meet her eyes.

"She's done it again," he said flatly.

"Wow, I'll say!" Jack applauded. "Hey, Gen, I never asked, do you gamble? If so, sweetie, you can hit the roulette table with me anytime."

Brent Blackhawk had come to the stern as well. Thor stared coldly as Blackhawk took the box from Jack. "Do you already know what it contains?" Thor asked.

Blackhawk shrugged. "It probably belonged to Anne," he said. "And there might be something in here that tells us more about her life."

"Because there's something she wants us to know, I take it," Thor said.

Brent shrugged. "We see what we choose, and read what comes in life in the same manner," he said with dispassion.

"There's a lock on it," Genevieve commented, peeling off her dive suit.

"We'll take it back to the lab. There's no reason

to destroy something that's hundreds of years old," Thor said.

"You're kidding," Jack protested. "How can you stand it? So what if we break the lock?"

"We're not just treasure seeking. We're preserving history," Thor reminded him.

Lizzie popped up at the back of the boat, followed by Zach. Staring at them, she knew immediately that there had been another find. "I don't believe it!" she cried. She looked at Genevieve and threw her a proud look. "You're too much."

"Too much," Thor murmured softly.

Genevieve walked past him. "We have some sodas in the ice chest, right?"

"Cheer up. Celebrate," Lizzie said as Zach cleared the dive platform. "We have someone who's better than sonar. This is great," Lizzie said.

Her enthusiasm brought a smile to Genevieve's lips. "Thank you, Lizzie." She stared defiantly at Thor as she spoke

He turned away from her and got on the radio. She heard him call the other boat. Jay's voice crackled in return, but she knew what he had said from Thor's reply. "Yep, it's great. Genevieve homed right in and found a box. We'll bring it in. Let's call it quits for the day. With any luck, we'll hear from Marshall soon."

A little while later, back in at the dock, Genevieve was greeted with amazement and cheering from the rest of her teammates—and Nikki Blackhawk.

.As the other woman gave her a hug of congratulations, she whispered, "Don't look so depressed.

Shower, change, then Brent and I will meet you in the parking lot and we'll go talk with Adam and Audrey. It's going to be fine."

It was going to be fine? Yeah, right.

She forced a smile. "Thanks."

Nikki caught her by the shoulders, looking at her sternly. "Open up," she said softly. "The ghost is trying to help you."

"That ghost is making me look crazy."

Nikki smiled and shrugged. "Ghosts will do that. I wish there had been a way for me to be the one diving with you, but we have to be careful. It won't do any good if everyone knows who we are and why we're here."

She stepped away quickly as Victor came up, lifting Genevieve, spinning her around. "Hon, you've just got to ditch that Norse god somehow and get back to being my partner."

There was general laughter all around, even Thor taking the comment good-naturedly. He even told Victor it was nice to be called a god. But then he turned away, saying he would take the box to the professor at the lab.

Genevieve closed her eyes for a minute, feeling dizzy, then glad he hadn't suggested that she accompany him.

She sped as quickly as she could manage from the docks, going to her own cottage, showering and changing with shaking hands and a trembling that wouldn't leave. She dressed quickly, afraid that any minute Thor would be there, staring at her suspiciously, suggesting she come with him.

But he didn't appear.

Paradoxically, she felt a sinking fear that he would never appear again. That he might really see her the way she looked at an exotic jellyfish—gorgeous when billowing in the water, deadly when wrapping its tentacles around its prey.

She couldn't—wouldn't—dwell on it.

She raced out of her cottage, heading away from the tiki bar and toward the parking lot. No one else was there yet.

As she waited, a late afternoon cloud covered the sun. Darkness seemed to descend in a great, ominous swirl. Around her, palms whispered as they swayed in the rising breeze.

She gritted her teeth, fighting the sensation that she was being watched. That a predator was lurking behind the benign palms and sea grapes. But then she heard something.

A shifting. Something in the trees. As if an animal were stalking her.

She closed her eyes for an instant, trying to clear her head.

She nearly screamed aloud when a voice said suddenly, "Hey there, gorgeous heroine of the deep."

She spun around. It was Jack. She was almost giddy with relief.

"Jack! Damn you, you startled me," she told him.

He shrugged. "What's up? I should buy you a big bottle of champagne." He cocked his head at an angle. "Or a beer?" he said hopefully. "Kind of surprised me that our mighty leader brought us in today.

I have a feeling we'll be working long, hard hours from here on out. So what do you say? Can I buy you a drink?"

"Sorry, Jack. I'm meeting Audrey," she said. "But how about a little later?"

"You got it. I'll be hanging around in the usual places. Crook your little finger, and I'll come running."

She smiled. "Thanks, Jack."

He waved to her and headed across the lot to the street beyond. As he disappeared into the crowd on the sidewalk, Brent and Nikki came forward. "Hey," Nikki said cheerfully. She looped an arm through Genevieve's. "Cheer up. You're going to be rich and famous. Oops, wait a minute. Government funding. You'll be *kind of* rich and famous."

I just want to be sane, she thought. And despite herself, that inner voice went on. Sane—and loved.

"There's a reason why you're seeing what you are," Brent said quietly.

Genevieve flashed him a rueful smile. "Always?"

He laughed. "No. Sometimes, people are…well, just seeing what they want to see. That's why we're not easily accessible. Adam tries to make sure there's really something going on before he calls in his people."

Again, she felt there was something very solid—sane in the midst of insanity—about Brent Blackhawk.

She hesitated. "So…do you see ghosts?" she asked him.

"All the time," he said softly.

She stared at Nikki. "And you…?"

"I've seen them most of my life. Shadows, a hint of something." It was her turn to hesitate ruefully. "They've only started talking to me recently."

The late afternoon sun was shining down again, though the heat was beginning to ease. Duval Street was crowded with tourists, and competing music escaped from different bars on different corners. This seemed like the most ridiculous conversation in the world, coming in the daylight, among so many of the laughing, partying, vacationing…living.

They reached the alley to Audrey's and turned. Adam Harrison was already there and opened the door for them. Apparently he knew his people well, because he greeted them warmly. Once again, Genevieve felt stronger in his presence.

"Hey, you!" Audrey called happily. When she entered her friend's parlor, Genevieve saw computer printouts, magazines and books everywhere.

"We've been looking up everything we can find," Adam explained. "About the attack on the *Marie Josephine,* the storm and the sinking. We've had a few minutes to speak, and Audrey has filled me in on what she knows. So I thought we should sit around and discuss what facts we have, add in what's happening, and see what answers we get."

"Genevieve found a box today, someone's private little treasure chest. It was locked," Brent said.

"Oh?" Adam said. "The ghost led you to it?"

She nodded.

"She likes you," Nikki said cheerfully.

"Great," Genevieve muttered.

"She might have picked you because she knows you're willing to help her," Brent said. He paused, looking at her. "Some people have a sixth sense, if you will, though most people have a habit of denying it. Who thinks that someone who sees ghosts is sane? You've probably always had the ability to sense something beyond the usual, but it's only just now that someone has tried to make contact. This ghost sees you as some kind of kindred spirit. It's a good thing."

"A good thing? She's nearly given me a heart attack several times," Genevieve protested.

"Yes, but now you're accustomed to her," Brent said. He always spoke so evenly, in such a matter-of-fact tone. The ridiculous seemed to make sense.

"What I don't understand," Nikki said, taking a seat and frowning as she picked up a batch of the papers, "is why Genevieve is seeing *pirates*. Supposedly the pirates survived and it was the ship's crew that went down. What we know about what happened comes from the pirates' letters and journals."

"Yes, that is interesting," Adam agreed.

"Then again," Nikki said, "how do we know the ghost is from the *Marie Josephine*? The body of a murdered woman was found on the beach," Nikki reminded them. She hesitated. "That means there might have been other victims. Other ghosts."

"Did you see her?" Adam asked Nikki.

Nikki shook her head. "I wasn't with Genevieve when we went down. We were lucky Thor Thompson even let us out on the dive. He knows we're your people, Adam."

Adam nodded gravely. "Well, she keeps showing Genevieve the pirate treasure. So let's assume she *is* from the *Marie Josephine*."

There was silence for a minute.

"Genevieve, you're going to think this is a bit schlocky, but we're going to try a seance," Brent said.

"A seance?" Genevieve said weakly. The idea terrified her. "Um…it's still light out," she murmured.

"It isn't a matter of light and dark, though ghosts do tend to prefer darkness and shadow," Brent said levelly. "But they also walk the streets in broad daylight. They frequently have some kind of a mission."

Genevieve winced. Good God, this entire conversation was ridiculous!

Brent Blackhawk must have sensed the emotions churning within her. He smiled. "I've seen them all my life. I told you that." He cocked his head at an angle and grinned. "Luckily, I'm half Native American. People think we're prone to the mystical." He hesitated. "Sometimes ghosts can't be helped. They walk the streets because they're punishing themselves for some evil deed they think they committed, and they have to come to terms with themselves before they can move on. But sometimes there's something happening in the world of the living that they're determined to straighten out."

Genevieve nodded, looking from him to Nikki. "They help solve murders," Nikki said.

"But…a seance?" Genevieve said uneasily.

"Don't worry, it's not like what you've seen in movies," Adam told her.

"The table is best," Audrey said. She shrugged. "It's where I pretend to contact the dead all the time."

They formed a circle around the table. Genevieve found herself between Brent and Nikki, and she was certain they'd planned it that way. Just joining hands with the two, she nearly jumped. There seemed to be a flow of electricity going through her.

"There are no gimmicks under the table, right, Audrey?" she asked.

Audrey looked at her, hurt.

"Sorry," Genevieve murmured.

"Not today," Audrey admitted with dignity.

"So…what do we do?" Genevieve asked softly.

"Just hold hands. Imagine your vision," Brent said.

She held tight, all the while thinking it was point-less and that despite the fact *she* had been the one having the visions—this was really ridiculous, a bunch of mature adults sitting around a table holding hands.

"Clear your mind," Brent said, his tone deep, yet oddly quiet. "Close your eyes for a moment."

Outside, night was coming at last. It was a time that folks waited for: sunset on Key West. The sky would be a burst of beautiful colors. In fact, there were few places in the world where sunset was quite so beautiful. Rays of last light playing atop the water, then diving into it, changing sea and sky at lightning speeds. Shadows falling…

She opened her eyes.

And there was the woman.

Jay drove Thor to the lab, which gave him a chance to quiz the police officer.

"You might have mentioned your new pals were with Adam Harrison," he said dryly.

Jay shot him a glance. "The captain said they were sent by the feds. Harrison wasn't mentioned."

"Right. And you didn't suspect anything?"

Jay shrugged uneasily. "Yes. But what difference does it make? You knew."

"Yeah, I knew." He was quiet for a moment. "I asked Harrison to stay away, but I guess it's not going to happen."

"The guy seems decent enough," Jay commented.

"Yeah? Well, the son is a smart-ass."

"The son?" Jay said, sounding surprised.

"The man's son is here, too. Josh Harrison. I met him this morning when I joined his father for breakfast."

"That's impossible," Jay said.

"What makes you say that?"

"Harrison had a son once, all right. And the kid's name was Josh. I don't know who or what you saw, but it wasn't his son. Josh died in a car accident over ten years ago."

13

The woman stared at Genevieve. For once her hair and clothing didn't seem to flow in the water, as they did in the sea and in her dreams.

Her eyes were a deep, almost violet, shade of blue. Her hair was the color of sunkissed wheat. Genevieve saw her more clearly than ever before.

The woman looked around the room.

Genevieve tried hard to keep her breathing even, tried not to blink. She didn't want to lose the vision.

She wasn't alone in seeing the woman, she quickly realized. Brent Blackhawk spoke softly to her. "Hello. Don't be afraid."

But the ghost didn't acknowledge him. She turned to stare again at Genevieve and gave her the usual warning.

"Beware."

"Beware of what? Please, help me."

The woman's arms stretched out, covered in the silky white cloth of her gown. "Help me," she whispered. "Help me. Beware."

"I want to help you," Genevieve assured her. "I want to help you. Tell me how."

The ghost was suddenly distressed. Afraid.

Was it possible for a ghost to be afraid? she wondered.

Possible or not, the woman looked around frantically with her huge blue eyes and then began to fade from sight.

"Wait! Please!" Genevieve begged.

But the woman was gone. And in her wake she left only the whisper of her warning.

"Beware."

Then there was nothing. Nothing, Genevieve realized, or the absence of *something*. There had been a subtle change in all of them. She looked at Brent, at Nikki, and realized she had nearly broken their hands, she had been gripping them so tightly. At the end of the table, Audrey was staring at her in shock.

Genevieve swallowed. "Brent, you saw her."

"Yes."

"Nikki?"

"Something…I knew she was here."

"Audrey?"

"Not a damn thing," Audrey admitted dolefully. "Some mystic I am."

Genevieve smiled. "It's just a good living, remember?" she said.

"Some of us have great eyesight, and some are born myopic. Some make great acrobats, while others are mathematicians," Adam said kindly.

"Yeah, but…" Audrey said with a sigh.

"I wonder why she disappeared the way she did," Brent mused.

"'Beware' and 'help me.' Not enough to give us much information," Genevieve said. She was stunned to realize she wasn't feeling terrified. She felt...relieved. There *was* a ghost.

Audrey brightened. "I know. The poor woman was murdered. She never had a decent burial. We need to have a service."

"Oh, Audrey," Genevieve said, "we don't even know who she is."

"Well, she hangs around with pirates a lot—were they here, too, by the way?" Audrey asked.

Genevieve shook her head.

"Still, you're looking for the *Marie Josephine*. She was attacked by pirates before the storm that doomed her. The ghost has to be Anne, the captain's daughter. We should just have a nice funeral service at sea and let her rest."

"I'm not sure...." Genevieve murmured.

Nikki Blackhawk shrugged. "It can't hurt."

"Actually, it could," Adam commented.

"How's that?" Audrey asked.

"Are you sure you *want* her to disappear?" Adam asked.

"Of course! If she's a ghost...wandering, suffering past pain and trauma, of course I want her to be at peace," Genevieve said. "Why wouldn't I?"

"She does keep leading you to treasure," Brent said.

Genevieve was thoughtful for a moment. "I don't want to disappoint the others, but...well, I think it's obvious we're on the right track. If there were a way to let her go, I'd gladly do it."

"I can get hold of Father Bellamy," Audrey offered. "We can hold a funeral service for Anne."

"We should probably get Thor's permission," Genevieve said uneasily. "And if the papers got wind of it, I'm not sure it would be a good thing."

"Not true at all. It could be spun into a nice human-interest story," Nikki said.

They were all startled by a knock at the door. Audrey rose quickly, collecting the papers from her coffee table. "Would you mind getting it?" she asked of no one in particular.

Genevieve walked to the door. She was startled, when she opened it, to discover an entire crowd. Bethany, Alex, Victor, Jack, Jay and Thor were all there.

Thor was wearing his shades, making his expression unreadable.

"Hey," she said, hoping she sounded surprised, but not nervous.

"Are we allowed in?" Victor asked.

"Uh…"

"Sure," Audrey announced, coming to the door. "Hi, Victor." She gave him a hug. "Jack…Jay. And you're Alex, right?" She gave him a hug, too, but she didn't approach Thor. "Come on in."

"Do we need any introductions?" Adam asked politely as they all entered.

"No," Thor said. "We didn't all mean to barge in like this. Jay and I were hoping to find Adam, and we just ran into the others along the way."

"Oh?" Adam said. "Well, here I am."

"They have bad information at the police station, and we're here so you can correct it," Thor said. "I told Jay I met your son this morning. He didn't believe me."

Adam Harrison stared at Thor, mouth open in shock. After a moment he regained his composure enough to speak. "My son died ten years ago," he said very softly.

Genevieve thought every single little muscle in Thor's body must have tightened. His face was like stone.

"Then who was with us this morning?"

Adam frowned, looking truly perplexed. "Mr. Thompson, no one was with us this morning."

"Come on," Thor said impatiently. "You had an English muffin, I ordered eggs, your son..."

"Yes?"

"He didn't order," Thor said

Adam looked down for a moment. "Others have seen him, too. Sometimes I get the sense of him, but..."

"What in God's name are you two talking about?" Victor asked, but the two men paid him no attention.

Thor stood stiffly for a minute, then turned to Audrey. "Thanks for opening the door to an entire horde," he said pleasantly, then turned and left.

They all stared after him. "What the hell was that all about?" Jack demanded.

Genevieve looked at Adam Harrison, who looked back at her and smiled. "Maybe a good thing," he said briefly.

"We're all frigging nuts," Jack said. "Well, hell, this *is* Key West," he said proudly.

"Anybody hungry?" Victor asked, looking at his watch.

"Sure," Jay agreed. But as he spoke, his phone rang. He excused himself, stepping back outside to take the call.

"Well?" Victor said. "Anyone else hungry?"

"Sure," Bethany murmured.

"Nikki? Brent? Audrey? Uncle Adam?" There was a twist on the last. Genevieve decided that everyone had somehow intuited at this point that Adam Harrison wasn't really Audrey's uncle.

"Dinner sounds like a fine suggestion at the moment," Adam said. "Audrey, what do you say?"

"Sure."

Victor slipped an arm around her shoulders as they left.

Bethany gazed at Genevieve and rolled her eyes. Genevieve just shrugged.

Thor returned to the hotel. He doubted the crew that had been on duty that morning would still be working, but he could at least find out how Adam Harrison was registered.

The clerk at the desk was a young woman. He was prepared, since she wasn't supposed to give out certain information. He didn't have the credentials to demand answers to his questions, but he had a number of different legal IDs from various associations that would make it appear he had plenty of authority.

He didn't need to use any of them. The young woman apparently recognized him and was quick to help him. "I'm sorry, Mr. Thompson, but no. Adam Harrison is registered alone. To the best of my knowledge, no one else came in with him. He'd be more than welcome to have two or three adults in the room, so I can't imagine why he'd pretend not to have company," she said very seriously.

He thanked her and walked back into the night.

The usual activity was going on, people wandering aimlessly, stopping to look, to shop, to buy a little trinket here or there from the sidewalk vendors.

He paused for a moment, just watching. Adam Harrison didn't need to have a roommate for them to have been joined by a young man at the breakfast table. Maybe it had just been some kid hired to put on an act. He found himself irritated to realize, looking back, that there had really been no interaction between the man claiming to be Josh Harrison and anyone other than himself. The kid hadn't ordered food. He'd never spoken to the waitress or to his supposed father.

It had been a sham, of course. But a convincing one. He should probably be visiting the local high school drama club. Tomorrow morning, he would find the waitress. She would know that Adam hadn't been alone.

He felt his anger rising, and it disturbed him to know he also felt unease rising beneath it. His anger, he decided, was righteous. The dive was going to hell. First off, Marshall had been sold to him as the ultimate professional. But a professional didn't disappear in the middle of a project, no matter what. A professional didn't even call in sick. The only way to get out of this kind of work was to call in dead.

He gritted his teeth, watching as a tall blond woman emerged from the hotel. She was attractive, but there seemed to be an edge to her. As he watched, she caught his eye. She smiled and sauntered over to him. "Hello. Lovely night. Have a light?" she asked, producing a cigarette from her small clutch bag.

Her skirt was short, her shoes high. Her blouse revealed a great deal of cleavage.

"Sorry, I don't smoke."

She nodded, dropping the cigarette back into her bag, her eyes remaining focused on his. "Are you looking for company?" she asked bluntly.

He shook his head. Working girl. "Sorry," he said softly. "And watch out, miss. A woman was found dead, you know."

She smiled. "Still gotta make a living. Well, I'm sorry, too, handsome. Have a nice night."

She headed off down the street.

Thor turned, walking down toward the water, determined to get back to Genevieve. He hadn't liked leaving her earlier, but at the same time, he'd needed some distance. Not from *her*, exactly, but from the craziness, the whole thing with ghosts and dreams and….

His own sense of impotence, his inability to

protect her. It had to stop. But by leaving that afternoon, he'd left her free to spend the day with Audrey and those government-sanctioned ghost hunters.

As he walked at a brisk pace, he nearly collided with Jay Gonzalez.

"Hey," Jay said, startled.

"Hello. You didn't go to dinner with everyone?" Thor asked. He still didn't know if Jay Gonzalez was on his suspect list or not. The man's wife had died under mysterious circumstances. And he'd been around for the previous disappearances.

"Duty called," Jay said.

"Oh?" Thor said sharply.

Jay shook his head. "No more bodies. No real ones, anyway. A fellow working garbage detail freaked out. Went to empty his truck and thought he had a bunch of body parts. In a way, he did. Someone hacked up a mannequin and disposed of it all along Duval Street."

"A mannequin? Did he find the head?"

Jay looked at him curiously. "Yeah. Why?"

"Was it blond?"

"Yeah, there was a blond wig."

"Have you got anything on it?" Thor demanded. "There's some kind of prankster out there."

Jay frowned, shaking his head. "Thor, it's not a crime to dispose of a mannequin."

"Genevieve claimed someone left a mannequin on her doorstep the morning the body was found. She thought the body was a mannequin, in fact, and then it turned out there was a real victim. Doesn't that strike you as something that should be investigated?"

Jay groaned. "Come on, Thor, there's a big difference between chopping up a mannequin and killing a flesh-and-blood person."

Thor just stared challengingly at him.

"All right. I'll put in a few hours tomorrow and try to find out which shopkeeper was missing a dummy, and who they sold it to or why it wasn't reported as stolen, if that's the story."

"Thanks. Anything new on the victim or the killer?"

Jay cast him a weary look. "A hooker found dead, any trace evidence pretty much gone. What do you think?"

"I think you're going to solve the crime," Thor said.

"A ghost tell you that?" Jay asked irritably.

"Actually, I was going on the premise that you're a good police officer. You don't want to go with that, fuck you."

Jay let out a sigh. "Sorry. Listen, I won't be on the dive tomorrow. We're running short of manpower. They'll still give you the boat."

"Anything more from Marshall? Has he called anyone at the station again."

Jay shook his head. "No."

"Aren't *you* getting a little worried?"

"Yes," Jay admitted.

"He wanted this dive," Thor said.

"I know. Look, I've got word out in Miami."

"No one knows where he's staying?"

"No."

"You could pull the phone records, find out where he called from."

"Yeah, I'd need to do some paperwork for that," Jay said. "But I will. And like I said, I arranged for you to have a police dive boat."

"Thanks." He couldn't help adding, "We have the mighty Brent and Nikki, right?"

Jay shrugged.

"Hell, this whole thing is about as professional as a party boat," Thor grated.

Jay grinned. "Some people have connections. You know that—you use them yourself."

True enough. "Point taken," Thor said.

Jay waved a hand in farewell. "They were going out somewhere for dinner. Check along Duval. You'll find them."

Thor did find them. By then Lizzie and Zach had found them, as well. "I think it's an absolutely charming idea," Lizzie was saying as he approached the table. There was an empty seat. He realized they had planned on him joining them at some point.

"What's a charming idea?" he asked, sitting down.

He was located between Nikki Blackhawk and Audrey. Audrey was the one who answered him. "A funeral service."

"A funeral service is charming?" he asked.

"A service for poor Anne," Audrey said. "To lay her ghost to rest."

His face must have looked like a thundercloud, and he couldn't help staring at Genevieve, seated farther down the table between Victor and Jack.

"There's nothing otherworldly about it," Audrey said. "Father Bellamy has been asked many times to do services for people lost long ago." She shrugged. "I happen to know he's available tomorrow morning. And I have a friend at the paper." She noted the wariness in his look and spoke quickly. "A friend who writes *good* things. We want your permission, of course. But she thinks it's a lovely story, a beautiful young woman caught between pirates, the love of her life and a strict father, then dying young. It's got all the elements. You're not superstitious, of course, but a lot of sea people are. So what do you think?"

He looked up and down the table. Jack shrugged. Victor grinned. Genevieve was just staring at him.

"Really, Thor," Lizzie chimed in. "Come on, the work is only going to get harder. Let's go for it."

Thor stared across the table at Adam Harrison. The man was looking at him impassively.

"Mr. Harrison, what do you think?"

Adam lifted his hands. "I certainly don't see any harm in it."

"Well?" Audrey asked anxiously.

Thor stared across the table at Genevieve. She hadn't said a word, but she was looking at him hopefully. He thought about the way she had homed right in on their finds. Directions from a ghost?

He didn't believe in ghosts.

But apparently she did. And maybe she didn't want to be shown anything by the undead anymore. He thought it was all in her mind, in her dreams, but there had been that seawater....

And Adam Harrison might well be playing him for an idiot. Staring at the man, he couldn't quite get a handle on him. He just didn't seem like the kind of guy who went around perpetuating elaborate hoaxes.

Hell, someone had played a trick on Genevieve—a real trick, with a real mannequin—but Harrison hadn't been here at the time. As far as he knew...

Maybe a funeral service could put a stop to all of it.

There was also a real murderer out there, a vicious killer who had allowed a woman to drown with no hope.

And why the hell did he feel that crime had something to do with the dive?

He stared at Audrey. "We'd better not get any bad press out of it. And, hey," he said, addressing the others, "I made the call to come in early today, but from now on we'll be making a minimum of three dives a day. We know we're in the right area, but we need to find the largest debris fields before the heavy equipment comes in. With or without Marshall."

"Where the bloodly hell is Marshall, do you think?" Alex asked, sounding annoyed.

"I don't know, but at least he's all right. According to Jay," Genevieve said. There was a note of worry in her voice, despite her words.

"It's not like him," Jack said. "I've known Marshall since he was a kid. He didn't get where he is by acting like this." He shook his head.

"Let's not get going on another anxiety fest, huh?" Alex suggested.

"Food's here!" Victor announced, pointing as two waiters approached them bearing large trays laden with plates, and the conversation moved on.

"Your place or mine?" Thor murmured softly, slipping an arm around Genevieve's shoulders as they left the restaurant.

Despite his words and his touch, Genevieve felt a strange reserve in him. She didn't know what he was really thinking, and it hurt, because she wanted to be close to him even more.

"Sure you want to keep sleeping with me?" she asked softly in return.

"If you're sure you want to keep sleeping with me," he assured her. "By the way, did you know Jay was called out because a garbageman found a dismembered mannequin in the garbage?"

Her heart thudded. "I knew he'd been called away suddenly, but not why. Um, a mannequin. Really?" Why was she lying to him? Protecting Victor?

"I'm curious—why was Jay called in on it? I think it's legal to throw away a mannequin."

"Legal, yes," Thor agreed with a shrug. "But I guess the fact it was in pieces scared the garbageman. And in light of what's going on…"

"So," she said slowly, "is Jay investigating?"

"He's going to find out if one was stolen or sold to anyone." He stared at her hard. "The joke was played on you. Don't you want to know who did it?"

"I suppose. Though to tell you the truth, I'm not sure I really care. I mean, everyone sobered up and got mature the minute the real body was found."

"Right. And how many people know the body you saw was not the same body found on the beach? Let's see—me. And Audrey and Bethany. Who else? Nikki and Brent, I bet. And how many people did Bethany tell?" he queried sharply.

"Obviously it has nothing to do with Brent and Nikki. They weren't here then. And Bethany can keep a secret. Anyway, what difference does it make? It might have been a mean joke, but I'm sure the mannequin *was* a joke. Nothing more."

"You know more than you're telling me," he said softly.

She groaned softly. "I just want…I just want to let it go," she said.

He didn't reply, just looked straight ahead. "Let's see what your funeral service will do tomorrow," he told her.

"What was that little discussion you had going with Adam?" Genevieve asked him.

"A little discussion," he said curtly.

"You know more than you're telling *me*," she echoed softly.

He grimaced humorously, still looking straight ahead. "They're staying at the resort, Nikki and Brent. I saw them before I met them," he said.

"They…they can be helpful," she said lamely.

"At least she can dive," he muttered.

They had reached the parking area, and everyone started waving goodbye to one another. Adam headed off down Duval Street for his hotel. Victor, Genevieve noticed, had disappeared.

"Where's your roommate?" she asked Bethany.

"He saw a blonde," Bethany replied.

"Oh?"

"I don't think he's bringing anyone back," Bethany said. "Although maybe I shouldn't be there tonight."

Alex laughed. "He would have asked you politely to get the hell out if he'd any such plans," he assured Bethany. "But you can come to my place, if you want."

"I'll be fine, but thanks, Alex."

"Good night, Bethany," Alex said, waving and walking off. "Good night all."

Thor's arm was still around Genevieve's shoulders. "Which way?"

"Your cottage, I guess."

He nodded. Despite the way he held her, the intimate way he spoke, she still had the terrible sensation she was losing him.

Inside, with the door locked, she touched his face gently with her palm.

"Look, honestly, you don't have to pretend or feel that you started something and you have to keep it going, that…"

He pulled her close to him. "Do we have to talk?" he asked.

She shook her head. "No."

"Then let's not."

His arms wound around her. Ghosts faded away in the vital reality of flesh and blood and the volatile power of his touch.

Losers. The guys here were a bunch of losers.

Ana Maria Strakowsky decided she shouldn't have come so far south. There had been talk about there being a lot of money in the Keys. So far, she'd seen retirees, beer bellies and men in Speedos who should never, never, be so exposed. She didn't particularly care about that, but they were cheap. And slow. They didn't seem to comprehend that she wasn't looking for entertainment or the charm of their company, just a business deal. Then there were the kids. Lordy. Kids, everywhere. And family men. Guys who might have eyes that strayed from their widening wives, but not guys with the gumption to do anything.

And the really sharp, good-looking one…

He'd probably never paid in his life. But that had been hours ago. She smiled. His warning had been nice. She didn't remember the last time anyone had said anything to her that had held the least note of concern. She had come to the States a long time ago. And though she had been barely sixteen, she had known exactly why her "sponsor" had paid for her to get in. Back then, she'd had dreams of using her body as no more than a stepping-stone. In the village where she'd grown up, she could have either married a farmer or gone to the city, where the men were ugly and cheap, anyway.

Strange, the American-dream thing. It hadn't gone quite the way she had expected. So here she was, getting older now....

Cosmetic surgery could do a lot for that. She had to admit, she looked damned good for her age, but she was no kid anymore. More young girls entered the business on a daily basis. *Young.* That was the key word. And she'd never quite quit when she should have. When she could have used her earnings for an education, pressed for more....

So here she was. Seeking new ground. And it sucked.

At least, as the night wore on, the kids began to disappear from the streets. As she passed from one bar to the next, she nearly collided with a man.

He apologized quickly, straightening her—his hands lingering on her shoulders as his eyes surveyed her face.

No hesitation there. He smiled immediately.

"Well...hello."

She smiled back. Took note of the way he was dressed. He might not be Trump, but he clearly made a decent income.

"Hello."

"Are you, uh, free?"

"Not exactly free. But negotiable," she teased.

"Great. I like to negotiate."

"I have a room," she said huskily, and told him where.

He did like to negotiate, as it turned out. He talked a good line.

She didn't even notice they weren't heading in the direction of her room.

Genevieve wondered vaguely if she groaned out loud. She was sure, in the distant nether realms of the subconscious, that her sleeping body inched ever closer to the man with whom she was entangled.

She knew they were coming.

Even when they were at a distance, she could sense them as if they were marching through a fog and were dimly visible. As if she saw them through a storm at sea.

Closer…closer…they marched, then thronged around her.

She was beginning to recognize them. The jawless one in the tattered poet's shirt with the sword. The fellow in the big, plumed, deteriorating hat. The one with the knee breeches and rough leather boots.

And the woman. The beautiful blond woman.

She was weary. Not afraid…just weary.

Why? she pleaded silently.

She knew the answer.

"Beware."

Beware of what? Please, please, please…

"The truth."

What truth?

Just as the ghost opened her mouth to speak, a look of extreme pain seized her. She seemed to double over in agony, even as she faded from view, her decomposing pirate escort disappearing with her into a field of fog.

Genevieve really had to hand it to Thor. He was stubborn. He pretended not to notice the seawater that permeated his cottage, the floor, the bedding....

He awoke early. Very early. It was still dark.

He kissed her forehead. "I've got something to do before we take off. Look out for the project for me— make sure Audrey's priest and reporter are on the up-and-up."

"Of course," she murmured, only half awake.

"I'm locking the door. Keep it locked until you leave."

"Yes...of course," she mumbled sleepily.

He left. She stayed in bed, half awake, half asleep. To her astonishment, she found herself talking to the ghost.

Please, come back. I want to understand. I want to help.

I need to know the truth.

Thor took the exact same seat he'd had the morning before. The same waitress walked over to him.

"Hi," she said cheerfully.

"Hi."

"How are you this morning?"

"Do you remember me?" he asked her.

"Eggs, whole-wheat toast...I forget. Hash browns or grits?"

"Well done," he congratulated her. "I'll take hash browns, please. And do you really remember yesterday?" he asked.

She grinned. "I'm twenty-two. No senility yet. Though my brother insists I'm definitely warped."

"That's a brother for you," he said. "Do you remember the people I was with yesterday?"

"Well, you were with an older man."

"There was a younger man, too. Sixteen…seventeen…maybe even eighteen or twenty," he said.

She shook her head, smiling warily, as if he were trying to play some kind of trick on her. "I'm sorry, I didn't see anyone else."

"He didn't eat. He just sat with us."

"You're pulling my leg, right?"

Her smile faded as she stared at his face.

"You honestly saw no one else, other than the older guy?"

She hesitated. He winced inwardly.

This was what it felt to be looked at like a crazy person.

"I'm sorry. I only saw the one man. Um, you wanted coffee, right?"

"Yeah, thanks."

A little while later, as he was leaving, he paused at the door. Turning back, he saw Adam Harrison coming into the dining room.

The kid was with him, trailing behind him. He was tall and thin. Lanky, but good-looking, serious, a little grim, even.

"Have a nice day, Mr. Thompson," the host called out.

Thor nodded, then walked over to him.

"You know Mr. Harrison?" he asked the man.

"Sure. Nice guy," the man said cheerfully.

"Is the younger man as nice?" Thor asked.

"What younger man?"

Thor let out a sigh of irritation.

"That young man," he said, pointing.

Again, that look.

"I'm really sorry, Mr. Thompson. I don't know who you're talking about."

Josh Harrison stared straight at him and waved.

Thor spun on his heel and departed.

He reached the street. It was still barely light.

He looked up at the sun, trying to peek out and start the day.

"I am fucking crazy," he muttered aloud, and started back for the resort and the docks, his strides long and angry.

14

There were no messages to Genevieve from ghosts or anyone else as she lay awake after Thor departed. She had actually tried to go back to sleep, actually wanted some kind of message. She was no longer going to be so afraid. And she wasn't talking to anyone except Adam, Brent or Nikki—especially not Thor—about anything she saw, felt or sensed. She wasn't going to fight the fear; she was going to find...

The truth.

Whatever that meant.

But she couldn't fall asleep. So she rose, showered, drank coffee and watched the morning come.

It seemed to do so slowly, especially since she couldn't sleep. Drinking her second cup of coffee, she was struck with guilt. She was going to have to call Jay. There was no reason for him to waste his valuable time looking for a culprit in the "mannequin murder." She was surprised to realize she really didn't care who had been trying to play a trick on her. It didn't matter anymore. Other matters were far too grave.

At last she grew tired of sitting alone in Thor's cottage.

She opened the door and walked out.

The sun wasn't really up yet. It was one of those overcast mornings. She hoped the storm clouds would quickly blow away, as they so often did. The heavy rains and thunderstorms didn't usually come until the afternoon. Then it could rain like blue blazes for twenty minutes before coming to a dead stop. The streets could all but flood, and then the sun would come out again with a burning glory.

There was no one at the tiki bar. Still, she didn't feel like being alone in the little cottage. She frowned, wondering why Thor had disappeared so early again that morning. She might be keeping secrets, but so was he. They shouldn't talk. They should just have sex. If only…

There had to be an explanation for everything that was happening. She had to believe it would all make sense in the end.

She didn't want to think too far ahead. They would have a prayer service that morning. At the very least, it would be a nice gesture.

As she sat there, the breeze picked up beneath the dark sky. It teased at her nape, snaked down the length of her spine. She shivered. It was a distinctly unpleasant, even eerie, sensation.

She couldn't help herself. She looked around for ghosts.

But she knew there were no spiritual beings trying to make contact.

Just as she knew she was being watched again.

She had the uneasy feeling she was being assessed, that her steps had been followed, her daily pattern mapped out, that someone was watching her with evil intent.

She wanted to laugh aloud at herself. Okay, so they were late bringing the coffee out to the tiki bar that morning, while there were heavy clouds up above. And the breeze had an odd, almost icy feel to it. Leaves were rustling, fronds making strange whispering sounds, but that didn't mean someone was watching her.

Did it?

She leapt to her feet, ridiculously afraid, sorry she had come out.

"Hey, what's the matter?"

She swung around. Thor was there, wearing his sunglasses despite the overcast sky.

With his words, her unease evaporated. The clouds seemed to break. Light filled in the shadows.

She shook her head, smiling. "I heard you coming up at the last minute. You startled me, that's all."

She was glad he smiled, that he pulled her close and brushed her lips briefly with a kiss. But then he pulled back. "The troops are coming. Look." He pointed toward the parking lot. "The Exorcist himself has arrived."

"He's not an exorcist," Genevieve murmured. "He's a nice guy. You'll see."

She left Thor and went to greet Father Bellamy, feeling guilty because she hadn't been to church in a while.

Next Sunday, she promised herself.

Surprisingly, Thor found that he did like Father Bellamy. The priest wore his collar with a lightweight suit, and he had a bag of dive gear with him, as well. His first question, after introducing himself to Thor, was whether he would allow him to enter the water as long as he swore to stay out of the way. It turned out he was an Episcopal priest, and he was dating the reporter, Helen Martin, who had also brought a dive bag. They were both in their midforties, down-to-earth, and both impressed him immediately.

"It's so nice that you're doing this—such a sign of respect to someone who died long ago," Helen told him. She grinned. "People in these parts can get excited about treasure, but they also want the past to be honored. I think this will make a wonderful piece. Thank you so much for allowing us to be a little part of this."

There was still no sign of Marshall, a fact they all seemed to silently accept as a bad sign. What the hell had happened to the man?

Thor assigned Jack to the police boat with Alex, Bethany, Victor, Lizzie and Zach. He brought both Blackhawks, Audrey, Father Bellamy and Helen, and Genevieve with him.

Out on the reefs, the boats tied on together, and Father Bellamy began his service.

Thor had to admit it was both appropriate and well handled. The priest addressed no ghosts; he merely spoke to God about those who had been lost to sea, adding a special addendum for Anne, a young woman who died due to the perils of the sea. Flowers and wreaths were thrown into the water.

Helen scribbled away on a notepad the whole time.

There was nothing occult about the proceedings. Nothing to make him uncomfortable in the least.

When it was over, Audrey looked at him with a questioning smile. He smiled back. She seemed to be trying very hard to do what was right.

"Father Bellamy, too, looked at Thor anxiously. "May we hit the water now?"

"Yes," Thor told him. He looked at Genevieve, who nodded. She knew they would remain dive buddies.

Bethany was staying topside with Nikki that day. On the other boat, Jack would be watching out for the divers, ready to assist anyone in trouble, keeping an ear out for the radio.

It was going to be a long day, Thor decided. This wasn't a professional and historically important dive anymore, he decided wearily.

He was running a party boat.

But there were times when it seemed appropriate to go with the flow. This kind of work could take months, even years. Best to get all the foolishness out of the way now.

Damn Marshall. Where the hell was he?

He watched as Brent Blackhawk calmly buckled on his tank. He didn't know why, but he had the feeling that Brent was the one with the deepest belief.

So? Wasn't he seeing a kid who'd been dead for over a decade.

No. There had to be a logical explanation. Maybe it was all a tremendously elaborate hoax. But to what end?

"Ready?" he asked Gen.

She was.

They went out on three dives. Sadly—or thankfully—all three were uneventful.

Somehow, the day, which had started out with the threat of rain, remained bright and cloudless after the first hours of the morning. They were able to work without once being disturbed by thunder and lightning.

It was well past six when they brought the boats back in at last. Despite the lack of any discoveries, everyone seemed happy. He realized that, despite where they lived, Father Bellamy and Helen didn't often get out diving, so they were especially pleased about everything they had seen that day.

As they neared the dock, he heard Genevieve speaking softly to Brent Blackhawk. "Do you think she's at rest?" she asked softly.

"I don't know," he told her. "I'm sorry."

It was an exhausted group that came off the boats. Helen hurried off to write her story; she wanted it ready to run in the Sunday paper. Father Bellamy had promised to meet with an elderly couple who were renewing their wedding vows, so he left quickly, as well.

Adam Harrison was waiting for them at the docks. He eyed Thor as they appeared, hauling their equipment from the boats to be hosed down.

"How was it?" he asked.

"Fine. You didn't join us," Thor replied.

Adam shrugged. "I had some research I wanted to do."

"Did you discover anything?"

Adam shrugged. "Maybe. I need to do some thinking."

"I see. In other words, you don't intend to share your information."

"I can't share it until I have it," Adam said serenely. "I'll be at the tiki bar," he said. The man walked away, straight as a ramrod. He was wearing a short-sleeved cotton shirt with palm trees on it and khakis. Thor had to grin, watching Adam. He might try to blend in, but no matter what, the man looked like the retired fed he was.

Genevieve seemed cheerful, Thor realized. She kissed him on the cheek, her eyes bright. He was glad to see her happy.

"I'm done. I'm going to your place to shower. See you at the tiki bar," she said.

Strange. And sad. They were on a treasure hunt, but the days she had discovered treasure, she had been depressed. Today, no treasure, but she was radiant. Saddest of all, he understood.

She walked away, turning once and offering him

a brilliant smile. He smiled back, but wondered why he was feeling as if their boat had sunk. He wanted this chapter in the hunt over.

He just didn't believe it was.

By the time he had finished rinsing down the boat, half an hour had slipped away.

He put in a call to Sheridan. "You won't believe what we've got!" Sheridan said excitedly.

"Diamonds?"

"No," Sheridan returned impatiently over the phone. "Something better. Letters. We're moving carefully. There was some erosion, even to the silver. But they were wrapped in a pig's bladder, and we're working to read them without causing any damage. This is a remarkable find."

"Great news."

"And today?" Sheridan asked.

"Nothing."

"Ah, well, you'll be back out tomorrow."

"Yep." He hung up.

By the time he reached his cottage, Genevieve was gone. He showered and changed for the night.

It was already getting dark by the time he neared the tiki bar. Jack was playing chess with Alex, while Lizzie and Zach looked on.

Victor had stepped away and was on the phone.

Genevieve was sitting beside Bethany, with Adam on her one side, Audrey next to *him*. Nikki and Brent were at the table, as well.

"Thor," Audrey said, and he thought it was almost as if she were announcing his arrival.

Silence fell, and the others looked up.

"We were about to order burgers," Brent said. "You in?"

Thor nodded, then sat down next to Brent. "So where do you come from?"

"New Orleans."

"Lots of reefs around there," Thor murmured dryly.

Brent smiled slowly, using his thumb to rub the condensation off his bottle of beer. "Not everyone lives where they dive, you know."

"True. What kind of Indian comes from New Orleans?"

He knew Genevieve was frowning. He was certain the question was rude.

"If you're asking my background, it's Dakota. Irish mom," Brent said.

Nikki was staring at him icily. "I'm straight from New Orleans," she told him. "I was a Du Monde. Would you like to see our passports?"

He shook his head. "I'm sure every document you possess is in perfect order," he said softly.

Brent started to rise; Adam lifted a hand.

Genevieve wasn't about to be stopped by Adam. "I'd forgotten what an asshole Mr. Thompson could be. Excuse me, will you? I have a phone call to make."

She walked away. He watched her with concern, fingers tensing on the arms of his chair. He should have been more careful. But he just couldn't shake the idea that he was being played.

It was either that or he'd had breakfast with a ghost.

He stared at the remaining group. Bethany and Audrey were both staring at him, wide-eyed. Adam was wearing a tired but accepting smile.

"Attack me, if you want, Mr. Thompson. Not my employees," Adam said, then looked around at the group. "My associates and I work in the field of the unusual, the unexplainable—the otherworldly, if you will." He turned his attention fully upon Brent then. "You see ghosts, right?"

"Yes," Brent said flatly.

"And when did that start?"

"When I was a kid."

"And you?" he asked, zeroing in on Nikki.

"I've always sensed them. Since a particular incident, I've been able to communicate with them, as well."

Thor shook his head apologetically. "Sorry. I didn't mean to be rude. I'm looking for facts, that's all," he said softly.

"You're looking for a black-and-white world. Something you can control," Adam said. "That's not reality."

"What's reality is the body of a woman that was discovered on the beach," Thor said.

Audrey frowned. "But, Thor, I don't see how her death can relate to the dive. Or to any of us. She was a prostitute. Prostitutes never know the men they pick up."

"Do any of us really know anyone?" Nikki asked softly.

"Do you want a drink?" Brent asked. "I was going to go up to the bar, order our burgers, just put them on the tab. I can get you a beer while I'm there."

Thor had to admit he liked the guy. He had acted like a jerk, but it would be worse if he was taken for a ride by these people.

"Yeah, I'll have a beer, thanks."

He kept an eye on Genevieve, who wasn't far away; she was on her cell, speaking intently.

To whom?

He realized that Nikki Blackhawk was staring at him, smiling.

He arched a brow to her.

She laughed softly. "You really are a good guy."

He lifted a hand, puzzled.

"You're watching out all the time," she said. "You'll be great—once you learn what to watch out for."

"And that would be?"

"We all learn as we go."

Bethany drew his attention before he had a chance to ask Nikki what she mant. "Thor, did you hear anything more about the little box? Was it silver? Was it filled with gold or emeralds and rubies—"

"Letters," he said.

"Letters?" Bethany said with disappointment.

"Letters?" Audrey was intrigued.

"Sheridan is pleased," he said. As he spoke, Brent returned and handed him a cold beer. He nodded his thanks. "I was just saying that the box Genevieve dug out a day ago contains letters."

"Oh?" Brent was intrigued. "Were they badly damaged?"

"They were packaged in a pig's bladder," Thor said.

"Ugh," Audrey murmured.

"Hey, pig's bladders and other organs were the first condoms, too," Nikki offered cheerfully.

"Okay, that is gross," Bethany said.

"Imagine, though," Audrey offered, "if you were a working girl back then."

"I thank God for my century," Bethany said.

Genevieve was back. She was behind him, but Thor knew she was there without looking.

"Speaking of centuries," Audrey said thoughtfully, "do you think ghosts from one century might hang around with ghosts from another? I mean, suppose you died in the 1700s and you met a ghost who died in the 1800s. Or last week, for that matter. What would you have to talk about? Are there ghosts who are stronger than other ghosts? Are there rules? Is there a way to learn how to be a ghost?"

Brent lowered his head, smiling. "A lot of it goes to simple belief," he said. "Most of the world's peoples hold some form of belief. Most religions find counterparts in one another, no matter how far apart they seem to be. Some worship one god, some worship several. But most believe human beings are something more than flesh and blood. That there is an energy within us, our spirit. It makes me *me*, and you *you*, more so than any compilation of DNA. The general belief is that flesh and blood dies—

earth to earth, ashes to ashes—but the spirit, or soul, moves on. It's generally accepted that ghosts are spirits who, for whatever reason, have not moved on."

"The way you explain it," Genevieve said, "things make sense."

Thor was startled to feel a stab of jealousy. Well, sorry, I'm not a ghost hunter, he thought, and realized he was almost bitter.

He wasn't accustomed to feeling like this. And he didn't like it. He gritted his teeth, fully aware that the power to change was his, and his alone.

But what change was he supposed to make?

"Do I think they communicate?" Brent asked Audrey. "Sometimes. Is there a book of rules? Probably not. Is there more in the world than science has yet explained? Definitely. Will we ever have all the answers? Probably not. Faith is as important to life as bald facts."

"Do you know what I'm thinking?" Audrey said suddenly, excitedly, looking at Genevieve. "I think your ghosts might be from different times. I mean, if you had a woman who was murdered by pirates, I think she'd be too afraid of them to get anywhere near them. Maybe she's from a different time, and she's protecting you from the pirates. What do you think?"

Genevieve groaned. "I think we need to stop talking about ghosts," she said firmly.

"Hamburgers!" Victor announced suddenly.

The chess game had ended, and the players and their team cheerleaders came over to join them.

Thor rose. "Let's push the tables together," he suggested.

He looked at Genevieve, wondering who she had called. She glanced over and saw the obvious question in his eyes. She flushed. "I called Marshall's cell and left a message. I'm really getting worried," she said.

"I've tried him a half-dozen times, too," Victor told her.

"Looks like he doesn't want to be found," Alex said.

"It's time the police looked into it," Thor said.

"They *are* looking into it," Genevieve told them, reaching for the ketchup. She paused, realizing everyone at the table was looking at her expectantly.

"I spoke with Jay, too," she admitted, her cheeks flushing. "He's called some friends up in Miami. The call from Marshall came from a hotel on the beach, but Marshall was never registered there. I told him I'd fill out a missing persons report tomorrow. If Marshall didn't want us hounding him, he should have had the sense to make sure someone knew what was up!"

Thor wasn't sure how he knew it, but he was certain Genevieve had called Jay about something more than Marshall's disappearance.

"They'll find Marshall, don't you worry," Jack assured Genevieve. "And don't *you* worry," he told Thor. "We'll find plenty more at the bottom of the sea."

After that, the conversation stayed well away

from ghosts. And it seemed that everyone was eager to call it a night. The diving had been exhausting, and they had another full day ahead of them.

Genevieve had kept a slight distance between them. He didn't press her, just headed to his cottage on his own, hoping she wasn't aware that he was watching her through the window, determined to keep an eye on her.

Still, perhaps absurdly, afraid for her.

As he watched the group at the tiki bar break up, he saw Victor offer to walk Audrey home. Adam waved to the group. Brent and Nikki went off, hand in hand, to their own cottage. Zach and Lizzie walked down toward the beach, he noted. Well, if nothing else, the two of them really seemed to be enjoying their time in the Keys.

At last Genevieve started toward the cottages.

Toward her own? Or his? At first he wasn't certain.

But then, halfway along the path, he saw her stop. She went very still, chin raised. The breeze caught the long tendrils of her hair, lifting it. Except for that slight movement, she might have been a statue, an elegant, perfectly formed, alabaster statue, she seemed so frozen in place.

Then she spun around, looking wildly around her.

She stared first at the trees surrounding the parking lot and cottages. Then she turned and stared back toward the water.

Once again, she stood still. Then she started walking.

Toward *his* cottage. Then she wasn't walking, she was running.

Heedless of being caught spying on her, Thor threw open his door and stepped out onto the porch. She all but flew into his arms.

"What is it?" he asked anxiously, smoothing back her hair, looking past her into the night.

She shook her head, staring up at him. "I…I don't know. Something ridiculous, I suppose. I just felt that I was being watched. By someone other than you."

"Sorry."

"No. Thank you," she said softly.

"I thought you were angry with me."

"I am. Furious. I can't believe how rude you were."

"I'm sorry. So why did you call Jay?"

She gasped, backing away. "I—I called him about Marshall."

"You're lying."

"All right. I called to tell him I helped Victor get rid of the stinking mannequin."

He was floored.

"What?"

"He said he didn't do it to begin with, but that the mannequin wound up in his cottage. And I believe him. I've known Victor all my life. He said they'd ditched the idea. But…" She paused. "Do you want me to leave?"

"No. I want you to get some sense. So you told all this to Jay, right?"

"Of course! I didn't want him wasting his time chasing down such a ridiculous case. And you're twisting this around. Just because you don't like Brent Blackhawk, you don't have to be so rude to him."

"I like the guy just fine."

"Then why be such a jerk?"

"Because I don't like what's going on around here."

"Because you can't beat up a ghost?" she demanded angrily.

He started to respond just as angrily, then paused. Hell, was that it?

"I'm sorry," he said coolly. "I'm afraid I don't believe in ghosts." Was that the truth? Or was he afraid of the truth.

Because she was dead right. How the hell did you fight a ghost?

"Then you don't believe in me," she said evenly, and started to turn. He was afraid she intended to leave. He caught her by the shoulders, pulling her around.

"Don't walk out on me," he pleaded softly.

"I wasn't walking out on you," she replied.

"All right, sorry. You were just so angry—"

"Yeah. So are you. But I wasn't walking out. You may not believe in me, but I'm sadly under the impression that this is what people call a relationship."

"Oh, hell! Of course it's a relationship," he snapped.

He pulled her into his arms. It was a relationship, all right. Anger just led to kisses that were heated, almost violent. She was just as wild, just as angry. Beautiful. Living alabaster. She touched him like burning lava, liquid and fluid, erotic and exotic; she excited and teased him, and finally sated him. When he held her in the end, in bed, he still felt the frustration, the anger, that he didn't know how to fight what was upsetting her.

Then she curled against him, flesh to flesh, her cheek resting on his chest. He stroked her hair and lay awake.

Audrey was barely inside the house with her shoes off when the doorbell rang. She let out a sigh, kicked the shoes aside and headed back.

She threw open the door and saw a familiar face. "Hey," she said. "What's up?"

He pushed his way in.

"Hey," she repeated, in irritated protest this time. "What the heck…?"

The door closed.

Her eyes widened. She was still entirely puzzled when he made his move.

By then, it was far too late to scream.

When at last he slept, Thor dreamed. In his dream, he saw a battle. Fierce and furious. A man with dark hair, in expensive nineteenth-century apparel, against another, more tattered, fiercer….

Shouts rang between the men, along with the clash of steel. Shouts, words, but he couldn't comprehend them.

He woke. As he woke, it seemed he could still hear the ringing of steel on steel

He realized Genevieve was wide-awake. She was lying in his arms, shaking, staring at nothing in the shadows of the night.

The sound faded and was gone, as if it had never been.

She realized he was awake and turned to him.

"She isn't at rest," she said softly. "Oh, God, she isn't at rest."

He just held her.

But he knew that when he stood, the floor would be flooded.

With seawater.

15

Whatever was happening, it wasn't good, Genevieve could tell that the moment she stepped outside.

Jay Gonzalez was at the tiki bar, deep in conversation with Victor, who was angry and gesturing emphatically.

Hoping Thor wasn't directly behind her, Genevieve hurried over, certain Jay was reaming Victor out about the mannequin business, and equally certain Victor was going to be furious with her.

He was. He shot her a cold glare as she neared them. "I'm trying to tell you, Jay, I don't know how the mannequin wound up in my room. I didn't take it. I didn't play the joke on Gen."

"But you do admit to dumping the pieces?" Jay said.

"Thanks," Victor muttered to Genevieve.

"Jay," Genevieve said. "I called you to stop a problem, not create one. I helped throw it away. I told you that."

Jay had his sunglasses on, so she couldn't read his eyes, but she knew he was irritated. "Genevieve, the problem is not that the mannequin was thrown away. It's not illegal to discard a mannequin. It isn't even illegal to pull it to pieces first. It is, however, illegal to steal a mannequin."

"I didn't steal it," Victor protested.

"Wait," Genevieve said. "When was it reported stolen?"

"When I made my initial inquiries, the staff at Key Klothing didn't know they were missing a mannequin. The owner called the station late last night. He'd figured it out, but he told me he thought some kids had spirited the thing out. He wasn't going to report it, but since we'd discovered the pieces, he wanted to let us know where it had come from."

"Key Klothing," Genevieve murmured. "That's right by Audrey's place."

"You're suggesting Audrey stole the mannequin?" Jay asked.

"No," Genevieve protested.

"Look, Jay," Victor said. "How long have you known me? If I wanted a mannequin, I wouldn't have stolen it. I know half the shopkeepers on Duval Street. I would have bought one. Are you really going to arrest me over this?"

"No. Not if you make good to the owner."

"But I didn't steal it!"

Thor would be joining them any minute, she knew, and she had to stop this before he got involved. She pushed her way between the two men. "Look, Victor, I'll pay for the damned thing. Let's just get it over with."

"But I didn't steal it."

"I believe you. But let's just make this end here and now. I'm begging you," Genevieve pleaded.

Victor stared at her, still indignant. "Genevieve, it might be important to find out who *did* steal it."

"Why?"

He shook his head. "I don't know. I only know that I didn't do it."

"Let's just make it go away, please? We have bigger problems. Please, Victor?" she said.

He let out a sigh. From the corner of her eye she saw that Thor was coming. She had to get this settled—*now*.

Victor shook his head. "Fine. I'll pay for it," he said.

"No, I will," Genevieve insisted.

"Don't be ridiculous."

"We'll argue about it later," she said. "Jay? Good enough?"

He nodded his assent just as Thor strode over to join them.

"Any word from Marshall?" Thor asked.

"No. But Gen's going to fill out a missing persons report today. Then we can do more than just have me calling old friends in Miami-Dade and asking for off-the-record help," Jay said.

"Something's wrong," Genevieve insisted.

"Or right. Maybe he's found the woman of his dreams," Victor said.

Genevieve shook her head. "This project meant too much to Marshall for him to just walk off it. He's a responsible person. He's built up a great reputation.

I can't believe he would slough it off all over some woman."

Thor nodded. He, too, was wearing dark glasses, so she couldn't read his thoughts.

At least he hadn't commented on the water, or the smell of the sea that permeated his cottage.

"I'm going to get some coffee," Thor said.

Genevieve's eyes followed him, and she saw that Adam was walking toward the tiki bar from the parking lot, and he had met up with the Blackhawks on the way. He looked upset.

Frowning, Genevieve hurried toward them.

"What's wrong?" she asked.

"Probably nothing," he said, forcibly easing the tension from his features as he tried to smile.

She shook her head. "Tell me."

"I'm sure Audrey just overslept—either that, or she simply forgot her appointment with an old man," he said lightly.

Genevieve felt her heart catapult. "You were supposed to meet Audrey?"

"For breakfast, yes," he admitted unhappily.

"And you went by her house? And she isn't answering?" Genevieve demanded.

"Please, don't panic," Nikki cautioned carefully. "Something important might have cropped up."

Genevieve spun around and rushed back to Jay. "Audrey's missing," she said flatly.

"Missing?" Victor said impatiently. "Don't be silly. I walked her home myself last night."

"She was supposed to meet Adam Harrison for

breakfast. She didn't show. And when he went to her house, she didn't answer the door. Jay, you have to do something."

"I can't just break into her house," Jay protested.

Genevieve whipped out her cell phone, staring at them all angrily. "What's the matter with you? Haven't you noticed that people around here keep disappearing!"

"Marshall hasn't disappeared. He called the station. Adults have the right to take off if they choose," Jay told her.

"That's a bunch of police crap," she snapped at him.

"I walked Audrey home, and she was fine," Victor said.

Genevieve had already punched in Audrey's number. It was ringing and ringing. The answering machine came on.

"Call me as soon as you get this," Genevieve said. Then she snapped the phone closed with dread in her heart.

Something was really wrong. Why couldn't they see it?

"I'm going over there," she said.

"Do you have a key?" Jay asked.

"No."

"Then what are you going to do? If you force your way in, I'll have to arrest you for breaking and entering," Jay said wearily.

"Please, Jay, I'm worried sick," Genevieve said.

He looked down. "I'm going to wind up fired after

all these years," he muttered. "You go out on your dive. I'll go to Audrey's place, okay? And if she's angry because I jimmied my way in, I'll never speak to you again. I won't be able to, because I'll be looking for a job slinging hash in a distant city!"

"Audrey would never get you in trouble. She'd know we were just worried," Genevieve promised.

Jay shook his head and started off. "She missed a breakfast meeting," he muttered. "As if we all haven't slept through breakfast at one time or another."

"C'mon. No lectures today. Let's get on the boats," Thor called out from the bar, where he was drinking his coffee. He didn't know anything about Audrey yet, Genevieve thought. Should she tell him, then insist they stay on shore for the day?

No, she decided. Jay would check on Audrey. And there would be some simple explanation. She hadn't been missing and out of action forever, not like Marshall.

She didn't need to put a hold on the dive. She could do her work; Jay could do his. He was a cop, and he was also a friend. He wouldn't let her down.

"Move!" Thor called.

When they reached the dock with their equipment, Thor started giving out their diving instructions for the day.

"Jack, stay topside on the police loaner. Bethany and Alex, as usual. Zach and Lizzie, you're with them. Victor…topside on my boat for the first dive, but we'll switch around later. Brent and Nikki, keep being a couple. Genevieve, you're with me. Everybody got it?"

There were nods all around, and they headed to the appropriate boats.

Genevieve noted that Adam wasn't there to watch them leave. She hoped he had gone with Jay and that, between the two of them, they would find Audrey. She fingered her cell phone, in the pocket of her cover-up. She couldn't take it down with her, but she would tell Victor to answer it if it rang.

Thor was at the helm. Genevieve chose a seat beside Nikki, who gave her hand a squeeze. "It will be all right."

"Will it?" Genevieve asked.

"Maybe the ghost is at rest."

"She isn't," Genevieve said flatly.

"No?"

"She still came to me in dreams," Genevieve said. "And she soaked the room while she was at it."

Nikki smiled gravely. "I'm telling you, she's here to help."

"Great."

Brent joined them in time to overhear the last part of the conversation, sitting next to Genevieve rather than his wife. "There *is* a reason," he assured her.

Victor sat next to Nikki. "Do ghosts steal mannequins and move things around?" he asked.

Genevieve wasn't sure if the question was genuine, or if he was just mocking them. Looking at him, she thought he was sincere.

He hadn't been the one to play the joke on her, she thought. But still, the niggling suspicion was there. Especially now that they had been caught getting rid of the mannequin.

Brent hesitated, looking at his wife before answering. "They have been known to gain the ability to move objects, but as to stealing a mannequin with a purpose...I don't know."

"What exactly *do* you know?" Genevieve asked.

"Please," she asked, to take the sting out of her words.

"Most of the time, spirits remain or return with a purpose. And usually that purpose is to aid the living in some way."

"Time to anchor and dive flag," Thor shouted, breaking off the conversation.

Genevieve quickly found her position and buckled on her tank.

On the platform, she glanced at Thor as she positioned her mask. He looked back at her, but she could read nothing in his eyes.

She realized she was dreading the dive.

She had forgotten her enthusiasm for the project, her love for what she did. All she was doing now was waiting.

Something else was going to happen. She was sure of it.

She stepped out into the water, felt her body fall, felt the rush of the sea around her. Bubbles surrounded her as she released air from her vest and began to sink.

Thor had moved them out into slightly deeper water today, she realized. They were following a path that led them past the reefs, then dropped down to deeper shelves.

She listened to the sound of her breathing. Slow and easy. She was proud of how long she could go on a single tank of air.

Look around, watch, feel, remember everything you love about this, she told herself.

But it wasn't working. The sense of dread that had first assailed her on the platform was growing. She found herself breathing far too quickly, too heavily. Her heart was hammering.

Small brilliant fish swept by her, unconcerned with anything but their next meal. The sun-kissed yellow of a tang, the stripes of a clown fish. To her side were dozens of pastel anemones, drifting in the easy flow of the current.

She was gaining control. The world beneath the waves was as it should be. A nosy barracuda was tracking them at a distance. Silver in the water, he stuck out his jaw, looking like a belligerent child. A giant grouper swam toward them, took a look, turned away.

Staghorn coral rose, followed by a field of brain coral. More anemones. More tiny, colorful, darting fish. A starfish began a slow trek across the sand. A tiny ray was disturbed by their passage and dug deeper into the sand.

She knew, her heart thundering, seconds before the body came into view that she was going to see it.

At first she denied it.

It was the ghost. Surely it was no more than the ghost, and she was there to lead Genevieve to the treasure, some new find....

But it wasn't the ghost.

It was real.

Like the body on the beach, this one was real.

Caught just the other side of a huge field of staghorn coral, this was not a ghost.

Not a mannequin.

Suddenly she felt a deepening certainty that it was Audrey.

Her heart seemed to scream. Her stomach pitched. Thor was just feet away from her, but she couldn't bring herself to reach out to him.

She didn't want to know.

She had to know.

She gave a thrust with her flippers and approached the body, desperate to know the worst.

Adam Harrison caught up with Jay before he left the parking lot.

Jay was annoyed. What the hell was with the guy? There was no reason for him to be so concerned so quickly.

Victor had walked Audrey home, undoubtedly made sure she was inside with her door locked before he left.

Then again, Audrey still wasn't opening her door. He'd tried her home phone, her cell and her business number, and there had been no response, only her cheerful normal voice on the first two, and her "business" voice on the last, explaining that it was very important to leave a message, then make an appointment to learn what the future held.

"Are you going in?" Adam demanded.

He'd promised Nikki he would. He had the tools in his car to pick a lock like Audrey's. He could do it easily enough.

"Shit," he swore out loud.

Adam Harrison just stared at him.

Jay threw his arms up in the air. "You're the great medium. Do I need to go in? Is she there? Is it life or death?"

"I'm sorry. I'm more of a coordinator than a medium," Adam said, totally unruffled. Of course he was unruffled, Jay thought. This wasn't his home, his life. These weren't his friends. Key West and all that happened here would fade from his memory once he stepped on a plane and moved on to the next... whatever.

"Are you going in?" Adam repeated.

Jay swore again, his language worse. He paced in a circle, then faced Adam.

"Yeah, what the hell. I can live on the fish I catch, I guess," he muttered. "Stay here."

He left Adam at Audrey's door and went to his car for his tools. He wondered just how discreetly he was going to be able to pick the lock. Genevieve had asked him to do this, he reminded himself. But frankly, Genevieve didn't have the right. *He* didn't have the right to do what he was about to do.

Probable cause…

Yeah, probable cause. Please, God, let someone else—like the brass—believe that was true.

He felt like a thief himself, as he carefully worked the lock.

"If you see anyone coming…" he started to tell Adam. Then he just swore again. "Never mind. What can they do? Call the cops? I *am* a cop."

The door opened. They both just stood there for a full minute.

"Audrey?" Jay called.

They stepped in. They both stood quietly at the entry for a moment. "Audrey?" Jay called again. "Don't touch anything," he told Adam.

"Of course not," Adam said with his customary smooth Southern dignity.

Jay walked through the small house. There was nothing to indicate there had been a struggle anywhere.

Until he picked the lock, he thought ruefully, there hadn't been any damage to the door whatsoever.

So, either Audrey had simply gone out…

Or she had let someone in. Who had then…

The bed was neatly made. Either Audrey had never gone to sleep the night before or she'd gotten up and made her bed this morning before heading out to…to not have breakfast with Adam Harrison. Nope, she must not have gone to sleep at all.

With a sinking heart, Jay walked back to Adam. He shook his head. "She didn't sleep here. But as you can see, there's no sign of a disturbance."

"Where do we go from here?"

Jay looked down with a sigh. "Lots of paperwork. I can't get started on Audrey till twenty-four hours have passed. At least Marshall has been gone long enough to be considered a missing person."

He walked past Adam, speaking aloud. "I need someone to agree to a crime-scene unit in here quickly. Shit! She opened her door to anyone with an appointment. Then again, she must have opened her door to someone really late, and now she's not here."

"I'll be combing the city," Adam said quietly as they left.

"Yeah, you do that," Jay muttered. "You just do that."

It slowly began to register on Genevieve, just as she swam around to see the corpse's face, that the woman was blond. Audrey was a brunette, with a touch of red in her hair, much like herself.

Not Audrey. *Not Audrey!*

For a moment the rush of relief eased the agony of what she was about to witness. Then the sad truth and blood-chilling horror set in again.

She'd never seen the woman before. She was wearing the bottom half of a bathing suit. Her breasts were bared.

Her eyes were open.

She stared at Genevieve in lifeless horror.

Genevieve blinked, freezing in the subtropic water. The woman was floating by the coral because she was attached to it. A rope around her ankles had tangled itself in the field of staghorn. Her ankles were chafed and bloody. She had fought desperately to free herself. She hadn't been killed where she was, Genevieve registered dully. The rope had broken off from whatever weight had originally held the woman beneath the water, but too late for her to escape.

The woman's bloody ankles were now of tremendous interest to dozens of fish, all swimming frantically about, taking tiny bites.

Genevieve's stomach heaved.

She nearly screamed, despite her regulator and the fact she was more than sixty feet beneath the surface, when hands fell on her shoulders. Startled, she turned.

Thor.

His expression was grave. He sternly indicated that she shouldn't touch the body, then signaled that she should surface. Her mind in a fog, she nodded. She realized he had summoned Brent Blackhawk, who had been exploring the seabed fifty feet to their left.

Brent swept effortlessly and silently over to them. Nikki in his wake.

Genevieve saw the horror with which the other woman viewed the floating corpse. But she immediately joined Genevieve and tugged her topside. Genevieve realized they had to radio in the information as quickly as possible, not that the police could possibly help the woman now, but she deserved justice.

As she swam upward alongside Nikki, Genevieve felt a new rush of ice in her veins again, wrapping around her heart.

Two bodies. Two blondes killed in the same way.

There wasn't just a killer loose in the Keys.

There was a serial killer at large.

For Thor, the worst part of it was the fact that he recognized the woman immediately.

She was the hooker who had propositioned him outside the hotel.

So recently alive, and now so newly dead.

He wasn't sure why he felt it was important to remain by the body until the police divers came, but he did. It seemed to take an eon. Brent Blackhawk stayed with them, neither of them touching anything, just staring into her sightless eyes until the police came.

A pall seemed to sit over the boat when they surfaced. They'd come here seeking treasure and history; they were finding horror and tragedy.

Jay Gonzalez was topside in a police craft that had tied on to Thor's boat. After doffing his scuba gear, Thor moved over to the other boat.

Jay looked grim. "It's definitely not Audrey, right?"

"Right."

"Thank God," Jay breathed.

"No sign of her yet?" Thor asked.

"None. Another body, no sign of Audrey or Marshall. What the hell is going on here?" he asked, sounding frustrated.

And scared.

"I recognized her," Thor told him.

"What? Who the hell is she?" Jay demanded.

"I don't know who she is, but I know what she did for a living."

"Another hooker?"

Thor nodded. "She was outside Adam's hotel the other day. I don't know if she was staying there or not, but she was looking for johns on the street." He hesitated. "I actually warned her to be careful."

"You didn't take her up on anything?"

Thor felt a bolt of anger surge through him. Then he realized Jay was only doing his job.

"No."

"All right, but she spoke to you, you knew she was a hooker, and you warned her to be careful. What then?"

"She told me she had to make a living. And that was all. She headed down Duval Street, toward the water and the bars, looking for customers. I'm assuming she found someone."

Jay nodded. "Yeah. She found someone, all right."

"Maybe the killer is getting sloppy. That would be something, at least," Thor said.

Jay winced. "In other words, this may have been going on for years, but he's getting careless and drowning the girls too close to shore?"

Thor nodded.

Jay nodded grimly in return. "Or maybe he's only just now made his way down to the Keys. Or he's just gotten started and he's an idiot incapable of securing a body to the ocean floor. Who knows? All I know is that now I've got two corpses, two missing persons, a bunch of ghost hunters—and no fucking answers." He looked across the water and shook his head. "Who the hell would have suspected, when Gen first thought she saw a body, that it would turn into this?" he asked morosely. He looked at Thor again. "You can take your crews in now. Tell them— all of them—that I may have some questions."

As he spoke, the police divers surfaced, one man calling out to him.

They had brought the body up on a light canvas stretcher designed to preserve whatever evidence might have remained on the corpse.

He heard a startled exclamation and looked around.

The borrowed police boat was anchored about twenty feet away. Lizzie, Zach, Bethany, Alex and Jack were standing at the stern, watching.

He didn't know who had cried out.

He looked over at his own boat.

Brent, Nikki, Victor and Genevieve were also staring at the sad remains of a life gone tragically bad.

"Take your crews in," Jay repeated curtly.

"Right. And you'll let me know the minute you find anything out?"

Jay stared at him. He could imagine what the man was thinking. *Yeah, right. I'm a cop, you're not. Count on it.*

Jay lowered his head. Maybe he'd regretted his own thoughts, unspoken but clear.

"Hell, yes, I'll get back to you. You'll just pull some of your government strings, if I don't, right?"

"I would appreciate it," Thor said simply, then hopped from hull to hull, returning to his own boat. He shouted out to Jack on the other vessel, "Bring her in."

There was silence as the boats raced across the water, returning to dock at the resort. The police boats weren't far behind.

News traveled fast. A crowd—being managed by uniformed officers—had formed around the docks.

Strangely, there was a sense of excitement in the air. As if people felt they were being a part of history, rather than witnessing a tragedy. News had traveled fast. It seemed everyone already knew it was another hooker who had been found, so as long as you weren't a hooker, you were safe.

Thor was still tying down when the police cruiser came in, when the corpse was removed from it in a body bag. One of the cops had been as sloppy as the killer.

The bag wasn't fully closed.

As two officers managed the weight, the top gave way. The woman's face was clearly visible, eyes still staring.

Thor heard a startled gasp from behind him.

He turned to see Bethany gaping at the corpse.

She saw him, and instantly, a shield came up over her eyes.

"You knew her?" he asked sharply.

She shook her head vehemently. "Knew her? No, I didn't know her."

"But you've seen her before?" he asked.

"Hell, yeah," Jack announced from behind them both. "She's Victor's blonde."

16

In his wildest dreams, Victor couldn't have imagined this.

The interrogation room was like those he had seen on television—stark.

And the way the detectives spoke to him... He kept wondering what the hell had happened to "innocent until proven guilty."

Jay wasn't there. He assumed the powers that be had decided Jay was too close to him, and that others should do the baiting. Because it *was* baiting, nothing more.

Detective Suarez was lean, dark and sharp-looking. Mertz...well, even without the name, Victor would have been reminded of Fred Mertz on *I Love Lucy*. Mertz was stout, balding and sixty-ish.

But he wasn't very funny.

"How many hookers have you done in?" Mertz demanded.

"Why did you kill her? And the one before?" Suarez asked.

"Don't be a jerk. This is a death penalty state.

Death penalty. We can keep you from the needle, Victor. We'll help you—if you help us."

"Where's your friend Audrey? What happened? She isn't the type you like to kill, so what happened? Did she suspect you were the murderer? You were walking her home, right? She said something, so you conned her into going with you so you could toss her overboard somewhere, too, is that it?" Mertz suggested.

"I didn't kill anyone!" Victor exploded, thinking back to the way he'd ended up here.

One of the officers had walked up to him pleasantly enough, explaining that they would be talking to everyone from the boats, because of the circumstances surrounding the finding of both bodies.

Of course, *he* knew the dead woman. Knew her in every sense of the word.

"I thought she liked me. I didn't know she was a hooker at first," he'd told Jay.

"They just want to talk to you at the station. Don't worry. It's routine. Help us out," Jay had told him. "Please."

So polite at first.

And now…

"She's dead, buddy," Suarez said. "That means you killed her."

"Yeah. That happens when you weigh someone down and dump them in the water," Mertz added.

"Talk to us. We'll help you," Suarez said.

"Come on, buddy. The others, they were strangers. Whores. You know what I mean? But Audrey was your friend," Mertz pressed.

"To the best of my knowledge, Audrey is alive and well."

"And missing," Mertz said.

"I walked her to her door. I watched her enter the house. I heard her lock the door after I left," Victor said.

"But then you went back," Suarez said.

"I did not," Victor protested.

"Imagine the needle slipping into your arm," Mertz warned. "They say it's better than Old Sparky. Hey, Suarez, remember when that guy went to the chair and his hair caught fire?"

"Yeah. Why the hell he had hair at an electrocution, I don't know," Suarez replied, shaking his head. "They say the needle is much better. They say you're unconscious before the heart goes into agony and the lungs shut down. But imagine what it must be like. Being strapped down. Feeling the needle. Knowing what's going on."

"For the last time, I didn't murder anyone, don't you get that?" Victor demanded.

"Was murdering a real woman kind of like chopping up that mannequin? Or are you going to tell us you didn't do that, either?" Mertz demanded.

"I need a lawyer," Victor said.

"You're not under arrest," Mertz said.

"Because you don't have any evidence, do you, assholes?" Victor demanded, standing. His temper had finally burst. "I'm out of here—unless you think you can arrest me."

Mertz grinned. "In that case, you're under arrest."

"For murder?" Victor asked incredulously.

"Theft," Suarez said with a shrug.

"What?" Victor said.

"The mannequin," Mertz said.

"But I didn't steal the mannequin," Victor protested.

"You broke it up and dumped it, right? Your friend Genevieve told Gonzalez all about it," Suarez reminded him.

"And she was going to pay for it, and no charges were going to be filed," Victor reminded them.

Suarez smiled grimly. "Imagine that. She was going to pay for it. Miss Wallace. She's a good friend, buddy. A real good friend. But she can't save you now. Trust me, we *will* find out the truth."

"If you want the truth, you should be out there looking for it. If you want to arrest me, do it—and get me a damned lawyer. If not, I'm leaving."

"We *are* going to arrest you," Mertz said.

Victor groaned.

"We've gotten the shopkeeper to file charges," Suarez informed him.

Victor slumped back into his seat.

"That is bullshit," he informed them.

"Hey, the mannequin was stolen. It was in your cottage. Miss Wallace found you breaking it up. Is that what you really wanted to do with the women you killed, Victor? Slice them up?"

"I didn't kill anyone," Victor said.

"We think you did. We think there are more."

"You think. *You think!* Think whatever you want,

but you don't have anything on me—you *can't* have anything on me—because I didn't do it." Was this how most confessions were obtained? Torture was no longer legal, so he'd heard, but with both these guys right on top of him...

Shit. He could begin to question his own sanity.

"But you did steal the mannequin," Mertz said.

"No, I didn't."

"You just chopped it up. *Murdered* it. Like you murdered those hookers."

"If I'm under arrest, I want a lawyer. Now."

"You should talk to us. We can get you a deal, keep you from the needle. No matter how many hookers you've killed," Mertz said.

Victor gritted his teeth. "I want a lawyer. Now. I know my rights." An idea occurred to him. "Hey, you guys forgot to read me my Miranda rights."

Score one for him. The detectives stared at each other.

Mertz began to drone out the Miranda rights.

Damn Genevieve. What had made her feel she had to go to Jay, confess that they had ditched the mannequin? She couldn't have known it would come to this. Still...

His hands twitched.

He fought the urge to throttle her.

Because everyone was talking, because everything was such a disaster, Genevieve had suggested they all get showered and cleaned up and come over to her house.

"A party?" Bethany had asked incredulously.

"No! But the police said they're going to question us, so they can find us all there."

The look on Thor's face had indicated that he wasn't fond of the idea, but she had already spoken. And so, by the late afternoon, they had all gathered at her place.

They talked in circles. "So what do you think Marshall having disappeared has to do with all this?" Alex asked.

"I wonder why they haven't called the rest of us in," Bethany murmured.

"I wonder why the hell they're keeping Victor so long," Jack mused aloud.

"I'm going to call the station and find out what's going on," Genevieve said, starting to rise.

Thor, at her side, placed a hand on hers. "What do you think?" he asked dully.

"They can't seriously suspect Victor," she said, horrified.

"They can," Brent said, leaning forward. "Genevieve, Victor knew the woman you found."

"So what? That's just circumstantial. I think."

"Right. And Victor would be smarter. He would have done a better job getting rid of the body," Bethany said.

"Bethany!" Genevieve protested angrily.

"What? It's not like I think Victor did this," she protested.

"No, it wasn't Victor," Alex said.

"No way," Jack agreed.

"You guys don't have any answers?" Lizzie asked, staring at Brent and Nikki.

"If we had them," Brent said, "trust me, we'd be sharing them."

They all nearly jumped sky-high when Thor's cell phone rang.

"Thompson," he said briefly.

He rose as he listened to the speaker, pacing toward the front of the house.

Out of earshot, Genevieve thought.

He snapped his phone shut after a minute. "I'm going to see Professor Sheridan," he said. "I'll be back. If anyone hears anything…"

"We'll call you right away," Lizzie promised.

Looking at him, Genevieve nodded.

She was surprised when Brent stood. "Mind if I go along?"

She was even more surprised when Thor studied him for a minute, then shrugged. "Suit yourself." He turned to the others.

"See you soon," he said to the room in general. Then he hesitated, before looking back at Genevieve. "Let's take a ride somewhere later tonight, huh?"

"All of us?" Bethany asked, frowning.

"I meant Genevieve," Thor said.

"Bethany, they want to be alone," Alex said.

"Oh! Of course," Bethany said. But then she frowned. "Now? In the middle of all this?"

"If Victor is delayed, Bethany, you can room with Brent and me," Nikki said.

"Thanks, but—"

"I can get you a room at the hotel," Adam said, sensing her unease.

"Thank you, but I'm sure Victor will be back." Her words carried more conviction than her tone.

"Adam, want to come along?" Thor asked, really stunning Genevieve.

"I'll keep watch here, thanks," Adam said. "In fact, I'm quite capable in the kitchen. I'll throw something together for dinner."

"All right. We'll be back," Thor said.

Genevieve watched him go with growing concern. Audrey was missing. Marshall was still a no-show. Victor was down at the police station—and their group had now discovered two corpses.

She didn't know what was going on, but she knew it sucked.

"That was Sheridan on the phone?" Brent asked as they drove.

"Yes."

"And...? This have something to do with the murders?"

"No. He's started working with some of the letters from the box Gen found. He's treating them with something—I don't really understand the preservation of paper—and he's been translating them from Spanish into English." Thor shrugged. "He's...an oddball. The type who feels you live by the sword, you die by the sword, and those women were living by the sword due to their profession. The present never interests him much. His biggest feeling seems to be irritation that the murders are disrupting the dive."

Brent lifted a hand. "Some people are like that."

There were several long moments of silence before Thor turned abruptly to Brent. "You know a lot about…ghosts, right?" he asked, unable to keep his tone from being slightly dry.

"I know this is really hard for you. That you aren't the type to believe in anything except what you see and touch yourself."

"You just made me sound completely closed-minded."

Brent grinned easily. "I didn't mean that. It's a tough world. You're a pretty tough guy. I wouldn't expect you to believe in the occult. You're a man who makes his living in the real world. It wouldn't do a lot for your reputation if you went around talking about pirate ghosts."

"I try not to spend my time protecting my reputation," Thor said.

"We do that to an extent. How do you think Adam has acquired his contacts and his ability to slip his people in wherever he chooses?" Brent asked.

"Okay, you've got a point. But what the hell good is any of this doing? Genevieve sees ghosts—but I don't think it's any ghost murdering those women. So where is any of this getting us?"

"I'm hoping what Sheridan has discovered might be of some help," Brent said.

"I hope so, too. Though, realistically speaking, I don't see how it can solve the current problem."

"I've never claimed to have all the answers," Brent said.

"No, you haven't," Thor murmured. He bore a grudging admiration for the other man that continued to grow. He had an ability to hold his temper and still stand his ground.

"Tell me more about Adam Harrison," Thor said abruptly.

"Adam? The last of the great gentlemen?" Brent said gruffly, his affection for the man evident. He lifted his hands. "He was born on a working plantation in Virginia to a family with a long history in politics. His wife died soon after the birth of their only son, and his son was killed in an accident after his high school prom. He was kind of like Harry Houdini, I guess, desperate to believe there was life after death."

"To the best of my knowledge, Houdini spent most of his life unmasking charlatans," Thor commented.

Brent smiled noncommittally.

"And he never made it back himself?"

"I have no idea."

"So you can't summon up whoever you choose?"

"No."

"I see."

"No, actually, you don't, and you don't need to humor me. I don't really care if you believe in an afterlife or not," Brent said. "I'm not trying to argue.

I just know what I can and can't do, and your opinion isn't going to change it any."

"So Harrison Investigations is completely on the up-and-up?" Thor murmured.

"I'm sure you know it is. I'm sure you used some of your own contacts to check."

"Of course I did."

"But you still don't really trust us."

"You're ghost hunters."

"We're not con men," Brent said.

"I'm still trying to figure out what the story is with my seeing a boy claiming to be Josh Harrison," Thor said.

"You probably did see Josh," Brent told him casually.

"A ghost."

"Yes, a ghost."

"Josh Harrison, son of Adam, ghost," Thor murmured. "I guess you're going to tell me you've seen him, too."

"I'm seeing him right now."

"Excuse me?" Thor demanded, his brow furrowing.

"He's in the back seat."

"What?"

Thor turned around.

He nearly drove off the highway.

Brent was telling the truth.

The boy was seated in the back seat, right behind Brent.

"Shit!" Thor gasped.

"Maybe I should drive," Brent said.

* * *

"All right," Jack said, rising. "I can't do this. I can't just sit around. Anyone want to join me? I'm going to hit some of the bars and find out myself if anyone has seen Audrey anywhere, or if she said anything to anyone."

"I'm going to try Audrey's numbers again, just in case," Genevieve said. She pulled out her cell, since she felt the need to pace while she talked.

All three numbers rang until Audrey's recorded voice asked for a message.

Genevieve flipped the phone shut, shaking her head.

"So we look for her," Jack said.

"If she had her phone...if she were reachable...she'd answer. She'd call me," Genevieve said. "I'm so worried."

"C'mon, she's a brunette, not a blonde. Just like you, Gen," Alex pointed out.

"And she's a quack, not a hooker," Jack reminded them cheerfully.

"I'm still worried," Genevieve said.

Jack walked over and gave her a hug. "We all are. And I'm restless. I know she's probably not barhopping, but we're not doing any good, all of us sitting around here, just waiting. We'll see if she did run into someone else. Who knows, maybe there's a relative somewhere we don't know about who suddenly called because they needed her. Maybe she had to go to the aid of one of her clients. Maybe she really conjured up a ghost or...well, who the hell knows. But maybe, just maybe, we can find something out. Anyone want to join me?"

Zach rose, reaching a hand down to his wife. "Sure. Though we don't know the locals like you do."

Alex rose. "Yeah, we need to do something." He looked at Genevieve ruefully. "I think I need to move, too. I'm going to go with Jack, too, if you're okay."

"I'm fine. But I'm going to hang in here until I hear from Victor or Thor."

Bethany laughed. "I'm staying with my new best friend," she said, indicating Adam.

"We'll call you if we hear anything," Jack promised as he and the others filed out.

There was silence for a minute after they left. Then Genevieve picked up the plates. Adam had concocted an interesting hash out of the leftovers from the barbecue, and everyone had eaten heartily. "I'll just put these in the kitchen," she said.

Nikki rose with her. "I'll help. Move it along." She glanced at Adam. "Actually, Gen, there's something we'd like you to try."

"Oh?"

"Hypnosis," Adam said, rising.

Genevieve nearly dropped the plates she was carrying, staring from one of them to the other.

"Past-life regression, or something like that," Bethany said.

Adam hesitated. "I don't know exactly what we'll discover. But I can question you while you're under, and maybe…. Don't be worried. We choose a safety word before you go under. That word will bring you back to the present, wide-awake, if you find yourself under duress."

Her hands were shaking and she didn't know why. Bethany stood and took the plates she was holding from her. "No reason to break the china," she said cheerfully.

"I won't do this unless you're entirely willing," Adam said.

"I…I am willing. If it can help. I'm willing to do just about anything," she said. She lifted her hands. "What do I need to do?"

"Just relax, and trust me. Nothing more," Adam said.

"That's what all the guys say," Bethany teased.

They all smiled. Then Genevieve looked seriously at Adam.

"I do trust you," she said.

"Then we'll begin."

Terrified he was going to kill himself and Brent and whoever else might be on the road, Thor forced himself to stay calm and drove onto the shoulder. They were almost at the lab, but he needed a break.

Throwing the car into Park, he looked in the back seat again.

It was empty.

He stared at Brent.

"There was just someone in the back seat," he said.

"Yes," Brent agreed.

"He's gone now."

"He probably thought you were about to have a heart attack."

"I nearly drove off the damned road."

"Yes, I noticed that." Brent smiled.

"I don't fucking believe in ghosts! What the hell is this bull you all are pulling on everyone? Smoke and mirrors. How the hell are you doing it?"

Brent didn't flinch. He just stared at him. "You tell me," he said, calm, quiet. "You're a logical man. You figure it out. Maybe there *are* things in this world that you can't explain. Maybe there really *was* a ghost in your back seat."

"I don't believe in ghosts," Thor repeated stonily.

"Okay. Don't believe in them. But shouldn't I drive?" Brent asked.

"We have about four blocks to go," Thor said. "I can drive."

He pulled back out onto the road. He didn't want to look into the rearview mirror, but he couldn't help himself.

The kid was back, staring at him.

"You're not there," he snapped.

And then he drove on. Cautiously.

A strange wind was blowing. She was accustomed to the sea, loved the sea, and yet today something in the air was disturbing…frightening.

Or was fear creating the disturbance within her own spirit?

No one believed her, not even her own father. But then again, he was such a liar. Yet, she dared not decry him too passionately, lest the truth be known. And the truth was far worse....

She stared toward the horizon, certain help would come.

Then she turned and looked nervously at the ship's guns. There seemed to be so many. She was a proud ship, but the ocean was vast, and any ship, no matter how proud, was but a speck on the sea.

She turned around, aware of the wind, and also aware of something else.

Silence.

A strange and eerie silence. The ship shouldn't be quiet.

A sensation of evil crept along her spine. She looked slowly around her. There should have been men in the rigging. The wind was changing and the men should have been shouting to one another, hurrying to trim the sails.

Not a single sailor was topside.

But he was.

Staring at her. With that smile she hated so much.

"What's going on? Where is everyone?" she demanded.

"Gone," he said simply, and smiled more broadly.

The chill along her spine became glacial.

"What do you mean, 'gone'?"

"They wanted to swim," he said pleasantly, approaching her. Slowly. Still keeping his distance. He was enjoying himself.

She watched him very carefully, then looked to the horizon again.

Maybe she was hoping, maybe it was real, but she thought she saw another ship on the horizon. But the weather was changing so quickly. Calm seas began to roil. A mist seemed to have suddenly sprung up over the water, a sure sign of changing temperatures.

She was worrying about a storm, she realized, while he…

She was worrying about a storm rather than face the truth.

"You have…you have taken over the ship? But…the men are loyal to…"

"Seamen, dear girl, are most often loyal to the highest bidder," he commented. "You forget the port from which we have just come. And that new men had to be hired on to replace those who took ill so seriously—and so suddenly. You forget so much—my dear."

"I forget nothing! You, sir, lived in the recesses of your mind and imagined truth where there was none."

"You betrayed me."

"Never."

"You betrayed us."

"There was no 'us' for me to betray."

He shook his head. "It doesn't matter anymore. History will tell the tale. And it will be the truth. The pirate destroyed all."

Her eyes widened.

It was then that she saw what he was about. Saw the two men emerge from behind a pile of rigging.

One was huge, with burly arms. She'd seen him

before, when the first mate had been railing at him for some dereliction of duty.

He was winding a length of thick rope.

The second man dragged a canvas bag of ballast with him.

"You should have loved me," he said softly.

She turned, desperate to crawl over the railing and cast herself into the sea while some margin of hope remained.

Too late.

She felt their hands, dragging her back.

She screamed. Screamed as if the sound could break the heavens, penetrate earth and sky, somehow bring salvation. But they were on her. Huge and heavily muscled. She had not a prayer. She knew that when the first blow struck her cheek and she went reeling. She fought the loss of consciousness, knowing her fate, disbelieving, and yet still…

Knowing.

There was a ship on the horizon. A distance away, still, but closing. Oh God, oh God, dear Father in Heaven, forgive me…

The rope was tied securely around both her ankles and the bag of ballast. Still, she bit, scratched, screamed, cursed….

She was lifted.

As she hit the water, she heard the first boom of cannon fire.

17

Sheridan's real facilities were in the northern part of the state. Still, he had managed to do a good job of making it look as if he had kept a research lab in town for at least a decade.

A grad student sat sentinel in the antechamber; specialists the professor had called here were busy at various locales throughout the complex of rooms—too many, Thor thought, considering the few artifacts they had turned up thus far.

Sheridan led Thor and Brent into his office, ignoring his people as if they were no more than honeybees buzzing around, expected to produce.

"The letter was written by Anne, and signed with a flourish. She had lovely penmanship," Sheridan told them, warming to his subject. His desk was laden with papers and books. Thor wasn't quite sure how the man could find anything.

Sheridan looked up at them triumphantly. "There was far more going on than one might have expected," he announced.

"Like what?" Thor asked.

"I'll read you my translation. The ink was poor in a few spots, but…imagine, almost perfectly preserved after all these years."

"Professor, if you would?" Thor said, trying to hide his impatience.

He didn't need Sheridan going all intellectually ADD on him at the moment. He'd been trying to keep it together since he'd slammed his way out of the car.

Who would have expected this dive would be the one on which he found the woman he loved.

And lost his mind.

If he'd seen a ghost, he should be considering a long vacation. If he hadn't seen a ghost, something criminal was going on with Adam Harrison and his gang.

He stopped thinking and started listening when Sheridan began to read.

Today I awoke afraid, as I had not been before. I was aghast at the lies being told, yet did not dare to utter the truth.

But I know he will come.

And for all that is reputation and all that is legend about the man, I know that one thing is true: his love for me. He will see the battle is swift and sure. He will see that the good do not die. He will be merciful. For me.

But while I wait, I am afraid, so I will write my prayers.

Sheridan stopped speaking and looked up at them as if he had just translated the Dead Sea Scrolls.

"That's it?" Thor asked.

"Yes, that's it!" Sheridan exploded. "Can't you see? There was a conspiracy going on aboard the *Marie Josephine*. Of course, I don't know why Anne was afraid, who she feared, or who she thought would come to her rescue, but...we will know more. I'll continue translating what I have, and you'll bring me more."

"Professor," Thor reminded him, "another body has been discovered."

"Yes, yes, sad."

"There's a killer loose in the Keys," Brent commented.

Sheridan stared at him, frowning. "And you're professional salvage divers. What's going on is sad, but I don't see why it has to delay your work."

"I'm afraid it's going to have to, Professor," Thor said. "The police have asked us to keep the area clear until they've had time to look for evidence."

"But you can help them—while you look for the *Marie Josephine*," Sheridan said.

"I'll get back to you as soon as I have more information," Thor told him, cutting the conversation short.

Sheridan rose. "We're working on grant money, you know. This lab...it costs a fortune to run. We've got to get back to work. We're going to need much more to justify our expenses."

"I'll keep you posted, I promise," Thor told him.

As they left the offices, Thor tossed the keys to Brent, who caught them, looking surprised. "Just drive," Thor said wearily.

To Victor's amazement, they didn't arrest him. Even after they had said they were going to do so.

Suarez was the one who let him go, after having shut him in the interrogation room alone for at least an hour.

He released him simply, opening the door, popping in his head. "You can go."

"What?" Victor said sharply.

"Leave. You can go."

"I thought you were pressing charges against me?"

Suarez shrugged. "Change of heart. I just work here."

Victor rose, telling himself that they didn't have a damn thing on him, and they couldn't get the owner of Key Klothing to press charges.

As he walked past Suarez, he felt his every muscle tightening, and he couldn't stop himself from saying, "I may be suing. False arrest!"

"You were never arrested."

"Police brutality, then."

"We never touched you."

"Mental cruelty."

"Hey, buddy, we're not getting divorced or anything here," Suarez protested.

"I promise you, I'll have my eye on you," Victor threatened.

"Funny. I was about to say the same thing."

Victor lifted his chin. He decided it was time to beat a hasty retreat before the detective found another reason to detain him.

Audrey awoke. Her mind was in a pea-soup haze. She was tied up, nearly smothering, and in pain, but she couldn't figure out where she was, or how she had gotten there.

Then it all began to come back to her.

She was terrified, trapped in tight quarters, a gag in her mouth, the lingering thud of the drug in her head, and the bindings chafing at her wrists and ankles.

As the fog cleared, she became more aware of her position.

She could barely breathe, down here in the hold; she needed to keep still, to save her oxygen.

Despite that, she cried. Wet tears that slid down the grime on her cheeks.

She remembered how it had happened, step by step.

And realized she was going to die.

So far…just the torture. Inflicted because her attacker had an ego that seemed to know no bounds.

How much more torture?

Could she do anything…play into it?

She wondered if air could get in? She realized all the things she didn't know about the sea, about boats.

She was going to die. When the game of torturing her grew old.

She could only put it off….

She resolved to herself that she *would* put it off. She would play along, say anything—good God, *do* anything—if it could keep her alive for one more minute.

Someone would finally figure it out, surely.

She wasn't the one he had really wanted, she knew. She was just a poor substitute.

Substitutes were so expendable….

No!

She had to fight, had to stay alive, say anything, do anything….

Oh, God.

Genevieve. Eventually she, too, would be here. And she, too, would die.

Despite the circumstances, Genevieve appeared to be in the best of spirits as she opened the door to see Thor and Brent standing on her porch.

"Victor is out," she said first, without preamble.

"Oh?" Thor asked cautiously.

"They have nothing on him, of course," she said indignantly.

He cleared his throat. "He was the last one seen with her."

"But ask Bethany—he couldn't have been with her long because he got back to his cottage too quickly," Genevieve said with a wave of her hand. "I'm onto something, though, but first—" she looked past him, smiling at Brent "—what did Sheridan have to say?"

"That there's more to this than meets the eye,

basically. Our Anne left letters in the box. She was afraid of someone. And she was waiting for someone else to come and give her assistance. It's kind of convoluted. She goes on about some truth, but the truth is worse than a lie. He's only translated one of the letters so far."

Genevieve smiled. "I have the truth," she told them.

"Oh?" Thor said.

"Come on in and sit down," she said.

"Any word of Audrey?" Brent asked.

Genevieve's brilliant smile collapsed. "No."

Adam, Nikki and Bethany were in the parlor. Someone had apparently just brewed tea.

"Want something?" Genevieve asked.

Thor's stomach was growling, but he shook his head. Information first. "Give us what you know," he told her.

"Anne wasn't desperately in love with Aldo. She despised him," Genevieve announced.

"Oh?" Thor said skeptically.

Genevieve nodded. "I don't know if you remember or not, but I've done a lot of reading on the *Marie Josephine*. Some of the letters and memoirs were written by pirates who sailed with Gasparilla, and they talked about his deep love for Anne. Remember there was the suggestion that Gasparilla hated being scorned, that he might have killed Anne? Well, he didn't. He tried to save her. There was a mutiny on board the *Marie Josephine*. Aldo— the supposed great love of Anne's life—was the one who killed her. Gasparilla was on his way to save her. He'd promised to do his best not to kill the crew and to see that her father was safe. But he was too late. Aldo was the one who couldn't bear the fact Anne had scorned him. He murdered her. In the same way these women were murdered now. He weighted her down and threw her overboard. Gasparilla was on his way. He attacked the ship, found the crew dead and battled the mutineers. The *Marie Josephine* was already breaking apart. Cannon fire did her in. Well, I'm speculating on some of this, but I swear I'm right."

Thor stared at her, frowning. "How do you know all this?"

"It was incredible," Bethany breathed.

"What was incredible?" Thor asked.

"She went back. She lived it all as Anne," Bethany said.

Thor felt his temper rising. This was ridiculous, so why did he feel…

Fear?

"What the hell are you talking about?" he demanded. He stared at Genevieve hard, then turned his glare on Adam Harrison.

"Hypnosis," Adam said evenly.

"What?" Thor exploded.

"Thor, stop it," Genevieve said. "Please."

"Hypnotism is a valuable tool," Nikki said. "People have quit smoking with the help of hypnosis. They've lost weight, made other important changes in their lives."

Thor wasn't appeased. "Go on."

"I simply painted a picture of the day," Adam said. "Then I asked Genevieve questions."

"You should have heard her. It was like she was living it." Bethany was so obviously still under the spell of what she'd seen.

Smoke and mirrors. The power of suggestion. Maybe it was all a form of hypnotism.

He folded his arms over his chest. "Great. You think you know what happened on the ship."

"It makes sense," Genevieve said. "And," she pointed out, "it fits in with everything Sheridan was telling you. Just wait," she said stubbornly. "Wait until he's read more of the letters. You'll find out I'm right."

In this group, he wasn't going to win so he simply ignored the topic and moved on.

"So Victor has been released. What about Audrey? Any word from the cops on the identity of the corpse? Or from Marshall?"

Genevieve's face fell. She shook her head. "Jack, Alex, Lizzie and Zach went out right after you left. They were going to see if Audrey was out…if anyone ran into her, if she said anything to anyone…anything at all."

"You haven't heard back from them?" Brent asked.

Genevieve shook her head. "But I can just call them."

"No, they'd have called you if they'd discovered anything. Want to head out with me?" he asked.

She frowned, her eyes indicating that she had company. "Where?"

"Miami," he said. "We're going to see if we can't find out something about Marshall." She kept staring at him. "We're not getting anywhere here," he added quietly.

"Are you going to drive all the way to Miami and back today? It is kind of late. And what about the dive?" Bethany asked.

"Sheridan doesn't seem concerned about the dead women," Thor admitted dryly. "But we have to leave the area to the cops for another day. That's assuming they'll sanction us going back down on Thursday. We'll be back by tomorrow night."

"Hey, Gen. I'm just leaving with these guys," Bethany called, interrupting them. She smiled assurance to Genevieve. "Don't worry. I'm sticking to this group like chewed gum on the bottom of a shoe."

"Keep in touch," Brent told Thor.

"Actually, we *are* getting somewhere," Genevieve said as soon as everyone else was gone. "And I want to get hold of Helen—that reporter who's Father Bellamy's main squeeze. I want her to do a story about what happened on the ship."

"We don't know anything yet," Thor reported.

"I'll have her write it up as my theory," Genevieve told him.

"You can call her from the car," Thor said curtly. He was suddenly in a hurry to get out of here.

He needed a little distance from all the insanity.

But could they really get away?

Or would they be followed?

By…? he taunted himself.

Ghosts.

He was back.

Audrey could hear his footsteps overhead.

From the noises, it sounded as if he were getting ready to take the boat out.

Oh, God!

It was time. If they went out to sea…

She could fight. Yes, now that she knew, she could fight.

And never win. Look where she was right now.

So this was it.

Tears sprang into her eyes again.

But then, very distantly, a phone began to ring. His cell.

She couldn't hear his words, only that he had answered, and his tone was as blithe as if he had a fish in his hold.

Then the noises stopped.

He had left the boat.

A reprieve?

The heat was terrible. She was sure her air was almost gone, although she kept trying to tell herself that oxygen was getting in to her somehow. The boards were wet beneath her. The whole place stank of fish.

She was going to smother or roast before she could drown, she thought.

Then a prayer rushed into her heart. No, no, I didn't mean it. I will survive. I *will*. Don't let him come back…!

"Are you sure this is a good idea?" Genevieve asked, settling into the passenger seat of his car. "I mean…should we be gone right now?"

He set his hand on hers where it lay on her lap. "I know you're worried sick about Audrey, and with all that's been going on, you have good reason. But everyone is out looking for her. I don't even begin to know where to start. It makes sense to take a trip to Miami. Marshall wasn't checked into the hotel his call came from. When I met with him to set up this dive, we met in Coconut Grove. There's public dockage there. I thought we would do some club-hopping on the beach tonight and rent a boat tomorrow. We can search the yacht clubs, marinas and waterways for his boat."

She nodded. "That's very logical. But by now, haven't the local police notified their associates up there? Aren't they on the lookout?"

"He's probably not at a public marina," Thor acknowledged. "But you can be certain law enforcement in Miami-Dade isn't seeing this as a serious situation. I'm not saying anything negative about them, but they've got their hands full with local crime, and they're not going to be overly concerned with a grown man who may have disappeared of his own volition."

"You're right," she admitted, then looked at him.

"So you have a plan. And here I was thinking you just wanted to get the hell out of Key West," she teased.

"That, too," he admitted. "We'll be gone twenty-four hours. Okay?"

She nodded.

"You feel all right?" he asked.

She laughed out loud. "Do you mean, am I slipping in and out of another lifetime? Do I have a ghost on my lap?"

He grinned at her through the rearview mirror.

He also checked out his back seat.

It seemed they were alone.

He was starving, so they stopped in Plantation Key for dinner, then moved on.

There were no traffic problems on US1 that night, and by the time they reached Miami, it was well past rush hour.

They checked into the Mayfair in Coconut Grove. Thor was in a hurry to go out, but Genevieve insisted that if they were hitting the clubs on South Beach, she had to shower and change.

Thor wound up joining her in the shower. And then they wound up slick and soapy and together.

Slick, soapy, and flesh to flesh, steam rising all around them. They were alone. In a massive marbled bathroom. With a huge king-size bed just beyond.

The bed wound up damp and just a bit slick, as well. Thor found himself wondering what it was about one particular woman that could make the rest of the world fade away. Sex, yes. The rise of excitement created by something so small as a smile, a touch…

A body, slick and soapy.

And still…

It was her. Everything about her. Her eyes, her smile. The shape of her face. The way her fingers felt against his. Little things he knew she would do. The way the palm of her hand felt against his buttocks, the way her lips felt on his, the way she teased with just the tip of her tongue…

The heat that exuded from her body, the very scent of her so unique…

Later, as he lay looking at the ceiling, he knew he was in love with her. Thor would accept anything in the world if…

But…ghosts?

There seemed to be none around them that night. Her fingers played across his chest for a moment as they lay there, just breathing, hearts slowing. "It's a good thing that prime time at the clubs is in the middle of the night," she murmured.

He leapt up. "Shower first—don't come in," he warned.

She laughed. But she waited dutifully until he was out. Then she rushed in.

She really had her virtues—beyond beauty, sensuality, diving ability and her smile. She could get ready faster than any woman he had ever met.

"All right, we're out of here," he said.

He was amazed to discover he had fun. He was

pretty sure, despite the fact that he might have been recognized a time or two, that they were admitted to every club without hesitation—despite occasionally lengthy lines—because of the way Genevieve looked and smiled.

At first, and well past midnight, it seemed they were on nothing more than a club-hopping tour. They danced. They paid exorbitant prices for drinks. He became best friends with lots of cocktail waitresses, while Genevieve flirted with bartenders, describing Marshall and asking if they'd seen him anywhere. Several knew him, but no one had seen him recently.

They found out nothing useful. Thor's frustration must have shown, because Genevieve slipped her arm around him and said, "Hey, it was a good idea. We did find out most of the bartenders know him, so if he *had* been there…"

They wandered into a little place on Washington, a piano bar.

It was much quieter than the places they had been. The pianist was good, the audience sedate.

He and Genevieve took seats at a small table toward the back. They ordered coffee, despite the fact that they would be heading back to the hotel soon to sleep. Hell, he needed to stay awake enough to find their way back.

"There has to be an explanation for his disappearance. He's not a prostitute—hell, he's not even an attractive woman," he said, trying to lighten the mood.

"Do you think he really called the police?" Genevieve asked worriedly. "You don't think that he was…I don't know, abducted for a different reason, and someone faked the call?"

"I don't know what to think," he admitted.

She was folding and unfolding her napkin. "I'm worried about Marshall, but…I'm even more worried about Audrey. She *is* an attractive young woman."

She stared straight at him then. "I'm worried, too," he admitted.

She smiled wanly, placing her hand on his. "Still worried about me?" she asked, and he knew she was referring to her sanity.

He didn't have a chance to reply. A soft female voice broke in on them.

"Gen? Genevieve Wallace?"

He turned as Genevieve looked up. They had been approached by a couple who had apparently been leaving but stopped at the sight of Genevieve, who frowned, before her face lit up in a smile.

"Kathy!" She grinned at Thor, who rose quickly as Genevieve introduced her friend. "Kathleen O'Malley, Thor Thompson. Thor, Kathy and I went to school together. She's an escaped Conch. And George." She rose, too, kissing the man on the cheek. "George Ryder," she said in a rush, remembering she was doing the introductions. "George also went to school with me."

Kathy laughed. She was tiny, with blond ringlets. George was taller, and very lean. He shook Thor's hand. "You're the diver, right? I've seen you in magazines."

Thor nodded. "Can you stay a minute? I'll draw up a few chairs."

"Yes, thanks," Kathy said. "Oh, we're both Ryders now. George and I got married four years ago."

"I had no idea," Genevieve said warmly, taking her seat again. "Congratulations. Weren't you voted 'Couple Most Likely to Stay Together'?"

George arched a brow. "Oh, stop," Kathy said, laughing. "Gen, you look wonderful. But I thought I read that you were on some dive now? Did you two escape or something? The prostitute murders down there have made the news up here. They just found a second girl, right?"

Genevieve nodded.

"Be careful down there. No wonder you guys wanted to come up here for a break," Kathy said.

"Hey," Genevieve said. "You know Marshall—my boss?"

Again, Kathy smiled. She seemed unfailingly cheerful, Thor thought. "Sure. He used to humor us all the time when we were kids. I still love boats and diving because of him. We came up here because George was going to law school at the University of Miami, and then he got a job up here...but I still miss the Keys. Anyway, yes, I remember Marshall."

"You haven't run into him anywhere up here recently, have you?" Thor asked.

Kathy shook her head. She was obviously the speaker. George was the quiet one.

"No, no, sorry. He isn't down there with you? Hard to believe Marshall would play hooky. I remember him telling us he'd have his own company one day, just like the big-time salvage guys. He managed it, too."

"Yes, he did," Genevieve murmured.

"Wow, imagine, running into you," Kathy said. "Of course, the distance isn't all that great, but I haven't been all the way down to Key West in years. We escape to Key Largo a lot, but that's just an hour away. Much easier when you only have a weekend here and there."

"I know. I almost never get up here," Genevieve said.

"Actually," George said, breaking in suddenly, "it's strange to run into you tonight. I've been thinking about you and Bethany and Victor. I thought you might be affected by what was going on."

"The murders, you mean?" Thor asked, frowning.

"Yes," George agreed, nodding gravely. "Do you remember back when we were in school? We were seniors, I think, when the paper had a spread on that woman who was on her way to being a super-model. Remember?"

"Yes, she just up and disappeared," Genevieve said.

"It's been bugging me," George said.

"Wasn't there something in the paper last year about another woman who disappeared? Did they ever find her?" Kathy asked, wide-eyed.

"Not that I know of," Genevieve said. "I should ask Jay."

"Jay," Kathy said. "Poor guy. He loved his wife so much. Did he ever remarry?"

"He's not married. If he's even dating, I don't know about it."

"Send him our love, will you?" Kathy asked.

"Of course," Genevieve said.

Kathy looked at her watch. "Yikes! We'd better get going. George's cousin is home with the baby. Oh, we have a little boy—George, of course," she said, rolling her eyes.

"Congratulations again," Genevieve told her.

"I wish we had seen you earlier. This was wonderful," Kathy said, rising. George and Thor did the same and Genevieve, too, got to her feet to give Kathy a warm hug.

"Really great," George added.

"And a pleasure to meet you," Kathy said to Thor. She assessed him, grinning, gave Genevieve a nod of what seemed to be approval.

"Really great," George said again, pumping Thor's hand.

"Oh, and listen. Best of luck with the treasure hunt. And remember, Gen, you knew us when."

Waving, Kathy was led away at last by her husband.

Thor stared at Genevieve, grinning.

"George was the smartest kid in class," she said, grinning back.

"And Kathy?"

"The most talkative."

He laughed, then sobered. Something about the conversation had disturbed him. As they paid their bill and left, he kept mulling it over in his mind.

He'd felt suspicious of those close to them before now.

Jay.

Who had lost his wife when she had drowned.

Victor.

Who had been with the prostitute.

As he drove back to their hotel, he knew George and Kathy had pressed something home to him.

It had all happened before.

So who had been around all that time? Strangers, of course. People he had never met. Key West could be a transient place. He was certain a lot of the people living there now had arrived since Genevieve had been in high school.

There was no reason to believe the murderer was close to them.

Except…

Okay, it was a long shot, but what if ghosts *did* exist? What if Genevieve's ghost kept appearing not because she wanted help, but because she wanted to give *them* help?

"Crazy," he muttered aloud.

Genevieve was half asleep in the passenger seat. She raised her head slightly. "What?"

"Nothing, sorry," he murmured. How was he supposed to respond? Hey, guess what? I'm seeing a ghost, too. Different ghost, a wise-ass kid, but still…

Gen was so tired he was tempted to pick her up and carry her to their room after they turned the car over to the valet. He refrained, slipping an arm around her instead. She crashed out on the bed, murmuring something about getting up in just a second to change.

She wasn't getting up again. Not that night, he knew. He managed to slip off her shoes, but he left her sleeping in her lilac halter dress.

Slipping in beside her, he drew her to him.

Close…

He couldn't shake the feeling that he murderer was close to them.

Who to trust? Lizzie and Zach—they came from the north and certainly hadn't been around years ago. But who the hell else? Marshall—who could be playing them all—was from Key West. The question was, when had he been working in the north and when had he been working in the Keys?

Alex?

Key Largo was too close for comfort. He would have been in high school when the model disappeared, but Victor would have been in high school then, too. That didn't exonerate either of them.

Jay.

For that matter, Jack had been around, too.

So…hell! That left the ghost hunters in the he-could-trust-them category.

He gritted his teeth, willing himself to go to sleep. It had been a long day and he was dead tired.

Dead…

* * *

He woke with a start the next morning when Genevieve cried out.

She was sitting up, soaked and shaking.

He leapt out of bed, turned the light on and rushed around, lifting her up and into his arms.

The smell of seawater was sharp and strong.

She stared at him with wide eyes.

"We have to go back!" she cried, and threw herself against him, trembling. The salt and the sea seemed to sink into his flesh, along with a stinging blast of ice-cold dread.

18

Genevieve tried hard to be reasonable—especially since she couldn't explain her desperate urge to return to Key West so quickly.

She told herself that at least Thor didn't seem to be feeling repelled by her.

He didn't even comment on the salty scent of the sea or the dampness that seemed to descend upon them nightly. Since he was choosing to ignore those very weird occurrences, she told herself, she could control the desire to leave long enough for them to take a motor boat out for a few hours to search for any sign of Marshall.

Despite their night, they were up early, thanks to her nightmare.

Maybe the ghost's directive had simply been meant to get them up and moving.

Thor was patient. "I understand," he'd said very softly, holding her as she had trembled when the woman in white and the pirates had faded into puddles around her. "But we're here. It's a long drive back. We can rent a boat, cruise around for a few hours and still be back by five. All right?"

Sheerly for the fact that he hadn't gone running, she had agreed that they could take the morning. As they drove to the marina, she made phone calls. Bethany was a bit perturbed at being awakened.

She woke Jay up, too. He sounded exhausted and disgusted.

Nikki Blackhawk was the only one who sounded not only cheerful but determined. "I'm not sure how much we've helped so far, but a teaser ran today for the story on the *Marie Josephine* and Anne, Aldo and the pirates. I think Anne would be pleased to see the way Helen is handling it. And I'm sure Gasparilla would like the world to know he didn't kill Anne."

"So you think the ghost is Anne?"

At that, Nikki hesitated. "I still don't know," she said.

"But you've seen her?"

"In a way. The thing is, just as only certain people see ghosts, only certain people are either seen or acknowledged by ghosts. This woman wants *you* to know something. So just do what you have to do up there. I swear to you, we'll be combing the streets, along with the police, looking for Audrey."

As she hit the end-call button on her phone, Genevieve had to smile. Despite her dreams, they were certainly living in the modern world. Thor was on his phone. He had already spoken to Jack and left a message for Sheridan; he had been speaking with Brent Blackhawk while she had been talking to Nikki.

"All right?" Thor asked her.

She nodded thoughtfully.

At the public marina in Coconut Grove, Thor was able to rent the speedboat he wanted. It was a perfect day to be out on the water; the seas were calm, there was a slight breeze, and the sky was almost crystal clear. Of course, that could change quickly, but for the few hours they needed, it looked as if they would have perfect conditions.

They turned off their phones, so they wouldn't be interrupted, and headed north first, circling Key Biscayne, following the Intracoastal Waterway at a barely legal pace, then turning back. Downtown Miami was striking from a distance, the buildings towering above the ocean, all the hardships and sore spots of a major metropolitan area hidden by the distance.

Thor seemed irritated with himself as they passed marina after marina with no luck, and when he turned back, he told her, "I don't know why, but I was certain we'd find Marshall here, even though I know someone might have called in using his name." Her eyes widened with alarm, and he quickly added, "I'm sure he's just fine."

Genevieve was worried for Marshall, but also pleased they were turning back, because she still felt driven to return to Key West as quickly as possible.

Then Thor said, "The river."

She almost groaned aloud. Checking out the Miami River could add hours to their day.

But she forced herself to stay silent, though she was chafing inwardly, anxious to head back.

Suddenly she found herself standing, gripping the console, as they passed through a residential neighborhood that took up both banks of the river.

"That's it!" she exclaimed. "That's Marshall's boat!"

"Where?" Thor demanded.

"Right there…at that really weathered-looking dock. Behind the house that looks as if it's gutted. Thor, that's *it!* I've worked on that boat for years. That's her. I know it is. Take a look at her. She's a working dive boat, not a pleasure craft."

He cut the motor to idle, slowly steering closer.

Genevieve gasped.

There was Marshall. Sunglasses on, hands laced behind his head, he was stretched out on the deck, a bottle of Scotch by his side.

She felt fury swell inside her. Before Thor could warn her to be quiet, she cried out in anger, "Marshall Miro, you son of a bitch!"

Marshall jerked up as if yanked by the hair. He looked at Genevieve with disbelief, then confusion, and then, to her amazement, abject fear.

"Marshall!" she cried again.

Thor had cut the motor. They drifted closer. Genevieve didn't wait. She raced forward and leapt to the other boat.

"Genevieve!" Thor shouted. "Wait! Damn it, wait!"

Marshall had leapt to his feet. He was in a pair

of khaki trunks, no shirt, and she headed straight for him.

"Wait!" Thor yelled again. He threw a line to Marshall's boat, racing after her.

She hit Marshall. Hard, both fists pounding against his chest.

"Genevieve!" Thor reached her, dragging her away, before Marshall could strike back.

But Marshall clearly didn't intend to hit anyone. He didn't protest Genevieve's wild rage in any way. He edged back, insisting, "I won't go back. I will not go back, do you understand? Damn it, why couldn't you just have left me alone?"

Genevieve stared at him, her anger drained by the sheer astonishment that seized her. "Marshall, what the hell are you talking about?" she asked. "We've been worried sick. We've been—"

"I called. I said I had business," he protested.

Marshall was a big guy, his size and musculature emphasized by his shaven head and tattoos, but despite that, he looked absolutely terrified.

"You sure as hell better explain yourself better than that," Thor snarled.

His fingers were knotted into fists at his sides, and his tone had aroused something in Marshall, too, because suddenly he was bristling, as well. The air filled with a sudden rush of testosterone. She kept her position between the two men, hoping to keep them from coming to blows.

"Calm down," she said, and glanced at each man in turn.

Marshall let out a long sigh, lowering his head. "There's no way I can make you understand. I barely got out with my life."

"What the hell are you talking about?" Thor demanded.

"There's something in the water," Marshall said. "Something that doesn't belong there. It tried to drown me," Marshall said. "It almost succeeded." He pointed a finger at Genevieve. "It's all your fault. Why the hell couldn't you just leave me alone?"

Genevieve opened her mouth, but words wouldn't come.

"Marshall, is this you talking—or the Scotch?" Thor asked.

"I didn't start with the Scotch until I encountered whatever the hell is down there."

"What was it?" Thor demanded.

"I don't know," Marshall said, staring at them defiantly. "I never saw it."

"You're not making any sense," Thor said.

"You had no right just to disappear. I thought you were one of the best men in the Keys."

"Once," Marshall said, shuffling his feet.

"Please," Genevieve said. "I don't understand."

Marshall stared at her, shook his head, winced. "There was something in the water. It kept tugging at me. It dragged me under. Let me up, dragged me under again. There were weird sounds, and…shit, you can't smell in the water, but I could *smell* decay. It was trying to kill me. I mean it. I'm not going back there…at least not for a long, long time. Not until someone finds out what it is and kills it or…exorcises it or something. Don't you understand yet? It was trying to kill me. And *you* brought it on, Gen. You brought it on when you went down and saw that…whatever."

Thor stared at him, his eyes narrowed. "Don't blame Genevieve," he said. "Blame the project, but don't blame her." He caught her hand. "Let's go."

"Let's go?" she echoed questioningly.

"You heard him. He's not coming back. And we *have* to go back. Just one word of advice, Marshall—lay off the Scotch. You feel like you can handle things again, you know where we'll be. Genevieve, let's go."

They returned to their rented boat. Thor had tied on to Marshall's with so much haste he'd caused some minor damage to the hull, which they would have to pay for.

Either he didn't notice or he didn't care.

He was obviously struggling to obey the speed limit as they headed back down the river. He stared straight ahead. She went to stand by him.

"He's really terrified," she murmured. She had worked with Marshall forever. She was angry, disappointed, hurt. But she still found herself defending the man who had been her boss—confident, professional, assured—for so many years. "And honestly, this isn't like Marshall. I've seen him face a million threats and I've never seen him cave like this."

Thor didn't look at her for a moment, but when

he did, he smiled ruefully. "I don't care what a guy looks like. Or a woman, for that matter. We all have some point deep in our psyche where we can be afraid. In Marshall's case…who the hell knows what went on? But it isn't your fault. You didn't cause any of this." He hesitated, staring straight ahead again. "I don't believe in ghosts," he said. Yet, the words were like a line in a script, like something he had said over and over that no longer held any conviction. "But if there *were* ghosts out there…" He shook his head. "I'll start over. I don't think anything intended to harm Marshall. Whatever happened, it just touched that raw edge deep inside where any human being can be vulnerable." He fell silent again for a second, then offered her another smile. "Hell. We found him. He's alive and well. We'll just tell the others that. That he felt he needed some personal time. That's kind of the truth."

"What if something down there *did* try to kill him?"

"I don't believe it," Thor said simply. "I *do* believe a flesh-and-blood murderer is out there, and because of that, we need to be…not afraid, but wary. I believe that…that there are questions that have to be answered."

She stood next to him, not replying at first. Then she said. "We've found Marshall. Now we have to find Audrey."

He was quiet. She knew he was thinking they might never find Audrey, and that, if they did, she might already be dead.

* * *

They made Genevieve's house before dark.

As they pulled into her driveway, Thor turned on his cell, which immediately began to ring.

"Where have you been? I've been trying to reach you for hours." It was Sheridan, and he sounded irritated.

"Driving," Thor said flatly. "What do you want?"

"I read another one of the letters, and it's too damn close to what that reporter rushed ahead and insinuated in the paper. If you've been on to something that you haven't been sharing, you are entirely outside your contractual bounds."

"We've given you everything we found," Thor said.

"You have to get back down there," Sheridan said.

"As soon as I have police clearance."

Sheridan let out an irritated snort. "Can they cordon off the ocean? There was no reason for the dive to stop."

"A corpse is a good enough reason for me, Professor. Is there anything else?"

"Can you get over here immediately?" he demanded.

Thor maintained his temper, grimacing at Genevieve as she arched a brow at him. "I'll run by. I'll check with the police first and see if they need more time."

"More time? It's an ocean, for God's sake."

Sheridan was probably right; Thor was simply in the mood to buck him.

"Are you off to see Sheridan?" Genevieve asked after he'd hung up.

"You want to come?"

"No," she said emphatically.

"I won't be long," he told her.

"Just go now, and then you can get back fast. I'm going to call Bethany, find out what everyone is up to, see if they're meeting later for dinner."

"I'll go in with you first."

"It's okay—I threw everyone out and locked the house," she reminded him.

"I'll go in with you first," he repeated.

She smiled.

They went through the same routine they had followed the first time. Thor didn't really believe anyone was lurking inside, ready to assault Genevieve, but he had a feeling that something was brewing and it was getting closer and closer to an explosion.

Her house, as he had expected, was empty.

"Sure you don't want to just come with me?" he asked.

"We went through the house, and I'll be fine," she assured him.

"Don't go off without me," he commanded.

She shook her head. "I won't. I'll be waiting."

She walked him back to the door, smiling. He wasn't sure why, but he hesitated. He felt as if his breath locked in his throat. He wanted to hold her, to refuse to leave her. He drew her into his arms instead and kissed her tenderly. When he eased his hold, she whispered, "What was that for?"

For the fact that I love you…

But he didn't say the words. He wasn't sure he'd ever before felt the way he did about her now. He had cared about women before, been deeply involved several times.

But he'd never been in love, never felt as he did now.

"Nothing. I'm going to get moving. Get this over with. It's been a long day, but you're right. I'd like to have dinner with the others, find out if anything they found out puts a new light on things. At least we can tell everyone Marshall's alive and well. In fact, you might as well get started on that right now. We probably should have called earlier. I was just so…"

"Mad?"

"Yes. And…hell, never mind. I can't explain it. I'll hurry."

He didn't need to explain. He knew she understood. He lifted a hand to her as he walked away and slid behind the wheel once again.

She smiled and waved.

He turned the key in the ignition, then he almost turned the car back off. Something was nagging at him, but he couldn't put a finger on it.

Reluctantly, he drove away.

Genevieve watched Thor go, wondering why she had actually been anxious for him to leave.

She locked herself inside, lowering her head pensively.

She knew why.

She was going to try to summon her ghost, and he wouldn't understand.

How to go about it?

She should call Adam Harrison, she thought. She should call him and the others immediately, just as she had told Thor she was going to.

But she was feeling the same sense of urgency that had plagued her all day. Yes, they had found Marshall, and Marshall was okay.

And Audrey, she somehow knew, was not.

Her heart was pounding as she went to the sofa and sat, closing her eyes and doing nothing but concentrating, trying to find out if it was possible to communicate with the dead, with the woman who had sought her out.

Please, don't let Audrey be dead already, she prayed silently.

She leaned back and closed her eyes.

Tried to relax. To clear her mind.

Easier said than done.

And so she let her thoughts free.

Help me. Please. You said to beware, but of what? Or of whom?

Please, don't let me be responsible for Audrey's death. You can help me.

Please...

At the police station, the desk sergeant spoke to Thor, then asked him to wait while he made a call.

Jay was apparently out on the street somewhere.

Detective Suarez walked out to speak with Thor instead.

"The sergeant said you've spoken with Marshall Miro," Suarez said.

"That's right. He's taking some personal time. He's docked up on the Miami River. I'm assuming the property belongs to a friend, or maybe he owns it himself."

"Well, there you go. Your friend and co-worker is fine."

"Yes. I'm much more worried about Audrey."

Suarez made a ticking sound of impatience. "She's probably off somewhere having fun, too. But I'll keep my eyes open. You know, your friend Victor was the last one seen with that hooker."

Thor discovered he disliked Suarez. The "hooker"—even if they didn't have an identity on her—deserved more in the way of respect.

"You questioned him," he commented.

"Yeah, and I would have held him. But the shop owner refused to press charges." He let out a strange sound of disgust. "These people—" he waved a hand, indicating exactly who, Thor wasn't sure "—they're like a closed group."

"You're not from here, I take it," Thor murmured.

"Nope, not me. I've lived all over," Suarez said.

Thor was glad he didn't specify a place; he would have hated to harbor a grudge against a certain area just because of Suarez.

"Yep, your friend's back out on the streets, so I'd beware," Suarez went on.

Beware.

"I work with the man," Thor said. "And you have no evidence against him, right?"

Suarez shrugged. "All I know is, this kind of thing has gone on before down here. That suggests the perp is someone who's been around for a while, and that fits your friend."

"That fits a lot of people here," Thor said coolly. Hell, even if he thought beyond a doubt that Victor was guilty, he would have defended him against this guy.

"I came in to tell you we're going back in the water tomorrow," Thor said.

Suarez shrugged. "Try not to dig up any more bodies, huh?"

Was he trying to be humorous?

"Good evening, Detective," Thor said.

More irritated than he had been already, he set out to see Sheridan.

Please…

She could sense it, smell the sea. Something different around her. Maybe just a charge in the air at first, a surge of energy…of electricity.

Help me, please.

The feeling that someone else was with her began to grow. She took a deep breath, then another. She wasn't going to be afraid. She was going to make this work. She was going to stay with the ghost until…

She nearly rocketed off the sofa when she heard a hammering against her door.

The electricity was gone. There was no longer any sense of the sea, or of anything but emptiness surrounding her.

She swore, rising.

The hammering continued as she walked across the room to the door. She looked out through the peephole and saw Victor.

"Calm down," she told him, throwing open the door.

He swept past her, ignoring her words.

"Those fucking detectives grilled me as if I were Ted Fucking Bundy!" he exploded at her.

"Victor, you can't blame them. It's their job."

"They don't have a real suspect. That's why they're going after me. I'll sue. This is harassment."

"Come on, Victor, they let you out," she said.

"You!" he accused her.

"Me?"

"You just had to call Jay and tell him you and I put that mannequin in the garbage."

"Victor, I had to. He would have spent hours investigating—"

"As if they're not spending hours investigating right now, trying to prove I stole the damn thing," he interrupted.

"Victor, do you want a drink? A soda or something?"

"Genevieve, I'm telling you, you don't know what it was like."

"Victor, I'm sorry, but quit acting like a two-year-old."

"A two-year-old? You didn't have to go through that."

He was pacing so angrily that she kept her distance from him. She had to remind herself that she'd known him all her life.

"Women!" he exploded next. He pointed a finger at her. "Always trouble—always teasing, and the next thing you know, they want money!"

"Come on, Victor. You're not the first guy to be taken in by a prostitute. And how can you still be angry? The poor woman is dead."

He was still pacing, acting as if he hadn't even heard her.

"Victor, stop it! I'm sorry, but under the circumstances, I did the right thing."

Suddenly she found herself sorry she hadn't gone with Thor.

How long before he returned?

A while, she thought, amazed to realize how nervous she felt.

It was suddenly as if Victor read her mind.

"Where's loverboy?" he asked.

"Back any minute," she said.

"Down with the cops, probably. Reminding them I've lived here all my life, so I could be guilty of anything."

"Victor, damn it, I told you—"

"Yeah, yeah, you're sorry."

"Yes," she snapped angrily. "And instead of feeling sorry for yourself, you should be worrying about Audrey."

"Sure. Let's all worry about poor Audrey."

"You were the last one to see her, too," she said without thinking, then practically gasped at her own foolishness in uttering the words.

He turned on her, furious, clenching his hands at his sides.

She'd never seen him so angry.

She was an idiot. She never should have opened the door to him.

"I should throttle you," he said softly.

She froze for an instant, shocked into stillness by the menace in his voice.

How well did she really know him?

He'd been angry at the prostitute.

Had he been angry with Audrey?

He'd been the last to see both women.

Had he lied about the mannequin? She couldn't help but remember the sight of all those plastic body parts.

She forced herself to remain calm.

"I'm getting a beer, and I'll get you one, too," she said. To her amazement, her voice was even. "Sit down. I'll be right back."

She had absolutely no intention of returning, of course. As she started toward the back of the house, she could still hear him pacing. She ran past the kitchen and out the back door.

19

Sheridan, Thor thought, was the most boring academic ever to try to make a name for himself.

It was true that the second letter gave credence to everything Genevieve had said. It *had* been Aldo, remembered as the lover determined to defy anyone for the love of his Anne, who had planned vengeance against the English, the ship—and the woman who had spurned him.

Sheridan was still talking, but Thor barely heard him. His mind was elsewhere.

The discomfort he had been feeling was growing. If Sheridan didn't shut up in sixty seconds, he was going to make up an excuse to bolt.

He didn't have to.

His cell phone rang.

"Thor, it's Brent Blackhawk. Where are you?"

"At Sheridan's lab."

There was a split second of silence. "Where's Genevieve?"

"At her house."

"She isn't answering her phone."

Thor's stomach tightened in fear.

"Mr. Thompson, perhaps we could just finish up here?" Sheridan asked hesitantly.

"We *are* finished," Thor said flatly, then turned on his heel and headed for the door, racing toward the parking lot while Brent continued speaking.

"I know you don't believe in…all this," Brent said, "but you need to get to the house. Find Genevieve. I'm on my way there now."

"I'm almost in the car," Thor said, sliding into the driver's seat. His heart was pounding.

He knew before glancing to his right that he was not alone.

Josh Harrison had graduated from the back seat to the front.

"You'd better be here because you're going to help me," Thor snapped.

"She's in danger—I know that," the ghost said.

"And that's it?"

"I know the killer is *alive*, but I don't know his every move. I just know that…hell, step on it, will you?"

"Genevieve, what the hell?"

She was hiding in the midst of her hibiscus bushes when she heard Victor come out the back door.

"Genevieve? Where the hell are you?" he called. She heard him muttering, "Now she's gone frigging nuts, too."

She knew he couldn't see her. Darkness was falling, and though it seemed to come slowly at first, she knew it would soon be night.

She bit her lip, wondering if she was being ridiculous. She loved Victor like a brother, but…

He had been with the prostitute.

He had been the one to walk Audrey home. And now Audrey was gone.

She stayed where she was. She wasn't going back in the house. The killer was probably someone they didn't even know, but still…

She felt ill and she didn't believe Audrey had taken off of her own volition, not like Marshall.

She had to get to town, back to the resort, she decided. As long as she was in a crowd, nothing could happen to her.

She regretted running out of the house without her cell phone, but she wasn't going back for it.

Nor did she dare take the street in front of her house. What if he came after her?

She hesitated, then turned and climbed over the fence to her neighbor's yard. As she did, she felt a strange chill.

She thought about the times she could have sworn she was being watched, that she was being followed.

Someone she knew was the killer.

The knowledge washed over her with complete certainty.

Victor?

Her heart and mind fought the possibility.

She cut through people's backyards at first, disturbed to feel there were eyes in the night, that she was even now being watched—being stalked.

That was sheer idiocy, she assured herself. She didn't know how anyone could have possibly followed her, the way she had left, the path she was taking.

She eased back onto Duval Street, feeling like a paranoid fool. There were people everywhere. She hadn't been followed. She almost laughed aloud at herself as she hurried on toward the resort, then sobered when she realized that if she should run into Victor alone now, she really would be scared. She'd walked out on him. He was going to be more furious than ever.

She took the half turn toward the water and the resort, her strides long and confident. It was when she reached the parking lot that the odd feeling returned.

She found herself pausing. The night had gone full dark. Streetlights created shadows under every leaf and branch. Clouds passed over the moon.

Why am I standing in the parking lot, shivering? she asked herself.

She realized that she didn't want to take the overgrown path to the tiki bar area and the bungalows.

She managed to make herself move at last. She hurried toward her own cottage, then paused.

There was a figure on the little porch, seated and hunched over. She couldn't tell who it was.

She started toward the bar, but there wasn't a soul at the tables. Clint wasn't even there, though the place was entirely set up. As she hesitated, she heard her name being called. Someone was coming through the parking lot in her wake.

Had she been followed?

She didn't want to be seen, didn't want to be caught alone, but she couldn't go to her own cottage. Silently, she hurried across the sand, heading for the docks.

She avoided the pier where the dive boats were berthed, choosing to move along the other. Jay's boat was there, as was Jack's.

To her amazement, Jay Gonzalez was on his boat, though he hadn't seen her. His head was bowed as he sat in the captain's chair, busy at something.

He was a cop, for God's sake. She should just go ask him for help.

But she didn't want to see anyone. Not until she saw *lots* of someones.

She kept moving then, certain he would look up if she moved back to land but all too aware that she was almost dead in front of him.

He still didn't see her, he was so completely absorbed in his task.

As she stared at him, she realized what he was doing.

Knotting and unknotting a rope, over and over again.

Her heart hammered; she needed to get past him. She hurried on, terrified that at any moment he would look up.

Her door was closed, but it wasn't locked when Thor arrived.

Brent Blackhawk was running toward the house

just as Thor got there. He shot Brent a frantic look, then burst into the house.

To his amazement, Victor was there, sprawled on the sofa, drinking a beer.

"Where is Genevieve?" Thor demanded, striding forward and catching him by the shirt, dragging him up from the couch.

"What the hell is the matter with you?" Victor cried out, torn between trying to wrench away and taking a swing.

"Hey! Take it easy, both of you!" Blackhawk ordered. "Thor let him go."

Thor eased his hold on Victor, who was staring daggers at him, teeth clenched in anger.

"Where is she?"

Victor shook his head, looking worried. "I don't know," he admitted sickly. "I was hoping she'd come back. I didn't mean to, but I guess I scared her. I—" He broke off in fear when he saw the murderous look that entered Thor's eyes.

Brent forced himself between the two men. "The important thing is that we find her," he said quietly. "Where did she go?"

"I'm not lying, I don't know. She said she was going to get me a beer, then she ran out the back door. I called her, but I didn't want to chase her and really scare her, so I figured I'd wait here for her to get back."

Thor realized he was still tense; his muscles were knotted and he wanted to shake Victor until he produced Genevieve.

"Go easy on him. I think he's telling the truth."

It wasn't Brent Blackhawk who spoke, but Josh Harrison, who had walked in and was standing behind Victor.

"What the hell do you know about it?" Thor demanded irritably.

"Who the hell are you talking to?" Victor demanded.

"Tell him," Josh said indignantly to Thor.

"You shut up," Thor muttered.

"Excuse me, but Gen is my friend, too," Brent said.

Something in his manner alarmed Victor. "You think something is really wrong, don't you? Look, I swear to you, I'm not the killer."

Thor took a step back, pulling out his cell phone. The killer was someone they knew. Someone who had been in the Keys a long time.

Not Marshall. He was still in Miami.

So assuming Victor was telling the truth…

Alex?

Not from Key West, though close enough.

Still, in his mind, only two suspects were left.

Both had been old enough to kill when the first woman went missing. One might have done away with his own spouse.

He dialed Jay Gonzalez's cell phone. No answer.

Brent Blackhawk was staring at him. "She probably went to the resort, where she would expect to find lots of people."

"Of course," Victor said. "I bet she's having a drink at the tiki bar."

"Let's go," Thor said.

* * *

She had made it past Jay unseen when she heard the strange noise, a kind of *thunk*. She didn't know what it was, and she didn't want to know. She just wanted to get away.

Ten feet to Jack's boat. She ran along the pier and took a flying leap, landing hard on the deck of the beat-up old fishing boat. She ducked down, waiting, certain Jay was somewhere, that he was coming after her. He'd seen her and had no doubt paused only to get a weapon.

She waited, her heart thundering. And waited some more.

And no one came for her.

Jack, thank you for docking your boat here, she thought.

She closed her eyes tightly. Still waiting. Still afraid to move, even afraid to breathe. Then she opened her eyes.

She felt a soft tremor in her heart, but not of fear.

The ghost was back.

Just as she saw the beautiful woman in white, she heard the noise. It was muffled, something knocking against the bottom of the boat.

The ghost stared at her with her huge sad eyes.

Beware.

Help…she needs help.

She?

The noise again. Staring at her unearthly friend, Genevieve slowly rose. There was no one on the dock. The moon shone down through a break in the clouds. The noise came again.

She nearly tripped on one of the oars for the little dinghy as she moved carefully to the small cabin. There was barely any light at all there, but it was enough for Genevieve to see that no one was there. Her heart was thundering.

She?

Audrey?

She realized there was a hatch offering access to the engine, just at the base of the stepladder that led from the deck to the cabin. A massive slide bolt held the hatch door in place. She fell to her knees and realized it wasn't even closed. She struggled with the door, which seemed to be stuck.

She struggled again, tugging with all her might.

It gave suddenly, and she fell back.

In the darkness, she didn't at first recognize the figure that rose from the bilge.

"Gen!"

She tried desperately to scramble to her feet, but she was only halfway up when an oar—partner to the one she had nearly tripped over on the deck—came crashing down on her skull.

Bethany was at the tiki bar.

Thor was sure he scared her half to death when he rushed up behind her, and grabbed her anxiously by the shoulder. For the rest of her life, she would probably be sure he was crazy.

"Where's Genevieve?"

"I don't know. I just got here."

"So did I," Alex said, walking up behind him.

"Where were you?" Thor demanded.

"Over there," he said, gesturing. "I didn't know where the hell anyone was and I was getting lonely, then I saw Bethany get here. So I came over. I did see Jay earlier. He was heading out to his boat. It didn't look like he wanted company, though."

"His boat?" Thor said.

"Over there," Bethany said, pointing. "A bunch of cops keep their boats here."

Thor was already running, the others behind him. Suddenly he stopped, not knowing which boat. Bethany nearly crashed into him.

"There—she's called *My Lady*."

He sped forward, leaping from the dock to the deck of the boat. There was no one there, but lengths of rope were strewn everywhere.

"Genevieve!" he bellowed out.

There was nothing. No sound.

"Oh, shit," Alex swore. "There!"

Thor looked into the water. A man's body was floating, facedown.

He dived in, Blackhawk behind him. Catching hold of the man, he flipped him; with Blackhawk's help, he quickly dragged him to the side of *My Lady*.

Bethany and Alex were there to help drag him up.

"It's Jay. He's not breathing," Bethany said as Thor and Brent pulled themselves from the water.

Alex already had Jay stretched out on his back.

"Bethany, dial 911. Fast." He ripped off Jay's sodden shirt, falling to his knees, ready to perform CPR.

"There's a knot on his head the size of an emu egg," Brent commented.

"What the hell…?" Thor murmured, hunkering down. He looked around. There was an empty berth next to *My Lady*. And the lines hadn't been untied; they had been severed.

"What boat docks there?" he demanded, taking Bethany roughly by the shoulders.

"Um…oh, Jack's old fishing boat," Bethany said, shivering, still in shock, staring at Jay's seemingly lifeless body.

"Get him on the dock!" Thor ordered. "Now!"

"Hey, I'm doing CPR," Alex protested.

"And this is a speedboat. Get off it!" Thor ordered. He bent down and lifted Jay himself, gritting his teeth, half hating himself.

But he needed the boat.

And for Jay, those few seconds wouldn't make any difference.

"Tell the cops. Tell them to get a boat out on the reef fast," Thor ordered over his shoulder, racing for the helm. "And keep up the CPR, no matter what, until help gets here."

Alex lifted a hand in acknowledgment. Bethany hurried to his side at the dock, dropping down beside him, then looked up at Thor.

"Oh, my God. Genevieve…."

He couldn't reply.

The key was in the ignition. He turned it, praying.

Beside him, Brent turned on the lights.

"You drive, I'll look," he said simply.

The powerful engine roared instantly to life.

Thor blessed the cop he had suspected for keeping the boat he never used anymore in good running order.

Genevieve was aware of the movement of the boat, the rush of the water, the heat thrown off by the engine. She blinked desperately, trying to move.

She felt a body next to her.

Panic seized her. She was trapped in the darkness with a dead body.

Audrey!

Oh, God, Audrey was dead....

She started to scream, but it didn't matter. She couldn't even hear herself over the roar of the motor. She fought for calm. She was still alive, and she desperately wanted to somehow stay that way.

But she might as well have been paralyzed.

Her wrists had been bound behind her back, and her ankles were tied, as well. Realizing her situation, she fought a nauseating wave of panic. When she had finally gained a grip on her sanity, she realized the body wedged next to her own was still warm.

"Audrey?" she whispered.

There was no response. She didn't know if Audrey was alive or dead. She only knew they were both in serious trouble.

She tried taking a deep breath, but her stomach turned at the stench of motor oil. She coughed, her lungs ripping in agony. She bit her lip and began working at the ropes binding her.

Jack. Good God, Jack was the killer.

It hardly seemed to matter. She was numb.

He couldn't get away with it. Not this time. Thor would have returned to the house. He would look for her....

He might find Victor and beat him to a pulp, but he would still keep looking for her.

Except he wouldn't know where to look.

She couldn't think that way. She kept struggling with the ropes, cursing the fact that Jack was an expert seaman and knew how to tie a knot.

Despite that, she forced herself to work steadily at her bindings. As long as she worked at them, she had a chance.

She had become so fixed on her task that she didn't even notice at first when the motor cut off.

Then she froze.

A second later, the hatch opened. "Gen, you came to. I'm sorry. I should have hit you a lot harder, saved you the panic, but when you think about it, it's your own fault. You started this. You're the one who brought it to light. You're the reason I'm going to have to keep going tonight after I...well, let's not go into that now. It's too bad, though. I really love Key West."

He didn't reach for her first, but bent down to lift Audrey from the hold. He laid her out like a rag doll. Audrey's hair was plastered to her head. Her clothing was drenched.

"Still warm," Jack said cheerfully.

"Jack," Genevieve said, finding she had no voice at first. "Jack, I don't understand."

"Oh, don't take me for an idiot. Do you know what I really am? A hero."

"A hero?"

He stood in the cabin, staring down at her, his hands on his hips and laughed. "Imagine me with a red cape, honey. I'm an avenger. Those girls were running around with their short skirts and bursting cleavage, taunting men—and giving the clap and crabs and AIDS to guys the whole time. They had to be stopped."

"Jack, the girl years ago…when I was a kid. She wasn't a prostitute—she was a model."

He burst into laughter before dragging her out to lie half on top of Audrey. She gritted her teeth against the painful way he twisted her arm.

"Model? That's what she wanted people to think. That little whore was getting her room, her food, her photographs—all of it by hopping from bed to bed. I knew her, knew her tricks. And then, when I helped her out, did she want to pay up?"

Genevieve tried to breathe, thinking furiously that she had to keep him talking as long as possible.

"She was the first?" she asked.

"First—and only—for many years. Then, after a while, there were a few others. That little hussy who came down here last year, she was number eight. But I only punished those who deserved to be punished."

"Jack—"

"Excuse me, for a minute, Gen." He rolled her over, reached down and lifted Audrey up.

"No, Jack, wait!" she cried.

He turned, one step up the ladder. "Hey, don't worry. I'll let you two go together."

He was gone. She heard Audrey's body land topside.

Then he was back.

"Jack, I don't understand."

He hunkered down by her as if truly concerned, fingering the skull and crossbones in his ear.

"What don't you understand, Gen?"

"Audrey isn't a prostitute! And neither am I."

He sighed, not looking at her. "Gen, you started everything when you thought you saw a ghost in the water," he told her. He actually sounded truly sorry. Her heart took flight as she prayed she could talk him out of his intent.

"Jack, I still don't get it."

He shook his head. "Gen, you thought you saw a woman. Then a dead woman popped up. I was the one who tried to scare you off with the mannequin, you know. It was Victor's idea, but I convinced him it was idiotic. I only meant to scare you—to make you stop. Didn't work, though," he said regretfully. "And then there you were, spouting off about different bodies. And Audrey! Her and her so-called ghost hunters. I had to shut her up." He grinned suddenly. "Don't you go kidding yourself. She worked hard to stay alive this long. Real hard. She knew how to pay up. It's almost too bad she has to die, but that's the way it has to be. And you, Gen, I'm so sorry. You were always the sweetest kid. And so pretty, too. You know, I remember when you were a kid and you used to come see me. I'd tried to make you feel better when the boys teased you for being so tall, calling you an Amazon. Remember how I used to tell you it was going to be okay? That you were going to be a real beauty and they'd all be sorry. By the time you were twelve, you'd proved me right."

"Thanks, Jack. Listen—"

"Sorry, honey. No more time. I've got to get moving. I'm going to the Bahamas. I know some people there who will be thrilled to help me out. I've uncovered a few treasures of my own, you know, diving this area. Hell, we didn't need Sheridan and all his charts. I've been picking up pieces from that ship for years."

He stood, reaching for her. She shrank from his touch.

"Gen, I told you, I wouldn't do this if I didn't have to."

"You *don't* have to do it, Jack," she pleaded.

She landed on the deck next to Audrey.

"Tell you what?"

"What?" she asked hopefully.

He didn't answer at first. She realized he had two heavy canvas bags of ballast ready. He started tying one to the ropes around Audrey's ankles.

"What, Jack?" she demanded, trying to divert him.

He kept working while he answered. "I'll let you pick. Who goes in first, you or Audrey?"

She stared at him. She still couldn't believe it. *Jack!* He'd been like an uncle to them, a friend, someone who had taught them, stood by them.

"Jack, if you're running to the Bahamas, anyway, there's no need for this," she begged.

"I'm sorry, but there is. I have to slow your boyfriend down." He had hunkered down beside her and started humming as he tied the second bag to the ropes at her ankles.

"My boyfriend?"

"Thor. He's on his way now. I reckon that's Jay's boat he's coming in."

He was staring out at the dark horizon. She could hear, above the slapping of the waves against the hull, the rising sound of a motor.

"Jack—" she began, then broke off. Staring past him, she could see the ghost. The woman in white.

She wasn't alone. The pirates were aligned beside her.

Her heart sank.

Beware.

Too late.

Help me!

This time she was the one crying the words, in her mind.

"What? You seeing ghosts again, Gen? Jeez, who'd have thought you, of all people, would be the one to go off the deep end." He laughed. "Hell, is there a deep end in the ocean? Okay, you won't choose, so I will. Audrey first!"

He bent down, scooping Audrey up. He threw her overboard, then picked up the canvas bag of ballast he'd tied to her feet and threw that overboard after her.

"Oh, God, Jack, no!"

She fought as much as she could as he reached for her. She was still dimly aware of the ghosts. They had moved, congregating together, the woman in white giving the directions.

They were moving toward the helm. They seemed to be…

She saw the key fall from the ignition.

Success, she thought.

But not in time to save her.

Jack picked her up, heedless of both the ghostly activity and her fierce squirming. "Damn, you're as slippery as an eel," he complained. Then he laughed again. "Look at it this way. You already think you know some of the people you're going to be joining. And since you're in love, you can come back and haunt Thor until the end of his days." He roared with laughter at that.

He threw her over the rail.

For a minute she was dangling from the hull, kept from hitting the water by the bag of ballast.

Then she saw him lift the bag and throw it.

The water seemed very cold and dark as it closed over her head.

They were still a distance from Jack's boat when Thor felt his heart stop.

There was a splash, and a burst of silver as the

moonlight caught the droplets of water that rose in the wake of the sound. Another splash, another, then another.

He swore, revving the motor higher. Blackhawk stood silently at his side.

How long?

He was dimly aware that the other boat wasn't moving. As they closed in, he could see Jack at the helm. He should have been long gone.

But as much as he wanted to kill Jack, Thor couldn't spare a second. He nearly capsized Jay's boat, bringing it to such an abrupt halt, sending it spinning.

He threw himself into the water. How long had she been down? How long could she survive? She was a diver, in excellent condition, but how much time would that buy her?

Thor was aware that Blackhawk had followed him in. But the water was all but black at night, barely illuminated a few feet down by the moon and the lights from the boat.

He was amazed, when, almost immediately, he came upon a body. He pulled his knife from his pocket and groped blindly for the rope holding the still form to the weight. He slit the rope, jackknifed his legs toward the surface. They were no more than forty feet down, but it felt as if he were rising forever.

He broke the surface, gasping for air. "Genevieve?"

But it wasn't Genevieve. It was Audrey, and she was blue and limp.

Blackhawk burst from the water at his side, gasping desperately for breath. He swam hard against the light chopping waves, grasping Audrey. For a split second Thor hesitated, his heart sinking. How much time did he have left? And how the hell was Blackhawk going to get Audrey—or her earthly remains—aboard an unanchored boat?

"Go!" Blackhawk roared.

It was all he needed.

She loved the water.

She had loved it all her life.

And, she thought, as she pitched downward, dragged by the heavy weight, she was going to die in it.

She could see nothing. The moon didn't penetrate this deep. Her wrists were bound behind her back, and she was also bound to the weight.

They had moved the key, she thought. Somehow, the ghosts had moved the key. Jack's boat was stationary. He wasn't going to get away.

Would she even know or care once she was dead?

Would Thor kill the man, or would he die by lethal injection? Or would he get away?

Jack was a serial killer. He didn't even know exactly how many victims he had sent to a watery grave. She still could hardly believe it.

She continued working furiously at the rope

binding her wrists. How long could she hold her breath?

Four minutes. She'd gone as long as four minutes once, she reminded herself. And she was working her hands free. She could feel herself making progress.

Her lungs were already burning.

At first he could see, but then darkness became complete as he plunged deeper. Desperation filled his heart and mind. He hit the bottom. Searched…

Hopelessness, bleak and debilitating, seized him.

And then he felt it.

Like a featherlight touch. A hand…guiding him.

Was he dying himself?

Suddenly there was a stronger light penetrating the water. At first he thought it had been sent from heaven. Then he realized that Brent had found a floodlight on Jay's boat and aimed it into the water for him.

But that touch…

He looked.

And he could see her.

She was blond. Beautiful. With huge blue eyes. And she was leading him.

He followed and there was Genevieve.

She was alive. She had freed her hands. She was fighting desperately with the rope that tied her to the weight. He shot forward, his own lungs burning, cut the rope and grabbed her by the shoulders, then kicked with all his power, shooting them toward the surface.

They broke the water gasping. Genevieve started to cough. He took her in a life-saving hold and kicked hard for Jay's boat, which had crashed into Jack's.

Gasping for breath, Genevieve managed a hoarse whisper. "Audrey?"

"Blackhawk has her," he assured her. He reached Jay's boat and grabbed onto the small dive platform at the rear.

It was then that Genevieve tried to scream. She managed only a croak, but it warned him.

Brent was bent over Audrey, and Jack was approaching him, one of his deadly oars in hand.

"Blackhawk!" Thor roared.

He didn't dare release Genevieve, sure she couldn't possibly have the strength of a kitten left. But she did.

She grasped the dive platform.

Thor was amazed at his own strength as he hurled himself up.

Brent turned in time, ducking the blow.

Thor charged.

Jack turned to swing, but he barely caught Thor in the upper arm before Thor tackled him and shoved him hard against the helm.

Genevieve was staggering up; she made it far enough to sit on the platform, though she looked as if she were going to slip back in. Thor turned his attention back to Jack, who bellowed and thrust hard against Thor. The two of them staggered in a ghastly dance, then crashed against the starboard rail of the boat.

Jack flipped out his knife and Thor realized then he had lost his own, dropping it after freeing Genevieve.

Jack lunged at him. He ducked, but Jack lunged again. Brent Blackhawk was reaching for the oar. Jack saw him and darted toward the dive platform, catching Genevieve just as she pulled herself fully aboard.

"Got ya now," Jack taunted. There was blood pouring from the man's mouth. He'd probably broken a tooth in the tackle.

But he had Genevieve. And a knife.

"Jack, you're insane. Thing is, I don't care. If you put a single scratch on her," he said softly. "I will kill you in a way that will teach you agony you've never even begun to imagine."

Jack started to laugh, then began to cough as the blood choked him.

Genevieve cried out in rage, kicking him squarely in the groin. He bellowed and doubled over, his hold easing. Thor stepped forward, wrenching Genevieve far from the other man's grasp. He threw her behind him and was ready to rage forward again like a maddened bull.

"Stop," Blackhawk cried.

He did.

Because he saw what Blackhawk saw.

They were coming from the water. Two of them… three, four…five…six.

Pirates. Tattered. Decaying. A gold tooth gleaming here. A bleached white bone sticking through a ragged sleeve there.

Sightless eyes in empty sockets staring…

They surrounded Jack, who began to scream as he was grabbed by ghostly hands.

Jack's eyes widened in horror, and he screamed out in an agony of terror.

"Stop! God, help me, stop!"

His body began to tilt as his bony assailants pressed at him. Then he, and they, went overboard.

There was dead silence on the boat for a minute. Absolute stillness.

Then they rushed for the rail.

Jack surfaced and he screamed again as a bony hand emerged, grabbed him, and he went down for the last time.

They were stunned, just staring. Then Genevieve swallowed audibly and looked at Thor.

"Audrey!" she cried.

Brent shook himself back to reality and responded. "She's breathing, and she has a pulse. Just barely. God knows what she went through. She was his captive for days. But I radioed for help. The police are on the way."

Genevieve took a deep breath of relief, then turned to stare at Thor.

"Did…did you see…?"

"Yes," he said simply. And he took her into his arms, shaking.

Epilogue

It was strange, Thor thought. Whereas Josh Harrison appeared solid and real, Anne was gossamer.

He had gone outside, needing to see the night sky and feel the breeze. There were too many people inside, he thought, staring out at the ocean.

Neither he nor Genevieve had lost their love for the sea, and they had returned to the *Marie Josephine* project. It was their willingness to go back after nearly losing their lives that had made an impact on Marshall.

That, or maybe Gen herself, talking to him for hours, convincing him that if there were spirits in the ocean, they'd been trying to tell him something, not kill him.

Of course, they never mentioned ghosts themselves. What had happened that night out on the water remained between Genevieve, Blackhawk and himself.

Victor and Genevieve had patched up their differences. Genevieve had been buying Victor apology dinners ever since.

As for the project, not even Jack had known

where to find the bulk of the treasure, but Genevieve had found a large section of the hull. The vacuuming equipment had been brought in, and a chest filled with treasure had been found.

It was with Adam, Bethany and the Blackhawks that he and Genevieve had pieced together the most important discovery, and that had been before the bitter end for Jack. Genevieve believed that Anne had needed the world to know that Aldo had been her murderer. In Genevieve, she had seen someone with the strength to help her, as well as the spirits of the girls who'd shared her watery grave over the years.

As for the pirates, they had apparently admired Anne, who, in her captivity—that time in which she had fallen in love with Gasparilla and he had apparently returned her devotion—must have been kind, charming and engaging.

Perhaps they had guarded the treasure they had never stolen in life. Perhaps they had merely stayed behind to help her find justice.

Audrey had gotten well quickly, though. She'd refused to discuss her ordeal with them. She had done what she'd needed to to stay alive as long as possible. The only one she'd been willing to talk to was Jay.

They had spent time recuperating together, and she'd helped him put together his case against Jack. Then they had surprised everyone by flying off to Vegas and eloping. They still seemed incredibly happy.

He and Gen had opted for a more traditional

wedding. Well, traditional, by Key West standards, anyway.

His bride had been beautiful in white—but shoeless. They'd been married on the beach at sunset, only a few hours ago, with Father Bellamy presiding.

Bethany, Victor and Alex had been half smashed before the wedding had begun, and they had cried throughout, hugging one another. A difficult feat, since Bethany had been the maid of honor and the other two had served as ushers. But Lizzie and Zach—who had taken work in Australia—had flown back for the wedding and done their best to keep the others in control. Everybody from the project had been there—Adam, Brent, Nikki, Marshall. Something had grown between them, a friendship that would endure.

But friendship or no, he'd needed some air, only as soon as he'd walked out he'd seen Josh, leaning against the back porch rail, with Anne beside him.

"You're not there. I don't see you," Thor groaned.

"I am here, tough guy, and you know it."

Thor looked at Anne. She was still so skittish, so afraid....

He trembled inside.

Where would he be now, without her? Without her and her band of pirates?

"Thank you," he said softly, as she began to fade away, her work done. "But I've got to go in."

Feeling like a fool, he waved goodbye to the ghosts, wondering if he would ever see them again.

Inside, he ran right into Victor. The music was high, laughter in the air.

"Where's Gen?" he asked.

"I think she went upstairs, looking for you?" Victor said.

Thor took the stairs two at a time. Gen was in their room, standing at the window, looking down at Duval Street.

She turned, smiled.

His heart fluttered. Her hair was long, rich, waving with lustrous highlights against the black satin of her silk dress. Her eyes... God, he was in love with her eyes, the sound of her voice...

"Hey you." She walked toward him, catching his tie, pulling him close, kissing his lips.

"I love you," he told her, kissing her back.

"I love you, too. Listen, I know you think I'm crazy—" she began.

He pressed a finger against her lips. "I believe," he whispered very softly. "I believe. And now that that's settled, please just shut up so I can kiss my wife properly."

She smiled.

He did, too.

Outside, the palms swayed and the breeze blew, and there might have been a hint of delighted ghostly laughter, fading into the night.

New York Times and *USA TODAY* Bestselling Author

HEATHER GRAHAM

When Sarah McKinley is finally able to buy and restore the historic Florida mansion that she has always loved, she dismisses the horror stories of past residents vanishing and a long-dead housekeeper who practiced black magic. Then, in the midst of renovations, she makes a grim discovery. Hidden within the walls of Sarah's dream house are the remains of dozens of bodies—some dating back over a century.

The door to the past is blown wide open when Caleb Anderson, a private investigator, shows up at the mansion. He believes several current missing persons cases are linked to the house and its dark past. Working together to find the connection and stop a contemporary killer, Sarah and Caleb are compelled to research the history of the haunted house, growing closer to each other even as the solution to the murders eludes them.

UNHALLOWED GROUND

REQUEST YOUR
FREE BOOKS!

2 FREE NOVELS
FROM THE SUSPENSE COLLECTION
PLUS 2 FREE GIFTS!

YES! Please send me 2 FREE novels from the Suspense Collection and my 2 FREE gifts (gifts are worth about $10). After receiving them, if I don't wish to receive any more books, I can return the shipping statement marked "cancel." If I don't cancel, I will receive 3 brand-new novels every month and be billed just $5.74 per book in the U.S. or $6.24 per book in Canada. That's a saving of at least 28% off the cover price. It's quite a bargain! Shipping and handling is just 50¢ per book in the U.S. and 75¢ per book in Canada.* I understand that accepting the 2 free books and gifts places me under no obligation to buy anything. I can always return a shipment and cancel at any time. Even if I never buy another book, the two free books and gifts are mine to keep forever.

192 MDN E4MN   392 MDN E4MY

Name	(PLEASE PRINT)	
Address		Apt. #
City	State/Prov.	Zip/Postal Code

Signature (if under 18, a parent or guardian must sign)

Mail to **The Reader Service:**
IN U.S.A.: P.O. Box 1867, Buffalo, NY 14240-1867
IN CANADA: P.O. Box 609, Fort Erie, Ontario L2A 5X3

Not valid for current subscribers to the Suspense Collection
or the Romance/Suspense Collection.

Want to try two free books from another line?
Call 1-800-873-8635 or visit www.morefreebooks.com.

* Terms and prices subject to change without notice. Prices do not include applicable taxes. N.Y. residents add applicable sales tax. Canadian residents will be charged applicable provincial taxes and GST. Offer not valid in Quebec. This offer is limited to one order per household. All orders subject to approval. Credit or debit balances in a customer's account(s) may be offset by any other outstanding balance owed by or to the customer. Please allow 4 to 6 weeks for delivery. Offer available while quantities last.

Your Privacy: Harlequin Books is committed to protecting your privacy. Our Privacy Policy is available online at www.eHarlequin.com or upon request from the Reader Service. From time to time we make our lists of customers available to reputable third parties who may have a product or service of interest to you. If you would prefer we not share your name and address, please check here. ☐

Help us get it right—We strive for accurate, respectful and relevant communications. To clarify or modify your communication preferences, visit us at www.ReaderService.com/consumerchoice.

J.T. ELLISON

Homicide detective Taylor Jackson thinks she's seen it all in Nashville—but she's never seen anything as perverse as The Conductor. He captures and contains his victim in a glass coffin, slowly starving her to death. Only then does he give in to his attraction.

Once finished, he creatively disposes of the body by reenacting scenes from famous paintings. And similar macabre works are being displayed in Europe. Taylor teams up with her fiancé, FBI profiler Dr. John Baldwin, and New Scotland Yard detective James "Memphis" Highsmythe, a haunted man who only has eyes for Taylor, to put an end to The Conductor's art collection.

the cold room